# ANGEL DANCE

by

# M.D. GRAYSON

cedar coast press

**cedar coast press**

Published by Cedar Coast Press, LLC
http://www.cedarcoastpress.com

This book is a work of fiction. Names, characters, places, and incidents are either the product of the author's imagination or are used fictitiously. Any resemblance to actual persons, living or dead, or to actual events or locales is entirely coincidental.

**ANGEL DANCE**

Cover designed by M.D. Grayson

Cover art:
Copyright © Fotolia # 9830058_L/Sunset in Oia Village on Santorini Island, Greece/Ljupco Smokovski
Copyright © Fotolia # 7208248/Seattle Skyline/www.RDUNPhoto.com

Visit the author website:
http://www.mdgrayson.com.

ISBN-978-0-9849518-0-2 (eBook)
ISBN-978-0-9849518-4-0 (Paperback)

Library of Congress Control Number: 2012932021

Version 2012.07.12

Printed in the United States of America

10  9  8  7  6  5  4  3  2  1

*This novel is dedicated
to Michelle,
with love.*

# Prologue

August 4, 2011
5:00 a.m.

DEA SPECIAL AGENT Regis Jackson leaned against a ponderosa pine and took three long, deep breaths. At six feet two inches and 190 pounds, the thirty-two-year-old Jackson was in excellent physical condition—he wasn't winded. He'd found over the years, though, that it helped to periodically take a deliberate meditative pause, even if just for a few seconds. The benefits were as much mental as physical: it helped to sharpen his concentration while slowing down his heart rate and relaxing his legs, hands, and arms.

Jackson and his twenty-man team of heavily armed and camouflaged DEA agents, Yakima Tribal Police, and Yakima sheriff's deputies had been hiking for nearly two hours in the dark, early morning. The slope was modest, but the terrain was rough in the far northwest corner of the Yakima Indian Reservation, forty miles southeast of Mount Rainier in Central Washington. The darkness and the need for absolute stealth added to the physical challenge. Now, as the sky began to turn from dark gray to pink in the east, the team members had reached their objective and were moving into their final assault positions.

In the clearing beneath Jackson fifty meters away, barely visible in the dim light, lay a large marijuana plantation known as a "grow" in law enforcement circles. He peered through the dim light until he was able to identify the approximate boundaries of the grow. It looked to him like the Intel report from yesterday's flyover was correct—the grow was about fifteen acres, probably something on the order of five thousand marijuana plants. He studied the field carefully for a few seconds. The plants were scattered in a random pattern to make them more difficult to spot from the air. They were tall—maybe six feet. Another three weeks or so and they'd be ready for harvest. *Gonna be a bitch to cut 'em down*, he thought. He could just make out the flexible PVC piping snaking through the field that the growers had installed to provide stream water to the plants.

"Unit Two—update?" He spoke quietly into his headset. Unit Two was a two-man scout team led by Jackson's second-in-command and good friend, Special Agent Mike Hamilton. Unit Two, in position on the opposite side of the grow, had made the hike on their own three hours before Jackson's assault team. Hamilton and his team member were specially trained to locate and neutralize guard dogs, sentries, and booby traps. They looked for land formations and vegetation patterns favorable to ambush, using their eyes—aided by night vision and infrared scopes—their ears, and even their noses to help literally sniff out an ambush. The team had moved slowly as they'd carefully cleared the entire route.

Once they'd reached the objective, they'd scouted the entire perimeter of the grow and looked for traps and nighttime sentries. Their advance report to Jackson had been quick and succinct: "No dogs, no traps, no sentries. Four gardeners, sound asleep."

Four gardeners. In Jackson's experience, the gardeners tended to be illegal aliens, sometimes with an older supervisor if the grow was big enough. Although they were young and they weren't fighters, they were usually armed, and this made them potentially dangerous.

"Unit Two in position. No change in status."

"Roger. By units starting with Three, update," Jackson whispered.

"Three's ready." Each of the remaining nine two-man units answered identically.

"Okay, guys," Jackson replied. "Official sunrise is at 0515," he glanced at his watch, then continued, "fifteen minutes from now. We'll go then. Get a few minutes of rest."

~~~~

*So far, so good*, Jackson thought to himself. The team was in position with fifteen minutes to spare. Since the anonymous telephone call had come in to his Seattle office yesterday morning, he'd been busy. He'd arranged for a flyover to confirm the report. He'd obtained Yakima tribal approval for the raid. He'd put together a twenty-man, cross-jurisdictional assault team plus a two-helicopter extraction team. Now, everyone was ready to roll.

*We should be getting pretty good at this*, he thought. There'd been three recent anonymous tips and each had led to sizable busts. At first, he and his bosses had been skeptical of the anonymous tipsters. The calls had all been from different people calling from different pay phones. Most marijuana farm busts originated when an innocent civilian accidentally stumbled over the operation while on a walk in the woods—a hiker out for a weekend stroll or a hunter literally bumping into the grow. Sometimes, these folks would be chased out by the gardeners—occasionally, at gunpoint. Perhaps a farmer or a timber man might notice an unusual waterline leading off into the forest and report it to the police. Although they usually wanted to remain anonymous publicly, these people were good citizens and were not afraid to identify themselves to law enforcement. From the DEA's perspective, preserving anonymity was no problem, because no witnesses were needed for prosecution. The plants were seized and, most times, the gardeners were caught red-handed. Recently, though, there'd been three anonymous tips in as many weeks by people unwilling to come in and identify themselves. This was, to say the least, unusual. After the first tip panned out, though, his bosses took the subsequent ones more seriously. As proof, this latest tip—number four—had come in yesterday morning at eleven, and by 8:00 p.m., he was ready to go.

Jackson was proud of his DEA team. They were well trained, they were experienced, and, if need be, they wouldn't hesitate to defend each other with their lives. He said a quick prayer that that would not be necessary this morning and that no one would get hurt.

~~~~

Jackson looked out over the grow and listened. The sky had lightened appreciably in the last fifteen minutes. There were few clouds in the sky. Although the predawn air was still and pleasantly cool at the five-thousand-foot elevation, he knew it was going to be hot by the afternoon. He looked carefully at the camp and saw no sign of movement—all was still. The birds in the surrounding forest were awake and singing, having already gotten used to the unusual presence of the assault team.

"Unit Two, update," Jackson whispered.

"Two's, ready," Hamilton replied. "No change in status."

Each of the other units reported ready to go.

At precisely five fifteen, the sun appeared over the eastern horizon. Jackson pressed the comm button at his side and issued the order. "Okay, guys. Here we go. On my go. Ready? Three, two, one, go!"

The men sprang into action. Jackson stood up and began sprinting toward the camp. Three different teams positioned in close proximity to the camp lobbed flashbang grenades into the center circle surrounded by the tents. The three grenades exploded nearly simultaneously in a brilliant burst of light and a single loud blast that slapped Jackson in the face as he closed on the camp, still twenty-five meters away.

Seconds after the blast, three young men staggered out of two of the tents. Two of the men were unarmed and had their hands pressed to their ears. The third man carried a rifle—what appeared to be an AK-47. He was disoriented by the flashbangs that had blasted him from sleep moments before. His gun was pointed toward the ground, and he stumbled and nearly fell as he staggered from the tent.

"Tase him!" Jackson yelled, simultaneously pointing at the man holding the AK while diving for cover behind a tree stump. A member of his assault team must have been thinking the same thing because almost immediately, a bright red laser dot appeared on the gunman's T-shirt, followed almost immediately by two Taser darts that embedded themselves in the man's back. As a charge of fifty thousand volts surged through his body, the gunman howled and flung his hands up, throwing the rifle into the air. He fell to the ground, writhing in pain, the rifle landing two meters away.

Just as the Taser was fired, a fourth man bolted from the back of the remaining tent. He was also armed with an AK-47 but, unlike the other gunman, he was not disoriented. Instead, he headed at a full sprint for the forest. He dove through a slim opening between two blackberry hedges—the same hedges where Unit Five and Unit Six were positioned on either side. In diving between the hedges, the young man effectively split the difference between the DEA agents and escaped the perimeter.

Realizing this, he jumped to his feet and bolted into the forest. As soon as he stood, all four members of Unit Five and Unit Six saw him. They took off after him in pursuit.

Jackson jumped from behind the stump he was using for cover and reached the center of camp along with the other members of his team. His men surrounded the gardeners with their weapons leveled. The two young men standing—teenagers, actually—looked terrified. They offered no resistance and quickly raised their hands when he shouted, "Manos arriba! Manos arriba!" They were shoved to the ground and handcuffed. The third young man who'd been tased was facedown on the ground moaning and was quickly cuffed as well.

"Tend to this one," Jackson ordered.

He stepped back and looked into the trees where units Five and Six had disappeared in pursuit. "Unit Five, come in!" he ordered.

"Five here!" came a breathless reply.

"Are you in visual contact?"

"Negative."

"Then halt in your position. Six, report."

"Six. We don't see him either. We're searching."

Jackson took a brief second to catch his breath and to consider what was happening. He made up his mind quickly. Bottom line—he didn't really care if one of the gardeners got away. He wasn't there to arrest illegal aliens—they were someone else's problem. He was after the plants. The gardeners were as low as low-level could be. They had no information; they knew nothing about the organization. The only contact the gardeners would have had with any cartel higher-ups was with a foreman known as a "lunch man," who'd recruited them and who periodically brought them supplies. In fact, Jackson knew that for every gardener he busted, at least twenty-five were willing to step in for the chance to make twenty thousand dollars for four months' work. Spending time and risking lives chasing them down into the dark forest made little sense.

After all, one thing was certain—this particular gardener was armed and almost certainly didn't want to be sent back to Mexico or, worse, to prison. This made him very dangerous. It also made the potential cost of hunting him down much higher than the potential reward of catching him. Jackson pressed his transmit button. "Both units, return to the camp.

Let's let the little fish with a gun go today."

"Good idea, boss."

~~~~

An hour later, Jackson had redeployed his men. The majority of the team started the hot, dusty work of cutting and counting marijuana plants. One man guarded the prisoners. As a precaution, a four-man security team was deployed in a loose perimeter defensive position, one at each point of the compass—Jackson hadn't forgotten about the man who'd escaped. Most likely, the young gardener was halfway to Spokane by now, but Jackson wasn't taking any chances.

At 8:00 a.m., a helicopter put down in the landing zone that the team had cleared. The first of nearly thirty officers from various law enforcement agencies that would arrive throughout the morning disembarked. The men began to unload the supplies they'd need to remove the marijuana plants from the site. In addition to hauling out the plants, they estimated they'd need to remove one thousand pounds of trash, PVC piping, fertilizers, and supplies left behind by the growers. Not counting the prisoners, of course, who were hauled out with the first load.

By noon, the temperature had climbed to ninety degrees. Many of the men had stripped off their shirts. All were hard at work cutting, gathering, counting, and baling marijuana plants that would be transported to the Yakima Sheriff's Department for eventual supervised burial in a landfill. Jackson was careful not to allow the men to fall victim to the heat. He instituted mandatory rest periods in the shade every hour. The team members downed more than a dozen cases of bottled water that had been flown in on the choppers.

Finally, just after sixteen hundred, their work was complete. All the weary men had been hauled out except for Jackson and his security team. The grow was clean and a single helicopter idled in the clearing, waiting for the men to load so that it could take off.

Jackson looked out over the former grow site. He'd been up for nearly thirty-six hours, the last half spent in hard physical work. He was hot, dusty, and tired, and he knew his men were, too. Above all, though, he was grateful that none of his team had been injured. "Did we forget anything or, worse, anybody?" Jackson asked.

"No sir, boss. We triple-checked," Hamilton answered. "We got it all."

"Good." Jackson said, nodding. He gazed out over the now cleared site for several seconds, and then said, "We did good work today. Things turned out well."

"What was it," Mike Hamilton asked, "five thousand plants or so?"

"Yeah, five thousand three hundred four," Jackson said, having memorized the count from his tally sheet. "Agrees with the Intel estimate."

"At twenty-five hundred bucks a plant, what's that—twelve, thirteen million bucks?"

"Yeah. Nice bust."

The other team members nodded their agreement.

Another moment passed, and then Jackson pointed to the helicopter and said, "Let's get the hell out of here."

# PART 1

# Chapter 1

SEATTLE IS SPECTACULAR in the summer. I think it's God's way of paying back Seattleites for making us endure the long, drawn-out Pacific Northwest winters. From late October to early June, the color palette seems to meld into a gray-tone monoscape. The sky is gray. The water's gray. Even the trees look gray. The later into the season, the grayer and the more monotone it seems to get. It's almost always cloudy in the winter, but it usually doesn't rain hard. Instead, it drizzles continuously—tiny misty raindrops. And it does so for days on end, pretty much nonstop. It's not uncommon for the airport to record thirty days of continuous rain—a performance that begins to approach biblical standards. Then, just as people are about to grow moss on their feet or go insane (or both), summer finally shows up.

This generally happens around the middle of June when the "June Gloom" gives way to clear skies. The sun comes out in all its glory for four solid months. The gray landscape is shoved to the back of people's minds, where it's quickly forgotten. Seattleites hang up their Gore-Tex jackets and break out their shorts and T-shirts. Temperatures climb into the low to mid-seventies in the afternoons. Super-saturated greens of verdant forests set against brilliant blue skies and deep-blue sparkling waters touch the eyes in every direction. The contrast is so striking that tourists—sometimes even locals—stop dead in their tracks to admire the view. Summertime visitors marvel at the stunning scene and say, "It's beautiful here! There's no rain—what's all this talk about rain? We should move here!" Some do. Then winter returns. Oops. Gotcha.

It's hard to imagine anything bad happening in the paradise that is Seattle in the summer, but of course it does. There's no slow time of year in my private investigation business. People take advantage of each other pretty much year 'round. Husbands cheat on wives. Wives cheat on husbands. Employees rip off employers. People skip bail, or sometimes just disappear. Here at Logan Private Investigations, we stay busy every month of the year.

Which explains why I was sitting on the balcony of my office on Lake Union on a fine Tuesday afternoon on the sixteenth of August, trying to finish a surveillance wrap-up report on my laptop. A client of ours who owns an electronics parts distribution company kept coming up short in her inventory audits. After bringing in her auditors and back-checking her internal control procedures, she finally deduced that one or more of her employees—most likely dock employees—must be stealing from the business. But she couldn't prove it. Our client asked us to place the dock under video surveillance. That's one of our specialties, so we agreed. We took our plain white surveillance van, stuck our "Ryan's Quality Plumbing" vinyl to the sides and parked it across the street from her docks late at night. Three days later, we had the evidence to prove she was right. Now, I was trying to finish the wrap-up report.

Truth be told, I wasn't making much headway. I kept getting distracted by a Laser-class sailboat regatta taking place on the lake directly in front of me. The windward mark was just forty yards from my chair, and each time the fleet of little boats approached the mark in a bunch, I noticed a very attractive blonde in a gray Laser with *Volvo 116223* painted on its sail. She was fighting hard, holding her position near the front of the pack. Her little boat heeled precariously, causing her to hike way out. Clearly, she was in it to win. Though I can't say if she won or not, I know for certain she was a very effective distraction from the report staring up at me from my desk.

This bout of three-steps-forward-two-steps-back mind-wandering came to a sobering halt when my associate, Antoinette Blair, buzzed in on the intercom.

"Danny, there's a man named Robbie Fiore here to see you."

Robbie Fiore—now there was a name from the past.

"Thanks, Toni," I answered. "Do me a favor and bring him on back to my office, would you?"

~~~~

I grew up in Seattle and knew the Fiore family. I graduated from high school with Roberto. Robbie and I ran with different crowds, but we were friendly. In fact, we were both on the track team—I ran the mile; Robbie was a pole vaulter. Through him, I knew his kid sister Gina.

Gina was two years younger than us. She'd show up at the track meets with her friends to root for Robbie. She was one of a kind. And short—maybe five two with a fiery personality, almost to the point of being cocky. Beautiful: thick, dark hair and a knockout figure, even in high school. Unfairly beautiful, with brains to match. I'd see her in the halls at school, surrounded by girlfriends and guys with stars in their eyes. She was the center of attention, to be sure. Even though I was older than she was, she intimidated the hell out of me in those days. I'd have loved to ask her out on a date, but in high school I could never find the nerve.

Now, Gina was missing. Gone. No trace. The story had been front page in the *Seattle Times* yesterday and this morning. Even the morning edition of the national news had picked up the story and started running with it. "Local Business Heiress Vanishes."

Her picture was all over the local television news. According to the reports, Gina had not been seen since last Thursday. No clues, no ransom demand—no nothing. The police effort had started slowly, as is typical in an adult missing person case, but the press reports indicated that this was changing now. Gina's lifestyle didn't seem consistent with someone who'd simply disappear. The papers said her purse, her driver's license and credit cards, and all her personal effects were found locked in her apartment. Her car was parked in its normal space. It certainly sounded unusual at the least. Maybe even suspicious.

When I first saw the newspaper accounts, I'd thought of calling the family to offer my services, but I hadn't. I'm not sure why. Finding missing persons is one of the things we do, but I don't know, maybe it was because the timing didn't seem right yet. The police were starting to get fired up over the case, and they probably wouldn't welcome my uninvited help. I couldn't figure out how to bring it up with the family—I didn't want to just barge in. Anyway, I hadn't made the call.

~~~~

"Robbie," I said, walking to meet him as Toni brought him into my office. We shook hands. "Good to see you."

"Hi, Danny. It's been a long time," Robbie said.

"It has. I'm so sorry to hear about Gina."

"Thanks. I guess you saw the news—seems everyone has. It's not too hard to figure out why I'm here." His voice wavered—he was clearly scared. I've seen people in this situation before and I felt really bad for the guy.

"She's gone, Danny," he said, "and my family's scared to death. My parents flat adore her. She's their baby." He paused, then added, "I swear, if anything bad's happened to her, it'll probably kill them."

I nodded that I understood.

"I'm here to ask for your help," he said. His eyes were surrounded by dark circles and looked as though they were on the verge of tearing up. He looked whipped. His normally stout, six-foot frame was bent; his shoulders hunched. There were lines that appeared to be etched into his forehead. He looked like he hadn't slept for days.

"I understand," I said. "I'm eager to help. Let's talk for a few minutes about what we might be able to do." I nodded toward Toni. "Robbie, first let me introduce Toni Blair. Toni's an associate of mine. If we end up deciding that my firm can help your family locate Gina, Toni will be in on it with me. She's been with me since I opened the doors here. If it's okay with you, I'd like her to sit in with us from the start. That way, she and I can compare notes later and make sure we don't miss anything."

Robbie looked at Toni and nodded.

"I'm glad to meet you, Robbie," Toni said, shaking his hand. "I'm real sorry about your sister." There'd been no time to brief Toni on what was happening, but it really wasn't necessary anyway. She's one of those unusual people—the kind that you never see studying, but they always seem to know everything that's going on around them. More than that, I've noticed she has the unique talent of being able to put people at ease quickly. Her sincerity is genuine and shines right through. People respond well to her, as Robbie did now.

"Thanks," he said, his face brightening a little. "I appreciate that."

I directed Toni and Robbie to the little conference table in my office. "Let's have a seat, and you can tell us what's happened." They sat down while I grabbed a notepad for me and one for Toni before joining them.

"Robbie," I said, "I should start by saying we don't know anything—only what we've seen on the news and in the paper. For a number of reasons, that's not always very reliable." At least at first, the press tends to report what the police feed them. Oftentimes, the police hold things back for tactical reasons. We needed all the information. I continued, "We're going to take notes while you start at the beginning and tell us every-thing—everything you know—even the little stuff."

He nodded. "Okay." He looked at the water outside for a few mo-ments while he seemed to gather his thoughts. He cleared his voice before starting.

"Gina works for the company—that is, my dad's company: Pacific Wine and Spirits. She and I both work there. This past Friday, she didn't show up for work."

Toni and I both took notes as Robbie spoke.

"We called her and left messages at her condo and on her cell. We got no answer, no calls back. I sent her e-mails and text messages—again no answer. This isn't like her—Gina never misses work. She won't even be late for an appointment unless she calls first. By Friday afternoon, we were really starting to get worried. Cindy Dunlap, our HR director, and I decided to go to her apartment and check it out."

"You have a key then?" I asked.

"Yeah. Gina and I have always exchanged front door keys and keys to each other's cars so we can help out in case the other is out of town or something."

"Or in case you lock yourself out," Toni said.

"Right. I opened her condo and went inside and saw that she wasn't there. At first, I was relieved. Then I noticed her purse was on the counter and her keys, too. When I saw the keys, I went back outside and saw that her car was in its parking space. I hadn't noticed it on the way in."

Toni raised her hand suddenly. "Let me interrupt you for a second, Robbie," she said. "Before you get too far into what's happened over the past few days—I apologize—I should have been more clear and asked a few background questions first. I need you to back up so that we can get a few basic things out of the way."

"Oh, sorry," he said.

"No, it's not you," Toni said, "but I don't know anything about Gina—only what I've seen on TV or read in the paper in the last day or so. For instance, I don't even know her full name or how old she is."

"Oh," Robbie said. "I see. Her full name is Angelina Theresa Fiore. She's twenty-seven, born on June 14, 1984."

"Her physical description?"

"She's five feet two inches, about 105 pounds. Long, dark hair."

"Any distinguishing marks? Tattoos, piercings—that sort of thing?"

"No, nothing."

"Married?"

"No, never."

"Home address?"

"Three twenty-seven West Olympic Place, unit 304, here in Seattle," Robbie said.

"That's right near where my dad lives," I said, thinking of the house where I grew up.

"Yeah, I guess we all end up coming back to Queen Anne sooner or later," Robbie said.

Toni scribbled furiously on her notepad. "How do you two guys know each other?"

"High school," Robbie said. "Danny and I graduated from Ballard High in 2000. Gina was two years behind us."

"And church, too," I said.

"That's right," Robbie agreed. "Both our families attend St. Joseph's on Capitol Hill."

Toni nodded. "I see. Did Gina go to college here?"

"Yes, she graduated from U-Dub with a degree in business finance in—I think—2006."

"That sounds right," I added. "I went out with Gina for a bit in late 2006. She'd just recently graduated then."

Toni glanced up at me for an instant, then looked back at her notes. She wrote for a minute without speaking. The room grew quiet.

"Anything else on the background?" I asked her.

She finished writing and flipped back a strand of hair that had fallen across her face before she looked up. "No, that's good. That helps for now," she said. "Okay, Robbie. Back to current time. You're in Gina's condo. You've noticed that her purse and keys are still there and her car, too."

"Yes. After I saw all of Gina's stuff—her purse and her keys—in there, that's when I started to get worried. She wouldn't go anywhere without telling us, and she certainly wouldn't go anywhere without her purse or her keys. So I called the police to report her missing."

"Did the police send someone out?" I asked. The notion that you have to wait forty-eight or seventy-two hours before filing a missing person report with the police is an old wives' tale. On the other hand, just because you filed a report, the police wouldn't necessarily do anything right away unless there was suspicion of foul play, or unless the missing person suffered from some sort of mental condition that could put him- or herself in danger.

"They did. They were very prompt, as a matter of fact. They sent two people—a detective and a patrol officer. They looked around her condo a little and filled out a missing person report. They told us that they'd file the report, but that there wasn't much that they'd be able to do, at least not initially. I went straight over to my parents' home right afterward and told them what was happening." Robbie paused and looked around, then said, "Would I be able to get a bottled water from you?"

"Of course," I said. I hopped up and grabbed him one off the credenza.

He took a long drink and then continued. "They pretty much freaked out. My dad called Gary Frohming—our family lawyer. Gary must have had some pull with some higher-ups at the police department because later that same afternoon, the police called back. They sent out two different guys. They interviewed us and took another report."

Never hurts to have friends in high places. I knew Gina's dad, Angelo Fiore. He was "plugged-in" socially and politically. If anyone had friends with pull, it would be Angelo.

"We're still talking about last Friday, August 12?" Toni said.

"Yes."

"Okay. Do you remember who these two guys were?" I asked. "If we're able to help out and take this case on, we'll have to coordinate with them."

"I do," Robbie said. "I have their cards." He reached into his jacket, pulled out two business cards and handed them to me.

"Dwayne Brown," I said, reading the names off the cards. "I know Dwayne Brown pretty well. I don't think I've met his partner, Symanski, but I've worked with Dwayne in the past."

"He's the guy that was at our open house?" Toni asked. "The one you worked with while you were in the army?"

"Yeah," I said. I was a U.S. Army CID Special Agent at Fort Lewis with the sixth MP-CID Group for three years from 2005 to 2008. Dwayne was with the Seattle PD. We worked on three or four cases together. "Dwayne's a good guy."

"He'll cooperate with us?" Toni asked.

"Most likely," I said. "Unless he's being told not to by his bosses."

"Okay," Toni said, focusing back on Robbie. "So Robbie, you said the police came out—where'd they interview you?"

"The second time, they talked to all of us at my parents' home."

"We'll talk to them separately, but did your parents have any information they were able to add?"

"No, not really. My mom said that Gina was supposed to have come over that Friday night. Dad didn't know anything at all."

"After the interview, did the police visit Gina's condo and do any sort of investigation there?"

"Yes. The next day—last Saturday—they sent a whole team of people out. They photographed everything and took some of Gina's things— pictures and bathroom stuff, mostly. They collected some fibers from the carpet. Oh, and they took a cup from the sink. On the way out, though, Detective Brown told me that there didn't initially appear to be anything unusual or suspicious about the condo—aside from the fact that Gina wasn't in it and all of her personal stuff was."

I nodded. "Okay," I said. "Sounds like a CSI investigation. I'll follow up with him about that."

"As a matter of fact, their jackets said 'CSI'" Robbie said.

I nodded.

"I have a question," he said.

"Shoot."

"The CSI people took her hairbrush and put it in an evidence bag. Why would they do that?"

I looked at him. "It's standard procedure. They're collecting a DNA sample. It's required by Washington law for identification in missing person cases."

"Identification?" he said. "Why don't they just—" He stopped and then said, "I see. It's so that in case they find a body . . ."

"That's right. In case they find a body, they can make a positive ID using a DNA sample, even if the body is otherwise unrecognizable. Don't try to read anything into this—it's standard procedure and good police work."

He was silent for a second, then he said, "I guess it's hard not to read anything into it when you're talking about collecting a DNA sample to potentially identify the body of your sister."

"I understand," I said, "but I honestly don't think it's going to come to that." I looked him in the eyes. "Look, Robbie, I've worked through several adult missing person cases over the years. And I know you're probably scared to death, and you have a right to be. But I need to tell you, the odds are very good that Gina's fine. She'll either come waltzing home all by herself or the police, maybe with our help, will find her and she'll be okay. It may be hard to think that now, but that's probably what's going to happen. Understand?"

He nodded. I continued. "The hard part for you and your family's going to be dealing with the unknown, and particularly, dealing with the wait—the wait while the process plays out."

Robbie nodded again.

"Because of this, you guys are going to face challenges and scenarios you're not used to. As you go through them in your minds, these possibilities will run from simply unpleasant to downright horrible—the worst things that could ever happen to a family. You'd never have to consider these things in your normal, day-to-day lives. We'll talk about these things—no sense locking them in a closet and then avoiding them altogether. As a matter of fact, when the time comes, we *should* talk about them so that you can develop rationally based expectations. Part of what we can offer is a little counseling—we can help provide you with some logic and context to all the possibilities. When we do this, you'll see that the reality is that the odds of these really bad things happening to Gina are very low, even though you're probably scared shitless now."

He nodded. "We are—scared, I mean."

I nodded. "That's understandable and to be expected. For now, though, my advice to you is this: don't dwell on the unpleasant possibilities. You'll just scare yourself even more. And if *you* are scared, then your *parents* will be scared to death—scared at a time when they need your strength the most. Make sense?"

He nodded.

"Be strong for your parents; they'll need your support. Take my advice. Bottle up the fears so you can channel your mental energy into something productive—liking helping to find Gina."

He nodded. "I appreciate that, Danny."

"No problem. But while we're on this line of touchy questions, have the police said anything about ransom demands?" I asked. "Have they set up a recording system or some sort of monitoring system on your phones? I'm assuming there's been no contact at all by anyone with anything to do with Gina regarding any sort of ransom?"

"Yes, they are monitoring my mom and dad's phone. They set it up Saturday. But you're right—we haven't heard a word from anyone that would make us believe she's been kidnapped," Robbie said. "No calls. No letters. No e-mails."

"Good," I continued. "Now back to our questions. Let's shift gears and talk about Gina and her behavioral traits. I know Gina from high school and from our brief time together in 2006, but this doesn't amount to much—especially now, five years later. What can you tell us about her?"

"Well," Robbie said, "she's supersmart. She works hard. She's outgoing. She's usually happy, although she does have a temper. She's focused. She's a great manager at work." This meshed perfectly with the Gina I remembered. It didn't sound like she'd changed at all.

"Question," Toni said. "When you say 'usually happy,' how had she been acting for the few weeks before last Thursday?"

"Maybe a little different," Robbie said. He thought for a few seconds, then said, "I wouldn't call it unhappy. She never seemed unhappy. If anything, I might call it preoccupied. Like when you have a big project at work and it demands all your attention."

"Was there anything going on at work that would have caused her to be preoccupied?" Toni asked.

"That's the thing. There's nothing. It's a pretty routine time for us.

No expansions, no new distributor lines, nothing."

"Business is good?"

"Business is very good," Robbie answered. "Seems the worse the economy gets, the more people want to drink. Since Gina took over the finance department five years ago, our profitability's gone through the roof."

This made sense. I'd have been surprised if she'd have been anything other than an excellent business manager. I said, "So she didn't mention anything at all that might have caused her to be preoccupied?"

"No—at least, not to me."

"How often do you speak to your sister?" Toni asked.

"She heads the finance department; I head operations. We work in different ends of the same building. We'd talk about business every couple of days, sometimes more often. We had weekly staff meetings with all the department heads. And we'd meet at mom and dad's place for lunch sometimes, usually on Sundays."

We scribbled on our notepads, trying to keep up. After a moment, Toni said, "Okay. Let's change topics again. Gina has no history of just up and disappearing? Never done this before?"

"Never," Robbie said.

"Okay," Toni continued. "I don't mean to be indelicate, but is Gina straight or homosexual?"

Robbie looked surprised. "I think she's straight," he said.

"How about boyfriends or girlfriends?"

Robbie shook his head. "Well, first off, I don't know of any boyfriends. Certainly nobody she brought home to meet the family. But that doesn't mean she didn't have boyfriends that I don't know about. She may have—she'd probably not have told me unless she thought I needed to know."

That was a pretty good summary of the Gina I thought I knew: she'd tell you if she thought you needed to know. She'd probably not tell you just to share information, like girlfriend-to-girlfriend chitchat.

"As to girlfriends," he continued, "I think she was friendly with a couple of the girls in the finance and accounting department. Those girls would be good for you to talk to—they probably know more about Gina's social life than I do."

"Okay," Toni said. "Does she use drugs? Any problems with alcohol?"

"As far as I know, she's never used drugs. She'll have a social drink or a glass of wine, but she's not an alcoholic or anything like that."

"Good," Toni said. She wrote in her notebook. "How about any sort of personal problems? Any history of mental illness? Depression? Anything like that?"

"No mental illness. No personal problems I'm aware of."

"Do you think she might be suicidal at all? Has she ever mentioned suicide?"

"Never."

"Okay. Can you get us some recent photos?"

"Yeah. Mom's got a bunch."

"Good."

I spent a minute reviewing my notes, then said, "Robbie, if we're able to go to work on the case we'll need a complete list of people from your organization that you think we should talk to—people who work with Gina or even just know her."

"Okay," he said, staring at the wall, concentrating intently on something.

"And—" I started to say when he interrupted me.

"Wait a second," he said, "I made a mistake."

"What's that?" Toni asked, looking up from her notepad.

"Of course there was one guy that Gina brought home to meet my parents."

My upper body tensed.

"Who?" Toni asked. "Do you have a name for this guy?"

"Yeah," Robbie said. He turned to me. "It was you."

~~~~

Toni looked at me, her mouth partly open, questions in her eyes. After a moment she recovered and said, "Danny? Anything you want to add?"

"Give me a second."

I pictured Gina in my mind the way I remembered her—laughing, witty, happy, on top of the world.

I thought about it and figured that, in front of Robbie, I didn't know how to say that I'd had a secret crush on Gina probably since the first time I saw her in high school. She was magnetic—everyone was attracted to her.

I didn't know how to say that I watched her in school for two years and wished that she was somehow as attracted to me as I was to her.

I didn't know how to say that after high school, I dealt with this by classifying it as a silly boyhood crush. That is, until I bumped into Gina in late 2006 and all the old feelings came back again. This time, at least, I'd grown up enough to find the guts to ask her out. To my never-ending joyous surprise, she'd said yes.

I didn't know how to say that I spent three of the best weeks of my life with Gina in November of 2006. She was two years younger than I, but she was the one who had all the answers. She was the one who seemed totally sure of what she was doing and where she was going. I was happy just to be there with her.

I didn't know how to say that I was crushed when I had to ship out to Quantico, Virginia, just after Thanksgiving that year for three months of FBI Advanced Training School and that during that time, our romance fizzled.

Finally, I sure as hell didn't know how to say that, at least as of November 2006 when we were together, Gina was damn sure straight.

I didn't know how to say any of this crap, so instead I just said, "No, I only saw her for a few weeks at the end of 2006. I can't think of anything to add."

~~~~

Toni stared at me with a cynical expression on her face that made it look like she was about ready to call, "Bullshit!" Rather than stare back at her, I did the manly thing—I looked away. It was quiet for a few seconds, then I turned back, avoiding Toni's probing glare, and said, "Tell you what, why don't we leave it at that for now, Robbie. That gives us some really useful background information. We're not going to solve the case this afternoon. We're just gathering some basic information to see if we're able to take the case on. If we do, we'll have a lot more questions. Toni, do you have anything else?" I turned to her.

Whether she did or not, she could tell I wanted to end the interview, so she looked down at her notes, flipped through a couple of pages and then looked back up and smiled. She said, "No, we're good for now." She glanced at me and added, "I think we've got plenty to work on here."

"Okay." I turned back to Robbie. "Robbie, to summarize, you want to hire our firm to find Gina—whether she's disappeared voluntarily for some reason or whether, God forbid, she's fallen victim to foul play."

Robbie nodded. "That's right."

"Alright, we'd like to help," I said. "Before we can answer you for sure, I need to do three things. First, I have to meet with Detective Brown and find out SPD's posture on our helping. We need them to approve our getting involved, or, at least, for them to have no insurmountable objections."

"I don't think that should be a problem," he said.

"Good." I appreciated his optimism. Chalk it up to friends in high places, I suppose. That's okay. I could use a little benevolence-by-association. "Second thing, I need to have a meeting with my staff to find out from my whole team whether or not we think we can actually be of service or if we'd just get in the way. We like to talk over the big cases like this as a group before we make a commitment. We need to be comfortable that we have the capabilities and that we'd actually be adding something."

He nodded, and I continued. "If both of those go well, the last thing I'll need to do is talk to you again, but this time with your parents. We need to get their stories. I think all of these things can happen by tomorrow. Based on that, are you okay if we set a tentative time for two o'clock tomorrow, at your parents' home?"

"Good," Robbie said. "The sooner the better." He stood to leave. "I want you to know that whatever happens, we'll be extremely grateful if you'd help us try to find her. We feel completely helpless and, frankly, that's not a position my family often finds itself in. My dad's a borderline Type A personality and Gina's the absolute definition of a super–Type A personality." He looked at us and the scared expression he'd been wearing when he arrived was back. "I'm not that way and neither's mom. When our family bumps into a problem, usually Dad—or recently, more likely Gina—will take charge and make things happen. With Gina gone, we're kind of floundering. We don't know what to do, and it's killing us."

I understood. Angelo Fiore may have been the head of the family, but it was sounding like Gina Fiore was the engine that made it run. Now that the engine was missing, the family was powerless and grounded—helpless and confused.

~~~~

Toni took Robbie to the door and said good-bye while I reviewed my notes. A few minutes later, she came back to my office and sat down. She hoisted her Doc Martens up onto the corner of my desk and stared at me while she chewed on the end of a pencil. She said nothing.

Finally, I looked up and said, "What?"

"What, nothing," she said, a bit of a smirk beginning to show on her face. I recognized the look. It meant different things at different times, but usually it meant that she was about to have some fun at my expense.

"What do you want, you—you little pain in the butt?" I asked.

She didn't look away. "Oh, nothing. I'm just waiting for you to tell me the whole story about you and this missing mystery woman." Toni's eyes sparkle when she's being mischievous, like now. She enjoyed seeing me on the hot seat, and she was instantly able to ascertain that, indeed, that's where I was.

Antoinette "Toni" Blair is a twenty-six-year-old Seattle grunge child blessed with strikingly good looks, kind of like a "grunge" fashion model. Think Katy Perry with tattoos. Taller, "grungier," but the same beautiful face, same breathtaking figure, same medium-length black hair, same brilliant blue eyes. No denying, Toni is easy to look at. She and I went to a charity black-tie function on behalf of the agency a couple of times and let me just say, she dresses up real nice. She swapped her leathers and her studs for a striking evening gown that covered up her tats while uncovering her dazzling cleavage. Her dark hair and blue eyes, not to mention her killer figure, immediately magnetized every set of male eyes in the room. Blam! Game over. I have to admit, it was a pretty cool feeling having her on my arm as we made our way to our table. No doubt the wealthy tech geeks who usually go to those sorts of things thought, "What's a knockout bomb like her doing with a shithead like him?" Ha! Get over it, propeller-head.

The sparkling blue eyes, drop-dead figure, and stunning intellect not-withstanding, I think my favorite Toni Blair feature just might be her smile. She actually has several she can use, ranging from a coy, seductive grin all the way to a full-power, stupefying Julia Roberts–like megawatt blast that can stop a train. I'm still figuring it out, but I think it has some-thing to do with the connection between the lips and the eyes. Actually, her whole face gets in on the act of smiling. She has a unique ability to convey a wide range of emotions with her smile. Without even seeming to try, she's a master at it.

Toni's parents were divorced when she was young. Her mom raised her and her younger sister while working full-time first as a waitress, then later as a manager of a restaurant in Lynnwood, north of Seattle. She saved money her whole life so that Toni would be able to go to college. I met Toni in 2007 when we were both seniors at U-Dub in the Criminal Justice department. I was still in the army at the time, and Toni worked part-time at the restaurant her mom managed—still manages, in fact. In 2008, after I was discharged from the army, I opened Logan Private In-vestigations. Toni basically hired herself and became my first employee. Turned out to be the best move I ever made.

Toni is a serious private investigator. Not only is she pretty to look at, but she's tough. And I don't mean girl tough. I mean take-your-best-shot, kick-your-ass guy tough. Dead shot with the Glock 23 she's always got tucked somewhere on her person. Also, she's damn good at Krav Maga—the Israeli army martial art that I picked up in Afghanistan and have been practicing ever since. Toni and I train together once a week or so. Woe be it to the fool who pisses her off. Pick your weapon, but if you go up against Toni, you'd better bring your "A" game.

Attractive as Toni is, I'd seen plenty of workplace romances end badly—most of them, I suppose. I knew better than to mix my work life with my love life, so I always considered her strictly off-limits. I exer-cised restraint (not always easy), and I never made a move on her. I knew she understood, and I think she felt the same way. But this didn't stop her from messing with me, just for shits and giggles. For instance, when we'd practice our grappling, if I started to get the better of her, she'd think nothing of grabbing me in the crotch and squeezing, then laughing when I immediately tapped out. Then she'd laugh even more when I'd get pissed afterwards—laugh herself silly, in fact. Shit like that.

She hates to lose. She's a kick, but she knows me so well that she could tell when she had me pinned down on something. She enjoyed it immensely.

"Give it up, Logan," she said, smiling. "I can't do my job unless I have all the details. I need facts, man."

"Alright, alright," I said, acquiescing. She wasn't going to give up until I told her. "It's simple. For two years in high school, I had a silent crush on Gina—same as probably 90 percent of the other guys at my school. Nothing came of it. Then, six years later, out of the blue, I bump into her at Starbucks. We start talking and end up spending an hour there. I guess I'd grown up, because in high school the thought of approaching her scared the shit out of me. Now, it was easy to talk to her. Asking her out seemed natural. Fortunately, she said yes."

"Did you fall in love?"

"No, I didn't fall in love," I said. "We were only together three weeks."

Toni smiled her little impish smile. She kept working me. "Did you— you know, did you two . . . consummate the relationship?"

I glared at her. "Fuck you, Blair—none of your goddamned business."

She laughed out loud, knew she'd gotten to me.

"Laugh it up. If you must know, we had a fabulous few weeks together before I shipped out to advanced training at the FBI Academy in Virginia. I had a dumpy little apartment in south Tacoma then, near Fort Lewis, where I was stationed. I'd drive up to Seattle most every night, and Gina and I'd go to a movie or out to dinner, or sometimes just hang out at her place. She'd just graduated from U-Dub and was working full-time at her dad's business. She had a nice apartment in Fremont. She took me home for Thanksgiving that year with her family."

"Go on," Toni said, when I paused to reflect how nice the holiday had been.

"Yeah. Well, three days after Thanksgiving, I shipped out. Our romance kind of fizzled then. It was hard on me, but I wouldn't say I was brokenhearted. I guess we'd not been together long enough for those kind of emotional ties to have set in. Disappointed was probably a better word. Not in her or in me—just disappointed in the circumstances that tore us apart." I thought back about those times—the highs followed by the lows.

Toni was respectfully silent for a few seconds; then she said, "Well, look at the bright side, Danny. When we find her, you'll be able to light a new fire there."

"Yeah? I don't know about that." I thought for a few seconds, and then said, "Actually, I see two problems with that."

"One?" she asked.

"One. We have to find her."

She shrugged. "If she's alive, we'll find her," she said, no doubt whatsoever in her voice. "What's number two?"

"Remember Thomas Wolfe?" I asked.

She thought for a second, and then smiled. "Ah yes," she said. "Here it comes. You're going to say 'You Can't Go Home Again,' aren't you?"

I was impressed that she guessed where I was going, though I probably shouldn't have been.

"Well, that's bullshit, you sentimental sop," she said. "You can do whatever you want."

I like Toni. She needles me a lot, but I think I'll keep her.

# Chapter 2

THE PARKING SITUATION at the Seattle Police Department headquarters really sucks. Basically, there isn't any. Visitors have to park curbside (good luck!) or at a remote lot. And I do mean remote. One time, I got back to the office so frustrated that I figured there had to be a better way. I looked on their website for what I was certain would be a nearby hidden lot that I'd failed to discover even after circling the building four hundred times. The website said, "Take mass transit." Seriously. Look it up.

Being an optimist, I told myself that this time it'll be different—this time I'll find a close spot, right by the lobby. Nope. I circled around and around the block for fifteen minutes looking for someone pulling out. Toni took it in good stride. She pointed to a guy on the corner, "Hey, isn't that the same homeless guy we saw on our last orbit?" she said. "And the one before?" Ha, ha. Finally, completely fed up with the whole business, I gave in and parked in a structure five blocks away, same as the last time here. We had a nice little hike back.

The Seattle Police Department is headquartered in the nearly new Seattle Justice Center, located just off I-5 on James Street in downtown Seattle. The idea behind the Justice Center was to house the police department and the municipal courts in the same building. Given their missions, this makes a certain amount of sense. Seattle City Hall is right across the street to the west and the Seattle Municipal Tower—the fourth tallest building in Seattle at sixty-eight stories—is across the street to the north. A tidy little package (if you're willing to overlook the lack of parking).

When the Justice Center was built in 2002, the architect thought it might be cool to essentially split the building design right down the middle to reflect the different characteristics of its two tenants. The southern half of the building houses the courts and is a light, airy, glassed-in structure meant to signify the transparency and balance of the judicial system. The northern half of the building houses the police department and is meant to look solid and secure. I think they missed, and instead, landed on stark and imposing. The two halves of the buildings are shoved together to form a single structure—sort of an odd-looking architectural chimera. Weird. Then again, I'm not very cool, so I probably don't get it. And besides, I was in Iraq marching in the desert when the building was designed. Nobody asked my opinion then, and it's damn sure too late now.

We made it to Dwayne Brown's floor, fifteen minutes late. I hadn't seen Dwayne for several years, and I was worried for two reasons. I had a slight concern that he might not remember me. I had a bigger concern that he'd remember me just fine and might not welcome the intrusion of a private investigator into the middle of his case. Usually, police departments need private investigators like ducks need roller skates. We checked in with the secretary on the eighth floor, pinned on our visitors' badges, and sat down to wait.

Two minutes later, Dwayne entered the lobby. "Danny Logan!" he said with delight. He shook my hand enthusiastically. "It is really good to see you, man. The last time was at your office's grand opening party. How've you been?" I breathed a little easier. The warm greeting was promising.

Dwayne hadn't aged at all in the past three years. At five ten, 180 pounds, he's just a little on the plump side. Short hair. Sharp dresser. He looked like a successful African American businessman. With a badge and a gun.

"Doing really well," I replied, relieved that he seemed glad to see me. "The agency's coming along—we're busy most all the time. How 'bout you—" I noticed the title on his name tag, "—Lieutenant? Moving on up, I see."

"Yeah, yeah, they bumped me up last year. Put me in charge of the Special Investigations detail."

"Excellent. Congratulations," I said.

I nodded toward Toni. "Dwayne, I don't know if you remember Toni Blair. Toni's an associate of mine."

"How could I forget," he said. "Good to see you again, Toni. You watching this guy here?" he said, laughing, as he slapped me on the shoulder.

"Like a hawk," Toni said, smiling.

"Good, good," he said. He turned back to me. "Danny, I know why you're here. You're here about Gina Fiore. I figured I'd see you sooner or later about this. Let's go back to my office and talk."

*That's an odd thing to say*, I thought, as we followed him back to his office.

Dwayne punched a security code into the keypad next to a door labeled *Authorized Personnel Only*. We followed him through.

"Come on in," he said, as we entered. "Have a seat over there." He motioned to a small table in the corner of his office.

"Thanks again for meeting with us," I said, as we sat down. "I assume you know who Roberto Fiore is."

Dwayne nodded.

"Yesterday," I continued, "Robbie came to our office and asked for our help in locating his sister. He told us you were handling the case for SPD. I told him that before we could accept the case on behalf of his family, we needed to clear things with you. My firm has an excellent relationship with SPD, and that's worth a lot to me. I won't do anything to jeopardize that—particularly by stomping around in a case where I'm not wanted."

"Appreciate that, but you can relax," Dwayne said. "That's how I knew you'd be here. I'm the one who told Robbie to call you."

"Really?" I said. "Well. I guess that explains why he didn't think there'd be a problem with the police."

"Yeah," Dwayne said, laughing. "I figured maybe we can help each other—just like old times, right?" Before I could answer, he continued. "Yeah. Oh well, the deal is—" he paused and then started again. "Well, better if I start from the beginning, so you'll understand what's going on." He opened a notebook that he'd brought to the table. "Last Friday—12 August—I get a call from my boss, Captain John Dwyer. I met with Captain Dwyer at 1630, and he told me that we had a potential high-profile missing person case coming in—that being Gina Fiore. It's potentially high profile partly because Gina Fiore is a very pretty young woman and

partly because her father Angelo Fiore is a longtime, well-respected Seattle businessman."

"Let me guess," I said. "He's a big backer of the mayor."

"Don't know, but it wouldn't surprise me in the least," Dwayne said.
He continued. "Our Special Investigations detail works only with certain
high-profile cases. As you probably know, most MP cases stay in the precinct where they originate. If they heat up—that is, if they become more
high profile, then sometimes the case gets bumped up to us. That's what
happened here. Somebody at West Precinct recognized the Fiore name,
and even though the investigating officers had determined that she didn't
appear to be an endangered person, they were smart enough to kick it
over to us immediately. Captain Dwyer and I went over the report filed by
the West Precinct officers who were first on scene. Then, at 1800—" he
turned to Toni and said, "That's 6:00 p.m. civilian time."

"I know," Toni said. She nodded toward me. "He does it all the time.
Either way's fine with me."

"Good," Dwayne continued. "At 1800, I went back out and interviewed the family again. The young lady had been missing since the previous evening. Even though her brother said nothing appeared out of place
in the young woman's condo, I suggested to the captain, and he agreed,
that we send a CSI team out to document the scene. You know that this is
something we don't do very often—use CSI to investigate a scene where
we're not even certain a crime has taken place. In this case, we thought it
might be prudent. We were worried that a normally reliable young woman
had suddenly dropped off the grid.

"CSI did an examination on Saturday morning, 13 August starting at
0900. They spent almost three hours on scene. Of course, a few people
had been in the condo before CSI got there while the scene was uncontrolled. But, her brother was first, and he said he found her condo door
locked with a deadbolt, which is the norm for the young woman. There
was no sign of forced entry. There was no sign of struggle and no signs
of anything out of place. They noted that the purse, keys, and car were
there. Aside from that, there were no clues at all, except for a behavior
anomaly—she'd never done this sort of thing in the past."

"The fact that all her stuff was still in the condo is pretty odd," I said.
"How about driver's license, credit cards, cash, that sort of thing?"

"All still in her purse on the kitchen counter," Dwayne said. "Strange, indeed."

"Did you get—" I started to ask a question, but Dwayne raised his hand to cut me off.

"Hold up for a second and let me finish this thought. Then you can ask all the questions you want," he said.

I nodded okay.

"I briefed the family on the results Saturday afternoon in a meeting at their house at fourteen hundred. I told them there was absolutely no initial sign of foul play. No signs of any sort of a struggle. I told them there was no reason to believe she'd been kidnapped, but we went ahead and set up a standard remote phone monitor on the parents' line. My impression—they seemed to be scared, but under control.

"By Sunday morning, another day had gone by and we hadn't heard from Gina directly nor had we received any sort of ransom call. Captain Dwyer and I decided that we wanted to get the word out and bring the public in. We made the decision to release the news to the press, which we did in a press conference Sunday afternoon—14 August—at 1500. The press has featured the story prominently since then. In fact, I'm told that a national news agency has picked up the story now."

"I saw it on Fox News yesterday and today," Toni said.

"There you are, then," Dwayne said. "Now I know you know that, statistically speaking, 90 percent of adults who go missing do it voluntarily and eventually turn up. There's no law against wanting to be left alone. With that in mind, you know it's hard for us to allocate resources to track down adult missing person unless there's some sign of a crime, or unless the adult has a history of mental illness. Technically, Gina Fiore meets neither of these criteria, so that means she falls through the cracks." Dwayne paused for a second.

I took the opportunity to ask a question. "Dwayne, normally when someone bolts, they take their credentials and, usually, their car with them," I said. "Does that alter your position at all regarding allocation of resources?"

"Good point, and yes it does alter our position. I'm a realist, which means I don't imagine that the fact that Ms. Fiore is Angelo Fiore's daughter hurts matters, either. That makes it hard for SPD to sit on the sidelines and not allocate resources to the case. Based on these two things, Captain Dwyer has authorized me to start an investigation into her disappearance. First, and most important, we want to find this young lady out of general principle—it's our job. But we also damned sure don't want to be accused of sleeping at the switch in case this turns out bad."

"Whatever the motivation, I'm sure the family will be grateful," I said.

Dwayne nodded.

"What's the makeup of your team," I asked.

Dwayne smiled. "Simple. Me and Gus. You probably haven't met Gus."

"Have not," I said.

Dwayne reached for his phone and punched in a couple of numbers. A moment later he said, "Hey Gus, come in here a second. Got someone I want you to meet."

Dwayne turned back to us. "While we wait for Gus, keep asking your questions. I'll do the best I can to answer them now."

"Okay," I said. "First question. Can you get us copies of the initial report, your interview notes, and the CSI report?"

He held up his hands and starting ticking off the requirements with his fingers, one by one. "One, if you are engaged by the Fiores; two, if they will sign a written release; and three, if you'll sign a confidentiality agreement, then yes to all of the above. Also, four, I want copies of the licenses and the CCW permits of anyone you're going to have working the case. Nothing gets released to anyone not on the list."

"Agreed. Next," I said. "Does SPD have any people you're already looking at in connection with the disappearance? Any leads, any witnesses?"

"None. Not yet. We haven't even started. We'll share whatever we develop and we'll expect you to do the same thing."

"Okay." I looked at my notebook. "Next question. We'll have a look at registered sex offenders. Along those lines, does your homicide unit have any serial killers they're working on in this area that we should be concerned with?"

"I've already made a call to homicide to find out," Dwayne said. "I haven't heard back yet. I'll check and get back to you with that as soon as they get back to me."

"We need to visit the crime scene," I said.

"Well, technically it's not a crime scene," Dwayne answered.

"True." I said. "Whatever you call it, though, we'll need to take a look at her apartment and her car."

"CSI is done. The scene's released. You can look anytime you want," Dwayne said.

"Okay. More specifically, we'd like to look at the scene as an integrated team. Toni and I and you and your team—I mean, you and Gus. I'd like to know we're all seeing things the same way."

"Alright," Dwayne answered, slowly. "That makes sense. Let me look at my schedule." He studied his mobile phone for a second, then said, "Assuming we get the paperwork handled, how about tomorrow morning at eight? I have a ten o'clock meeting back here, but that should give us enough time."

"Good," I answered. "Make sure you bring the CSI report and all their exhibits—sketches, pictures, everything."

"I will."

"Okay," I said. "Next, if we do take this case, how do you see us fitting in? How should we coordinate?"

Before Dwayne could answer, a short, round middle-aged man with only thin strands of hair and wearing a plaid sport coat entered the room.

"Ah," Dwayne said. "Sergeant Gus Symanski, meet Danny Logan and his partner, Antoinette Blair."

"Call me Toni," Toni said, hopping out of her seat and extending her hand to Symanski.

"Charmed," Symanski said to Toni, clearly not having expected to see someone like her when he entered the office. He recovered quickly though, and turned to me. "Danny Logan," he said, reaching to shake my hand. "Lieutenant Brown's mentioned you a few times over the past couple of years. Army Special Forces. War hero. Silver Star."

"No Special Forces. No hero. Just regular infantry, 101st Airborne," I corrected. I didn't want anybody to think I'd been a snake-eater. And, despite the medals, I was uncomfortable with the hero moniker.

"Glad to meet you." He handed me a business card that read Detective Goscislaw Symanski. "I was regular army during Desert Storm. First

Infantry Division."

"Really? First Infantry," I said. "Big Red One. You guys were the point of the spear, weren't you?"

"Damn straight," Gus answered. "One day I'll buy the beers, and we can bullshit about the army."

I nodded at my fellow soldier and said, "Hooah."

"Sit down, Gus," Dwayne said. "I was just about to lay out some ground rules for our private investigator friends here."

Gus took the fourth seat.

"Okay, Danny. You guys have more time and are probably going to be better paid than we are. You can focus on one case. We have—" he looked at Gus.

"Fourteen," Gus said.

"Fourteen active cases," Dwayne said. "So you may find yourselves in a better position to expedite things than we are."

I nodded in agreement.

"Then again," he continued, "We're not going to be sitting on our well-dressed, bureaucratic asses over here, waiting for you to solve this case for us. We'll be working our own plan, developing leads, conducting interviews—you know, police shit."

I nodded again.

"Unfortunately, counting Gus and me, our department consists of two people. Fact is, we're mostly managers these days. We coordinate the different assets of our organization to bring cases to a resolution. Now, you guys get to be one of our assets."

"Sounds fun," I said.

"We may be able to grab some people from different departments around here, from time to time. I assume you'll be using the same procedures, just like in your army CID days. This means that the likelihood of tripping over our respective dicks—" he looked at Toni and said, "Pardon me, ma'am—no disrespect intended."

"No offense taken," Toni smiled.

"Anyway, the likelihood of us . . . bumping into each other during the investigation is pretty good. So the only way this can work between us is if we share everything—preferably before it happens. If you're going to interview someone, you need to know if we haven't already talked to them, and vice versa. We each need to know what the other team's come up with. We've got to get coordinated and stay coordinated. We can't be tripping over each other out there. Bad for business and with all the press likely to be around, we'll look like jackasses. And that, my friend," he said, pausing to straighten his tie as if he were about to go on camera, "is something we never do."

"Understood. How about regular meetings?" I suggested.

"Agreed. Next on my list, actually," he said. "Weekly's probably not enough and daily's probably too much. So we'll go with weekly meetings for now supplemented by lots of phone calls. Make sense? Just to be clear: nobody makes a move without letting me know first. This is my case and my ass on the line. I want your help—probably even need your help. But it has to go my way."

"Got it," I said. "That's not a problem with us. Where and when do you want to meet? And please don't say here. This place is a pain in the ass to park at."

Dwayne smiled. "Same time next week. Same place." He looked at Gus. "Gus, hook these guys up with a lot pass, will you?"

Gus nodded.

~~~~

"How well do you know Dwayne?" Toni asked, as I drove us from the police station to our office. "Are you concerned that we might not be able to do the job with him breathing down our necks?"

"I think we're okay," I said. "My job at Fort Lewis was to investigate felony crimes committed by soldiers. There's a good deal of overlap and cooperation between CID and local police departments. That's how I came to meet him."

"He's okay to work with?"

"Yeah, he's great. He's been a cop for twenty-some odd years. Worked himself up from patrolman. He's honest and he works hard. He likes busting bad guys."

We drove without talking for several minutes before Toni said, "Danny, when you talk about the army, you always talk about your time at CID, but you hardly ever mention your time before that in the war unless you're with another soldier."

"It makes me uncomfortable," I said.

"I can see that. It's because of the hero talk, isn't it?"

"Partly that."

"What else?"

"Partly because I don't think people will understand. They won't re-late."

She thought about this. "You could explain things," she said.

"Maybe," I said. I thought for a second, and then added, "The other thing is I think the experience of being in combat is so vivid, so intense, that after it's over and you're lucky enough to make it home, you can get to the point mentally where nothing else measures up. Then, before you know it, you find yourself in a position where the most intense, most memorable thing you ever did in your whole entire life is in the past. Rearview mirror shit. I've seen a lot of guys like that. They're still mentally stuck in Vietnam or Kuwait or Iraq—wherever. They seem to base their entire self-identities on their military experiences. They define themselves by it. Like I said, the high point of their lives is in the past. I understand this and I can see why it happens, but I don't want to be one of those guys. For my own sanity, I need to believe, firmly, that my best, most intense days are ahead, not behind. I don't want the best part of my life to already be over. That idea sucks. The military experience will always be there, part of who I am. It's helped shape me, helped influence me, helped me grow up. But the actual combat experience itself is just a part—not the whole thing."

Toni considered what I'd said for a minute. "Interesting," she said. "But even if you don't define yourself by your military experience, and you certainly don't, it's still a part of who you are—even if just a small part. I still don't understand why you never talk about it at all. It's not like some evil genie that if you let it out of the bottle, it'll take over your mind and soul. You can choose to not allow it to take over, you know."

"I know. The other thing, I guess, is that some good people died—friends. They were in the same place doing the same exact thing as me. One guy was standing four feet away and he got hit. They didn't make it, and I did. Pure, dumbass luck. They don't make it home and they get a flag for their parents. I'm standing four feet away and I do make it home and I get a medal. That makes me uneasy. My sacrifice seems pretty pale in comparison to theirs."

"But I read your commendations. I think you're downplaying what you did. You didn't get the medal for just standing around. You did some pretty brave things. Incredible, really."

"It's a little embarrassing when I try to explain what happened. I wasn't thinking about any of the stuff the commendations talk about when we were under fire," I said. "It was almost involuntary. Actually, I saw my friends getting hurt and it scared the shit out of me. Then it really pissed me off, so I lost my mind—I lost my fear, anyway. Then, I just did what I had to do. Nothing special. If you live, later on maybe they call you a hero. But it wasn't something I was after. It was an involuntary response to a nasty situation. Like when someone swings at you, you swing back."

She thought about that for a second, then said, "Maybe by celebrating our heroes—the ones who fought and made it home—it helps us to deal with the loss of those who didn't make it. Maybe celebrating our heroes is important and necessary."

"Maybe. But I didn't sign up for that, and I'm not comfortable with it." I glanced over at her. "By the way, who made you psychologist of the week?"

Toni smiled. "Just trying to put the pieces together, boss."

# Chapter 3

LOGAN PI'S OFFICE is located on Westlake Avenue, directly on Lake Union across from Chandler's Cove, on the south end of the second floor of a fifty-year-old, two-story building. The building has wood siding that used to be a faded hue of drab green until they repainted earlier this summer with a new, bright, shiny version of drab green.

This is okay by me because I didn't select the place for its color. My office is located in the back of our building, which means it's on the water. This is what I was after. Even better, the rear of the building is built on piers, so I have a balcony outside my office that actually sits out over the water. If you fall over the rail, you're swimming in Lake Union. I tried it once—dove in on purpose: one and a half, pike position. Nailed it. Toni was impressed.

The conference room is next to my office, also on the water. Through its large glass doors, it has access to the same balcony. When we moved in, the conference room, like the rest of the office, had fifteen-year-old commercial carpet in a color that they used to call "Harvest Gold" in the day when people would actually buy harvest gold anything. The walls were dingy beige, and the ceiling was stained a dusty, dirty gray. In a desperate frenzy of design inspiration, we ripped out all of the carpets and replaced the flooring with walnut hardwood and area rugs. We painted the walls bright white—even added wainscoting and crown molding. We yanked down the old curtains and replaced all the ceiling tiles. Bingo! Instant renovation. What was once a dark, dank space was transformed into a light, airy place with fantastic views from most offices.

The new, traditionally styled decor even made our second-hand furniture actually look good—promoted it automatically from junk to antique, just like that. My old, beat-up conference table suddenly wasn't old and beat-up anymore—it was "distressed." What used to be pits, scratches, and gouges became a design feature that I'd probably have had to pay extra for if it were new. The rickety chairs that surrounded the table that I'd bought second-hand from a real estate broker suddenly looked like part of an expensive "shabby chic" interior design master plan. All in all, the transformation was remarkable, both for the small amount of money it took to achieve and for the dramatic change when it was complete. We were happy here.

By the time Toni and I had worked our way through downtown traffic, parked, and then made our way upstairs, we were ten minutes late and most of the other members of my team were already waiting for us in the conference room.

Kenny Hale was doing what Kenny usually does—banging away on a laptop computer, oblivious to everything around him. Kenny is about five eight and skinny—maybe 140 pounds—with an unruly mop of dark hair. I think he's the model on which all computer geeks are created. He's on my payroll as IT Director but he also moonlights for half a dozen tech companies around here. We joke that when Microsoft runs into a real stumper, they call Kenny. Kenny doesn't have a college degree, most likely because there's no one at U-Dub who knows more than he does about computers, and he's not shy about reminding them of that. Sometimes he seems to have trouble remembering that other people have feelings, too. He has a sharp wit and is truly the smartest guy in the room. Just ask him. He looked up when we entered and said, "There you guys are. I was about ready to hack your cell phones and track you down so we could make sure you were okay."

"Very funny," I said, walking past him and setting some files down on the conference room table. "Can he actually do that?" I whispered to Toni. She nodded. *Great.*

"Sorry we're late," I said. "We got behind looking for parking at SPD this morning and we never caught up."

"It happens," said Richard Taylor, who was sitting in the conference room chair, back to the table, watching a floatplane take off from Lake Union. He spun back toward us and smiled. "You know, they actually built those civic center buildings downtown with no parking," he said.

I nodded. Technically speaking, Richard is not on Logan PI's payroll. I bought the company from Richard in February 2008. He'd owned Taylor Private Investigations for nearly twenty years. I've had Richard paid off for the purchase of his business for more than a year, but he still likes to sit in on case conferences. I welcome his input—Richard's seen almost everything in a law enforcement career that's spanned almost fifty years—thirty as a detective with SPD, followed by twenty doing PI work. Richard is a tall, lanky, seventy-something-year-old with bright blue eyes and a head full of pure white hair. He's as sharp as he ever was, which is to say, very sharp indeed.

"I'm eager to hear about this case. Toni told me just enough to tantalize me," he said. "A new case makes my fingers tingle."

"Could also be because your Viagra didn't wear off yet," Kenny said.

"Only your mother knows that for sure, runt," Richard fired back. He takes no shit from Kenny.

"Where's Doc?" I asked as Toni and I joined the others at the conference table.

"Right here," said Joaquin Kiahtel as he entered the room. "I had a call."

Joaquin "Doc" Kiahtel is 100 percent, purebred Chiricahua Apache Indian. He claims to be a direct descendant of Cochise, and I've no reason to argue with him. Besides, my mother didn't raise a fool—Doc's not a guy you want to get in an argument with. He's a highly decorated former U.S. Army Ranger. A quiet man, particularly when it comes to his experiences with the Rangers, he speaks about four or five words per month on the subject. Still, after several years of this, I've been able to piece together that he spent most of his eight years in the army hiding behind enemy lines on one covert mission or another, either chasing or being chased by bad guys. He talks about his wartime experience even less than I do. His inner demons remain bottled up. Joaquin is six feet four and probably weighs around 230 pounds. All muscle. He's pure warrior—absolutely fierce, and an expert in all forms of combat—hand-to-hand, firearm, or his favorite: blades. Makes me cringe just to say it. I'm damn glad he's on my side.

I met Doc when I was stationed at Fort Lewis. Doc had put four local punks in the hospital in a fight outside a Tacoma bar. The local

DA wanted to hammer him with felonious assault charges because of his special army combat training, which, as a dedicated soldier, I was simultaneously amused and pissed off by. I investigated and found that the four idiots had actually instigated the fight—they each had records of strong-arm robbery and general thuggery. They'd seen Doc, alone at the bar, and their pea brains had singled him out as their next victim. In so doing, they made a near-fatal miscalculation in victim identification. The outcome of the fight in the alley outside the bar was never in doubt; trust me. The only question was would Doc kill them or spare them. He spared them. I ended up working with him on his defense, and all charges against him were eventually dropped. We'd developed a friendship and, when Doc discharged about eighteen months ago, I had a place waiting for him at the agency. He took a seat at the conference table, and I got started.

"First off, thanks for allowing me to push this meeting back to 10:00 a.m." I said. "Yesterday, Toni and I met with a guy I know from high school named Roberto Fiore. His sister, Gina, has not been seen since last Thursday—you've probably seen the news. The Fiores want to hire our firm to find her. This morning, Toni and I met with Detective Dwayne Brown at SPD's Special Investigations unit. Essentially, they're inviting us in, subject to a few coordination and confidentiality rules."

"I didn't even know they had a Special Investigations unit," Richard said. "Must be new."

"It is," I said. "I think SPD formed it to coordinate their efforts with outside groups on high-profile cases."

"Interesting," he said. "Is he proposing their standard coordination and confidentiality rules?" he asked.

"Yeah, easy stuff—nothing we can't live with," Toni said.

"They've agreed to provide us a copy of their initial responders' report and Brown's notes from the interview with the family, as well as the CSI report of the investigation done at her condo."

"They had CSI out already?" Richard asked. "I'm impressed." He pondered this information for a couple of seconds, then said, "That means Dwayne's covering his ass and checking off boxes in the event the case turns out bad."

"Sounds like," I said. "One of the benefits, I suppose, of putting the case into Special Investigations. They'd have never been able to get CSI out this quickly if the case were still at the precinct level, given there's no evidence yet of a crime."

"The Fiores want to hire us? I assume they'll pay well," Richard said. He's a pragmatist, who was in business too long not to recognize the necessity of actually getting paid in order to survive. He was as good a mentor on the business side of things as he was on the ins and outs of investigation.

"I imagine," I answered. "If we decide that the case makes sense for us, Toni and I will interview the family this afternoon. We'll talk business then."

"The Fiore family is a well-known Seattle Italian-American family," Richard said, leaning back in his chair. "As I recall, Angelo Fiore came to Seattle in the late 1960s as a young man. He opened a liquor distribution business—Pacific Wine and Spirits. It's in the SoDo district, over by the Mariners' stadium. He built it up from a start-up to a point at which, now, I think they've got exclusive rights to supply nearly all of the best beer and wine brands to restaurants and grocery stores in the Northwest. They also sell hard liquors to bars and hotels."

"This is our type of case; pretty much right up our alley," Doc said. "Assuming it pays, is there any reason why we shouldn't take it, now that SPD has basically signed off?"

"There's a couple of things we should consider before we decide," Toni said.

I looked at her, wondering what she was referring to.

"Angelo Fiore," she continued, "is a first cousin of John and Peter Calabria."

I knew this but considered it common knowledge. I hadn't thought about the possibility that the others might not be aware of it. "I'm sorry I didn't mention that," I said. "You're right. The Fiores are related to the Chicago crime family John and Peter Calabria. But Angelo Fiore is not part of that."

"You certain about that?" Toni asked. "Where'd he get his money to start his business? And did you know that the Calabria family is distantly related all the way back to Al Capone?"

"Haven't you ever heard of the six degrees of separation?" I asked. "Hell, we're all probably distantly related to Al Capone."

"He might be," Doc said, pointing to Kenny. "I'm an Apache."

"Doc is excepted," I said.

"I believe the six degrees refers to friendships, not relations," Richard said. "In any case, I prefer to think I'm from a different genealogical branch as well. That said, Toni's is a valid question. Fortunately, it's already been asked and answered many times before. The Calabrias were once a major force in Chicago crime—drugs, prostitution, loans, the like. I say *were* because I believe that the Calabrias themselves are essentially retired—no longer involved with operations. Although the name of the organization remains the 'Calabria family,' the actual day-to-day operations are run by younger generations now. Peter and John are out of it." He paused and sipped from a water bottle before continuing. "Actually, what happened is that Peter and John Calabria were both rung up on federal RICO charges in the nineties. They both spent several years in a federal prison. They got out and that was that—they were done. In any case, the Fiore branch of the family here in Seattle has always been clean. When I was at SPD, we knew Angelo Fiore was related to the Calabrias, and we watched him pretty closely. The Feds would also drop in from time to time and have a look. As far as I know, no one has ever been able to even accuse Angelo of any mob dealings, never mind convict him of anything. From anything I've ever seen or heard, he's an upstanding member of the community—active in politics, patron of the Seattle Symphony. He's squeaky clean. But excellent due diligence, my dear," he said, nodding to Toni.

"Thank you," Toni said with a smile. "Since you are both so well informed, I suppose you're aware of Angelo's current troubles with the federal government?" This time, Richard and I both stared at her.

"What?" Richard asked.

"Turns out that Angelo has a very serious IRS problem."

"Really?" I asked.

"Yep," she said. "In fact, two years ago he was indicted in federal court for income tax evasion. His trial is scheduled for later this year."

"Where'd you get that?" I asked.

"I'm a detective," she said. "I detect."

"Yeah, right," I answered. "Give it up. Where'd you get it?"

"Same place I got the info on the Calabrias. I had Kenny dig it up on the Internet."

I looked at Kenny, and he was grinning. "True," he said. "I pulled the federal records, and Angelo Fiore was indicted over two years ago. It's taken this long to get to court, but his trial is set for December."

The room was silent for a second. Then Toni said, "The question is, do either of these two little tidbits a) have anything at all to do with Gina Fiore's disappearance, or b) have any impact on whether we accept the case?"

"What would the Chicago mob have to do with Gina's disappearance?" Richard asked. "It's hard to know what goes on inside a closed organization like that, but it seems unlikely that they have anything to do with this. After all, Angelo's been running clean and untouched for forty years."

I didn't relish the thought of getting tangled up with organized crime, but I had to agree with Richard. I couldn't see any reason why the Calabrias would have had anything to do with this. "I tend to agree," I said. "The bigger issue might be if the Calabrias try to send muscle from outside to help the family out. We'll have to watch out for that. As to the tax problem, I don't care about that except to make sure we get paid. I'll talk to Robbie about an advance retainer."

Toni and Richard nodded.

"We've got the manpower, and we've got an opening," Doc said.

"And we've got the experience in missing persons," Kenny added.

"Anyone see a reason why Toni and I shouldn't make a deal with the Fiores?" I asked. There were no objections.

"Alright. We'll go tell them we're in. Toni and I already have a meeting set up with the family this afternoon."

"Cool," Kenny said. "Does this mean we get to keep getting paid?"

"Cross your fingers," I said. "We'll need you to start working on our standard missing person protocol—bank activity, credit card activity, cell phone use, the works. Keep in mind that, at least in theory, the police may be doing the same thing. Be careful not to trip over them."

"Please," Kenny said with a disgusted look.

"Amends," I said. "Doc, why don't you pull the Sex Offender Registery. We'll start working that angle just in case. Let's see if someone stands out."

"I'm on it," he answered.

~~~~

The Queen Anne neighborhood, where the Fiores live, is not far from our office. Since it was a beautiful summer day, we took the Jeep with the soft top pushed back. I popped in "Times Like These" by the Foo Fighters—the acoustic version—and we listened as I drove. I rested one arm on the windowsill while Toni took in the sights.

The Queen Anne area is always in high demand. While neither the size of the lots nor the size of the homes on them could be considered extreme, the central location, the historical architecture, and the urban panache of the area make the price of entry here such that only the very well-heeled can afford to buy in. Once-beautiful houses that have started to show their age are typically purchased by wealthy techies who are not afraid to spend incredible sums of money to restore the homes to their former beauty—or even beyond. It's an area that hasn't been hit too hard by the nationwide real estate recession.

Ten minutes later, halfway up the Queen Anne Hill, we pulled up to the Fiore residence. The large yellow home featured Victorian architecture and was set back from the street by a large lawn and a veritable sea of roses and rhododendrons. Ornate, white wrought-iron fencing that was partially covered by a Photinia hedge protected the home. Large maple trees served as a backdrop.

"Damn," Toni said, looking in awe as we drove past. "I've been hanging with the wrong crowd."

I chuckled. "I've never showed you where my dad lives, have I?" I asked. "He's about half a mile north of here."

"Is it like this?"

"Yeah, a little," I said. "It's a Victorian, like this one. Very old. My great-great-grandfather built it in 1920. Different color, thank God."

"If it's anything like this," she said, looking wide-eyed at the large, impressive home, "then the answer is yes."

"Yes? Yes what? What's the question?"

"Yes, I will marry you and have your children. When do we move in?"

I laughed. The white-iron entry gates were open, so I swung around and parked in the circular drive. Promptly at 2:00 p.m., we rang the bell.

"Danny, Toni," Robbie said when he answered the door, "Thanks so much for coming. Please come in."

Robbie closed the ten-foot doors behind us, and we found ourselves in a foyer with bright white wainscoting and shiny dark-oak flooring. Centered above us was a crystal chandelier, perhaps six feet in diameter. A large vase of stargazer lilies sat atop a walnut entry table to our right. On the wall to our left was a huge French Impressionist painting of a seacoast village. "Is that real?" I asked Toni. I couldn't tell.

"Hard to say," she said. "Looks real." She'd taken art history in college and it was a hobby of hers. Real or not, the overall effect of the home was very impressive—all the more so because it achieved an elegant style without seeming to try very hard.

"Please come this way," Robbie said, walking with us. "My parents are waiting for us." We followed him to the back of the home where the family room was located. Floor-to-ceiling windows trimmed in gloss white formed the back wall. The room overlooked a backyard that featured a brilliant blue swimming pool set amid red-brick decking and rich, well-tended landscaping. The mature trees completely sheltered the yard from the surrounding urban area.

Natural daylight flooded the room. We stepped from the wood flooring into the carpeted room, and it felt like I sank in up to my ankles. A large flat-screen television was on, tuned to a news channel with the.sound muted. As we entered, a small man and a taller woman rose to greet us.

"Mother, Father," Robbie said, "I don't know, but you may remember Danny Logan—Gina had Danny here for Thanksgiving dinner with us several years ago. And this is Miss Toni Blair, also of the Logan agency. Danny, Toni, my parents Angelo and Carina Fiore."

"Mr. and Mrs. Fiore," I said, reaching to shake hands, "we're very pleased to see you. We only wish it could be in happier times."

"Thank you," the woman said. "We're very grateful to have you here."

Angelo Fiore was a short, thin man who appeared to be in his late sixties. He hadn't changed much since I'd last seen him, five years before. His hair was still full and, along with his goatee, was still mostly dark, not much gray. His face, though, was lined with wrinkles, which gave away his age. His eyes were more tired than I remembered, but this may have had more to do with the stress brought on by his daughter's disappearance than with his age. He was dressed neatly in gray slacks and a yellow knit shirt.

Carina Fiore was a striking woman—it was easy to see Gina in her. She was in her mid-fifties and was five five or five six—nearly as tall as Angelo. She had a very attractive figure. Her hair was mostly blonde with maybe a little gray mixed in. Her eyes were a deep blue, but swollen and lined with red—she'd been crying recently. She was very pretty, but her distress was obvious.

Carina Fiore nodded and said, "It's very good to see you again. Please, sit down." She pointed to a sofa. "Let's talk. May we bring you something to drink? Iced tea, bottled water?"

"Yes, please. Water would be very nice," Toni said. I nodded in agreement. Robbie stepped away to the kitchen while the four of us sat down.

There was silence for a second, then Angelo leaned in and said to me, "You're the soldier."

I nodded. "Yes sir, I was in the army when Gina had me over." I glanced at Carina. I had no idea what Gina had told them about why I was there for dinner with them those several years ago or, maybe even more important, why I seemed to disappear from her life shortly thereafter.

"I do remember, indeed," Carina said. "My daughter bringing any man home is something to remember, for certain. She seemed to like you a great deal, as I recall, but then you had to go off to school." So—Gina'd told them the truth.

"That's right. I was a special agent for the U.S. Army Criminal Investigation Division. I had to go back east for more training."

Angelo stared at me. "I'm not on all that good of terms with the federal government at the moment, young man. Let me ask you—do you have any connection with the federal government now?"

"None, sir," I answered. "I was discharged in December 2007."

Angelo nodded. "Good."

"Have you seen my daughter recently?" Carina asked.

"No ma'am, I'm sad to say I haven't seen her since shortly after our Thanksgiving dinner here in 2006. We hadn't been seeing each other for very long before the dinner. After I left, we eventually lost contact altogether."

"People flow into and out of each other's lives, don't they?" she said. I nodded. "That's true."

"And you," Angelo said to Toni. "This guy tell you about any of this—this history?"

Toni looked directly at him for a moment, and then blasted him with the dazzling megawatt smile. "He tells me everything, Mr. Fiore."

Angelo was only human. He couldn't resist. He melted and smiled back. The ice was broken.

"My daughter's gone," he said, sober again. "Can you help us?"

~~~~

The last time I'd been at this house, Gina had been laughing and happy. She was twenty-two then, a recent magna cum laude graduate from the University of Washington, and on top of the world. At that time, the home had been decorated for Thanksgiving and had a warm, comfortable feel about it. Gina and I had arrived around noon. I remember making small talk with her dad, but mostly I'd wanted to talk to Gina. I was hooked—completely enthralled. She knew it, and she played with me, but I didn't mind. I was done. Stick a fork in me.

It had been a rare sunny November day, and after dinner we'd decided to go for a ride. We drove over to Gasworks Park at the top of Lake Union and found a bench that looked out over the water to the south. I had my arm around her as she explained her idea. "Let's take a couple of weeks off just after New Year's and go to Hawaii," she said. "By then, we'll be sick and tired of the gray Seattle winter. I want to share a Hawaiian sunset with you. We'll have them bring us boat drinks—the kind with the coconut and the pineapple slices and the umbrellas. We'll get a little drunk, but not too much. We'll watch the sunset. Then we'll run back to our room and get naked." I reminded her of the fact that I was due to report to the FBI Academy in Quantico, Virginia, for Advanced Training. "No problem," she'd said. Just reschedule it. Truly nothing sounded better to me than spending two weeks—or two years for that matter—in Hawaii with Gina. But she didn't know about the realities of the military—my world.

I never got to take that trip with her. I reported for training in Virginia and what started as nightly phone calls quickly turned into weekly phone calls and then, within a month, no phone calls at all. I got a one-week leave for Christmas, but when we talked over the phone about it, it seemed like the enthusiasm had waned—maybe for both of us. I ended up going to St. Thomas with a couple of guys from the school.

I think that the idea of having absolutely no control over things was most likely too hard for Gina to deal with. She wasn't used to things she couldn't control, and even Gina couldn't control the U.S. Army. It didn't matter if she got pissed and jumped up and down; if the military said go, I had to go. Period. In the end, I don't think she was prepared for that. That little conflict ended us before we ever even really got started. My last happy memories of us together were sitting on the park bench together, my arm around her, watching the sailboats on Thanksgiving Day on Lake Union.

Now, of course, she was beyond reach. All I could do was take everything I'd learned, including some of the stuff from the very class that split us up, and try to find her and keep her safe. That is, if she wasn't already gone.

~~~~

"Let me begin by saying, sir, that we're starting with a completely blank slate. Not even a hint of a clue. This isn't necessarily bad. In fact, in the schools I've attended, I've been trained not to jump to any conclusions early in any case. We've been taught to let the facts speak for themselves. What that means is that if we come to an agreement here this afternoon, then my team will begin to methodically collect evidence until the evidence itself speaks to us and tells us where to find Gina. We'll do that as quickly as we can."

The Fiores both nodded, so I continued.

"Now if I may, I need to be honest—brutally honest—for a minute."

"Go ahead," Angelo said.

I continued. "In all of my training and in all of my experience with missing person cases, I've found that there are basically three possible scenarios. As of right now, I don't have any reason to believe that Gina's disappearance is unique to this, so I'm going to give them to you in no particular order. Again, I don't know what's happened and I don't have any clues or evidence yet."

"Scenario one is that Gina's been kidnapped. Somebody who wants something—it's usually money—has grabbed her. Typically, some sort of ransom demand is made within forty-eight hours or so—most often sooner. Usually this demand comes by phone, sometimes by mail or even by courier. The initial problem I have with this scenario is that apparently, there's been no ransom demand. Have either of you heard from anyone in any manner that might suggest a kidnapping? A ransom demand? A note? A phone call? Even an e-mail or a text message?"

"Nothing," Angelo said. Carina shook her head to signal no.

"Robbie?" I asked.

"Nothing," he said. "Nothing at all."

"Exactly," I said. "The question I have is why go to the trouble of kidnapping somebody to get something, and then not go ahead and make a demand? Because there's been no ransom demand after Gina's been gone for more than four days, I doubt this is what has happened to her. The police have already placed a monitor on the house line here. Aside from that, if we all jointly decide that my firm will be helping you look for Gina, we probably won't spend any time on this scenario."

The Fiores nodded their understanding.

"Second scenario. And I remind you, I have no reason to believe this is what's happened. It's just a possibility that we must face. Gina's been abducted by a predator—either a serial murderer or a serial rapist. This is hard to say, and I hate to say it, but I have to tell you that if this is the case, she is almost certainly already gone. This type of person would have probably killed her within the first few hours after abduction, almost certainly by now. The good news is that I believe the probability of this happening to Gina is quite low, but it is a possibility and this might have happened."

The Fiores were stone-faced. They'd surely already danced around this possibility in their minds, probably even out loud to each other. But hearing it from an outsider tended to make it more sobering.

"I should add that if we go to work for you, we will spend some time on this scenario, probably just at first. Eventually, though, we'll want to shift our focus and our resources to scenario number three—and the one that I think is by far the most likely. That is, Gina's gone because she wants to be gone. She's hiding. She's either run away with someone, or she's run away from someone, or she has some other reason to disappear. I don't know her all that well, but I think I know her well enough to say that she's a very smart girl. I don't know what might be driving her to want to disappear, but my guess is that she's out there, and she thinks she has good reason to vanish." When I looked at them, I saw hope in their eyes that Gina herself might be responsible for her own disappearance. I knew I'd said the right thing. Certainly, from my perspective, I wanted to believe Gina was alive.

"I will commit my four-person staff full-time to this case. If she's hiding, we'll do our best to find out why. Then, we'll do our best to track her down and find her. We're experienced at finding missing persons. I've already cleared this through Detective Brown at the Seattle Police Department—I believe you talked to him last week. He welcomes our help. In fact, as you know, he recommended us. We'll be working as a team. We can go places and do things that he cannot. He recognizes this and is glad to have our participation because of it. When I was in the army, Detective Brown and I worked together on several cases. We get along well."

"Again, if Gina's alive—and I believe she is—we'll find her," I said with confidence, glancing at Toni. She smiled at me.

Angelo and Carina nodded, almost in unison.

"Good. Do you mind if I ask a question that came up in our internal meeting earlier today?"

"Go ahead," Angelo said.

"Could there be any possible connection between Gina's disappearance and your relatives in Chicago?"

"You mean is the Chicago mob involved in this somehow?" Angelo said, a puzzled look on his face.

"Yes."

"No. No chance," he said resolutely. "I talk to my cousins from time to time, but none of us has anything to do with the business of the other—completely separate. No connection at all."

"Okay. Thank you," I said. "I didn't mean any offense, just had to ask."

Angelo nodded. "Given the reality of the family connection, I suppose I'd have questioned your competence if you hadn't."

"Don't want that to happen," I said, smiling. "Would you do me a favor? It's completely up to you if you want to turn to them for help. But if you decide to ask for their assistance—please let me know."

"I'm sure I won't be asking my cousins for help, but if I do, I agree to notify you."

I smiled. "Thanks. Then, as to our business arrangement—"

"Mr. Logan," Angelo interrupted, "Let me interrupt you. My wife and I have been fortunate. We don't worry about money anymore. We'll pay your going rate."

"Thank you for that, Mr. Fiore," I said. "But don't you want to know what it is?" Before he could answer, I said, "You need to know that, as a four-man firm, we bill out at two thousand dollars a day, or sixty thousand dollars per month plus expenses."

Again, Angelo interrupted. "Mr. Logan, I apologize. I should have phrased it differently. I realize that even though my wife and I don't have to worry about money, I'm quite aware that you, as a young businessman, are not yet in that position. Your employees certainly have their own money concerns. I don't want you worrying about money when I would prefer you should be thinking about my daughter." He turned to Robbie. "Roberto, please have a check drawn for $120,000 on account for Mr. Logan." He turned to me. "Will that be satisfactory?"

"Thank you. More than sufficient, sir."

"Good," he said. "You're hired." He stood up and reached for my hand. "Now, please. Stop wasting time. Go find my daughter and bring her home to us."

# Chapter 4

THE NEXT MORNING, Wednesday, August 17, at 8:00 a.m., Toni and I met Dwayne and Gus in the parking lot of Gina's condo. The day was bright and sunny and already warm with just a couple of little, puffy cumulus clouds drifting in from the southwest.

"I see they have no dress code at Logan PI," Dwayne said, as he and Gus walked up to meet us. I think he was talking to me because I was wearing faded jeans, Nikes, and a short-sleeved Hawaiian shirt that I hadn't tucked in. Then again, he could have been talking to Toni because she was wearing black denims and her Doc Marten black shit-kicker boots that made her nearly six feet tall. She wore a pink V-necked blouse with no sleeves. Her sleeve tat on her left arm and the Celtic armband tat on her right were on full display. Each ear had three pierced earrings, including a bar that pierced the same ear twice. Plus, she had some sort of tiny diamond stud in her nose. The effect was memorable.

"Unlike you fat cats, we don't work on a union pay scale," I said in our defense. "We can't afford the fancy suits."

Dwayne fingered his lapels and smiled. "I assume you're referring to me. Pretty snappy, isn't it?" he said. Then he turned and nodded toward Gus, who was wearing another plaid sport jacket. "I gotta balance out Gus, here. He does his shopping at the bargain bin at Joseph A. Bank."

Gus acted offended until Toni said, "I think Gus looks quite dapper."

"Dapper?" Dwayne said. "Dapper? I never knew anyone who looked dapper before. I'm impressed."

"As well you should be," Gus said, beaming at the compliment from Toni.

"Anyway," Toni added, "When we dress in plainclothes, we actually try to not look like cops."

Dwayne laughed. "Touché."

"Sweetheart," Gus said, reaching for Toni's hand and kissing it. "Let me say that you look absolutely lovely this fine morning. And you don't for one second look a goddamned bit like any cop I've ever seen."

"See?" Toni replied, batting her eyelashes at him. "It worked."

I smiled. "This is going to be fun, guys." I noticed Robbie driving up to let us into the condo. "Robbie's here. How about we get to work." I pointed to the door of Gina's condo. "Let's start inside first; then we can take a look at her car."

At the landing in front of Gina's condo, Dwayne handed me a large envelope. "I got your paperwork in my e-mail. Thanks for that. This is a copy of the first responder report, a copy of the missing person report, a copy of my interview notes, and a copy of the CSI report. We've already filed with NCIC and WACIC."

"Thanks," I said. "Yesterday afternoon, we met with the Fiores. I assume you know that Angelo is directly related to the Calabria family in Chicago."

"Yeah, we knew that," Gus said.

"I asked Angelo if there's any way Chicago might be involved. He was pretty adamant—said no way. I asked him to notify me if this changes."

"You think he might ask them for help?" Dwayne said.

I shrugged. "I don't know. I think it's something we should consider. If it was my kid missing, and my cousins had the necessary muscle and skills, I might be tempted to ask the family for a little assistance. I'd probably do anything to get my daughter back."

Dwayne nodded his agreement as Robbie walked up. He said, "Yeah. Keep us posted." Then he pointed to the envelope he'd just given me. "Let's pull out the CSI report and walk through it. CSI already released the scene, but let's act professional anyway. Does everyone have gloves and shoe covers? Good. Let's put 'em on now."

We all covered up and went inside.

~~~~

An hour later, we'd gone completely through Gina's condo and compared what we saw against the CSI report. We found no discrepancies. The condo appeared completely undisturbed—nothing was amiss. There were no signs anywhere of any sort of struggle. There were no signs anywhere of forced entry—the windows were all locked from the inside. There were no unusual odors, no unusual stains. The bed was made and there were no dirty dishes lying about, although the CSI people had taken a coffee cup from the sink to test for fingerprints. There was a small amount of laundry in a clothes hamper in the bathroom. The trash cans were completely empty. The refrigerator was nearly full. The closet was full of clothes, with no empty hangers like you might expect to see if someone had packed for a trip. The bureau drawers seemed as full as you'd expect. The hall closet held two pieces of luggage. There didn't appear to be anything missing; there was no room for anything else in the small closet. The bathroom shelves did not appear to be abnormally empty—no blank spaces, that sort of thing. Nothing appeared out of place.

Gina had a small desk in the corner of her living room. It held a cup filled with pens and pencils and a cordless telephone. The phone had no voicemail messages and no records of any recent phone calls. A small bulletin board was attached to the wall above the desk. The bulletin board held a calendar with no markings and a photo of Gina and her parents printed on plain paper. Most of the rest of the board was full of business cards tacked to the cork with colorful little thumbtacks. Gina had pasted a number of Post-it notes around the edges of the board. I had Toni take digital pictures of all the business cards and notes. When she was done, I had her shoot three dozen more pictures of the entire condo, top to bottom—even the inside of the refrigerator.

Bottom line—except for the fact that Gina's keys were conspicuously on the counter next to her purse—the place seemed just like the owner had cleaned up and gone to work.

After we locked up the condo, we looked at Gina's car, a near-new BMW 528. At first glance, the car seemed completely empty. When I looked in the pocket on the side of the door, however, I saw a Chevron receipt for a gas purchase. "Look at this," I said to Toni. She looked at the receipt and said, "August 11. The last day anyone saw her." Robbie had a key, and the car started normally. The tank was full. I had Toni photograph the interior of the car and the gas receipt.

After we finished the car, we huddled in the parking lot to com-pare notes. "Did we miss anything?" I asked after Robbie locked the car. "Seems like we pretty much got it all covered."

"Seems that way," Dwayne said.

"Scene matches the CSI description exactly," Gus said.

"Sure seems to," I said. "Very curious. Anyone got any ideas?"

"Just tossing out theories here," Toni said, "but if she was abducted from here, it doesn't look like there was a struggle. If there was, whoever snatched her did an almost perfect job of cleaning up the place and mak-ing the scene look normal. That doesn't seem very likely."

"Question," Gus said. "How did the deadbolt get locked from the outside if her keys were inside?"

"There's other front-door keys floating around," I said. "Robbie has one. There must be more."

"And either Gina, or the person who abducted her, left everything as it sits, and then used the spare key to lock up, all nice and neatlike," Dwayne said.

"And then drove away in a waiting vehicle other than this one," I said, pointing to Gina's BMW.

"Either way, somebody went to a pretty good deal of trouble to leave us this confusing scene," Dwayne said. "They're trying to throw us off."

"Got that right," I said. "Seems to me that the voluntary disappear-ance scenario is pretty straightforward. She staged the place to look nor-mal, she locked up using a spare key, and she left in another vehicle, either one she'd stashed or with another person." Toni nodded her agreement.

"And the involuntary disappearance plays out one of two ways," she said. "Either she locked up like Danny just said, and then drove off with someone who turned out to be a bad guy, or she was snatched, the bad guy cleaned up and used a spare key to lock the door, and then he drove off with her. Either way, it doesn't look like there was any struggle here."

"Could she have been grabbed somewhere else?" I suggested.

"If that were true, how did all of her stuff end up back here—her purse and her keys?" Toni asked.

"Good point."

"Do we have a last known sighting yet?" Dwayne asked.

"No interviews yet," Gus said.

"The last I saw her was about five thirty last Thursday," Robbie said.

"Our plan is to start in with interviews at Pacific Wine and Spirits to-day," I said. "Maybe we'll be able to locate someone who was either with her later or at least saw her later that night."

"Good," Dwayne said. "We haven't done anything yet, so you won't be stepping on our toes. Give us a list of whom you talk to and a copy of your notes when you're done. So that we don't double up on people and piss them off, we won't schedule any interviews until we hear from you."

I turned to Robbie and said, "Robbie, would you get us a list of everyone at your company who Gina works with or who she might have been friendly with on a social basis? If you can schedule time with them starting at about 3:00 p.m., that would be great."

"Sure," Robbie said. "I can set you up in a conference room if you'd like."

"Perfect."

"We're trying to find out who saw her last, and when that was, what was she wearing, what was she doing, what kind of mood was she in, that sort of thing," Dwayne said. "And we also want to find out who her friends are, does she have a boyfriend, who she hangs out with, where she goes at night—all that kind of stuff. Even little things could be helpful."

We agreed that we'd call with an update later in the afternoon.

Before breaking, Robbie said, "I have to say, I'm impressed with the procedures and the methodology. I guess I didn't know how you guys went about solving cases, but, somehow, seeing the process makes me a little more hopeful."

"What'd you think," Gus said, "we just sit around like Colombo and wait for clues to fall into our laps?"

"I honestly didn't know what to think," Robbie said. "Fortunately, I've never been through anything like this."

"Well, we don't sit around and wait," Dwayne said. "We develop the clues. We go after them. I was kind of trained on the job as I went, but this guy—" here he pointed to me, "—this guy got the best training that money can buy in the U.S. Army and at the FBI. Special schools, that sort of thing."

I said, "Like a lot of other problems, solving a missing person case lends itself to a logical, step-by-step procedure. We all know the procedure—we don't have to reinvent it. Experts have worked it out over the years, and the four of us are pretty well versed on the steps to follow. We simply apply the procedures we've been taught to the facts as they exist on each case. When we flush out a clue, we modify our approach to accommodate it. If we follow the steps and get a little lucky here and there and things work out like they should, we should be able to develop a chain of clues that ends up leading us straight to Gina."

"With a whole lot of legwork and questions and answers along the way," Dwayne said.

"Sounds reassuring," Robbie said.

We don't have all the answers, but we know the steps. Poor Robbie doesn't know any of this—he's completely in the dark and probably has no idea how the process works, or for that matter, if there even is a process. I imagine suddenly discovering that crimes get solved by following playbook-like procedures developed over the years would be somewhat comforting to a logical person like Robbie. He seemed much relieved.

"Alright," Dwayne said. "Robbie, thanks for opening up the place this morning. Now, we all have jobs to get to. Let's get it done." The group began to break up, but Dwayne grabbed my sleeve and whispered to me, "Hold up a second."

~~~~

When Robbie had driven away, Dwayne said to Toni and me, "I talked to the homicide guys yesterday afternoon after you left. It turns out they do have a possible serial killer working in this area. Apparently, they've just recently discovered a pattern in about four killings in the greater Seattle area, about one per year."

Just the possibility of this happening to Gina was enough to raise my blood pressure. Unfortunately, my hometown is infamous for being ground zero for some of the worst serial killers of our time. I'm talking about the real nice fellows like Ted Bundy, the Green River Killer, and the like. I think there's something in the Seattle weather that triggers some sort of short circuit within these lunatics. Someday, scientists will nail down the connection.

Dwayne continued. "This sick bastard who's doing it tends to torture his victims before he kills them. Then he has sex with the body."

Toni looked confused. "That describes maybe a dozen different serial killers," she said.

"That's true," Dwayne said. "Unfortunately, that in and of itself isn't what makes this guy unique. What does is that after he's killed the poor girl, he mutilates her body the same way each time. Homicide wouldn't tell me what or how, except to say it involved dismemberment."

"I guess that would make the crimes tend to stand out," I said.

"True. Fortunately, there haven't been very many victims. Unfortunately, this has made it so that the pattern got missed until now."

"That's not good," I said. "Any lifestyle pattern to the victims?"

"Young, pretty, all live alone."

"Prostitutes?" Toni asked. Many serial killers focused their attention on prostitutes, thinking, correctly, that the shadowy lifestyle of women engaged in prostitution made them less likely to be missed than your average woman.

"Two of the victims haven't been identified yet, but the other two were definitely not prostitutes. One was a U-Dub student; one was a nurse. The U-Dub student lived in the U-District, the nurse lived off Eastlake Drive on Lake Union."

"Great," I said sarcastically. "Right in our area."

"It gets worse," Dwayne said.

"How's that?"

"Like I said, there've been four killings in the last five years. So far, they've discovered a body each summer."

"And—?"

"And they haven't found a body yet this summer that matches the MO." Dwayne paused, then said, "If he's killing one girl each summer, the bastard's due."

Although the odds of Gina having fallen victim to this particular maniac were low, it didn't stop a dread from instantly filling my body, almost as if a flatbed truck had suddenly parked on my chest. If nothing else, it made the possibility that Gina could have been abducted and killed by any number of twisted psychos all the more real. It didn't have to be this guy—there were plenty of madmen to go around. Dead is dead.

My mind raced, but didn't land on an answer. "I don't know how to respond to this," I said, finally. "With no facts, no evidence, nothing, I think we should keep this little nugget to ourselves unless the family brings it up directly. They're scared enough as it is. No sense creating any more dread in their lives."

"We agree completely," Dwayne said.

~~~~

Toni and I hopped in my Jeep and drove back to our office. Neither of us spoke. I guess there's nothing like the potential threat of a sadistic serial killer to throw a wet blanket on the mood. *Gina*, I thought to myself, *I sure as hell hope you're running some sort of scam, some sort of deal. I know you probably think you're tough and in control, but there are some really sick sons of bitches out there, and I hope to hell you haven't met up with one of them.*

Finally, Toni couldn't take the silence any longer. "Boss, I know what you're thinking."

"Yeah?"

"Yeah. You can relax. I'm convinced. Gina didn't get caught up by this shithead, or any other for that matter."

"I hope you're right. Why do you say that?"

"Too many odd things about what's happened—mostly about the condo, I guess. That place is clearly staged."

"You think?"

"Oh, hell yeah. I think everything we've found is exactly the way somebody wanted it to be found. Right now, I think the most likely some-body is Gina herself."

I swerved to avoid a double-parked delivery truck, then straightened back out. "You sound pretty sure of yourself. Why would she do that?" I asked.

She was quiet for a few seconds. "I don't know that. Yet. But I'm go-ing to find out. Anyway, that's my theory."

"Well, I hope you're right."

"Count on it."

Toni's smarter than I am. I found her confidence somehow reassur-ing.

~~~~

Later that same day at three, we pulled into the parking lot at Pacific Wine and Spirits in the SoDo industrial district on the south side of Seattle, near the Mariners' ballpark. As he'd promised, Robbie had a conference room reserved for us. The view through the room's large picture window featured a nice vista of gritty warehouses and busy loading docks. Through gaps in the buildings, the big orange overhead cranes on the waterfront several blocks to the west were visible. Not exactly a five-star view, but the room itself was nice—big conference table, comfortable chairs.

In the first hour after we got settled in, we talked to four different people from the finance section. Each of them had been with the company since Gina had graduated from college and started working there, five years ago. They all knew Gina because she'd been their boss for the entire time. Unfortunately, they were also married with their own family lives outside of work and none of them hung out with Gina or even considered themselves friends. In fact, they agreed that although Gina was friendly enough at work, she did not seem to make friends easily. If she had an inner circle, they agreed, none of them were in it.

Nonetheless, we were able to ascertain that all of these women had a good deal of respect for Gina as a boss. All four agreed that Gina was a very focused, driven person and that she wasn't prone to small talk or office chatter. She was fair, hardworking, very shrewd and very hard-nosed. Shortly after she'd arrived, she uncovered the fact that the previous controller was skimming money from the company and cooking the books to cover it up. Gina went to her dad, and the offender was summarily fired. Gina got the controller's job. Now, five years later, she was the company's chief financial officer. Today, if a supplier or a customer tried to take advantage of the company, she hammered them without mercy. There was unanimous agreement that Gina had turned a floundering business with a questionable future into a very profitable ongoing concern in five years.

Next on the list was a woman who each of the others had identified as being Gina's closest confidante at work. Ms. Regina Campbell was the company's current controller—she answered directly to Gina. She entered the conference room at 4:00 p.m. on the dot. She was probably thirty years old, blonde hair, average height and weight; not beautiful, but better than cute—call her pretty. No wedding ring. I introduced us and asked her to have a seat. She told us to call her Reggie.

"Reggie, thanks for talking to us this afternoon," I started. "As you've probably heard, we've been hired by Gina's family to help locate her."

Reggie nodded.

"We've just gotten started, and one of the first things we wanted to do is talk to the people she works with."

She nodded again.

"Maybe you can start by telling us what you do here and how what you do interacts with what Gina does?"

She nodded. "First off, I appreciate you talking about Gina in the present tense," Reggie said, sniffling. "I get these ominous vibes from the press. They seem to think she's already dead."

"We don't think so," I said. "In fact, if we thought that was the case, there'd be no reason for us to be doing what we're doing. We're working on the assumption that she's not dead. We don't know why she's disappeared, but we want to find out. If she's in trouble and needs help, we want to be there."

"Good," she said. She reached for a tissue from the box on the table. "I moved to Seattle five years ago—about the same time Gina started with the company. Gina's probably my best friend. As the company controller, I work closely with her—you probably already know she's the CFO. I talk to her maybe a dozen times a day."

"Did that contact lead to your friendship?" Toni asked.

"For me, yeah. We work together a lot. We're both single. We both went to college—I feel like we have a lot in common."

"When you say—'for me'—what do you mean?" I asked.

"Well, if you know Gina, you'd understand," she said. "How should I put it—Gina doesn't share much. She keeps her feelings pretty well bottled up inside. I think it was the way she was brought up. I know Mr. Fiore, and I think he's a nice guy, but I get the impression that they had a pretty strict upbringing—Gina and Robbie. Anyway, she doesn't open up very easily."

"I'm not sure I understand," Toni said. "You said Gina's your best friend. How does that jibe with this?"

"She's *my* best friend," Reggie said. "I'm not sure I'm *her* best friend. For that matter, I'm not sure she has a best friend. It would have to be someone from outside work." She sniffed and dabbed her nose with a tissue.

"Did the two of you go out together after work?" I asked.

"Yes, from time to time," Reggie answered. "We'd talk on the phone after work and sometimes we'd go out—movies, bars, that sort of thing. She had me over to her parents' home a couple of times."

"Do you know if she went out with other people here at the company?" Toni asked.

"Maybe occasionally. But I think that of all the people here in the company, Gina probably spent the most time outside of work with me. Not counting Robbie, of course. But the thing is, she didn't spend all that much time with me. We'd talk on the phone and every couple of weeks, we'd go out."

"Were you able to share things with her?" Toni asked. "For example, if you had a boyfriend, would you talk about it?"

"Sure, I could tell her things," Reggie said. "But much as I wanted her to open up herself, she really didn't. I can't help but think that I was the one who did most of the sharing. I talked; Gina listened."

"Did she ever talk about boyfriends with you?" Toni asked.

"Never. She'd talk with me about my boyfriends, but when I'd ask her about her love life, she'd just laugh and say she was too busy working. If she had boyfriends, she never mentioned it."

"Based on the amount of time she spent with you, would she have had time for other friends from outside the company?" I asked.

"Oh, yeah," she answered quickly. "Like I said, we didn't hang out all that often. She'd have had a bunch of time left over for other people."

"Did she spend a lot of time alone?"

She thought about this for a second, then said, "I'm not sure. She didn't tell me one way or the other."

We were going to need to find out whom Gina was seeing from outside of the company. "Got it," I said. "That's helpful. Let's move on. When you and Gina went out, was it ever for lunch or was it just after work? Did you ever go out on a weekend?"

"No, it was always after work. Gina used to go out for lunch, but lately she ate lunch at her desk or with Robbie. When we went out, it was usually on a Friday night after work."

"Where did you go?"

"We went to a few different places. Naturally, Gina always chose them. At first, we went to this piano bar in Pioneer Square called—I forget what it's called. It's the place with the two pianos. . ." she searched for the answer.

"Chopstix," I suggested.

"Yeah, Chopstix, that's it," she said. "Sometimes we went to Tula's."

"The jazz place in Belltown?" I asked.

"Yeah," she said. She paused, then shook her head and said, "But lately, she had us going to a place called Ramon's Cantina down in Kent." She shuddered visibly. "That place creeps me out a little."

"Really? How come?" Toni asked.

"It's scary," Reggie said. "A lot of lowlifes go there. It's not a very friendly place if you're not Mexican."

"Yet Gina took you there," I said. "Any idea why? She suggested it, right?"

"I don't know why, but yeah, it was her idea. We went a couple of times. She seemed to be fine there. She almost looks Mexican, with her dark hair. I sure don't," she said, lifting a section of her long blonde hair.

"Ever have any trouble there?"

"No. I guess I'm surprised, but we never had any trouble. I just didn't find it very comfortable."

"When you were with her, did she seem to know anyone there?" Toni asked.

"Yeah, a few people," Reggie answered. "The bartenders know her. And she knows this guy named Eddie—we met him there both times we went. She seemed pretty friendly with him."

"Boyfriend-type friendly?" I asked.

"I don't know," Reggie said. "I never saw them kiss or anything. But they always hugged when we went in. He would sit next to her whenever we went there."

"Did she ever talk about him, other than when you went to Ramon's?" Toni asked.

"No, never."

"You wouldn't happen to have any pictures, would you?"

"I think I do, on my cell," she answered. She reached into her purse and pulled out her phone. She scrolled through the pictures and then handed the phone to me.

The picture showed four people sitting in a booth—Gina, Reggie, a man who I assumed to be Eddie, and another woman.

"This is Eddie?" I asked.

"Yes."

"Who's this woman on the end?"

"I think her name is Karen, or Carolyn—something like that," Reggie said. "Gina seemed to know her pretty well."

"You don't know anything about her—where she lives, where she works, that kind of stuff?" I asked.

"Sorry. I don't know anything about her except that she met us just this one time at the bar when Gina and I came in. That's when I got this picture."

"Okay," I continued. "When was the last time you and Gina went to Ramon's together?"

"About three weeks ago," Reggie answered.

"Toni, do you know how to send this picture to Kenny?" I asked, handing her the phone.

"I think I can probably figure it out," she said. About 2.2 seconds later, she handed it back. "Done," she said, with a Cheshire-cat smile.

"Thank you," I said, smiling back.

I turned back to Reggie. "Was there anything going on at work last week that might have been particularly stressful?"

"No, nothing. It gets busy at the end of the month, but in the middle of the month our workload is pretty light."

"The business is operating profitably?" I asked. "No strain there?"

"We're making more money than we ever have," Reggie said. "Gina opened up all of the supplier contracts for new competitive bidding last year, and we lowered our costs by about 10 percent overall. It went right to the bottom line and doubled our profit."

~~~~

"Did this upset any of the suppliers that got replaced?" Toni asked.

"At first. But eventually, most of the people we'd already been working with lowered their prices to match the other bidders. Gina gave them the opportunity to do that because of the long-standing relationships. They appreciated that and, like I said, most of them came to the table and kept the relationship."

"Any vendors leave with hard feelings?" I asked.

"A couple got dropped, but we never hear from them."

"Alright," I said. "Well, do me a favor. Would you put together a list for us of the vendors who lost your business because of the rebidding? It's a long shot, but who knows? Maybe someone got hurt financially and might have wanted to take it out on Gina."

"Sure," she said.

"Okay. This has been very helpful," I said. "Let's wrap up with some standard questions. When's the last time you saw Gina?"

"Last Thursday at about 5:30 p.m., when I left work. I stopped by her office and said goodnight."

"Did she mention anything about what she was doing that night?"

"No. We didn't talk about that."

"What was her mood like last Thursday?"

"It seemed fine. No different than usual."

"Do you remember what Gina did for lunch that day?"

"I think Robbie came by, and they went out together."

"Do you remember what Gina was wearing last Thursday?"

"It was a navy shirt and beige slacks. I remember because I told her the shirt looked pretty. She said it was new."

I studied my notes for a few seconds and saw that I'd covered everything I'd written out in advance. "Well, I think that about wraps it up for me. Toni, do you have any more questions?"

Toni shook her head. "Nope."

"Reggie, anything else you can think of that might be helpful to us?"

"No. Has this been helpful to you? I sure hope it has."

"Very helpful," I said. "We appreciate your cooperation."

"I just hope you find her."

"We'll try."

# Chapter 5

WE TOOK I-5 south to the 405, then headed south on 167 toward Kent. The landscape changed as we headed south. Compared to most East Coast cities, Seattle developed through the years without any significantly pronounced ethnic districts. Historically, there's always been a small Asian concentration in the International District and a small Scandinavian concentration in Ballard, but that's pretty much it. Although there were a few particular bars best avoided, I've never felt that there was any particular part of the city where it was unsafe to drive or go to a restaurant.

Times are changing now, though. In some areas, a certain critical mass seems to have been achieved, and ethnic groups—mostly Hispanic—are becoming more and more prevalent in some of the small towns on Seattle's outskirts. Supermarkets, bars, and restaurants are being re-cast in Latino flavors. Advertising signs are strictly in Spanish. By itself, this doesn't bother me. Most of these new folks are hard-working family people chasing the American dream. More power to 'em whatever their background. Don't get me wrong—I kind of miss the character of the old towns I grew up around—but then again, times change and places change. You roll with it.

The problem is, in some of these areas, half the new residents don't have jobs. A sizable number have incomes below the poverty line. I suppose it should come as no surprise that crime is escalating. Instead of seeing quaint, historic small towns like I used to when I drive through, now I see tagged overpasses and the angry stares of bored young men and women hanging around on street corners. Some of these areas are just dripping with a big-city, twenty-first-century, in-your-face attitude. Gang activity is increasing rapidly. Nothing like Los Angeles yet, but clearly, violence is on the rise. In south King County, there's probably a gang-related homicide every other week now.

The area just south of the town of Kent is one of these areas. Here, on a side street off Highway 167 is a little garden oasis called Ramon's Cantina. In a previous incarnation, the cantina had a well-deserved reputation as a dangerous place. All the action started inside but eventually got settled in the parking lot. Drug deal? Make the deal inside; make the exchange in the parking lot. Disagreement among patrons? Don't bleed on the floor—settle it in the parking lot. Romantic encounter? Get a room. Or go to the parking lot if you can't wait. Eventually, the local authorities got tired of the parking-lot murders and assaults and drug deals, so they yanked the owner's liquor license, closing the place down. It stayed boarded up for several years. When the area converted to a Latino population base, new owners reopened the bar as Ramon's. Unfortunately, they didn't change the place's character any. In my humble opinion, it looked like the only differences from the old joint were the sign and the paint color. Let's just say I'm pretty certain that they weren't holding church bingos at Ramon's.

We pulled into the parking lot at about seven. The sign featured a neon-green saguaro cactus. To its left the words *Ramon's Cantina* were spelled out in neon except that the *ina* on the word *Cantina* wasn't lit. The lit part of the sign flashed *Ramon's Cant* on and off. Fortunately for Ramon's, at 7:00 p.m. in the summertime it was still broad daylight outside and the malfunction was hardly noticeable. I'm not sure any of the patrons would have cared anyway.

The lot was nearly full, but I found a space in back behind the building. From the outside, the place looked like a cross between a biker bar and a low-rider convention. Loud music burst out into the parking lot anytime the doors swung open and someone entered or exited. A bottle broke somewhere on the other side of the lot. From somewhere nearby, I heard sounds coming from one of the cars that suggested an act of intense romance was under way. Hooah.

"Do you think we should disarm?" Toni asked, looking concerned. We both have concealed weapons permits valid anywhere in the state of Washington. Anywhere, that is, except government buildings and bars. I can understand no guns in government buildings. I suppose this provision of the law was included because the legislature perceived a need for self-preservation. And, at first glance, I can understand the prohibition against carrying guns in bars. The good legislators figured that there was no need for the drunks to be armed. So they wrote the law such that if we, as duly permitted concealed weapon carriers, got caught with said concealed weapons in a bar—even if we were stone-cold sober—we ran the very real risk of being charged with a felony.

Unfortunately, this law overlooks the fact that bars and the areas immediately surrounding them are precisely the type of places where a firearm might come in handy. If we went into Ramon's Cantina and started asking potentially provocative questions without the ability to defend ourselves, they might end up carrying us out feet first. We'd definitely be guilty of terminal stupidity. Go figure. Bottom line: you can take a gun to church where you're not likely to need it, but you can't take one with you to a bar, where you might need it very badly. This created something of a dilemma for an otherwise law-abiding citizen such as me. For maybe a half second or so.

"Hell no, I'm not going to disarm. Are you nuts? For all we know, this Eddie character killed Gina. Just a guess, but he might not be all warm and fuzzy if we get to talk to him. And he might have friends. I'll take my chances on getting busted. At least we'll be alive."

"I was just asking about you," Toni said. "No way I go near this shithole unarmed."

Before we'd left, we stopped by the office and picked up copies of the photograph Toni had e-mailed to Kenny. The lens on the iPhone used to take the picture was tiny, but the resolution was surprisingly high. After Kenny downloaded and Photoshopped the file to clarify and enhance it, he was able to print us out a five-by-seven group photo, plus, with a little skillful cropping, individual blow-ups of each of the four parties. The photos were quite clear. They'd certainly work for our purposes.

We walked around to the front of the building and entered the bar. Inside, it was dark and loud. It took a second for my eyes to adjust. When I could see clearly, I realized that we'd somehow been beamed to downtown Ensenada. A large Mexican flag—maybe eight feet high and twenty feet wide—was pinned on the wall across from the entry. Even at 7:00 p.m., the place was busy. Not surprisingly, most of the patrons were Mex-

ican—the "he's" outnumbering the "she's" by two to one or so. Most of
the booths were full. All of the pool tables were in use. There was no
band playing, but the PA music was cranked up loud. There were eight
flat-screen televisions on the walls, all tuned to soccer games and music
videos with the sound muted. The PA music made the bar patrons have to
yell at each other to be heard. All of the yelling was in Spanish. Washington State had recently passed a law that made smoking illegal in bars, but
apparently, this law hadn't made its way to Ramon's yet. A haze of smoke
loitered near the ceiling. I saw two empty barstools and pointed to them.

"Over there," I said, loudly, to Toni.

Dressed as she was in dark jeans and boots, and with her dark hair,
and tats on conspicuous display, Toni fit in much better than I. From
behind, anyway, she could even pass for Latino. My Hawaiian shirt, on
the other hand, was probably not the best choice if one wanted to be
incognito at Ramon's Cantina. People looked at Toni as we passed, most
in appreciation. They looked at me, and most seemed pissed. *Wonderful.*

The female bartender on our side was pretty and had a nice figure.
She wore a white long-sleeved shirt, rolled up at the sleeves, and a black
vest. She wore heavy silver-blue eye makeup and bright red lipstick. Her
long dark hair was pulled straight back. "What can I bring you, amigos,"
she said, nearly yelling to be heard over the music.

"Do you have Mac & Jack's?" I asked.

She didn't even answer—she just made this little grimace thing with
her mouth and stared at me like I'd just asked for a glass of chocolate
milk. I guess she thought the question was so stupid it didn't warrant an
answer.

"Bohemia for me," Toni said.

"Same for me," I said.

"Dos Bohemias," the bartender replied, with a bit of condescension
in her voice.

She brought us our beers.

"Eight dollars," she said.

I thanked her and put a twenty-dollar bill out. I noticed she had a
tattoo of a butterfly just above her left wrist, barely visible beneath her
sleeve.

I nodded at it. "I like your butterfly," I said. "Mariposa, right?"

"Sí," she answered, her voice sharp.

"What's your name?" I asked. I needed to soften her up.

"Rita," she answered. "You can call me Rita."

"Good to meet you, Rita," I said. "I'm Danny. This is Toni. It's loud in here!"

She nodded but didn't say anything. She didn't smile, either. So much for softening her up.

"I wonder if you might be able to help us out with a couple of questions." May as well get down to business. I put the group photo on the bar in front of her.

"You know any of these people?" I asked.

Rita looked at the photo for a second; then she looked back at me.

"You guys cops?" she asked.

"Now, Rita," I said, "do we look like cops?" I looked at her with my most non-cop-like smile. I shook my head. "We're not cops."

She wasn't impressed. "Good," she said. She looked back at the photo, then back at me. "In that case, since you're not cops, maybe you'd better get your gringo asses the fuck out of here."

That was surprising. "Rita, that's pretty rude. We just got here," I said, a little condescension in my own voice. "What about our beers?"

"I'll give you a to-go cup. Take them with you. It's for your own good."

I tilted my head—a habit I have when I hear something I don't like. "That's starting to sound like a threat. Is that a threat?" I stared at her.

She stared back without speaking.

After a few seconds, I raised my left hand and said, "Okay. Alright. You don't want to help us. I get it." I shrugged and nodded that I understood. "You're scared. Fine. How about you call your manager and tell him you've got a problem and you need his help. Maybe he'll answer a question or two."

"Besa mi culo," she said, nearly spitting the words at me. Kiss my ass.

I like a succinct answer, but not that one. Fortunately, the place was so loud that no one could overhear us.

I smiled. "Rita, there you go again," I said. I paused and the smile left. I stared at her a second, then said, "Look, you don't need this trouble, and I sure as hell don't want it, but we really need to get some questions answered. If not from you, then we need to talk to your boss. And Rita, if you don't call him out here—right fucking now!"—this part I said plenty loud enough for people around us to stop what they were doing and look. I quieted down and pulled out my cell phone—"then I'm going to put in a phone call to my friends out there in the parking lot. What if we are cops? What then? My friends are going to come inside here and start busting this place up, taking people down and ruining your whole goddamned night. Is that what you want? Or would you rather just call your boss?"

Rita stared at me for a few seconds, her eyes firing daggers. Then she turned and picked up a telephone. She spoke into the phone, and then hung up and walked ten feet or so away. Less than a minute later, a middle-aged man in slacks and a short-sleeved white shirt hurried out to meet us.

"Amigos," he said with a smile as he opened his arms, "Please—come join me in my office."

"Thank you." I said. I took the ten-dollar bill from the stack of change. "Rita—keep the change," I called out. From the scowl I got in return, a wild guess told me that Rita was not happy with me. Also the extended middle finger helped clear up any confusion I might have had.

~~~~

"I am Jorge Sanchez, owner of this establishment," the man said as we entered his office. He pointed to two vinyl-covered diner's chairs in front of a desk buried in papers.

The little office was crammed with file cabinets. The walls were covered with State of Washington posters with clever little sayings like "Employees—Know Your Rights!" and the like, conveniently printed in Spanish as well as English.

"I thought this place was Ramon's Cantina," I said. "Where's Ramon?"

"Ah," Jorge said, smiling, "there never was a Ramon. When I started this bar, Ramon's Cantina sounded better than Jorge's Cantina. You know what I mean?"

"Interesting," I said. "I suppose."

I looked at Toni. She weighed the two names. "Ramon's, Jorge's—I think he's right," she said.

I shrugged. "Okay."

"I'm told you are looking for some people," Jorge said. "I'll tell you what I know, because I want no trouble with the police."

"I appreciate that," I said, choosing not to tell him we weren't the police, "but no offense, this place doesn't exactly have a reputation as being a family joint—one where you go to avoid trouble."

"Alas, to remain profitable, we have been forced to cultivate a certain public image to attract a certain type of clientele," Jorge said. "It's part of our marketing efforts. Some of these customers are rough characters—rougher than we'd like. But they pay well. Besides, we don't usually know about that until they've created a problem, and then it's too late. Meanwhile, I try to keep things in balance as long as they behave themselves here. But, you should know that the bar itself—behind the scenes, we always cooperate with the authorities. We're squeaky clean. I went to U-Dub, you know. MBA."

"Really?" Toni said, smiling. "I'm impressed. We both went to U-Dub as well. Good to see a fellow alum."

"Yeah, it is. I can switch from barrio-speak to banker-talk on a dime in three different languages—all depends on the audience," Jorge said, smiling. "But the important thing is I wanted you to know that I know how to run my business the right way. I play by the rules."

"Maybe with the possible exception of the lovely Rita out there," I answered. "She seemed a little agitated."

Jorge cringed. "For that, I apologize," he said. "I will speak to her."

"No need," I answered. "It's over. Besides, she already hates me. No need to get her even more upset. She might blow a fuse."

I laid out the photo of Gina on Jorge's desk, along with the group photo. "This girl here is Gina Fiore—you may have seen her on TV. She's gone missing. We've been hired by her family to help the police find her. It's been reported to us that she frequents your bar in the company of this man here—we think his name is Eddie." I laid the next photo down. "And this girl here, probably named Karen or Carolyn or something along those lines." I laid down the last photo. "We are trying to identify these two people so we can see if they might help us find Gina."

"His name might be Edward, Eduardo, something like that, as well,"

Toni said.

"I recognize him," Jorge said. "His name is Eduardo Salazar." He'd suddenly become very serious. "He is a real chingón—a badass. And he has very bad friends."

I wrote his name down in my notebook. "Why do you say that?" I asked.

"I'd prefer not to say," he said, the fear in his eyes obvious. "My information is all second-hand, anyway. Trust me, amigo. From what I hear, he is a dangerous man. One of those rough characters I referred to. Between you and me, if he chose another cantina, I'd be happy. Let's just leave it at that."

I nodded. "Okay. When did you see him last?"

"I haven't seen him for a week or so. Like I said, if I don't see him anymore around here, that's okay. I want no trouble with anybody, including the police."

"Do you know where he lives?"

"No, but if I did, I could not tell you. Not out of disrespect, but because of who he is and who his friends are."

I nodded. "Alright. I understand."

"Do you know who this girl is?" Toni asked, pointing to the unknown woman.

"I think I may have seen her," he said slowly as he studied the photo. "I might recognize her, I'm not sure." He studied the other photos. "I've definitely seen this one," he said quickly, pointing to the picture of Gina. "She's been in often. Several times I've seen her with Eduardo Salazar."

"Is that right?" I asked. "Is it possible any of your employees might know this girl or might be able to shed some more light on Eduardo Salazar?"

"Probably not. If I ask anybody around here to talk to you about Eduardo Salazar, they'll likely quit right on the spot. They might talk to you about the girl, if they know her. But not if you start talking about Eduardo Salazar first. If you ask about him—even show his picture—they'll clam up. They won't answer any questions. I can ask around about the girl separately if you'd like, tell them her parents are looking for her, or something like that."

"That would be helpful," I said, handing him the photo of the mystery girl along with one of our business cards.

"We understand about the problem with you-know-who," Toni said. "It'd probably be better if we'd never even visited."

"I can handle my business," Jorge answered confidently. "If asked, I'll tell them I sent you away empty-handed."

The room was quiet for a moment, then Toni suddenly stood up, smiled, and said, "Mr. Sanchez, you've been absolutely no help at all."

"Good!" Jorge said, smiling broadly as he stood.

I looked from one to the other for a second before I saw what Toni was doing. I stood up and said, "I'm certain your name or your establishment will never come up in the course of this investigation."

"Good!" he said again, beaming.

"We're very sorry to have bothered you, sir," I added. "We didn't mention any names at the bar. Tell anyone who asks that we're looking for the girl."

"Excellent!" he said, still smiling. "Thanks for coming. And don't come back!"

~~~~

"Strange," Toni said as we left the bar.

"You got that right," I agreed. "Jorge was petrified by this Eduardo Salazar character."

"No shit. He seemed more afraid of him than of the police, of us, or of anything we could possibly do to him. Who scares a guy that much?"

"Someone with a nasty rep," I answered.

"True. At least we got a name," Toni said.

We rounded the corner of the building, headed toward the back parking lot and saw three Mexican men standing near my Jeep. When they saw us, they began slowly walking toward us. One of the men split off from the others and started circling to our right in a not-so-subtle attempt to flank us. All three men were probably in their mid- to late twenties. All wore some sort of outer garment—either vest or denim jacket. *Great*, I thought—the better to hide the automatic weapons under. I focused on the two men in front of us while Toni concentrated on the guy circling to our side. One of my guys was tall and looked like a body builder. He was bald and completely covered with prison tattoos. The other guy was shorter and more round, but no less bald. He did have a mustache. He wore a vest over a white T-shirt. His arms were also covered with prison ink.

"Look confident and mean," I whispered to Toni, trying not to move my lips.

We approached to within about ten feet, and then stopped. They stopped as well. "What's up?" I called out. "Going inside?"

"Maybe in a minute, esse," Mr. Short and Round said quietly.

"We were just leaving," I said. "Nice place. Ask for Rita. She's a hoot."

"Yeah, real nice," he said. He gave me a mean glare for maybe ten seconds—long enough for Mr. Scout to reach a decent flanking position. Toni had turned completely around to stare the bastard down, her back to mine.

Mr. Short and Round said, "We hear you're looking for a friend of ours."

I was ready. "Really? Maybe you can help us," I said. "You know this girl?" I walked forward with the photo of Gina in my left hand, extended. My right hand I kept straight down to my side, ready to go for my Les Baer Thunder Ranch 1911 handgun, .45 caliber. I'd have no cover, but I was a damned quick draw. And I was 100 percent confident that by now Toni had her hand on her Glock and had already determined where her closest cover was.

I handed the photo to Mr. Short and Round. He looked at it for a few seconds, then looked back at me.

"I don't know her," he said, confused and maybe a little disappointed. "This who you're looking for?"

"Yeah," I said. "Who'd you think?"

He looked at the photo, and then at me, but didn't answer

"You probably saw her on TV," I said, continuing my story. "She's gone missing. Her family hired us to help try and find her."

He handed the photo to Mr. Big and Tall, who stared at it a moment. I could see that he recognized her immediately. He fired off a string of rapid Spanish to Mr. Short and Round, all the while nodding his head.

"He's seen her?" I asked.

"On TV," Short and Round replied. He seemed confused. "You got other pictures?" he asked.

I figured that Rita, our clever little bartender, had phoned these guys while we were talking to Jorge and told them we were snooping around with pictures of Eduardo Salazar—thus the greeting committee. Short and Round expected us to be looking for Salazar and, therefore, he expected me to present photos of Salazar. Presenting photos of Gina instead had caught him by surprise, as I'd hoped it would. I hoped Rita hadn't been very specific about what type of photo we had. The head shot of Salazar might make it seem more like we were looking for him by virtue of the fact that he'd been singled out. The group photo might allow my story that we were focusing on Gina, not Eduardo, to continue. So I handed him the group photo.

"See here, this is a picture of the girl with some friends of hers at this bar. That's why we came here. We wanted to ask if any of these people could help us find her. Do you recognize any of them?"

He studied the photo, then quickly handed it back to me. "I never seen none of 'em."

"Too bad. Nobody inside recognized them either," I said. "Well, I appreciate your help. You guys have a good evening. We won't take up any more of your time."

He turned and silently looked at Mr. Big and Tall with a confused look on this face. While he was still considering his options, I walked past and then turned and watched. I was ready to jump in if needed, but Toni walked past with no incident. The men stared at us, but they did nothing.

We climbed into the Jeep, and Toni said, quietly, "Whew! That was intense!" I don't know if she meant intense thrilling or intense scary.

I fired up the Jeep and looked back to see the three men, still standing in the parking lot talking to each other.

"That little bitch Rita called in the welcome wagon, didn't she?" Toni said indignantly.

"Looks like it," I agreed. "Looks like Jorge was right—this Eduardo Salazar guy is dangerous. Hell, we didn't even make it out of the damn parking lot before they were on us."

It was quiet for a second, then Toni said, "That was good thinking back there, boss. I was wondering how that was going to play out. You confused the hell out of that guy. That could have gotten ugly fast if he thought we were looking for Salazar."

"True," I said. "Better to not have to fight your way to the car if you can avoid it. Speaking of which, did you have the flanker covered?"

"Of course. I made sure he noticed I had my hand on my gun."

"Good. Avoiding a fight is one thing, but no sense in us looking like pussies." I thought for a few moments. "I don't know what the hell is going on here, but it's pretty clear that these people are way fucking dangerous. I sure hope Gina's not gotten herself involved with them."

# Chapter 6

DWAYNE AGREED TO meet us at the police station first thing next morning after I called him and told him about Eduardo Salazar and our experience at Ramon's. Gus met us in the lobby and took us back to Dwayne's office.

"Heard you had a little excitement last night," Gus said.

"Yeah, a little," I said. "We met up with some mean-looking chulos in the parking lot at Ramon's Cantina."

"Ramon's Cantina, eh?" he asked, laughing. "You trying to impress your partner here by taking her to an uptown establishment like Ramon's?"

"Yeah, something like that. She likes to live life on the edge."

"The gentlemen in the parking lot seemed to take offense at us looking for Eduardo Salazar," Toni said.

"Did they try to muscle you around?" Gus asked.

"They were about to," Toni answered, "but golden boy here whipped out a verbal razzle-dazzle on them. Confused them with so much quick-talking bullshit that they ended up with stars in their eyes. We just walked right past them, hopped in the Jeep, and drove away. They were still there arguing with each other there in the parking lot, trying to figure out exactly what Danny said. Might still be there, for that matter."

Gus laughed. "Nice work. No sense creating a lot of extra paperwork."

We walked into Dwayne's office. "Were they gang members?" Gus asked.

"What do you think, Toni?" I asked.

"Too old. Too big," she said.

"That's what I thought, too," I said. "These guys didn't look like your normal Yakima/Tacoma skinny, teenaged gangbangers. I actually thought they looked more like La eMe types."

"Really? Prison gang? Mexican Mafia?" Dwayne asked.

"Yeah. Older than your typical MS-13 kids. Wiser. Maybe a little less macho-psycho fire in their eyes, but colder, more calculating, actually more menacing. Somehow I get the feeling that the guys last night are much more dangerous."

"They were bigger, that's for sure," Toni said. "One guy must have been six five and two-fifty." She paused, and then added, "Oh, and two out of three were bald. Lots of ink, too."

"Okay," Dwayne said, pointing to the conference table. "Have a seat and tell us what happened from the start."

We sat down and recounted the events of yesterday afternoon at Pacific Wine and Spirits and of last night at Ramon's, of meeting the bartender and then Jorge, and finally of meeting the three bad guys in the parking lot on our way back to the car. We didn't leave anything out.

"Here's some enhanced photos that Kenny made," I said, handing copies of all the photos over to Dwayne.

Dwayne studied them for a moment, then asked, "Who's this?"

"That's Reggie Campbell. She works with Gina."

"And this?"

"We haven't identified her yet. Karen, or Carolyn—something like that. We're working on trying to ID her now."

Dwayne pulled the photo of Eduardo Salazar forward and stared at it for a few more seconds. He said, "And you think the scumbags in the parking lot were upset with you because you were asking about this other scumbag here named Eduardo Salazar?"

"Technically, we never asked anyone about Salazar, specifically," I said. "They had to assume that all on their own. Not counting these guys, we only talked to the bartender and to Jorge Sanchez. We just handed the bartender the group photo—never even told her who we were looking for. I'm guessing that she jumped to a conclusion and notified her buddies out back that we were asking about Eduardo Salazar. I doubt she cared about Gina or the others."

"Maybe she was worried about covering something up," Gus said. "Maybe something happened to Gina and her friends were involved."

I thought for a few seconds. "Could be," I agreed. "But if that were the case, then why would they have let us pass in the parking lot after I showed them the pictures of Gina and said we were looking for her? I took a bit of a gamble in assuming they were interested in protecting Eduardo Salazar when I told them we were focused on Gina. As far as he understood, we considered Eduardo and the mystery woman here as nothing more than information sources to help us find Gina. This seemed to defuse him."

"Confuse him, more likely," Toni said.

"Actually," I said, "he seemed almost disappointed, like he'd been looking forward to messing us up. If he were there because of Gina, I doubt this little ruse would have worked. I think the quick explanation caught him totally by surprise."

Dwayne stared at the ceiling and thought about that for ten seconds or so. Then he looked back at us. "I think you're probably right," he said. "Unless there's some reason to think these guys are connected with the mystery girl here, then the only other reason they'd have been annoyed at you specifically had to have been if you struck a raw nerve with them when they thought you were asking about Eduardo Salazar. Even if you never did actually mention his name. The bartender must have jumped to the conclusion that that's what you were doing without you actually ever having mentioned him. They moved quick."

"They're nervous," Gus said. "Like a virgin in prison."

"They must be," I said. "So who is Eduardo Salazar? You find out anything?" I asked Dwayne.

"Yeah," he said, opening a file. "After you called last night, I started making some inquiries. Eduardo Enrique Salazar, aka Eddie, aka Eddie Stiletto, has been in our system here since last year." Dwayne turned a mug shot right-side up for us. The man staring back had a Manson-like glare in his eyes that made it clear he'd just as soon cut you up as look at you. He had long, thick, dark hair and long sideburns. He looked to be wearing the same black shirt he wore in the photo with Gina. "Eddie was busted last October for assault with a deadly weapon. He cut up his old lady," he turned over the next photo of a young Mexican woman who had two vicious knife slashes on her cheeks, one on each side. "Apparently, the good Mr. Salazar was miffed because she smiled at another guy."

"Nice guy," I said. "Let me guess. He's here on one of those high-tech worker visas."

"Yeah, right," Dwayne laughed. "Actually, Eddie's a Mexican national from Baja, here illegally now on an expired work permit. No current known place of employment. No job, but he posted one hundred thousand dollars bail last year and then—surprise—all the witnesses disappeared. We ultimately had to drop charges."

"Not only is he a sick bastard," Toni said, staring at the photo of the mutilated young woman, "He's a rich sick bastard."

"Looks that way," Dwayne said. "And he has a volcanic-sized temper. And, apparently, it doesn't take much to set him off."

"Yeah, just ask her," Toni said, nodding at the photo of the girlfriend.

"Got a last known address?" I asked.

"We do, but it's almost a year old and certainly obsolete," Dwayne answered.

"Probably, but we'll still check it out," Toni said. "We'll take everything you've got. A neighbor might remember something. It's better than nothing."

It was quiet for a few moments, then I said, "How the hell would someone like Gina get mixed up with an idiot like this?"

"Boggles the mind," Gus said. "But I've seen plenty of instances where well-bred rich girls are attracted to outlaws."

I racked my brain to try and answer my own question, to no avail. I couldn't agree. The Gina I thought I knew would not even give this low-life the time of day. I was stumped.

"Why don't we just find him and ask him?" Toni said.

"Good idea. Might be you find him, you find Gina," Dwayne said.

"That's right," Gus said. "Or maybe you can ask mystery lady here." He pointed to the photo. "If you can't find Eddie, maybe she knows what's going on."

"Could be," I said, rising to leave. "We'll start asking."

"Be careful," Gus said. "Sounds like you're starting to stir up a shit-storm. Make sure you don't get splashed."

~~~~

I was lost in thought as Toni and I drove back to our office. I kept hearing the words of my investigation instructor at Fort Leonard Woods in Missouri during my CID basic training over and over again: "Never jump to a conclusion. Never fixate on an unproven solution. Never fill in the blanks. Let the facts speak totally for themselves." The human tendency is to grab on to what appears to be a logical solution. Then, invariably, the mind focuses on that solution to the exclusion of all others. A person will start to rationalize every bit of evidence to fit the preconceived notion. When you fall victim to this sort of tunnel vision, the real solution can walk right past you completely unnoticed.

Because of this, I reminded myself that Eduardo Salazar, nasty and suspicious as he might be, was just one of many possible scenarios. We needed to keep it in that light. He might have something to do with Gina's disappearance. He might not. Could be that Eddie Salazar was nothing more than a play toy for Gina. Just because Eddie Salazar's a sadistic shithead doesn't mean he had anything to do with Gina. Coincidence? Maybe. Take a further look? You bet. Stop looking elsewhere? No way.

~~~~

"How many?" I asked, incredulously.

"More than seven hundred," Doc replied. "Seven hundred twenty-eight to be exact."

I had a rule that when we were working a case, we tried to meet as a team every morning, first thing. We called it our daily briefing meeting. After we left Dwayne's office, Toni and I had hurried back to the Logan PI office for our meeting. I'd just asked Doc how many registered sex offenders were on the list in Seattle.

"Wow," I said. "That's incredible."

"Yeah, must be something in the water up here," Kenny said.

"No shit," Doc agreed. "How am I going to make sense of this, Danny?" he asked.

"You aren't. You obviously aren't going to be able to go through each one carefully. By the time you're done, whatever you find will have become ancient history."

"Agreed."

"So you have to come up with some way to filter the list," I continued. "All you can do is look at each record and try to make a judgment
call on whether or not the pervert in question is into women of Gina's
description. Each record has some sort of report you can use, like an MO.
I'm pretty sure that a  sizable percentage of the people on that list won't
match our profile."

"That's right," Richard said. "Who's that lady teacher who got busted
for having sex with a student a few years ago? The one who ended up
having the kid's baby?"

"Mary Kay Letourneau," Toni answered.

"Right," Richard continued. "She's probably on that list."

"Good point," I added. "I'm sure she's not a suspect in our case."

"Okay," Doc said. "I'll try and whittle it down."

"Good. Now, let's take a minute and talk big-picture strategy," I said.
"We've decided that of the three possibilities—predator disappearance, kidnapping, and voluntary disappearance—that because there's no
ransom demand, we're going to ignore kidnapping and focus on the other
two, right?"

Everyone nodded their heads.

"And we decided that if we're talking predator disappearance, the
clock is running. In fact, odds are that Gina might already be dead, right?"

Again, everyone nodded.

"Yet so far, all the angles we're working focus on the predator disappearance possibility. One: Eduardo Salazar. Two: registered sex offender.
Three: serial killer. We haven't focused at all on the voluntary disappearance possibility."

"For good reason," Toni said. "We knew when we got into this that
if Gina got abducted by a predator, and if she's not already dead, her days
are surely numbered. We'd need to be lucky to find her in time. You're
right—the clock's running."

"That's right," Richard said. "The vast majority of women abducted
by predators are killed within seventy-two hours or so—three days. In this
case, it's already been almost a week. If she's been abducted by a predator and she's still alive, it would almost have to be some sort of sex-slave
type of scenario. You know, the kind where the pervert locks her in a
basement."

I said, "You guys think we should just ignore the voluntary disappearance possibility for a while then?"

"I think we have to, boss," Toni said. "There's only the five of us." She looked at Kenny. "And that's counting shithead here as a whole person." Kenny looked indignant. Doc and Richard laughed. "I think we have to focus our efforts on the most time-sensitive possibility first. If Gina's been abducted by a predator, and we can find her and rescue her in time, we need to do this." She paused for a moment, and then continued. "That said, I've told you before what I think—that she's gone underground on purpose and has orchestrated the whole thing herself."

"But," I interrupted, "you're not willing to risk her life on that."

"No, I'm not," she said. "It's just one theory. I don't want to fixate."

It was quiet for a second, then Richard said, "I believe that if we can't locate Gina in another few days, then we're probably not going to find her alive anyway. At that point—today's Thursday, say by next Monday—we should switch entirely to the voluntary disappearance possibility. Until then, we owe it to her to keep pounding away on the predator possibility."

"It's a sobering thought, but it makes logical sense to me. What do you guys think?" I asked.

Everyone agreed. We weren't jumping to conclusions, but we were being realistic.

~~~~

The office phone in the lobby rang. Toni got up and walked out to answer it. A few seconds later, she walked back in and said, "I think you're going to want to listen to this." I looked at her curiously as she reached over and punched the button on the speakerphone sitting in the center of the conference room table.

"Go ahead, Mr. Salazar," she said.

No shit. Eddie Salazar decided to cut through all the crap and just give us a call—the direct approach.

"Hello," he said, his voice coming through strong and confident over the phone. "Is this Danny Logan?"

"I'm here," I said. "What can I do for you?"

"Good. I got your business card. I hear you're looking for someone—perhaps someone we both know."

"Could be," I said. "We're actually looking for two people," I said. "First, we're looking for Gina Fiore. I believe she's a friend of yours."

He was quiet for a second. "I know her," he said. "Too bad she's gone." He paused, as if considering his next statement. "Why you? How come the police aren't looking for her?"

"Oh, they are," I said. "My company and the police are working together, although my company is technically working for Gina's family."

"Oh," he answered. "So you know anything? You got any leads? Maybe I can help."

"No thanks," I said. "I don't think we'll need outside help on this one." Obviously, even if Gina were sitting right in front of me, I wouldn't have told this scumbag. "While I have you on the phone, though, when's the last time you saw her?"

He was silent; then he said, "Been a long time—I'm worried about her, esse. There's lots of bad people out there. Maybe she hooked up with the wrong crowd."

"That's true," I said.

"You say you're looking for two people. Who's the other?"

"Why, that'd be you," I said. "We're looking for you. You know, if you really want to help, why don't we get together, talk things over?"

He laughed. "Soon enough, holmes," he said.

"Yeah, sure," I said. "By the way, I think we bumped into a few of your friends last night. When we left, they seemed a little confused. How are they doing?"

He laughed again. "My friends are fine." He was quiet for a second, then said, "They tell me they're eager to see you again."

"Me, too. Anytime. Sounds like fun," I laughed. "I'll tell you, maybe after we return Gina to her family, we can all have a celebration party. I think our friends at the police department have even offered to host it. What do you think?"

He was silent for a second. Then he said, "I was thinking more of a private party."

"Oh, that's good. A private party. That's okay, too. Like I said, anytime."

"Maybe soon," he said. "Maybe sooner than you think." He paused for a second, then said, "By the way, I'd like to meet your associate. I hear she's one fine *mamacita*. Watch for us, holmes." He hung up before I could answer.

~~~~

At first, no one said anything. Kenny broke the ice. "It was blocked, boss," he said, referring to the caller ID number. "Most likely, it was something like a prepaid cell phone anyway."

I nodded. "That was an unusual phone call," I said.

"Sure was," Toni said. "Scary, too."

"Bullshit," I said.

"What's with all the 'homes' talk?" Kenny asked.

"'Holmes,' not 'homes,'" Doc said. "Consider it a term of endearment."

Kenny looked confused.

"What was he really saying?" Richard asked. "Was he saying he doesn't know where Gina is and he's fishing to find out what we know? Or was he saying he does know where she is and he's trying to warn us away?"

We thought about this for a second. Then I said, "If it's your first choice, then we're more useful to him alive than dead. He can set up on us and follow us to Gina. If it's your second choice, then he'd probably rather see us dead so we don't try to find her and lead anyone to him."

"He might also just be a rabid dog. Bite anything that comes near," Doc said. "I've seen lots of assholes just like him who were that way. Couldn't think five minutes ahead."

"That's right. If we were in Mexico, he'd probably just bomb our office building with us in it," Kenny said.

"Either way, he's basically telling us that he's going to be watching us—either to have us lead him to Gina, or in preparation for taking one or more of us out. I think we need to bump up our security level," Doc said.

"That makes a lot of sense," I said. "Pay attention, everyone. This bastard could be parked across the street right now. If these guys are out there essentially stalking us, we need to be able to recognize them and counter it. Everyone needs to be armed at all times. If anyone sees anything unusual—a car, people, anything at all—hunker down and call Doc or me. We'll be right there. Got it?"

"Great," Kenny said. "So basically, you guys are saying that we've managed to find a psychotic, homicidal maniac and, without even meeting him, we've pissed him off to the point that he either wants to follow us and then kill us, or maybe just save time and go right ahead and kill us straightaway? Is that it?"

"Almost, but you got one thing wrong," Doc said to him. "He's not interested in following you."

"That's right, you little coward," Toni said. "You don't know anything. No reason for him to follow you."

"Good," Kenny said. "I'm safe."

"No, no. That's not what I meant," Toni said. "What I meant was, you don't know anything worthwhile, so he won't waste time following you. Instead, he'll just kill you straightaway."

"Oh, great."

Everyone laughed, except for Kenny.

"Okay," I said. "Game's heating up. Be careful."

# Chapter 7

AFTER OUR STAFF meeting, Toni and I drove past Memorial Stadium at the eastern end of Seattle Center on our way to Gina's condo. When I was in high school, the state championship track and field meets were held at Memorial Stadium. In my senior year, I remember running the mile in the state finals there. The race was four times around the track. The favorite was a fast kid from Spokane with a personal record of something like four minutes, twenty seconds. My own personal record was four minutes fifty. I knew going in that it would be tough, and it was. Bell lap and I was gassed. I'd managed to stay with the Spokane kid for the first three laps, but it was tough. Then, after the bell, he turned up the heat a little, just to see if I could hang with him. I did, but it hurt and he knew it. So he did what good runners do—he turned up the heat a little more. This turned the event into a two-person race: him leading, me struggling to hang on, everyone else falling back fast. Coming off the final turn, he started his kick, as I knew he would. In response, I did my own version of a kick, but it was pretty obvious that I couldn't hang with him. I started to fall back myself.

Yet even as I began to falter, my teammates and our supporters yelled for me, encouraged me on, urged me forward. And somehow, right in the middle of the screaming throng, I remember seeing Gina. To my weary eyes, she was a vision. Strikingly beautiful, smiling, confident, waving me forward. I felt a breath of inspiration. I was renewed. I had to do better, dig deeper. Spurred on by the sight of that beautiful high-school sophomore, I found a burst of energy and was able to kick it up to a new gear that I never knew I had. In the last fifty yards of the race, I closed the distance on the leader. I felt like I had wings.

Unfortunately, as I drew near, my opponent heard me closing. Turns out that on that day, he had the bigger wings, and he was gone. I crossed the finish line several seconds later, in second place. Afterward, I was disappointed but not devastated. I'd known I was an underdog and that my chances were not great. I jogged a little to cool down, and then returned to the team area.

My teammates congratulated me for running hard and taking second place.

"Noble effort, dude," Robbie said.

"Thanks. Thought I might get him for a second," I said, reaching for the towel he handed me.

"You were awesome," said a girl, standing behind me. I turned around and saw that it was Gina. She looked at me and smiled. "You know you ran a four-thirty."

"Really?" I asked, shocked at the result and even more shocked that she was talking to me.

"Yeah," Gina said. "Four-thirty. Damn good. You beat your own PR by twenty seconds. That's fantastic. I'm impressed." She smiled at me, then turned and walked back to her friends.

*No shit*, I thought to myself. I didn't think that she even knew who I was and it turns out she not only knows me, but she knows my stats. I could have finished last—it didn't matter. I was on cloud nine.

~~~~

Gina's condo was a corner unit on the second floor of an eight-unit building in Queen Anne. Toni and I started interviewing Gina's neighbors at one in the afternoon. We managed to catch four of the seven at home, which I thought was pretty good for a Thursday afternoon. Three of the four recognized Gina and had seen on the news that she'd gone missing. One guy was pissed that we'd woken him up, and then said he'd never seen her before anyway. Most commented that they'd seen the police cars at the condo over the past few days.

One by one, we showed the neighbors the group photo plus the isolated head shots of Eddie Salazar and the mystery girl. Most importantly, we were looking for the identity of the mystery girl. Secondly, we were interested in determining if anyone had ever seen Eddie Salazar around Gina's place. We struck out. None of the four neighbors had ever seen either Eddie or the mystery girl.

Just after three, we walked back to my Jeep and were getting ready to leave when a silver Toyota Prius hybrid glided silently into the lot. As we watched, an elderly lady got out. She removed a single bag of what appeared to be groceries from her trunk and took the elevator to the second floor. We watched as she entered unit 303—next door to Gina's apartment.

"Should we talk to her now?" I asked wearily. "We're going to have to come back to talk to the others tonight or tomorrow night anyway."

"Poor baby," Toni said. "We're here, she's here, we're getting paid. You can take the elevator if you're tired." She got out of the Jeep without waiting for me and headed for the stairs.

Have I mentioned that Toni can be a little bossy sometimes?

We went upstairs and knocked on the door for unit 303.

A few seconds later, the door opened and a lady who looked to be in her mid- to late seventies looked us over. She was probably five four with silver hair pulled tightly back. She was neatly dressed, wearing a pink knit sweater over a print dress.

"May I help you?" she asked.

"Yes, ma'am," I answered. I introduced us and handed her our business cards. She studied them intently for a minute, then looked up at me.

"Ma'am," I continued, "we've been hired by the family of the young lady who lives next door to you to try and find out what's happened to her."

"Gina? That poor, poor girl," the lady said.

"You know her, then?" I asked.

"Yes, certainly," she said. "I've come to know her well since she moved in last year. I hope and pray that nothing bad has happened to her."

"Thank you, ma'am," I said. "It says on the register that your last name is Perkins?"

"Yes, Elizabeth Perkins."

"Miss Perkins, do you mind if we ask you a few questions?" I asked. "Questions that might help us locate Gina."

"It's Mrs. Perkins," she said. "My Vernon passed many years ago. I'm a widow. I don't at all mind answering your questions. Please, come in."

We entered, and she said, "Do you mind if I put these groceries in the refrigerator first? I don't want anything to spoil."

I smiled. She reminded me of my grandmother.

"Please, take all the time you need," Toni answered.

"Thank you," she said. "You two are welcome to sit on the sofa there if you'd like."

We thanked her and sat down. Her unit appeared to be identical to Gina's—at least as far as layout. Of course, the decorating was nothing like Gina's. Whereas Gina's condo was stark, modern, and minimally furnished, Mrs. Perkins's unit looked like my grandmother's—that is, it featured painted and wallpapered walls, overstuffed furniture, and pictures and knickknacks everywhere. There was hardly a square inch of wall space without a picture or countertop space without some sort of figurine.

"May I bring you two some iced tea on a hot day like today?" she asked.

"Please," Toni said. "That would be delightful. Would you like some help?"

"No, thank you, dear," Mrs. Perkins answered, smiling sweetly, as she shuffled back to her kitchen. She laughed and said, "I believe I can still manage to bring a couple of glasses of iced tea all by myself."

A minute later, she came from the kitchen carrying a small tray with a pitcher and three glasses full of ice. She placed the tray on the small table in front of us and said, "Please, help yourselves." She sat down. "Now," she said, "how may I help you?"

Before we go out on an interview, we always build a standard list of questions that we call our PQL—our Program Question List. This helps us make sure we don't forget to ask a question that might make it necessary for us to come back later. Things like what's your full name, how long have you lived here, how well do you know Gina, when did she leave for work, when did she usually get home—that sort of thing. Mrs. Perkins felt she knew Gina reasonably well, but in a neighbor-to-neighbor sort of way. They did not socialize. We asked if Mrs. Perkins knew whether or not Gina went out often. Seemed like three or four nights per week. Did Gina bring men home? Occasionally. When was the last time she saw her? Last Thursday morning when Gina went to work.

When we completed our PQL, we broke out the photos. We first showed her the picture of Eddie Salazar. "Do you recognize this man?" Toni asked.

"Wait a minute," she said. She reached into her sweater and pulled out a pair of reading glasses with lenses that were nearly a quarter-inch thick. She put them on and stared at the photo for a minute. "No, I've never seen him," she said resolutely.

"Okay," I answered. "How about her?" I handed her the picture of Reggie Campbell.

"No," she answered. "I don't think I've ever seen her before, either." She looked up at me. "Sorry I'm not being much help," she said.

"Don't worry about that," I answered. "Right now, it's just as important that we know who doesn't come here as who does. You're being very helpful." I handed her the picture of the mystery woman. "How about her?" I asked.

She looked at the photo for a second, then she brightened and said, "Oh, yes! I know this young woman. I've seen her here many times."

Toni and I were both surprised. "Really?" I said. "Is that right?"

"Oh yes," she answered. "I recognize her."

I was a little worried about the size of Mrs. Perkins's glasses. "How can you be so sure it was this girl and not possibly another?" I asked.

"Because I bumped into the two of them outside once," she answered, "Gina introduced us."

"That's interesting," I said. "Do you happen to remember her name?"

She thought for a second, then said, "I think Gina said her name was Tara—no, wait, it was Kara—something like that."

"Could it have been Carolyn or Karen?" Toni asked.

"No," Mrs. Perkins said. "Now that I think about it, I'm almost certain it was Kara. I remember thinking that it rhymed with Tara from *Gone with the Wind*. One of my favorites."

"Mine, too," I said, truthfully. I wasn't lying. "That's very useful. Gina never mentioned where Kara lived, did she?"

"No," Mrs. Perkins said, "but I do recall Gina saying that they worked in the same business together. You probably know that Gina works in her father's business."

"Yes, we do," Toni said.

We chatted for another fifteen minutes or so before concluding. "Mrs. Perkins, is there anything else you can think of regarding this Kara girl, or any other thing you think we might be able to use?" I asked.

She thought for a moment, and then said, "I don't think so. But I have your card. If I think of something, should I call you?"

"Absolutely," Toni said, rising. "We really appreciate your help today, Mrs. Perkins. This is great information. You've been a big help this afternoon. You've given us a lot to go on." She smiled, then said, "And, I must say, you make the best iced tea."

"Thank you, dear," Mrs. Perkins said, smiling. "It's sun tea. It brews all by itself in a jar in the window. I'm glad if I was able to help you. I hope you're able to find Gina and bring her home safe and sound."

"We're certainly going to try," I said.

We thanked her and reminded her to call us if she thought of anything else.

We left and walked down the stairs to the parking lot. "Sweet lady," Toni said. "Aren't you glad you sucked it up and did one more interview?"

"I'd have been back here tonight or tomorrow anyway," I said. "But, that said, yes, I'm glad you guilt-tripped me into one more interview this afternoon. It was a good call."

"Damn straight," she said.

~~~~

"You still think she's hiding out?" I asked Toni on the way back to the office. She hadn't said a word since we'd left.

She thought for a second, then said, "No reason to think otherwise. Not yet, anyway."

"What about Eddie Salazar? How does he fit in?"

"Don't know," she said. "He sounds nasty, but we don't know how he fits in or, for that matter, even if he fits in at all—or anything else about him yet," she said. "All we know is that we need to be careful where we go trying to find him. He's got mean friends."

"And he likes to make veiled threats over the telephone," I added.

"True. Still, he might be nothing more than a jilted lover with a bad case of macho-ego, for all we know." She paused. "But I want to reserve the right to change my mind after we find this Kara chick and talk to her."

"Fair enough," I said. I changed lanes. "Got any bright ideas on how to find her?"

"Well, that sweet Mrs. Perkins said she thought that Kara and Gina worked in the same business. What could that mean?"

"Coworker? Let's check with Robbie when we get back to the office."

"Maybe. Odd no one would have mentioned her, though. Besides, if I were Gina and the boss of a whole group of subordinate employees, I probably wouldn't make any of them my first choice of hangout buddies," she said. "I'll bet it's hard to be the boss in the daytime and a best friend after work. From what I hear about Gina, she's nothing if not efficient. My money says Kara's not an employee of the company."

She had a good point. "You're probably right. But it's easy enough to check with Robbie anyway. I forget the name of the HR lady he said they had, but it should only take a second to crosscheck names."

"Okay," Toni said. "But how about a vendor or a supplier—maybe some sort of wholesaler. Might be that's their business connection."

"That's good," I said, impressed. "Same basic concept—how about a customer?"

"Yep. My working theory then—at least for the moment—is that Gina met Kara from her activities at work. Kara is most likely a reasonably high-ranked financial officer from a supplier or customer."

"First thing in the morning, let's go past Pacific Wine and Spirits. We'll get a list of employees' names from HR and then talk to Reggie Campbell about finding a list of supplier and customer contacts. Then we'll start making some phone calls."

~~~~

We made it back to the office by four, and I was glad to see that Richard was still there. When I bought Richard's company a few years ago, I discovered pretty quickly that he wasn't completely comfortable with the idea of stepping away from the work altogether. He needed to sell the business for health reasons—he's not really able to perform some of the physical aspects of the job anymore. Even the relatively easy stuff like sitting on a stakeout for five or six hours is hard on him now. Yet, despite the fact that the business no longer carries his name, he has a strong mental need to stay involved. Truth is, mentally, he's as sharp as ever, and he's addicted to working cases. If ever there was a born detective, it's Richard. Anything from crosswords to murder mysteries, he can't resist. And, after fifty years at it, he's damn good.

Not being completely stupid, I realized that I might be able to take advantage of his need to stay involved. If I simply provided him with an office, a phone, a business card and a place to hang out, I got the benefit of his massive database of expertise. What's more, he does it because he likes it! I don't have to pay him. What a deal. It's not really taking advantage, I suppose. We both get something out of it. And we're both aware of each other's motives. One of those I-know-that-he-knows-and-he-knows-that-I-know-that-we-both-know-what-each-other-is-after  sort of deals.

"Got a minute?" I asked him from the doorway of his office.

"You bet," he said. "I was just wrapping up to go home." Richard and his wife live in Ballard, just west of Queen Anne.

I slid into one of the chairs across from his desk. "We got a first name on the mystery lady this afternoon. It's Kara."

"Kara," he said slowly. "That's good news. How are you going to track her down, and what do you hope to accomplish if you find her?"

"We have a lead that Kara is in the same business as Gina. We have a hunch that she might be some sort of finance person employed by either a supplier or a customer of Pacific Wine and Spirits. Hopefully, if we find her, she might have some insight as to what Gina's up to. She seems to be pretty close to Gina. Gina's next-door neighbor said she's seen Kara at Gina's place a few times."

"Sounds like a good hunch, then," Richard said.

"Yeah, I hope," I said. "Step by step, right?"

"Step by step," he repeated.

"What are your thoughts about this case so far anyway? What's your experience tell you about what's happening here?"

"Well, let's look at the numbers. I checked the Internet. Nationwide, about 180 women are reported missing each day of the year. Of these, probably 80 percent are running away from something or someone—in essence, hiding. Fifteen percent are insane or have some sort of mental problem. The other 5 percent have been abducted and, most likely, are dead within a few hours of abduction. Except for the deceased, most of the others eventually return home or are tracked down."

"So you're saying I should find some comfort in these numbers?" I asked him.

"Sure, the numbers are in your favor," he said. "Unless she's one of the unlucky 5 percent. The numbers most decidedly did not work out for them."

"Thanks a hell of a lot."

"Well, that's the point, isn't it," he asked, leaning back in his chair and locking his hands behind his head, smiling. "She's not insane, so if you just go by the numbers, you tell the parents to go home and wait. Odds are excellent that she'll be back. She's most likely simply run off for the moment. The problem with this approach is that you're talking about a young woman for whom a disappearing act like this is completely out of character. And you're talking about someone's daughter—not a number in the FBI's national crime statistics. Why would this young lady run off? She has no known troubles. No known drug problems. No abusive husband. No known abusive boyfriend—although I grant you that Eduardo Salazar may turn out to be a motivation. But for the moment, there's no reason that we can see for anyone to be after her. Therefore, why would she take off and hide?"

"Exactly," I said.

Richard smiled. "So what do we do then? Do we throw in the towel and play the odds? Of course not. The way I see it, the problem we have is that fundamentally, we don't know this girl well enough to understand if any of the things that I just said are factual. Just because she doesn't have a legal husband, just because she doesn't have a record of disappearance, just because she doesn't have any other visible historical manifestation that could lead a rational person to conclude that she was likely to up and disappear doesn't mean that such manifestations don't exist. It's like the old saying, 'If a tree falls down in the forest and no one is around to hear it, does it make a sound?'"

Richard sounds more and more like a college professor every day.

He's also fond of sayings. He has one for every situation. This one made a weird kind of sense, though.

"I imagine," he continued, "the tree makes a very loud sound indeed, particularly if you happen to be standing directly beneath it. And I also imagine that there's something in this girl's past that's led to her disappearance, that's caused her to run. We don't know what it is. We have to dig until we find it."

I nodded. "This is true. Of course, there's the other explanation," I said.

He looked at me without smiling. "Of course," he agreed. "She could just be one of the unlucky 5 percent."

~~~~

After I called Dwayne and updated him, I wrote up my daily report, a habit I'd gotten into in the army. I said good night to Toni and left the office about six-thirty. I live in an apartment on Dexter Avenue, which is located on a bluff on the next street above my office and about a half mile north. This still puts me at the southern end of Lake Union. I like the water. Something about it soothes me. Lake, ocean, river, you name it— I've always liked the water. So my apartment, like my office, has a balcony that allows me an unrestricted view of the south end of the lake. I look right over the tops of the offices on the water, and I can see the eastern shore of the lake—the apartments, the marinas, and the restaurants of Chandler's Cove. If I look to my left, which is north, I can see the float house where *Sleepless in Seattle* was filmed. If I look to the right, I can see the Kenmore Air floatplanes seaport. They take off and land all day long. When the wind is out of the northeast, the landing approach path brings them directly over Chandler's restaurant. I love to watch the unsuspecting restaurant patrons dive for cover when a de Havilland Beaver suddenly appears out of nowhere and roars forty feet overhead on final approach.

Tonight, though, I wasn't looking at any of that. As soon as I got home, I changed into shorts and a T-shirt and poured a mug of Mac & Jack's from the growler in my refrigerator. The sun wasn't down yet, and the early evening was still balmy. I popped in a Brandi Carlile CD and listened to her tell me about her dreams. I plopped myself down on a lounge chair on my balcony and considered the case.

Richard's argument regarding the odds made sense, but I don't always trust the odds. I don't know if I'm burdened with a bad-luck charm, or what, but whatever it is, I've had my share of unlikely calamities. The second time I got wounded was on the outskirts of Tikrit in Iraq in 2003. I was crouched behind a rock wall—excellent cover, in theory. But I still got hit when an RPG blew up in front of the wall where I was hiding and sent a piece of shrapnel whizzing past the wall and into the rocks behind me, from which a good-sized chunk ricocheted back and hit me in the right thigh, just below my butt. I was the only one to get hit. Put me in the hospital for a week and a half. What are the odds of that happening? So, based solely on the odds, the 5 percent theory made me nervous. And the overdue silent serial killer, not to mention several busloads of registered sex offenders, didn't help.

# Chapter 8

IT DOESN'T RAIN all that often in the summer in Seattle, but by Friday morning, it hadn't officially rained for forty days straight, and that was newsworthy. Warm and dry—again. Last night, Toni agreed to meet me at the office at 8:00 a.m. The plan was to drive together to Pacific Wine and Spirits for the nine o'clock appointment I'd made with Robbie. Before we talked with Reggie Campbell about supplier and customer lists, I wanted to speak to Cindy Dunlap in the HR Department and get a copy of the employee names.

We arrived at Pacific Wine and Spirits with five minutes to spare. After we met Robbie in the front, he took us back and introduced us to Cindy Dunlap. He then excused himself, saying he was late for a meeting.

Cindy Dunlap was a short, middle-aged woman with hair that was half brown, half gray. She wore a gray dress suit. First thing, I asked for an employee list.

"Do you need all the employees?" she said. "There are 417 of us altogether, in three states. If you'd like, I can distill the list to just our Seattle employees, or even to those who worked in Gina's department."

"Good question," I said, considering our resources. "Why don't we start with just the Seattle employees."

"Okay," she said. "I'll get started on the printout. There are 274 employees in our Seattle operation. It will only take a minute."

"Two hundred seventy-four," I said. "I think we're just looking to match up a name. That shouldn't take long."

"Before you get started," Toni said, "you've met pretty much everyone in the company, right?"

"Yes. I generally do an orientation with every new employee—at least those in Seattle."

"Good. Do you recognize this person?" She took the picture of Kara from me and showed it to Dunlap. "We believe her name is Kara. We don't have a last name."

She took the picture from Toni and stared at it intently for thirty seconds or so. "I'm sorry, I don't recognize her at all."

It only took a couple of minutes for Cindy to run the query through the company's computers and print us a list.

"Thanks for doing this," I said, as she handed me the paper.

"No problem," she answered. "I hope you can find Gina. We sure need her around here."

"We're working on it," Toni said. She took the list from me. "One other question, Cindy. We haven't had a chance to interview you yet. Last Friday, as I understand it, you accompanied Robbie to Gina's condo to check on her. Find out why she hadn't come to work?"

"Yes," she said. I looked at Toni. These questions were a surprise—something we hadn't discussed.

Toni continued. "Robbie already told us what he saw, but it might be helpful to hear another perspective, just in case we missed something or in case something new comes out."

"Okay," Cindy said. "We were actually only there for a few minutes. The front door was locked, but Robbie has a key. He unlocked the door and we went in. The curtains were drawn, so it was a little dark. We turned on the lights inside and looked around."

"What did you see?" Toni asked.

"Nothing, really," Cindy said. She thought for a second before continuing. "Gina wasn't there, of course. We checked the whole condo. But nothing looked out of place or out of order. Her keys and purse were on the bar by the kitchen. Then Robbie looked outside and saw Gina's car. After that, we turned off the lights and locked up. We came back to the office, and Robbie called the police. We were careful not to touch anything the entire time we were there."

Toni wrote all this in her notebook. "That's it, that's all I needed. Thank you."

Toni turned to me and held the list so we both could scan it. At about the same moment, we saw the same thing on the first page.

"What about this?" I asked Cindy, pointing to a name. "It says there's a girl named Karen Brown in the shipping department. This resembles the name we're looking for. Does this Karen Brown look anything like the girl in this picture who we thought was named Kara?"

Cindy laughed.

"What's so funny?" I asked, turning to her.

"It's just—well, you're looking for the girl in the photo—a blonde-haired, blue eyed Kara. Karen Brown who works in accounting? She's black."

"Oh."

~~~~

After this unfruitful encounter, Cindy took us back to the accounting department where we met up with Reggie Carpenter. Robbie rejoined us a couple minutes later.

"Any progress?" Reggie asked, after we'd said our hellos and sat down.

"A little," I said. "We've learned that this guy," I pointed to the group photo, "is a genuine pillar of society named Eduardo Salazar."

"Actually, he's an illegal alien also known as Eddie Stiletto who was arrested last year for attacking a girlfriend with a knife," Toni said.

"Holy shit," Reggie said. "He seemed weird, but not that weird."

"He's a real piece of work," I answered.

"We also learned that he's got some dangerous friends," Toni added.

"That's right," I agreed. "They nearly jumped us in the parking lot at Ramon's just for asking questions about him."

"Great. Is there any way that this lands on me?" Reggie asked, suddenly looking concerned. She flipped a strand of hair that had fallen across her face.

"No way," I answered. "We have the only copies of the photos—us and the police, anyway. The only thing Salazar's thugs seemed concerned about was our interest in Eddie Salazar. I'm 100 percent confident you don't have anything to worry about." This was mostly true. I was actually about 95 percent confident. There's that pesky 5 percent risk again. Like they say, shit happens.

"Good," Reggie said. She seemed to believe me, and I suppose that for now, anyway, that was the best.

I continued. "We're also pretty confident now that the girl in the picture you couldn't identify is named Kara. You were close when you thought it was Karen. We've been led to believe that Kara is someone who works in your industry. We thought there was a slim chance that she might be an employee here, but that doesn't appear to be the case."

"I've never seen her around here," Reggie said. "I know most of the people here. I'd have recognized her."

"True. We probably should have asked you first," I said.

"I didn't recognize her, either," Robbie said.

Toni nodded. "She probably doesn't work here," she said. "It was just a shot. We think it's actually more likely that she works for one of your suppliers or maybe one of your customers, but we wanted to make sure. We want to talk to her to see if she knows anything more about Eddie Salazar."

Reggie nodded. "I can run a report of vendors and customers on our accounting system," Reggie said. "It will just take a few minutes."

"Do you also keep records of contact people at those companies?" Toni asked.

"Yes—it's part of the same database on the accounting system."

"Can you add that to the report?"

"It's already there. We have a standard vendor report that will give you company name, address, phone, and contact. The customer report will do the same."

"Perfect," I replied. I considered this for a second as I referred to my notes. Then I turned to Robbie. "Robbie, we haven't seen Gina's office yet. While the report's running, would you mind unlocking Gina's office so I can have another look around?"

~~~~

Robbie took us back to the corner where Gina's office was located and unlocked the door.

"We've kept it locked in case you guys or the police needed something," he said as he flipped on the lights. "I wanted it to be in exactly the same condition as the last time she was here. I had our IT guys set it up so that I automatically get copies of her incoming e-mails, so the business doesn't suffer. Or at least, suffer much. I'm not nearly as good at what she does as she is. I can't negotiate and make arrangements like she can. My talent seems to be in operations. Shipping, receiving, that sort of thing."

We went inside and I said, "Robbie, speaking of e-mails, there was no computer at her condo. I'm wondering how she gets e-mails when she's not at work."

"I'm not sure. I think she used to get them on her phone, as well as on the computer here," he said. "They must be tied together somehow."

"I'd like to take a look at her e-mail records and see if I can find anything, if that's okay with you."

"Sure," he said. "Go ahead. I haven't seen anything that looks suspicious as the message copies have come across my desk, but you're welcome to have a look." He pointed to the chair at her desk. "Please, have a seat and take a look."

I sat down at Gina's desk and looked around. There was an eight-by-ten photograph of Gina and her family in a frame on her credenza. A motivational poster was hung on her wall—one of those lone-hang-glider-against-a-sunset sorts with the snappy saying on the bottom. A silk ficus tree was in the corner. That was pretty much it for decorations.

A half-dozen Post-it notes—none of them consequential—were stuck to the frame of her computer monitor. I pressed a key on the keyboard. The PC beeped at me, and the locked-screen notification appeared.

"PC's locked," I said to Robbie. "Do you know her password by chance?"

Robbie thought for a few seconds, and then said, "Try PTCROIS-SANT1747."

I had him spell it for me as I typed it in. It worked and her desktop opened up. She used Microsoft Outlook, and I was able to look at her e-mail logs. I was initially interested in the dates. There was no outgoing activity after the eleventh of August—her last day at work.

"Do you mind if I browse the individual messages to see if any of the posts might be relevant?" I asked.

"No, Danny," Robbie said. "Go ahead."

I did, and they weren't. Like Robbie had said, unless there was some secret code being used, all of the e-mails—there were about a hundred—appeared to me to be either business-related or junkmail of some sort.

"I guess I didn't really expect to see anything here," I said. "But, you never know. And anyway, at least I'm able to confirm that the account hasn't been used to send anything over the past week. Or at least, this PC hasn't been used."

"Is there another PC she might have used?" I asked.

"Nothing else here at the office," he said. "Like I said, I've seen her reading mail on her phone. But in the entire time she's been with the company, she's always worked right here in this office."

"No other locations?" I asked.

"Nope," he said. "None. Right here in this office the whole time."

We started to leave when Toni suddenly said, "Danny, excuse me for a second. I just thought of something. I need to go outside and give Kenny a call."

"Okay," I said. I turned to Robbie. "I'm ready to head back to Reggie's and see what she's got."

~~~~

Reggie had printed a vendor report seventy-six pages long and a customer report 214 pages long. She'd been kind enough to place each report in its own three-ring binder. She even slipped a cover sheet into the plastic covering on the binder. Sweet.

I found an empty office and started flipping through the reports while I waited for Toni. Once I found where the contact name was, I was able to get a system going and fairly well blaze through the pages. There were three records—three contact names—per page. Once I knew where to look, I could quickly scan the page and flip to the next in about four seconds. I looked at my watch when I started. It took six minutes to look at the vendor report and there was not a single "Kara" listed in the contact name field. I was about to start in on the customer report when Toni came back into the office. She closed the door.

"Want to see something interesting?" she asked.

"Sure," I said.

"Look at this." She handed me her iPhone.

On the display was a photo of a Post-it note that read K—Nu Cell: 206-438-3992.

"What is . . . is this—?" I started to ask.

"Is it Kara's cell phone number?" she said, finishing my sentence. "I think so, anyway."

"Where'd you get it?"

"When we were in Gina's office and I saw those Post-it notes stuck on her monitor, I suddenly remembered that she had notes stuck on the bulletin board at her condo as well. You had me take pictures of them, remember?"

"Yeah."

"After I took the pictures, I gave my phone to Kenny. He took the pictures off my phone and stored them on the server at the office. For whatever reason, seeing the notes in Gina's office triggered something, and I vaguely remembered seeing a phone number on one of the notes. I didn't make the connection at the time. I called Kenny and asked him to pull them up and have a look. This is what we found."

"Damn," I said. "This might be great news. I'll call Kenny and have him start trying to work backwards and verify the name and get an address."

"I already told him to get started."

"That's damn good work, Toni. Thank you."

"I know," she said, smiling smugly. "What would you ever do without me?"

~~~~

Because of construction activity, it took nearly forty-five minutes to get back to the office. Seems Paul Allen decided to demolish the entire area around south Lake Union and rebuild it in his vision, and he's doing it all at once.

"Those questions you were asking Cindy Dunlap," I said as I drove. "Were you trying to corroborate Robbie's statements?"

"Very good," she said. "Until now, he's been the only one with access to the condo-slash-potential-crime-scene. Both we and SPD—including CSI—have assumed that what he said is truthful. It's also a little discon-

certing that he has a key to the condo. A smart person with enough unin-
terrupted time can do a lot to manipulate a scene."

"Makes sense," I said. "The questions, I mean. I don't think Robbie
had anything to do with the disappearance of his sister, but the questions
are logical."

"I don't really think he did, either," Toni said. "I just don't want to
be surprised."

I nodded as I pulled into our parking lot. "I agree. But now that
Cindy's backed Robbie's story, Robbie's closer to being in the clear. He
still had access to the condo—could have been there anytime Thursday
night or Friday morning."

"Right," Toni said. "Then he brings people out Friday, pretends to
be surprised at what he sees when it was him that staged it all along." She
thought for a minute. "I just have one major problem with this scenario."

"Aside from Robbie not seeming to be anywhere near swift enough
to pull that off?" I asked.

"Bingo," Toni said. "That's it—we're thinking alike. I like Robbie.
He seems pretty bright. But he doesn't seem like he's devious enough or
tough enough or resolute enough to be able to dream this up and execute
it and not crack in front of his parents, in front of us, and in front of
several sets of police officers. That's just not Robbie, unless he's the best
damn actor in the world. I don't think so. My money lands on someone
else, not Robbie."

"Agreed," I said as we walked into the office. Kenny was standing in
the lobby, waiting for us.

"Saw you drive in," he said. "Do you want the good news or the bad
news?"

*Great.* "Bad news first," I said.

"There is no bad news," he said, smiling. "I'm messing with you. The
good news is that the phone belongs to a Miss Kara Giordano. She lives
at 756 East Green Lake Drive, unit 212. It's at the top of Green Lake just
past the park."

"Outstanding," I said, beaming. "Good job, guys."

"There's more," he said. "I printed out her last two months' telephone activity. There were numerous calls to Gina's cell phone—nearly
daily. That ended abruptly last Thursday afternoon. The last call to Gina

that went through was at 3:34 last Thursday afternoon. Nothing since then. Nada."

"Interesting," I said. "Does that mean that she didn't try to call Gina, or that she may have tried to call but didn't get through?"

"Could be either," Kenny said. "The minute meter only rolls when the connection is made."

"Wow," I said, trying to think. "So Kara either knew that Gina wanted to disappear and wasn't using that phone or she didn't know anything and kept trying to call but Gina never answered."

"On account of the fact that Gina's cell phone is in her condo," Toni said.

"I'm checking every number Kara's called since last Thursday," Kenny said. "I'll try and pin down anything that looks suspicious."

*Progress?* I hoped so.

# Chapter 9

KARA'S CONDO WAS located about five miles from our office. We took Highway 99 northbound and crossed Lake Union on the Aurora Bridge. Two miles later, 99 skirts the western edge of Green Lake. We exited onto Green Lake Drive. The lake is always popular in the summer and today being another gorgeous sunny day, it was packed. People were everywhere—walking, skating, sitting at the benches and tables, riding bikes. Looking out on the water, I saw several radio-controlled sailboats—the same type my parents had given me for my twelfth birthday. Good memories here at Green Lake.

Not much further north, Green Lake Drive circled the top of the lake and swung to the east. "Seven fifty-six Green Lake. I think it's up ahead on the left," I said to Toni.

"Gray lap siding, two-story building," she answered immediately.

"How the hell do you know that?" I asked.

"I see it. It's right up there. There's a sign."

I searched for what she was looking at and located a sign that said Green Lake Terrace. The address was printed just below.

"Got it. Good eyes," I said. "Looks like there's a parking lot right in front."

A second later, I swung the Jeep beneath a sign that said Residents and Guests Only and parked in the last remaining empty spot. "Three o'clock in the afternoon and the lot's nearly full," I said. "I think we're a guest, don't you?"

"You bet," she answered.

I parked, and we walked up the stairs and across the landing to get to Kara's unit. The curtains were drawn but, as we walked past, there was the very slightest ruffle of drapery fabric inside. We walked past the window.

"See that?" Toni whispered.

"Yep."

By habit, we assumed a tactical position at the doorway—one of us on either side of the door, not directly in front. If anyone inside was inclined to start shooting, statistics indicated that they tended to aim for center mass, right through the middle of the door. Bad idea to be standing there on the other side.

I looked at Toni, and she nodded. I knocked on the door.

No answer.

I knocked again.

This time, the doorknob started to turn. Toni and I both had our hands on our guns, both on belt holsters on our right hips.

The door opened two inches and a male voice said, "Who is it? What do you want?"

"Good afternoon. We're here to speak to Kara Giordano," I said loudly enough to be heard inside. "We're private investigators and we're friends of Gina Fiore's family. We've been hired by the family to help find Gina and bring her home safely."

"There's no one here by that name," he said.

"I mentioned two names," I said. "Which name do you mean?"

"The first one you said."

"Okay. Kara Giordano. Well, does Kara Giordano live here at least?" I asked.

"There's no one here by that name," he said again.

"You already said that," I said.

The door opened enough so that we could see a medium-height, dark-haired man wearing a dark blue short-sleeved shirt over a white T-shirt. He wore khaki shorts with no shoes. He looked to be in his early twenties. His eyes were wide open, darting around, looking behind me—he was clearly nervous. He looked at me. "There's no one here by that name," he said yet again.

"Jesus," I said. "That's the third time you've said that, dude. We get it. We just wanted to know if Kara Giordano lives here."

He was silent for a minute, then he said in a more menacing tone, "You should leave now." He slowly pulled back his shirt to reveal some kind of compact Glock semi-auto tucked into an inside-the-belt holster.

I held up my hands in mock surrender, trying to calm the fellow down. "Whoa! Okay, we'll leave," I said. "We don't want any trouble. But dude, you're not very friendly, you know? Tell you what, before you shoot us," I raised my voice now, just in case Kara was inside listening, "do you mind if we leave a business card with my phone number to give to Kara—just on the off chance that you happen to bump into her?"

He stared at me and said nothing. I shook my head and turned and looked at Toni. "Do you think he heard me? Does that mean it's okay?"

"He heard. I think it means it's okay," she said.

"Okay," I said, nodding my agreement. Then again, loudly, "Here's my card with my cell phone. Please ask Kara to call me. I'd like to talk to her about Gina Fiore, and I have some information that she might find useful."

I handed him my card and kept my eye on his hands. Now that I could see him clearly, I didn't want to have to shoot the poor bastard if he made a move for his gun, so I planned instead on giving him a quick, measured poke in the eye. Hard enough to hurt like hell and incapacitate him, but not hard enough to blind him permanently.

Fortunately, it didn't come to that. He took my card and closed the door. We headed back to the Jeep.

~~~~

We climbed in, but I didn't start the car.

"Jumpy kid," Toni said.

I nodded. "Yeah."

"Now what?" she asked.

"Now we wait."

"Wait?" she said. "How long?"

"For a few minutes, anyway. If she's there, she should call."

Two minutes later, my cell phone rang. Toni looked at me, surprised.

"I'm a professional," I whispered to her as I looked at the caller ID and saw that it was Kara's cell phone.

"Hello, Kara, this is Danny Logan," I answered.

"How did you find out about me?" the female voice on the line asked.

I ignored her question. "Kara," I started, "I'm a private investigator. I've also been a friend of Gina's family for many years. Earlier this week, the police department recommended to Gina's family that they hire a private investigator. Since the family knows me, they hired my company. We've been working on the case, tracking down leads ever since. We mean you no harm whatsoever, and we might be able to give you some information and maybe some advice that might help you out."

I paused to let this soak in, then said, "Will you let us come up and talk to you in person?"

There was silence on the other end for a second, then she said, "Come up."

"Good," I said. "And Kara—please tell your boy up there not to shoot us."

~~~~

This time when we knocked, the door opened and Mr. Jumpy said, "Come in."

We entered the condo, and I glanced around. The front drapes were still drawn, but the lights were turned up bright. The television was on, but the sound was off.

I turned back to Mr. Jumpy and pointed to the gun on his waistband. "We okay now?" I asked. "No shoot-outs at the O.K. Corral?"

"Sorry," he said, looking somewhat flustered. "I'm Nick Giordano, Kara's little brother."

"Hi, Nick. I'm Danny, and this is Toni." I pointed again to the spot where the gun was hidden on his waist. "Do you know how to use that thing?" I asked.

He nodded. "I have a permit."

"That doesn't mean you know how to use it, though. Here's a quick hint, Nick. Never lift up your shirt and show your weapon or try to threaten someone with it the way you did. Keep it hidden, or pull it out and point it. Otherwise, you completely lose the element of surprise and that's a real good way to get killed."

He nodded. "Sorry, you're right. We're a little nervous around here."

"Why's that?" I asked.

"Have a look," he said, pointing to Kara as she entered the room from the bedroom area. The left side of her face was a sickly yellowish-purple color and puffy. Her left eye was surrounded with a nasty black bruise and was nearly swollen shut. Her lower lip was split and also swollen.

"Now you can see why I'm being careful," Kara said.

"Holy crap," I said, "what happened to you?"

"I got the shit beat out of me," she said. "What does it look like happened?" Her swollen lip caused her words to come out like "I got the thit beat out of me."

"It looks like what you said," I said, nodding in agreement.

Toni walked over to Kara and looked at her closely. "Have you been to the emergency room?" Toni asked. She reached forward and tilted Kara's head back so she could inspect her wounds.

Kara allowed Toni's touch and said, "No."

"You look like you should go."

"See?" Nick said. "I told you you needed to go to the hospital."

"When did this happen?" Toni asked.

"Last Thursday the eleventh."

"Is there any other damage?" Toni looked Kara up and down. "Stuff that we can't see?"

"No," Kara said. "I just got slapped around a bit." Thapped around.

"Sweetheart, you didn't just get slapped around," Toni said. "You were right the first time. You got the shit kicked out of you." She pointed to the sofa. "Let's sit down and talk." Toni took over the meeting.

Kara sat on the chair at the end of the sofa, and Toni sat on the end of the sofa next to her. I took the chair on her other side, while Nick sat across from me on the other end of the sofa, next to Toni.

"Who did this to you?" Toni asked.

"If I tell you, you got to promise me you won't tell anybody—even the cops."

Toni shook her head. "No. We can't make that promise," she said. "We're working together with the police to try and bring Gina home." Kara didn't look too happy about this. Toni continued. "I can say that whatever you tell us will not be used in any way to bring more heat down on you. The two detectives we're working with are very discreet."

Kara thought about this for a few seconds, then said, "I don't want to have to testify against anybody."

"If it ever comes to testifying against anybody, that will be totally up to you," Toni said. "Nobody can make you testify, and nobody is going to release your name. That I can promise."

"Okay," Kara said, nodding her head quickly. "I'll tell you what I know." She reached for a pack of cigarettes on the table but then hesitated. "Will it bother you if I smoke?"

"Go ahead," I said.

She grabbed a cigarette. She had trouble holding her hand steady enough to work the lighter. I reached over, took the lighter from her and held it until she finally got her cigarette lit.

"Thankth," she said.

I nodded. She leaned back and slowly blew the smoke up toward the ceiling. Then she looked straight at me for a second before she quietly said, "I got beat up by a Mexican prick named Eddie Salazar."

Toni and I looked at each other. Kara noticed. "You know him?" she asked.

"His name's come up," I said. I pulled out the group photo and showed it to Kara.

Her eyes flared, and she nearly panicked. I've seen scared people many times and Kara fit the bill, no doubt. "That's him," she said, her fear clearly visible despite her swollen face. She studied the photo. "Where the hell did this come from? The very last thing in the world I need is to have my picture taken with this psychopath. He'll kill me if he knows this is out there."

"It's okay," Toni said, trying to soothe her. "He hasn't seen it, and he won't. You're safe." When it appeared that Kara had settled down a little, Toni continued. "Let me tell you what we know. First off, the picture was taken on a cell phone camera owned by this girl here who's a friend of Gina's—someone she works with." She pointed to Reggie in the photo.

"Shit," Kara said, her hand trembling as she smoked her cigarette. "Eddie must not know this is out there. I swear he'd kill us all."

"We're the only ones with a copy of this photo," Toni said. "We were able to find you because of the photograph and a note on Gina's bulletin board at home."

"Do you know Eddie? Have you ever see him?" Gina asked, still basically petrified. "Did you ever talk to him? He's insane."

"No, we've never seen him," Toni said. "We talked to him over the phone. We agree—he's an asshole. He threatened us. The closest we got in person is when we went to Ramon's Cantina in Kent. We almost got jumped in the parking lot just for asking a question."

"That's the way this guy is," Kara said.

"Why did he do this to you?" Toni asked.

"He wants Gina. He wants her real bad. He said he's going to kill her," Kara said.

Toni and I glanced at each other.

"Really," I continued. "Did he say why?"

She shook her head. "Not a word. Not to me. He just asked where she was. I said I didn't know, that I hadn't seen her or talked to her in a couple of days. I wasn't going to lie to him, not after the stuff I heard about him at the bar."

"What kind of stuff is that?" Toni asked.

"They said he's some kind of hot-shit Mexican gangster. They told me that he's killed people before. I believed it then, and I really believe it now—he's a sadistic son of a bitch. Just look what he did." She started to cry.

"You're okay now," Toni said, reaching over to pat her on the shoulder as Kara grabbed a tissue. "We're not going to let anything happen to you now."

Kara nodded, wiping away her tears.

"Can I ask you to do two things?" Toni said.

Kara looked at her without answering, so Toni continued. "First, I think it would be helpful to get a couple pictures of you, particularly of your bruised face. I can use my cell phone."

"Why?" Kara asked.

"Just to make a record," Toni said. "I won't show them to anyone outside our team without your permission. But if we ever need to document what this bastard did to you, we won't be able to do it after your bruises and cuts have healed."

"Okay," Kara said. "But no one sees them without my permission."

"Agreed," Toni said. She snapped off a dozen photos of Kara's face, neck, and arms from different angles. While she did this, I considered Eddie Salazar. He was already on my shit list for being an asshole over the phone and threatening us, particularly Toni. Now, though, he'd threatened Gina and beat up Kara as well. Congratulations, Eddie, I thought. You're now my new public enemy number one.

"Second thing, why don't we back up for a second and have you tell us how you know Gina?" Toni continued.

Kara nodded. "Gina's dad owns Pacific Wine and Spirits—you probably already know that," she said. "Gina runs the finance operation there. I run finance for Northwest Evergreen Markets. We buy beer and wine from Pacific. Gina and I met at a seminar we both attended."

"About how long ago was that?" I asked.

"Two years," she said. I scribbled in my notebook.

"We started going to lunch, and then, seeing as how we're both single I guess, we started going out together at night."

"Do you know if Gina has any boyfriends?" Toni asked.

"No one serious," Kara said. "That didn't seem to be her style. She'd go out with a guy for a few dates, then move on. No one really connected with her, I guess."

"Why's that, do you think?"

"I don't know," she said, thinking. "She's like, twice as smart as anyone else. She's always in control, even when it seems like she isn't. Nothing surprises her. Nothing seems to get to her. Most guys can't even begin to keep up with that. I think she gets bored with them and just moves on."

*Been there and done that*, I thought.

Toni was reading my mind. "Seems consistent with your experience, Danny?" she asked.

*Ouch.* She just had to get that in. I smiled my best "fuck you" smile. *Thanks a bunch.*

"How did the two of you end up going to Ramon's Cantina?"

"It was Gina's idea," Kara said. "I normally wouldn't go within ten miles of a dump like that, but I think she liked to live on the edge. She took me there a couple of months ago."

"How did she meet Eddie Salazar? Was it there?"

"The first time I went with her to Ramon's, she already knew him," Kara said. "I don't know how she met him. He was hanging all over her.

First, she would tease him; then she was cool to him. I could tell it was driving him nuts. She was playing with him, and he never seemed to catch on."

"When was this?" I asked.

"June. Two months ago," she said.

"How often did you go to Ramon's after that?"

"Maybe once a week or so. I don't think we ever went more often than that."

"Did you see Eddie Salazar every time you went?"

"He seemed to always be there. Looking back and knowing Gina like I do, she may have told him that we were going to be there in advance, and she just didn't tell me."

"Do you think that Gina would have gone to Ramon's without you?"

"Sure. She told me she did."

"Interesting," I said.

"Did you ever notice Eddie hanging out with other people—other guys—at Ramon's?"

"Oh, yeah. He seemed to know a lot of people. They all treated him with respect, like he was an important guy. When we went there, I don't think I ever saw him buy anything. People would send over drinks all the time."

"So it was like a private party there at Ramon's?" Toni asked.

"Yeah, sort of," she said. She thought for a second before adding, "I guess it was fun in a weird, scary sort of way."

"Did the party ever move to other locations?" Toni asked.

"Not for me, it didn't. Not for Gina, either, at least not whenever we were together. I'm not sure about what she did when I wasn't there—I know she knew where he lived because she told me she'd been to his house a couple of times. I always got the impression that she was teasing Eddie, and it's possible they had some sort of history together. But she never provided any details. She was kind of private that way. And she never got passionate with him in the club, at least not that I ever saw. I think part of the fun for her was driving him nuts."

"You say she knew where he lives? Did she tell you where? Do you know what kind of car he drives?" Toni asked.

"I saw him driving a silver Mercedes once," she said. "It looked pretty new to me. Gina said he rented a house across from a cemetery in Kent."

Toni turned back to her notes for a second, and then turned to me again and asked, "Enough background?"

"Yeah," I answered. I turned to Kara and said, "Let's talk again about last Thursday. As accurately as you can remember, what happened?"

"I talked to Gina earlier in the day, and she said that we'd get together that weekend. At about eight thirty that night, I get a knock on my door. It's Eddie. I didn't even know he knew where I lived. He barged right in past me and slammed the door. He started asking me questions about Gina. At first I was pissed. But then, I discovered that he was really angry. Then I got scared instead. He asked me where Gina was. When I told him the truth and said I didn't know, he hauled off and slugged me." Kara started crying again as the pain of the recollection hit her. She dabbed at her eyes with the tissue she was holding. "He slugged me, the bastard. I was stunned. I never knew something could hurt like that. He knocked me down and it felt like my fucking head exploded. I saw stars. Then, he dragged me back to the sofa, real rough like. Now I'm petrified. He slammed me down and he asked me again. Like I suddenly remembered, right? I told him the same thing—that I didn't know—and this time, he slapped me, hard! This went on for about twenty minutes or so, before I guess he either got tired or maybe he believed me."

She sniffled and fought back the tears, then continued. "Then he pulled out a knife and put the point under my chin. See?" She leaned back, and I saw a healing wound from a knife point. "He told me if I saw Gina, I'd better call Ramon's immediately and leave a message for a guy named, Armando—let me think—Armando Martinez, that's it. I was supposed to call and leave a message for Armando Martinez to call me back. Then I was supposed to tell him what I'd seen. He told me if I didn't do what he said, or if I told her he was looking for her, or if I called the police, he'd be back and he'd cut me open." She cried for a second, then got control of herself.

"I take it you've not heard from Gina," I said.

"No, not a word. Next morning I called in sick at work. I spent the weekend in bed, doing nothing. I felt like I'd been run over by a damn delivery truck. I still looked like shit on Monday, so I called up and arranged a two-week vacation. I didn't want to go in and be seen like this, and I didn't want to have to explain what had happened. I called Nicky and he's been staying with me ever since. That's pretty much it."

"Have you heard from Eddie since last Thursday?" Toni asked.

"No, nothing—thank God."

"Wow. That's quite a story," Toni said. She turned to me. "What do you think, Danny?"

"I think this guy Eddie Salazar is a psycho nutcase, that's what I think. And based on the way he's been acting, and the people he surrounds himself with, he's dangerous. I think it's pretty obvious, Kara, that you're in danger here. And," I continued, glancing toward Nick, "it's the kind of danger that Nick isn't going to be able to do anything about with that Glock in his waistband. If Eddie Salazar shows up and he wants you dead and you're here, you're dead. Period. End of story. He'll show up with three or four of his flunkies, and they'll just blast the whole damn building. If Nick is here, he'll be dead, too. You can see that this guy won't think twice. He most likely has no conscience that we would recognize." I paused for a second, thinking, then continued. "I have no idea what game Gina might have played with him, or might still be playing with him, for that matter. But if he caught her, it's pretty damn clear that she's dead, too."

I let all of that sink in, and then I said, "I hate to say it, but I think the only way you can be truly safe now is to get out of town until this thing sorts itself out. In all honesty, if I were you, that's what I'd do. You said you just put in for vacation. Go ahead and take it somewhere you can't be found. Give us a chance to find this idiot before he comes back here for round two."

Kara started to cry again. "What about the police? Can they protect me?"

"They didn't protect you last time," I said. "Chances are, they won't be around next time he comes calling either. They're not going to give you a personal bodyguard."

"Do you guys do that?"

"We do, but we already have a case—we're trying to find Gina. The good news is that us working that case also helps you out."

She sniffled and reached for another cigarette. "Do you really think he'll come after me?"

"He might. He already has once. You're a loose end, and it wouldn't surprise me if he suddenly figures he doesn't like loose ends. That's bad. Worse, he told you he wanted to kill Gina. Apparently, he doesn't care that you know that. That's scary. He was probably going to just watch you and see if you lead him to Gina or if she might show up around here. But I wouldn't put it past him to come back. I definitely think you'd be safer somewhere where he can't reach you. At least for a while."

"Give us some time, Kara. We'll find him." Toni said. "We're going to get him, and then it will be safe for you to come back."

Kara looked at Nick. He nodded at her. She turned back to me.

"When does this end?" she asked.

"When we catch the sick bastard," I said. "How soon can you leave?"

~~~~

Kara assured us that they'd be gone in two hours and that they'd call us when they got to their destination, which I told her I didn't need to know. We said our good-byes, and Toni and I left the apartment.

"She's scared to death," Toni said as we walked down the steps to the parking lot.

"Yeah, well, that's probably healthy for her," I said. "Salazar can't get to her if he doesn't know where she is."

Just as I stepped off the bottom stair, I saw from the corner of my eye a large stick making a fast arc directly for my head. "Look out!" I yelled to Toni as I ducked and simultaneously threw my left arm out to block the blow.

The stick—turned out to be a two-by-four—glanced off my forearm, deflected off the very top of my head and thwacked into the wall behind me, throwing a shower of stucco chips into the air. I heard Toni scream, but I was unable to look back or help her because attached to the other end of the stick was the tall bald-headed Mexican gangster we'd confronted at Ramon's two nights ago. My left arm hurt like hell, and I'd seen stars when the two-by-four had whacked me in the top of my forehead, right where my nose had been one second earlier. I felt the blood trickle down my face. I staggered forward, determined not to go down. Still bent over, I looked up.

For his part, Mr. Big and Tall apparently hadn't considered he might miss me with the two-by-four at point-blank range. Having it slam into the wall must have surprised him for a moment. He stared at me, wondering whether I was hit or not, wondering whether I was going to go down. The blood on my head added to his confusion. When he saw that I was still alive and well, he started to regain his wits. He began to pull the board back for a second go at me. This wouldn't do—I didn't want him taking another swing. I was halfway dazed, but I recognized an opportunity. Since I was already bent forward and down below him, while he recoiled to swing at me again, I hit him with an uppercut to the groin with everything I had as I stood. The force of the blow, backed by my full 180 pounds, nearly picked him up off the ground. His eyes went wide, and his mouth made a little O—no sound came out. The two-by-four fell out of his hand. In that instant, before he could recover, I head-butted him across the bridge of his nose, and he dropped to his knees, as if ready to pray. He knelt there, motionless, for a second, before collapsing forward in a heap.

I turned to help Toni just in time to see her drive a hard elbow into the gut of Mr. Short and Round, who had appeared behind her and tried to put her into a choke hold. He held on. She elbowed him again and then once more before he let her go. I took a step toward her, and she yelled at me, "Get back!"

I looked at her face as she spun around to face her assailant. There was no fear—only rage. Krav Maga teaches us to change from defense to offense as soon as possible. She confronted Short and Round and automatically dropped into a fighting stance. He threw a big sweeping right hand at her head, which she easily ducked. In response, Toni threw a sharp left jab, which smacked solidly into his nose. He blinked his eyes. Before he could recover, she hit him again in the exact same spot. Then, she started a flying back kick. Not technically a Krav Maga move, the kick was nonetheless very effective if you knew how to pull it off. Toni did. Her Doc Marten connected at full speed directly on the nose of Mr. Short and Round and essentially pulverized it. He screamed as blood gushed down his face and onto his shirt. He fell to the ground.

"Asshole!" Toni yelled at him, stepping back and watching him fall.

With both assailants down in only a few seconds of intense action, I was about to tell Toni to watch out for others when a gunshot exploded in the parking lot, directly behind us. We both spun around to see Eddie Salazar standing in the lot, smoking revolver pointed in the air. He leveled it at me before we had a chance to reach our own weapons. He stared at us for a few seconds, no emotion visible on his face. Then he seemed to get pissed.

"*Pendejos!*" he screamed, not at us, but at the two men we'd dispatched. "One skinny gringo and his *puta*, and you *chingóns* go down in seconds? I never been so embarrassed in my whole life! *Mueven sus culos al coche!*"

The two men staggered to their feet and started to shuffle off to a car parked in the street. Salazar watched them pass. At the sound of the gunshot, several people had dropped to the ground or ducked behind cars. Most were peering out now, trying to see what was going on. A nearby patrol officer must have also heard the gunshot because a siren suddenly started blaring a few blocks away.

Salazar stared at us for another moment, then he smiled. "Amigos," he said. "Well done. Now I know more about how to approach you." He paused, then added, "And you should rest assured, our business is not done. We'll meet again." He started to turn to leave.

I tend to get pissed when people threaten me, so I started to step toward him. Toni grabbed my arm and held me back. "Don't be an idiot," she whispered, still breathing hard. "It's over. We're okay here."

She was right. I took a deep breath and tried to relax as Salazar and his men loaded up and sped off to the west on Green Lake Drive.

I took another deep breath and saw stars all over again. "Fuck me, my head hurts."

"Yeah, you should see yourself," she said. "You're covered in blood. I thought you were dead."

"I heard you scream."

"I screamed when I saw you get hit. I couldn't help it. Then that fat bastard grabbed me from behind and tried to choke me."

At that moment, Nick appeared at the top of the stairs. "You guys alright?" he shouted.

"Yeah," Toni said.

Nick looked at me with horror. "Did he shoot you? I already called 911."

"No," I said. "They hit me with a two-by-four. They were hiding behind this wall when we stepped off the stairs. He fired into the air so they could get away."

"Holy shit!" he said.

~~~~

Two minutes later, a police cruiser pulled into the lot. Toni was on the phone with Dwayne explaining what had happened. Nick brought me a couple of towels for my head. Three more police cruisers and a paramedic unit were on the scene within fifteen minutes. There were several witnesses who told the same story—a couple coming down the stairs got jumped by two Mexican gangster–looking guys. When the attacked couple turned the tables and kicked the gangsters' asses, a third gangster stepped in and fired a shot in the air. Words were exchanged, but the Mexicans drove away in a silver Mercedes.

Satisfied that neither Toni nor I had been the ones to fire the shot, even though we were both armed, the cops left us to the paramedics. They cleaned my scalp wound and told me to go to the emergency room. Toni drove.

Before we left, I called Nick over.

"Thanks for calling the cops, Nick," I said. "Might have made a difference. When Salazar heard the siren, he decided to leave. Now that those guys are gone, they're probably off licking their wounds somewhere. Perfect time for you to take Kara and get her away from here before Salazar regroups. No doubt, he'll be back."

~~~~

"Jesus, Danny," Toni said as we entered my apartment after spending two hours at the emergency room. "I saw all that blood, and I was scared to death. I thought they might have taken your head off."

I smiled. "Well, I appreciate your concern. Scalp wounds bleed a lot. No big deal." I hadn't even needed stitches—the doctor just X-rayed my arm, taped my head, and sent me on my way.

"I know, but still," she said.

"Anyway, speaking of taking people's heads off, you were a fucking tiger. I thought you were going to behead that guy with that back kick of yours."

She smiled. "Connected pretty solid, didn't it?"

"Sure did."

"I was pissed," she said.

"I saw it in your face," I said, smiling. "No fear, just anger."

"I thought they hurt you. I wanted to finish my guy in case I had to go after yours. I didn't see you take your guy out. Even with you being all bloody like that, you still got him. Looks like the Krav Maga stuff really works."

"Worked out nice, didn't it?" I said. I smiled at her. Nice to have someone like that who cared.

She looked in my eyes, then nodded. "It did," she said.

# Chapter 10

AT THE END of the summer of 2000 after graduating from high school, I joined the U.S. Army. My personal game plan was four years for my country as an infantry grunt, and then four more years for myself as a special agent in the Army Criminal Investigation Division learning a trade other than infantry. My idea was that in the second four years, I'd be able to prepare myself for a career in civilian law enforcement.

It played out pretty much as I planned, although two separate tours of combat duty with the 101st Airborne Division in the Middle East were not something I'd originally expected. I served with the Second Battalion Raider Rakkasans in the Shah-i-Kot Mountains of Afghanistan in Operation Enduring Freedom and later with the Third Battalion Iron Rakkasans in Iraq during the first months of Operation Iraqi Freedom. We were one of the first units into Iraq when the "Shock and Awe" bombing ceased. Through a combination of excellent U.S. Army training and preparation mixed in with a little blind-assed luck, I survived my two tours, although I was wounded twice in Iraq—first by an insurgent with an AK-47, and then two months later by that piece of shrapnel from a grenade. The shrapnel wound was actually the more dangerous of the two, though neither kept me out of action more than ten days. I was lucky. Hooah.

I had mixed feelings about leaving the infantry. My friends were in the infantry, and I was good at what I did. We looked down our noses at the pogues in the rear. The occasional adrenaline rush was huge. But even though I picked up sixty college credits through a correspondence college, the downtime was a drag. Also, getting wounded twice in two months may have been some sort of cosmic warning sign. "D-Lo! D-Lo! Get the hell out before your number's up!" Anyway, I had a plan, and

I was determined to stick with it. When our unit left Iraq and shipped back to Fort Campbell in January 2004, I took advantage of my original deal with the army and switched military occupations to Criminal Investigations Division—CID. With CID, I learned the business of law enforcement as it applied to felons within the U.S. Army. I was trained in legal procedures, criminal investigation procedures, arrests, warrants—the whole spectrum of law enforcement. In four years assigned to the Sixth MP Group (CID) stationed in Fort Lewis, near Tacoma, I ran across the same sorts of crimes that a civilian detective in a large metropolitan city typically encounters: murder, rape, robbery, burglary—we even had a few gang members stationed at Fort Lewis that we eventually busted for weapons charges.

Of all these, as is the case with most law enforcement personnel, I learned to reserve a special hatred for the bastards who killed, hurt, or otherwise abused women and children. For some reason known only to God, there are some guys who completely lack any semblance of a moral compass. They have no conscience, probably not even a soul. They don't consider the people they hurt to be people. To them, their weaker victims are not somebody's wife or mother or daughter or sister. These guys have a short circuit in those pea brains of theirs that enables them to believe their victims are their own personal play toys to be used as they want, and then thrown away when they're done. Move on. No remorse. No second thoughts. They would think no more about hurting or even killing someone than most people would think about swatting a mosquito. It just didn't register for them.

As far as I'm concerned, the depths of hell can't possibly be hot enough for these bastards. I hate them. And now, one of them was after someone I cared about. It's fair to say that he had my full attention.

~~~~

We don't take regular days off when we're in the middle of a case. Weekday, weekend, holiday—all the same, makes no difference. The next day was a Saturday. We met as usual at 9:00 a.m.

Dwayne and Gus, being civil servants, do take days off. Still, I invited them to dial in on a conference call and join our meeting, and they agreed.

"Dwayne, are you there?" I talked to the speakerphone in the center of our conference room table.

"Here," he called back.

"Gus?"

"Yo!"

"Good. Thanks for calling in, guys. I'm here with Toni and three other gentlemen who work with the firm here and whom I don't believe you've met yet. Kenny Hale is here—he's our technology expert."

"Good morning," Kenny called out.

"Joaquin Kiahtel is here. He's our security expert."

"Gentlemen," Joaquin said.

"And Richard Taylor is here. Richard is our consultant emeritus."

"Hey, Richard," Dwayne called out. "Good to talk to you again. It's been a long time."

"Good morning, Dwayne," Richard replied. "At my age, any morning you wake up above ground is a good one. It's good to still be around and involved."

"I hear you," Dwayne said, laughing.

I started the meeting. "We've made steady progress over the past five days." I spent twenty minutes reviewing the events of the past week, including our trip to Ramon's Cantina, discovering Kara's identity, right up through our fight with Eddie Salazar's troops yesterday afternoon, and my subsequent trip to the hospital.

"Holy shit," Gus said. "You guys lead an interesting life for civilians."

"I'm not certain interesting is the word I'd use," I said. "After all, I did get hit in the head with a two-by-four."

Dwayne laughed. "Sounds interesting as all hell to me. Looks like Eddie Stiletto is acting true to form. And he's out in the open now. He's on the hunt, and now it's Gina that he's after—maybe Kara Giordano, too. He doesn't seem to care whom he runs over or whom he hurts. Gina must have done something pretty nasty to piss him off, don't you think?"

"Sure sounds like it. Sounds like she's playing teasey windup on purpose with a homicidal maniac," Gus said. "Do you think she knew what she was doing? And who she was doing it with?"

"Yes, and yes," Toni said.

I looked at Toni. "What are you saying?" I asked.

"Look," she said. "I don't know Gina, never met her. I don't want to speak ill of her, and I'm not trying to lay down an indictment against her now. But everything I've ever heard about her in the past week paints a picture of someone who is definitely the smartest one in the room. Without fail, everyone we've talked to says she's always in control. She's always got a plan. She's always a few steps ahead of everyone else. Why would this suddenly change now? Why would she start screwing up now?"

She paused for a second to reload, then she continued. "I can't think of a single reason why she'd purposely cozy up to a maniac like Eddie Salazar, but if past form is any indication, I'd put good hard money on the notion that she did it on purpose, and she knew exactly what she was doing when she did it. The part about it that pisses me off is that whatever game she's playing, she's got a whole bunch of other people dragged into it now. And some of these people are starting to get hurt." Toni was angry. "I still haven't seen anything that doesn't support this theory."

It was silent for a few seconds as everyone considered this. She almost sounded like a prosecutor. Somehow I felt like I needed to try and calm Toni down, and at the same time, defend Gina. "What you're saying is possible," I said, "but it could also be that she didn't know who she was dealing with, or, like you say, she did know but she miscalculated and pushed him too far."

"Well, if that happened, it sounds to me like it would be the first time in her entire life that she's made a mistake in just about anything she's ever done," Toni said sharply, looking straight at me. *Oops.* I wasn't able to outmaneuver Toni when she was on a roll, like now.

"You'll look pretty silly saying that if it turns out she's dead," I said.

She stared at me for a second, then said, "If she's dead, I'll kiss your—"

Richard interrupted the action. "Folks, what's our timeline here?"

Toni continued to glare at me for another moment before looking away.

Kenny answered. "Kara Giordano said the last time she talked to Gina was last Thursday afternoon. The last time we know of anyone seeing Gina is Robbie Fiore seeing her leave Pacific Wine and Spirits at six thirty the same evening. Then, Kara gets jumped by Eddie Salazar at eight thirty the same night. Next day, Gina's disappeared. And we don't have any idea, except for Ms. Blair's theory, which for the moment is impossible to either prove or disprove."

"One thing we do know, though," Richard said. "Eddie Salazar is out there and, for whatever reason, he's behaving poorly. And he's dangerous."

"Well said," Dwayne said. "We may as well focus on that for now. How do we find him?"

"No record of him with Department of Licensing," Kenny said. "No driver's license, no vehicle registrations, no titles."

"According to Kara, Gina said that Eddie lives in Kent across from a cemetery," I said.

"Can't be too many cemeteries in Kent," Gus said. "You guys going to check them out? It's a little south of our jurisdiction down there."

"Yeah," I said. "We haven't mapped it out yet, but I was going to ask Kenny and Joaquin to do that so Toni and I could scout out the areas."

"If we get lucky and you find him, we'll have to coordinate with Tacoma PD," Dwayne said.

"I think I'll run Eddie Salazar's name past the gang guys here and in Tacoma," Gus said. "Maybe they're working something on Eddie Salazar."

"Speaking of names," I said, "Kara said that Eddie told her to call Ramon's Cantina and leave a message for . . ." I tried to remember the name.

"Armando Martinez," Toni filled in, reengaged.

"Right," I said. "Armando Martinez."

"We'll run that name, too, and let you know what we find," Gus said.

Dwayne said, "Danny, good thing you told the Giordanos to bolt. I'm not certain that we could adequately protect them considering the resources we have to work with. Better to be hard to find for a while. Are they going to call and let you know how to reach them?"

"She's going to call me and let me know," I said. "I should add that, short of having Eddie on a slab, I doubt she'll talk to you. She's scared shitless."

He nodded. "That's good enough for now. Later, though, we may need her testimony."

"Let's cross that bridge when we get there," I said.

"Based on the testimony from Kara," Dwayne said, "we'll probably have sufficient probable cause for an arrest warrant and a search warrant if we need it. At the very least, we've got him on assault against Kara."

"We have to be careful that we keep Kara on board," I said. "If you asked her to testify against Eddie Salazar today on the assault beef, I'm pretty sure she'd tell you to take a hike. She's too afraid of him coming after her when he gets free. And I can't say I blame her."

"We're not there yet anyway, people," Richard said. "Whatever we decide to do, we need to find Mr. Salazar. Then, unless he happens to be holding Gina Fiore at gunpoint in public, we'll most likely want to watch him for a while and see what we've got. If he has her, we need to find out where. If he's killed her, we need to study his habits. If he's still looking for her, maybe he'll lead us to her and we can rescue her if need be. Better to know where he is and keep him in our sites, rather than to go off half-cocked, blow our case, scare the hell out of him, and watch him disappear into the weeds. Trust me, I've made that mistake a few times."

The room was quiet for a few seconds, then Dwayne said, "Once again, I agree with Richard. Tell you what, Danny, why don't you write up your notes and send them to me. Also, give me possible locations for Eddie's residence. If you locate him, call it in and we'll figure out the best way for surveillance. Meanwhile, Gus will run the names through his contacts. We won't be bothering Ms. Giordano at the present time. Does this make sense to everyone?"

Everyone agreed, and we ended the meeting.

"Good call," I said to Richard. He smiled and nodded. He gestured with his head to where Toni had been sitting—she'd gotten up immediately after the meeting and left. "Better smooth that out," he said.

I nodded. *Great.*

~~~~

After the meeting cleared out, I tidied up the conference room and switched off the lights. I checked for messages on the phone system. Right before I started doing something really productive like running around and filling the paper clip dispensers, I finally admitted to myself that I was stalling. I needed to clear the air with Toni. So I walked down the hall to her office and poked my head in. She was typing something on the computer. "Got a minute?" I asked.

"I do," she answered without looking up. "I'm typing up a report of our activities yesterday for Dwayne."

"Good," I said. "Thanks." It was silent for a few seconds except for the clacking of her keyboard. Finally, I said, "Toni—are we okay?"

She stopped and turned to look at me, and then nodded. "We are," she said. "I'm sorry for being an asshole in the conference room. I acted like a jerk."

"I hope you're not pissed at me," I said.

"I'm not," she looked away. "You know I have patience issues. Sometimes it's a little hard for me to be methodical when the answers seem so clear in my mind. Especially when people I know are getting hurt because of someone else's actions."

I smiled. "People like me, you mean?"

She nodded. "Yeah. I'm sorry. It's a problem, I admit it, and I'll work on it so it doesn't pop up again." She sounded resolute.

"I'm touched that you care that much."

"I need the job," she said, dismissively. "I can't have you getting whacked." Then she smiled.

I laughed. "Well, there's that. Obviously, you still think Gina's alive. Eddie Salazar doesn't bother you?"

"Personally, no. As a threat to Gina, no. I believe she's most likely way ahead of him. To us, he's a suspect. To Kara, he's a psycho-threat. To Gina, though, I think he's a pawn. There's no way a smart person like Gina hooks up with a thug like Eddie Salazar unless she's using him for something. To her, he's nothing more than a useful idiot."

"She couldn't be authentically attracted to him? You know—a good girl falls for the outlaw type?"

"Puh-leeze," she said, rolling her eyes. "You've been watching too many movies."

"And the odds of her miscalculating and pushing him too far?"

She shook her head. "For her? Slim," she said. "Frankly, I'm interested to see how she wraps him up. She has to know the guy's a friggin' loose cannon."

"Hmm," I said.

"But Danny," she added, "I really am sorry I got bitchy. I'll try to be better. I don't mean to undermine you in front of the others."

I smiled. "No apology needed," I said. "My ego can handle different opinions. I just want to make sure we're okay. That's important to me."

She smiled.

I smiled back. "And I want you to know something," I said.

"What's that?"

"You think Gina's smart, right?"

"Everyone says so."

"Well, I know her, and you're right. But when it comes to smarts, Gina Fiore has nothing on you."

She smiled. "Flattery becomes you, Logan. I like it. Even if you do have a patch on your head."

# Chapter 11

JUST AFTER LUNCH, Kenny and Joaquin completed their research into cemeteries in Kent. There were three. They used maps and Google Earth and found that two of the three were in commercial/industrial neighborhoods just off Highway 167—probably not the most desirable residential areas. Therefore, since Eddie Salazar supposedly lived in a residential area across from a cemetery, they decided that the most likely possibility was the third cemetery—the Hillcrest Burial Park, just east of the Green River. The maps showed a small residential neighborhood just north of the cemetery.

It wasn't the strongest bit of detective work I've ever acted on, but I figured we didn't have anything to lose by taking a cruise down to Kent that afternoon and driving through the neighborhood. Who knew? Maybe we'd get lucky and turn something up, maybe even spot the car. Eddie didn't seem to be the kind of guy who always thought things through. If he didn't suspect that we might be looking for him, maybe he'd have no reason to hide.

"Let's go in my car," Toni said. "Those guys might remember your stealth-Jeep." She looked at the Jeepster with disdain. Then she looked at me and shook her head. She said, "You really need to get a more nondescript vehicle for this kind of work, boss."

My Jeep is dark red—I think it's called candy-apple red—and I've raised it six inches to accommodate my twenty-inch Rockstar wheels and thirty-five-inch tires. I installed a big winch on the front and another in the back. Either could probably pull me straight up one of those big cedar trees in the Hoh River valley. I enjoy driving around the back roads of the Olympic Peninsula, but I don't enjoy getting stuck while I'm out there—

help can be a long time coming. But I had to admit that in this context, Toni was right. The Jeepster does tend to stand out in a crowd. Of course, generally our suspects aren't looking for us at the same time we're looking for them, so it's not a problem. Now, though?

"Yeah, you may have a point, but does that mean I have to descend all the way down to a recycled beer can like this?" I asked, gesturing at Toni's silver Toyota Camry.

"Be nice," she said. "Besides, I insist. Hold your nose and cover your eyes if you must, you crybaby. But you've got to admit, no one ever notices a silver Toyota."

This was true. Probably because every other car on the road up here is either a green Subaru station wagon covered in "Save Tibet" stickers, or it's a silver Toyota. Honestly, is silver the only color Toyota has?

"Let's go," I said, reaching for the door. At least we weren't likely to get ID'd and shot at.

Toni drove. We went south on I-5 to where it met I-405. We took the Highway 167 exit south. We ended up in Kent about forty minutes after we left the office.

~~~~

Whenever I drive down to Kent, the law-enforcement guy in me can't help thinking of the tragic events of the past that took place in that area. In July 1982, a city worker discovered the body of a young woman in the brush along the banks of the Green River, a picturesque river that meanders peacefully through Kent, maybe fifteen miles southeast of Seattle. Over the next two months, five more bodies turned up in or near the river. The press soon labeled the person responsible for these crimes the "Green River Killer"—an apt name for the homicidal maniac responsible for the eighteen-year reign of terror that was to follow. A steady stream of victims was discovered in the ensuing years. Some of the bodies were found in a posed position. In some cases, it was clear that the killer had returned to the scene and had sex with the dead body. When Gary Leon Ridgway was finally arrested in 2001, he admitted that he'd killed seventy-one young women over the years. Maybe more because, as he put it, he killed so many that he lost track. In a later statement, when asked, Ridgway said that murdering young women was his career. Today, there are at least eighty unsolved cold-case murders of young women between Portland and Vancouver. Ridgway remains a prime suspect in most of them.

In order to get information from this psycho that would lead to closure in dozens of missing person cold cases, prosecutors made a plea bargain deal with Ridgway. He pled guilty to murdering forty-eight women in exchange for forty-eight life sentences without the possibility of parole plus one more life sentence plus ten years for tampering with the evidence. I'm not sure exactly how many years this adds up to, but I know it's a long damn time. For Ridgway, who now sits in Washington State Penitentiary in Walla Walla, it's forever. Personally, I hope the scumbag rots. After which I hope he gets to be the main course at the big wienie roast in hell. He deserves no better.

Needless to say, I always get an odd feeling driving into Kent near the Green River. The place has ghosts and they're calling out. I hear them. It gives me the heebie-jeebies. As I contemplated the place's past, Toni turned off the arterial into a housing subdivision situated just north of the Hillcrest Burial Park. The cemetery is located just 250 yards northeast of a bend in the Green River. *Weird.*

~~~~

"What's our plan?" Toni asked. "Just drive up and down the streets looking for a silver Mercedes parked in one of the driveways?"

I shrugged. "Bit of a long shot, I admit. But you never know." I studied the map Kenny had printed for us. "It's a small subdivision, only about fifteen streets or so. Shouldn't take more than an hour tops to drive it. Also, Kenny knows how to get into the Department of Licensing database. He's pulling a list of late-model silver Mercedes and cross-referencing plate numbers to this immediate area. He might turn up something that could be useful."

We spent the next hour slowly cruising the neighborhood—up one street then down the next—looking for anything that might provide a clue. The houses looked to be around thirty years old and were situated on lots that ranged from one-quarter to one-half acre each. For the most part, they were well kept. It looked like a pretty decent area. But we didn't see a silver Mercedes.

Toni pulled over next to a forested area at the north end of the sub-division. "How about plan B," she said. "Instead of looking for a single silver Mercedes, maybe we shouldn't assume that he lives alone. Maybe he has a group of guys with him? Do you remember seeing any groups of guys outside?"

"There were a few," I agreed. "We could look for houses with a cluster of cars."

"Or with a cluster of people," she said.

"True. We just need to remember to be a little careful. Remember, Salazar said he wanted to get to know you, you being a hot babe and all."

"I am, aren't I?" Toni said, smiling at me.

"Drive."

We started over. We looked for groups of men. We looked for cars that might belong to guys associated with a badassed Mexican gangster. Not that we knew what kind of cars guys associated with a Mexican gangster drove. We just looked for any clusters of cars or clusters of people.

Some of the houses were front-loaded, that is, the driveway is right off the street. Others were alley-loaded. In order to really determine how many cars were at each house, we had to drive up and down each street looking for cars parked in front, and then up and down the alleys in the back, looking for cars parked in back. We decided not to count cars that looked like junkers or restoration projects—it had to be a real automobile that looked capable of actually being driven. We also set a four-car mini-mum target, assuming that any self-respecting gangster-type safe house would have at least four automobiles. Weak reasoning, admittedly, but you have to start somewhere.

~~~~

After searching for an hour, we ended up with a list of eight houses that each had four or more working-condition cars parked there. Four of the eight had young Mexican men outside, mostly sitting around talking or, in one case, working on the cars. One of these homes was located directly across the street from the cemetery.

We drove back to a convenience store near the entrance to the subdivision and pulled off to consider our next move.

"What now?" Toni said. "Got a plan C? Just start walking up to the front doors and asking if Eddie can come out and play?"

I laughed. "That might not be the smartest thing we've ever done," I answered.

"Or the healthiest," Toni said.

"I could call Dwayne—" I started to say, but then I noticed a car at the gas island. Or rather, I noticed the guy putting gas in the car at the gas island.

"Son of a bitch!" I said urgently but quietly, instinctively slouching down in the seat. "Look!" I pointed to the gas island. One hundred feet away, Mr. Short and Round calmly filled up his dark blue Honda. He had a big bandage across his nose.

Toni looked and immediately lowered her visor. "Good thing I drove," she said.

"True. Fancy meeting him here," I said.

"We should tail him and see where he leads us."

"Right. Maybe he and Eddie live at the same place. If so, he can lead us right there," I said.

"As long as he's going home and not somewhere else."

"We'll just follow him for a while and see where he goes."

Two minutes later, Short and Round pulled out and we followed, a discreet fifty yards back. We got lucky. He turned into the neighborhood. He was going home, just a few hundred yards away. He drove to the house directly across from the cemetery on East Maple Street—the same one we had noted on our drive-by. He pulled into the driveway and waited for the automatic garage door to open.

"Keep on driving the same speed," I said. "Just drive right on by."

As we passed the house, I was able to get a glimpse inside the two-car garage.

"See that?" I asked.

"She looked. Yeah—silver Mercedes. Hello, Eddie Salazar. What do you want to do?" she asked.

My heart was beating quickly, the way it does whenever I'm zeroing in on a bad guy. I thought for a second as Toni continued driving slowly down the street. "Turn right up here. I'm halfway tempted to pull up to the guys in the front yard and ask them if Eddie's there. But that won't really accomplish anything except tip him off."

"And maybe get us shot," Toni added. "Think about it. Right now, we have the upper hand. We know where he is, but he doesn't know that we know."

"True," I agreed. "Let's call Dwayne."

~~~~

An hour later, at seven in the evening, we were at the Seattle Police Department headquarters downtown. After I'd called Dwayne on the cell phone from the car and told him what we'd seen, he agreed to meet with us in his office. Our goal was to go over what we had and bring in the King County District Attorney's office to discuss strategy and options. We didn't have any real evidence that Eddie Salazar had done anything to Gina, all we had were suspicions based on threats he'd made to Kara and implied to us. Still, it didn't hurt to go over what we had with the DA to help develop legal strategies.

We met in the conference room on the eighth floor. Toni and I, Dwayne and Gus, and Harold Ohlmer and Denise Freeman from the King County District Attorney's office huddled around half of the large conference table.

Some ADAs were a pain in the ass, more intent on protecting their win/loss record in preparation for an eventual run for governor than they were in yanking bad guys off the street. Ohlmer had a strong reputation for not being one of those guys. He was a tall, lanky, gray-haired assistant DA who was known as a straight shooter among law enforcement personnel. He'd been an assistant DA in King County for twenty-five years, and he was not interested in elected office. I knew him only by his reputation. I'd heard that he was keenly interested in putting bad guys away and that he was willing to take chances, within the law, in order to do this. He didn't need an ironclad case in order to prosecute. Ohlmer had the demeanor of someone who knew what he was doing. We were lucky to have him on our side. His partner, on the other hand—I didn't know anything about her. All I could tell was that Denise Freeman was young. She seemed to be along just for the education.

We spent an hour walking the DAs through the events of the past week, bringing them up to speed, culminating in our discovery of Eddie Salazar's apparent residence less than two hours ago.

When we finished, Ohlmer said, "Thank you very much for the briefing. It seems very thorough. Before I comment, is there anything else anyone wants to add?"

No one responded, so he continued.

"Let me start by saying that, like all of you, we would love to see this case resolved and the guilty persons put away," he said. "Furthermore, if that young lady is still alive, our first priority is to rescue her, and second, to prosecute the case. In that order."

Made sense to me. I nodded my agreement.

"That being said," he continued. "Can somebody tell me what crimes, if any, this man Salazar has committed? If you're asking me to go to the judge on a Saturday night and ask for arrest warrants, what's the crime?"

There was silence in the room as we considered the question.

"If we want to arrest him, this is supposed to be an easy question," he said.

He waited another few seconds, then said, "Let me help you out. While we may suspect him of a lot of things, I see us actually able to charge Mr. Salazar with a felony assault on Kara Giordano at this time. It's obviously against the law to beat someone as he has, and I can definitely get us an arrest warrant for that. It's not what you're after, but it will give us a good, solid legal reason to get him off the street. Except, apparently there's one pesky little problem, which your collective silence seems to confirm. The victim's disappeared and there's no one to testify against him. Is my understanding correct?"

"It is," I said. "Unfortunately, as we pointed out in our briefing, after our interview yesterday and particularly after the altercation at her condo, we advised the victim to find a secure location and hole up for the moment. We asked her to call us once she'd done that and let us know how to reach her. Apparently, she's taken our advice as to the first part—she left. We guarded her exit and made sure she got on the road safely. But for some reason, she's decided not to take our advice as to our second suggestion: she hasn't called in yet to let us know how to get in touch with her."

"She probably thought you had shifty eyes," Dwayne joked.

"I suppose," I said. "But in any case, she's not available to act as either a victim or a witness. At least not now, not until she calls in."

"That's what I thought," Ohlmer said. "That means that the warrant for felony assault is off the table for now. At least until we're able to produce a victim. Beyond that, though, what has the man done? You've presented several possibilities. Theories, really. Kidnap, murder, drugs—who knows? This woman Kara Giordano says he told her he wants to kill Gina. But by her own admission, she doesn't know anything else. I don't think a hearsay threat made to a third party—a party who isn't even available—rises to the level of probable cause for us to charge this man with any crime against Gina Fiore. I hate to say it, but except for the assault charge, which is off the table for the moment, I'd say we are unable to bring charges against Mr. Salazar. Right now, we seem to be long on hunches, but short on evidence."

Ouch! Unfortunately, the guy's logic was right on. We could be absolutely certain in our gut that he was guilty, but without evidence leading to probable cause, he'd never be arrested, and certainly never convicted. I've had good defense lawyers take apart my cases in the past by whittling away at my evidence. They'd point out a weakness in our procedure and, bam, the judge tossed the evidence. Next thing you knew, the squeaking noise you were hearing was the sound of the hinges as the guilty guy walked out the door. I hate when that happens, so I always try to be super careful. I understood where Ohlmer was coming from. If we were going to do this, we'd better do it right.

He stood up to go. "Unless there's anything else," he said, "I believe we'll be running along. I'd like to get home to my wife, it being Saturday night and all. In summary, I'd say you need to get back to the drawing board and bring forth some real evidence before we can charge him with anything. Meanwhile, if you're worried that he poses a threat to Gina Fiore, perhaps you should consider inviting him in for an interview. If he won't agree to that, why not simply show up on his doorstep and try talking to the guy. If he's already murdered her, you've got nothing to lose. You need to start pressing him. If he's trying, but he hasn't found her yet, then you'll probably disrupt his search plans. Most folks can't play offense and defense at the same time. Either way is good for you."

I couldn't argue with his logic. We said our good-byes to the DAs and then sat back down at the table.

"Guy makes things pretty clear, doesn't he?" Dwayne said.

"Yeah," I answered. "I may not like what he has to say, but it's hard to argue with his thought process."

"Gus and I suspected that he'd say what he did. But sometimes it helps for the team to get together and hear it."

"That makes sense," I said. "Seems we have two choices now: surveillance or interview."

"We could always do both," Gus said. "See what we can see."

"Or both," I agreed. "Harold raises an interesting point about disrupting Eddie simply by visiting him. Sooner the better, I say. How about a Sunday morning visit to the house in Kent to rattle his cage and let him know we're alive? Tomorrow morning—say nine o'clock?"

"Turns out we've got a prior commitment," Gus said.

"This is important," I said. "When can you get free? What time do you think?"

"I mean we have a prior commitment—you guys and us. It's early—won't cause us to put off our visit to Mr. Salazar by more than an hour or so."

"Really? What's up?" I asked.

"One of my informant's leads might be paying off. We've got a meeting set up with a guy who knows something about Eddie Salazar and his background."

"Really?" I was suddenly intrigued. "When and where?"

"Paddy Murphy's. Eight thirty."

Paddy Murphy's is one of Seattle's most famous Irish bars and restaurants. It's at First and Madison in downtown Seattle. "Paddy Murphy's. Been a long time." I turned to Toni. "Ah—a real authentic Irish breakfast," I said in my best Irish brogue. "Toni, darling, prepare yourself for a wee bit o' heaven. Sure, you're in for a treat. Then we can pay a little visit to Mr. Salazar—this time on our terms."

~~~~

Toni dropped me off back at the office. We agreed to meet at eight the next morning. I spent the drive home thinking about the long day we'd had. Long, hard, frustrating, but ultimately productive. We'd gotten lucky, and we were zeroing in on Eddie Salazar. We might not be able to bust the little bastard just yet, but starting tomorrow, he was going to hear from us. He'd have to start looking out for us, and that meant there was that much less time he'd have to hunt for Gina.

Then again, the move wasn't without risk. Eddie Salazar had friends, and they weren't the kind of guys you'd meet for lattes at Starbucks. We'd found that out the hard way. We were going to have to be careful. I sent Toni a text message telling her to bring her vest tomorrow. I'd decide in the morning whether or not we'd put them on. I thought back to my squad leader in Afghanistan, Staff Sergeant Harry Wendall III. Sergeant Wendall was a Southern boy, full of wonderful sayings. One of his most memorable was when he'd check our gear before going out on patrol. He'd invariably yell out, "Vests are like rubbers, ladies! Much better to have one and not need it than need one and not have it." Hooah.

# Chapter 12

MY DAD FIRST brought me to Paddy Murphy's in 1985. That day, after the Seattle Gaels Irish football club played their Saturday morning game, half of the folks in the stands formed a parade and moved the party over to Paddy's to watch the "real" games tape-delayed from Ireland. Given my wee tender years, my dad and I were restricted to the restaurant-only side of the establishment. But it didn't matter. I thought I'd died and gone to heaven. Today, the place smelled exactly the same as when I was a kid, except no more cigarettes. The televisions in the corners had the sound off and were tuned to taped versions of last year's All Ireland Gaelic Football match between County Cork and County Down. Because of the hour, the crowd was not too heavy yet. The bar was nearly empty. Once my eyes adjusted to the relative darkness of the bar, I saw Dwayne and Gus seated alongside a third fellow at a table near the back of the restaurant by the kitchen doors. Gus waved us over.

"Hey guys," he said as we drew near. They all stood as we approached.

Dwayne said, "Toni and Danny, this is Mr. Javier Galindez." Galindez was a round, middle-aged Spanish man with swept-back gray hair. He was dressed neatly in gray slacks and an untucked light blue short-sleeved shirt. "Javi is an old friend of mine from the days when I was a patrol cop. Javi used to own a small grocery store in SoDo, but you moved that—when?"

"We moved in 2002 to Kent," Javi said. "I'm very honored to meet you," he said, reaching to shake my hand. He spoke with the slight accent of a man who had emigrated from Mexico and worked hard to master his adopted country's language. "Dwayne has told me much about you and your heroic service to our country. It is deeply appreciated."

"Thank you," I said, shaking his hand. "You know that Detective Brown has been known to exaggerate from time to time?"

"Two Purple Hearts plus a Silver Star for personal gallantry, young man," Javi said. "That's not easy to downplay. That's genuine hero stuff."

"Thank you. I appreciate the kind words. Please allow me to introduce my associate, Ms. Toni Blair."

"Toni Blair—just like the former Prime Minister of England," Javi said.

"Right," she said, smiling.

"But prettier, and with more tattoos," I said.

"And I can probably whip the Prime Minister's skinny little butt," Toni said, drawing laughter from the group.

"I don't doubt it, young lady," Gus said. He pulled a chair out for Toni. After she sat down, the rest of us followed.

Our waitress came over to take Toni's and my order. "Number one," I said, without referring to the menu. "Two eggs, sunny-side up, bacon, black-and-white pudding with rosemary potatoes, black coffee," I said, reciting a childhood favorite of mine.

"Ah, you've been here before, I see," the waitress said.

"I have, indeed." I answered. "My father used to bring me here when I was a kid. Very fond memories." I looked at Toni. She was intently studying the menu.

"You'll not be finding any tofu here, darlin'," I said in Irish brogue.

She looked up and smiled. "Darn," she said. "Number one you said? Let me see." She checked out the menu, then said "Okay, I'll have the same thing as him then. Just throw on some Lipitor sprinkles for me, will you?"

Everyone laughed. "You are a funny young lady," Javi said, laughing.

Toni laser-beamed him with one of her best smiles. He seemed to melt.

After we were done ordering, I said to Javi, "Dwayne says you know something about Eduardo Salazar."

"I do," he said. "After Dwayne called me yesterday, I made a phone call to my cousin in San Diego. My cousin's an immigration attorney. He called a friend of his who's on the Tijuana police department." He paused as a waitress walked past.

"According to the Tijuana police, Eduardo Salazar is a member of the Tijuana-Mendez drug cartel. They have photographs of him having lunch with known high-level people within that organization on several occasions."

I'd heard of the Tijuana-Mendez cartel, but I'd never had need to pay attention before. I knew that they were a drug-smuggling operation, constantly at war with the other drug-smuggling operations in Mexico. "Refresh my memory, please," I said. "Tell me about the Tijuana-Mendez organization."

He nodded. "As best I know it, the Tijuana-Mendez organization is one of the oldest drug cartels in Mexico," Javi said. "I think they were formed in the late seventies or early eighties by a man named Felix Mendez. They started off smuggling marijuana across the Southern California border. Today, Felix's two sons, Hector and Luis, run the organization. They still smuggle marijuana, but now they've branched out into gun, cocaine, and heroin smuggling, even human trafficking as well."

"They are one of five or six large organizations in Mexico that control the drug trade across the border," Dwayne said.

Javi continued. "Like most cartels, they are very territorial and extremely violent. Unfortunately, if anything, these tendencies have gotten worse in the past several years during the Calderón administration."

Basically, not a nice group of guys. Unlike the American crime families, the Mexican cartels have more in common with some of the Asian criminal organizations. They have relatively more power in their countries than the American crime families enjoy here. The cartels have not had to learn how to live with a strong government and a strong law enforcement presence. In America, if an organized crime family crosses the line, someone gets busted. As a result, they work hard to stay under the radar. In Mexico, there's no line and very few constraints. In fact, they take the opposite tack—they rely on intimidation.

"Any idea of where Salazar fits in?" Toni asked.

"Good question," Dwayne said. "Seeing as how he's having lunch with known higher-ups of the organization, then it stands to reason that he's probably mid-level to upper-mid-level himself."

He was bad enough when I thought he was just a homicidal maniac. Now I find out that he's a homicidal maniac who's backed by a whole organization of homicidal maniacs. "Great," I said. "What the hell is he doing here?"

"My cousin speculates that he is here to manage cartel operations in Seattle," Javi said.

"Cartel operations in Seattle?" I asked. "The cartel has operations big enough in Seattle that they need to be managed by someone like him?"

"Marijuana operations, Danny," Dwayne said. "They grow marijuana in clearings in the forest throughout the state. They're called grows. It's a damn big business, and it's getting bigger by the year. The Washington State Department of Agriculture acknowledges that marijuana is the number two or three crop in the state. It might even be the biggest, but they won't say that. The conditions are near perfect here. We've heard that the cartels are pushing hard to get control of the pot cultivation business here. Eddie Salazar being sent here to help oversee that fits."

"I guess it does," I agreed.

"That could explain why he's here," Gus said. "And being the type of outgoing fellow that he is, he feels the need for a little entertainment, so he takes to visiting Ramon's Cantina. It's probably just like a little slice of home for him."

Dwayne added, "And since Gina was apparently looking for a little excitement, she also visits Ramon's Cantina. Presto! The two brightest stars at Ramon's Cantina come into contact with each other."

Something didn't make sense to me. I suppose that if you didn't know Gina, then maybe Dwayne's theory fit. Problem was, I did know Gina, and I couldn't see any way that Gina would have approached this guy. This wouldn't have been in her character, at least as far as I remember her. Then again, it's been several years. Who knows? People change. One thing's for sure: Gina's a very attractive woman. It's not hard to believe that Eddie Salazar felt he needed to hit on her. The hard part was imagining her reciprocating.

"Along those lines, I regret to add that my cousin said that Eduardo Salazar is wanted for murder in Tijuana," Javi said. "He's apparently a very bad man—ruthless and willing to kill someone with no hesitation for the slightest affront, real or imagined. The man has no feelings of remorse whatsoever. He's a very dangerous man."

*Great.* After this news, the Irish breakfast didn't taste as good as it should have.

~~~~

In the parking lot after breakfast, Toni and I talked to Dwayne while we waited for Gus, who'd pit-stopped on the way out. "Does it change anything for you guys, knowing who we're up against? Any adjustments to strategy knowing this guy could be a front man for a cartel?" I asked.

Dwayne leaned against his car and considered this for a second. Even though it was Sunday, a steady stream of cars drove southbound on Second Avenue. "No, not really," he said. "Not for me, anyway. We already knew the guy was a psychotic scumbag son of a bitch. Didn't really hear anything different this morning."

"I suppose," I answered. I paused, then added, "We did learn what team he plays for. And we learned that his team is in the big leagues."

"True," Dwayne said. "But I don't think it matters. We're not after the team, thank God. We're just looking for the missing girl. If Eddie Salazar's linked to her, then he becomes of interest to us. But not the Tijuana-Mendez group. That's someone else's job."

I nodded. "I agree. We're not interested in the cartel," I said. "Let's just hope that when we bust their ambassador to the Pacific Northwest, the cartel doesn't become interested in us."

"Occupational hazard," Toni said as Gus joined us. "Screw 'em."

"Spoken like my favorite lady detective," Gus said.

Toni smiled at him.

"Just to play a little CYA, do you think you should notify the DEA and let them know what we've found?" I asked.

Dwayne shrugged. "Probably," he said. "But remember the DEA guys are Feds. They don't work weekends. We'll call them tomorrow."

So we decided to go ahead and pay a visit to the house where we'd seen Eddie Salazar's car yesterday. Nothing like spending a nice Sunday morning talking to a psychotic drug cartel maniac.

~~~~

Forty-five minutes later, we gathered our forces in back of the parking lot of the same convenience store where Toni and I'd stopped yesterday afternoon. Although our purpose was only to talk to Eddie Salazar, not arrest him—or anyone else for that matter—it made sense to be prepared. Dwayne had called Kent PD just in case. They sent two narcotics detectives in an unmarked car and two uniformed officers in a black-and-white to accompany us. The detectives both wore sport coats and slacks.

We gathered around Dwayne's car, and he laid out his game plan. "We have reason to believe that Mr. Eduardo Salazar either stays at or visits the house at 5470 East Maple Street—right across from the cemetery. We have an interest in talking to Mr. Salazar in connection with the disappearance of Gina Fiore—you guys have probably seen the case on TV. They've got television down here now, right?"

Both Kent detectives laughed. "Yeah," the tall one said. "Last year."

"Good. Anyway, if we can gain legal access—that is, if we can establish probable cause from outside, then we'll go inside and take a look around, just to make sure that Ms. Fiore is not being held against her will inside the home. If that turns out to be the case, and an arrest is made for any of the occupants, then Kent PD will make the arrest. Make sense?"

Everyone nodded.

"Will you be picking Salazar up if he's there?" one of the Kent detectives asked.

"Not unless he's smoking a joint or doing something else equally as stupid," Dwayne said. "Even then, we'd just have you bust him. We are not here to make an arrest in conjunction with the Fiore disappearance. We just want to talk to the man—let him know that we're watching him, send him a message. If we are unable to establish probable cause, then we won't enter. We'll just leave our cards and call it a day."

"Alright," the tall detective agreed.

"Now, as to how we go about doing this," Dwayne said. "We need to be careful. There's a possibility that these guys have some sort of connection to a Mexican cartel. We should assume they are armed and dangerous. Not that they're likely to shoot us for simply wanting to ask questions. But you never know. With that in mind, do you guys mind covering the back? If anyone bolts, detain him and call me. If we have to go in to secure the home, our first move will be to come through the house and let you in. Don't shoot us when we come outside, okay?"

"No shooting?" the short detective joked. "How are we supposed to

have any fun then? They told me this was supposed to be a fun assign-
ment."

"Wiseass," Dwayne said. "We'll let you in, and the four of us can
clear the house safely."

"Okay, then," they answered.

Dwayne looked at me and said, "When I say 'the four of us' I mean
the four law enforcement gentlemen standing here before you—the ones
with the suits and ties and the shiny gold badges. You and your partner
are not to enter the home. Understood?"

"Agreed," I answered for us.

He turned to the uniformed officers in the patrol unit. "You guys
hang back a block or so away so you don't ruin our surprise. Once we're
secure outside, I'll call on your radio, and you can roll up out front to
control the front entry."

The officers nodded.

"Any questions?" Dwayne asked. He paused a second, then said,
"Good. Let's do it." He turned to the Kent PD detectives. "You guys go
up the alley. I'll call on the radio when we're about to enter the property.
If the yard is empty, I'll let you know when we're about to knock on the
door."

"Got it."

Dwayne turned to us. "You guys follow us and park as close behind
as you can."

~~~~

"Vests?" Toni asked as we followed Gus and Dwayne's blue Crown Vic.

"They're in style," I said, looking around. "The cops are all wearing
them. No sense in us standing out. Let's put them on when we stop."

"It'll look a little conspicuous," she said.

"Putting it on or wearing it?" I asked.

"Both."

"Who cares? That's the point now, isn't it? We *want* to be seen. We
want them to know we're out here watching."

Two minutes later, we parked on the street two cars behind Gus and
Dwayne, who themselves were parked two houses east of our target. We

donned our dark-blue Kevlar vests before joining them.

"Very stylish," Gus said, nodding toward our vests. "A lot nicer than ours."

"Glad you approve," Toni answered.

"Didn't know they made 'em in ladies sizes," Gus said.

"Careful - you're treading a thin line there, Gus," Dwayne said. He turned to the house. "Let's get going. They're probably watching us. Let's move before they get all their guns loaded." He looked at me and said, "You two—no closer than the front porch. But make yourselves useful. Watch our backs and make sure nobody behind us gets frisky."

"Got it," I answered.

We reached the walkway from the sidewalk to the front porch and turned to approach the house. Dwayne made the radio call to the patrol unit and also confirmed that Kent PD was in position in back, ready to detain anyone who tried to bolt into the alley. Seconds later, the black-and-white rolled to a stop at the curb behind us. Three young Mexican men sat on the front porch and watched us warily. They said nothing until we reached the steps.

"Buenos dias, amigos. What can we do for you?" the oldest of the three asked. He was probably late twenties, maybe five ten, although it was a little hard to tell since he was seated.

"Good morning, gentlemen," Dwayne said. "Sorry to disturb you on this fine Sunday morning."

"We're just sitting here, enjoying the morning, minding our own business," the man said. "Who are you? What do you want, amigo?"

"Seattle Police Department." Dwayne held up his badge. "We're here because we need to talk to Eduardo Salazar."

"Who?" the man asked, looking as if he'd never heard the name.

"Eduardo—Eddie Salazar," Dwayne said again.

The man took a few seconds and acted like he was thinking. Then he shook his head no. "Never heard of him," he said again, with a smile.

"That's too bad," Dwayne said. He appeared to think for a few seconds, and then, as if the thought had suddenly flashed inside him, said, "Maybe someone inside knows the good Mr. Salazar. How about if we ask them?" He turned and took a step toward the door. All of the Mexican men started to rise in unison.

"Sit yourselves back down," Gus said, using his "command voice." "We can manage to knock on a door without your help."

I watched carefully to make sure none of the men reached for a gun.

Dwayne knocked on the door. Several seconds later, it swung open and who should be standing there, but Mr. Short and Round from Ramon's Cantina. He still wore the large bandage on his nose.

He looked at Dwayne and Gus, then he looked past them and saw Toni and me. I waved. I thought it was the friendly thing to do. He didn't wave back. He was probably in a bad mood.

"Good morning," Dwayne said. "We're here to speak to Mr. Eduardo Salazar."

"Don't know him," he said.

"Maybe this will help," Dwayne said. He showed Short and Round a picture of Salazar.

Short and Round continued to stare at Dwayne without looking at the picture. He was probably an awesome poker player. His face gave nothing away. "Never seen him," he said.

"What's your name? What happened to your nose?"

Short and Round looked down and fidgeted uncomfortably before he quietly said, "Armando Martinez."

"Mr. Martinez," Dwayne repeated. "What happened to your nose?"

Martinez looked past Dwayne and glared at Toni. "I fell down some stairs," he said.

"That's too bad," Dwayne said. "You've got to watch that." Dwayne looked past Martinez into the home. "Mind if we come inside and take a look around?"

"You got a warrant?"

"Not right now, but we can go get one," Dwayne said.

"Then go get it."

"Let me ask you this, first," Dwayne said. "Have you ever been arrested?"

"Why?"

"Why? I'm guessing you have. I see the 'M' ink all over your shoulders. I'm thinking you're a member of the Mexican Mafia and that you've spent some quality time at one of the lovely state resorts run by the Washington State Department of Corrections—maybe Walla Walla. Am I wrong?"

"Stockton, California," Martinez answered.

"California!" Dwayne said. "Even better."

"Why do you say that?" Martinez asked, confused.

"Because I wanted you to know that you are going to be well taken care of after today," Dwayne said.

"What are you talking about?" Martinez asked.

"What I'm talking about is this," Dwayne said. "Look behind you on that shelf."

Martinez turned.

"See the plant in the red vase sitting on that shelf over there?" Dwayne asked. "See that thing next to the plant? Tell me what that is."

Martinez said nothing.

"It's a gram scale!" Dwayne answered for him, as if delighted. "That's right. A gram scale, in plain sight from the front door. And just to the left of the scale there, what's that?"

Again Martinez said nothing.

"Right again!" Dwayne said. "It's a big-assed bong. And it looks like a whole collection of roach clips, papers, you name it." Dwayne pointed to something else. "And what's that rolled up in that baggie? Would that be marijuana there?"

"Looks like he's all set up to do some entertaining," Gus said.

"Sure does, doesn't it?" Dwayne said.

Martinez was stone silent.

"Now," Dwayne said, "last question. What do they call all that stuff here in the state of Washington? The legal definition? Not counting the pot, of course. We just call that pot."

"Paraphernalia!" Dwayne said, answering his own question. "You are too good at this, Mr. Martinez, really. Drug paraphernalia, to be exact. And you know what that means, don't you?"

"Yes—you've got it!" he said excitedly. "It means you're under arrest for possession of drug paraphernalia. Why don't you go on ahead and put your hands behind your back." He grabbed Martinez, spun him around, and leaned him against the wall. He frisked him.

The three men on the porch again started to get up, but Gus was watching them. "Sit your punk asses back down. Now!" he ordered. They sat. "Danny? You watching these mutts?" He asked.

"We've got 'em," I answered.

"*Chingada!*" Martinez said to Dwayne before turning around. "This is bullshit. I'll be out in an hour."

"An hour? Really? What do you think, Gus? Think this mutt will be out in an hour?"

"Maybe. Maybe not," Gus said. "Say," he added, "you wouldn't happen to be on parole, would you?"

Martinez was stone-faced and said nothing.

Gus smiled and said, "I thought so."

"We'll just have to have us a little chat with your PO," Dwayne said. "Maybe not just an hour then, huh?" Dwayne said. "What do you think?"

Dwayne led Martinez back to a solid post at the front porch and handcuffed him to it. "Don't go anywhere," he said. He turned to the other men.

"Gus, let's cuff these other guys up just to be safe." He asked one of the patrol officers to come up to the porch to help out.

Between the two of them, Dwayne and Gus had exactly three remaining pairs of handcuffs; they used one for each of the remaining men. They shoved each back down into a sitting position.

After they were through, Dwayne turned to us. "Ladies and gentlemen, we have illegal drug paraphernalia in plain view from the doorway of the residence. I deem that to mean that we have sufficient probable cause to enter the residence and seize said drug paraphernalia. When we do this, we'll need to secure the residence for our own safety. We'll be taking a quick peek around, just to make certain there are no other bad guys lurking about. Make sense?"

"Agreed!" Gus answered enthusiastically.

"Good," Dwayne said. He turned to Toni and me. "Your job—" he turned to include the officer on the porch, "—and yours, too, is to watch these guys. I've got four bad guys here now. Count 'em: one, two, three— plus the idiot cuffed to the post makes four. I want four bad guys here when I come out. Try not to let them get away while we're inside. And if a number five or six suddenly materializes, you sing out, you got that? Don't be a hero."

"Got it."

Dwayne made the call to Kent PD in the back, and he and Gus entered the building.

While the police secured the inside of the house, we kept watch outside. Five minutes after they'd entered, Dwayne popped back out.

"No one else inside, guys."

That answered one question. Neither Eddie nor Gina was there.

"Silver Mercedes?" I asked.

"Nope. Not here," Dwayne said. He went back inside.

A few minutes later, Martinez started laughing.

"Something funny there, Armando?" I asked.

"Yeah, sure is, holmes."

"What's that?"

"I might be going to jail, but you know that girl you said you're looking for? The sweet little one with the big *chi-chis*?"

I nodded.

"She ain't coming home, esse. You ain't never going to see her again."

I stared at him, but said nothing.

"Yeah, she dancing with the angels now."

I continued to stare.

"And something else," he said. The smile left his face and was replaced by an angry, mean look. "After this here is all over," he said. "After this is all over and I'm out, I'm coming for you and that sweet little bitch there." He nodded toward Toni. "I'm going to cut you up bad. Then while you're bleeding out, I'm going to fuck your lady there right in front of you like she ain't never had it before. Fuck her 'til she screams." He paused and then smiled again—a dangerous, evil smile. "Then I'm going to kill you both."

I stared hard back at him. I wasn't smiling. I don't respond well to threats. In fact, they piss me off. "That right, Armando?" I answered. I leaned closer to his side and slipped a business card in his vest pocket. I spoke softly. "Here's my card, so you won't have any trouble finding me. I'll look forward to meeting up with you. By the way, how's that nose?"

His smile vanished. He glared at me, eyes full of hatred. "Fuck you and your *puta*," he said.

"I don't think so," I said. "Have fun in prison." I slapped him on the back of the head—just a little going away present for threatening Toni. I didn't mean to slap him hard, but I guess I was a little pissed. He wasn't ready for it, so his head snapped forward and his already broken nose smacked into the post he was handcuffed to with a sickening crunching sound. He screamed and fell to his knees. Seconds later, blood gushed down his face onto his shirt. Dwayne had to call the paramedics. He pretended like he was pissed.

# Chapter 13

WE DECIDED AS a group that since we weren't overflowing with leads, it wouldn't be a bad idea to watch the Salazar house for a while in hopes of catching Eddie coming back. Kent PD had arrested Armando Martinez on drug paraphernalia charges and on possession of controlled substance charges for the three ounces of weed and five grams of blow that we found after we searched the house. Upon checking police records, they discovered that he was indeed on parole, and, in light of his transgressions, California wanted him back for five more years.

They decided not to arrest the three other guys who'd been sitting outside since they weren't actually in the house and none of them even appeared to be permanent residents of the home. No doubt Eddie would hear that we'd paid him a visit. Hopefully, though, he'd feel the need to come back—perhaps to talk to someone, perhaps to retrieve some item that we hadn't noticed.

Since we were just looking for someone and not actually gathering evidence to be used in a prosecution, SPD decided it would be okay to team up with us and take turns on surveillance. This was helpful because everyone's resources were limited. Logan PI would take even-numbered days; SPD would take the odds. Monday morning, August 22, we were up first.

Our strategy was to move back to low-key tactics. Now that we'd sent the message to Eddie, we needed to get out of sight again, or we'd not likely see him. The job called for clandestine surveillance, one of Logan PI's specialties. We've even got a few "stealth" surveillance vehicles—two service vans and an old Winnebago—that are set up on the inside to make surveillance duty something less of the grueling pain in the butt that it otherwise is. All our stealth surveillance vehicles have a desk with a couple of comfortable chairs, a refrigerator, and—most important—a small bathroom. They all have video recording equipment for use in recording the comings and goings of our targets. We curtain off the working area in the back from the driver's seat in front. No one ever suspects us.

Today, Joaquin and Kenny took the first shift: eight to noon. We approached at a quiet time when nobody was out. I had them park the Winnebago across the street from Salazar's house, about four houses down. This put the Salazar house in front of us, to the left. The cemetery was on our right, to the south. After I made sure they were squared away, I drove back to the office. Monday morning traffic in Seattle being what it is, I didn't get in until just after nine.

~~~~

Toni was reading the *Seattle Times* with her feet up on her desk, eating a Red Vine, when I walked into the office. She saw me and said, "Hey, boss. Guess who called and left a message this morning?"

"I give up," I answered.

"Kara. She left a number."

"Kara! Excellent. Let's give her a call on the speakerphone."

"It's an Ohio prefix."

Ohio? Must have been a long drive—all the better to hide from Eddie. I was anxious to talk to her. At the least, I needed to know how to get in touch with her. Ideally, I'd like her to agree to testify against Eddie on the assault charge. That way, we could get an arrest warrant, and SPD could hunt him down and bust him. This would be much easier than finding him, inviting him in for an interview and playing a game of twenty questions.

We went to my office and dialed the number. Three rings in, an elderly lady answered. She put Kara on when I identified myself.

"Hello, Kara," I said. "I'm very happy to see that you're all settled. That was smart."

"We're good," she said. "We're scared, but we're okay. I wanted to let you know where we are. We're staying—"

"Hold on," I interrupted. "We don't need to know where you are.

Keep that to yourself. We see your area code, and we have a general idea. That's good enough for now. Mostly, we just need your phone number so that we can get in touch with you, if need be. Now we have that, too. Thank you for calling."

"No problem."

"Did you have a good trip? Any problems?" Toni asked.

"Long. We drove straight through the weekend."

"Good. Is Nick there with you?" I asked.

"Yes."

"That's good, too. Did you tell anyone here where you were going?" Toni said.

"No. After we left the apartment, we drove straight up I-5 to Everett and found a motel for the night. We did a little shopping at the mall the next morning, and then we left. We got most of the stuff we needed. We didn't sleep much that night."

"At least you're safe now," I said. "Have you told the people you're staying with not to mention that you're there?"

"Yes, I'm staying with—" she stopped herself, then said, "Yes. I'm sure that won't be a problem on this end."

"Excellent. I'm glad we won't have to worry about that," I said. "Let me bring you up to date on what's going on here. Based on what you told us, our team did a search of cemeteries in Kent. We found one that looked promising, and Toni and I did some driving there Saturday afternoon. We didn't notice Eddie Salazar's Mercedes, but we got lucky and spotted one of his guys at a nearby convenience store—one of the guys that jumped us in your parking lot. Remember the name Armando Martinez? Turns out he was one of the guys we bumped into at Ramon's Cantina, and he was also the guy at your apartment whose nose Toni shattered. We followed him to a house across from the cemetery."

"That was Armando Martinez?" Kara asked.

"Yep."

"And the house he went to was across from a cemetery—just like Gina said?" Kara asked.

"That's right. When he opened the garage to park his car, we could see inside. There was a silver Mercedes parked there."

"Awesome," Kara said. "Did you call the cops? Did they arrest him?"

"We called them, but they were unable to arrest him," I said.

It was silent for a second. Then Kara said, "Why not?"

"We don't have enough evidence yet to arrest him for anything involving Gina. The only thing we can arrest him for now is for assaulting you. And we didn't know where you were or how to get ahold of you on Saturday. All we knew is that you'd said you didn't want to testify."

The line was quiet for a few seconds, then Kara said, "Shit, that's just great. If I don't say anything about this creep, then I have to look over my shoulder for the rest of my life. If I do say something, then maybe he gets put away, maybe he doesn't. Either way, after he's out I still have to look over my shoulder."

"It's worse," I said. "If you agree to cooperate on an assault charge, he'd probably get convicted. For assault though, he wouldn't be put away for very long. He'd be out in a year—maybe less. The only reason to testify against him now would be in the hope that while he's in jail, we can pin something to do with Gina on him. Then it could turn into a long sentence."

The line was silent. "I know it sucks," I said. "But that's a pretty clear assessment."

A couple of seconds later, she said, "All the way driving out here I got more and more pissed off at this bastard. He's trying to hurt Gina, and he might try to hurt me."

"*Again*," Toni said. "He might try to hurt you *again*. And he's come after us."

"Right. And that's fucked up. Why should I have to run off and hide because of him? What gives him the right to make me have to leave a good job and turn my life upside down? He's the one who's done something wrong—not me."

"He may have the ability, but he doesn't have the right," I said. "You can choose to either play his game, which is what you're doing now, or you can fight back and tell the DA you'll testify against him. That way, we can bust him when we find him."

"If you're worried about retaliation," Toni said, "at least you won't be alone. Yesterday, we went with the police to the house across from the cemetery to try and talk to Eddie Salazar. This time Salazar wasn't there, but Martinez was. He ended up getting arrested for drug charges. He said he was going to rape me while he made Danny watch. Then he said he was going to kill us both. So naturally, Captain America here slapped him and broke his nose again. Then he gave him our business card and told him he couldn't wait to meet him when he got out of prison."

"I didn't think you heard that," I said.

"Yep." She was stone-faced. "Heard the whole thing."

I stared at her, looking for a clue as to what she was thinking. "You liked it," I said to Toni. I was fishing, but what the hell. May as well guess optimistic.

"I did," she answered, suddenly smiling. "I was so proud." Her tone was that of a mom who's ne'er-do-well kid suddenly brought home an A on a report card. Better than I was expecting, actually.

"Really?" Kara said, laughing. A few seconds went past, then she said, "I've changed my mind. I already had, but now I really have. You guys inspire me. I want to testify against Salazar. I don't want him to do what he did, and then just think he can run around scot-free, intimidating people. That's bullshit. I want to fight back, like you guys do."

"Fantastic," I said. "That's the only way to stop assholes like this. The DA said he could get a warrant if you'd testify. I'll set up a conference call and call you back with a time. It's going to take a bit, though. They'll arrange to take your statement over the phone, and they'll figure out a way to get the necessary signatures from you. We'll have them call you, if that's okay."

"Okay," Kara said. "Just one thing."

"What's that?" I asked.

"You guys have to promise to look out for Nicky and me if we testify."

"No problem," Toni said. "We're all in the same boat. We can all look out for each other."

"One other thing, Kara," I said.

"What?"

"Until we find him and arrest him, you guys just keep doing what you're doing. Stay where you are, and stay out of sight."

~~~~

Excellent morning! I called Dwayne and let him know what had happened. He patched Harold Ohlmer in. An hour later, Harold took Kara's statement over the phone. Kara authorized Toni to release the photos Toni'd taken of Kara's injuries last Friday to the police. Harold took the photos and Kara's testimony and procured a warrant for the arrest of Eduardo Salazar an hour later.

Toni and I were in a good mood when we relieved Joaquin and Kenny at noon.

"Lots of traffic," Joaquin said, "but no silver Mercedes."

I looked at the log and saw that they'd recorded eleven separate cars coming and going from the home in four hours.

"Looks like a drug house," I commented. "But we searched it yesterday. There aren't any drugs there."

"At least there weren't after we left yesterday," Toni said.

"Maybe they moved some in last night after we were done. They might have thought that once we'd searched the house, it wouldn't get searched again, at least not for awhile." I set the logs down. "Good job, guys," I said. "Were you bored?"

"I noticed you didn't assign yourself to sit with this little peckerwood for four hours straight," Doc said, nodding to Kenny. "I had to listen to him brag about his girlfriends the whole damn time."

I laughed. "Girlfriends? Is that what he calls those jailbait teenagers he hangs with?" Doc laughed.

"They're all legal!" Kenny protested. "They're young, but not children."

"Are any of them even out of middle school yet?" Toni asked.

"Aw, that's bullshit!" Kenny said. "They're young women—all nineteen or twenty years old."

"But still in middle school, right?" Doc said. "No honor students in the bunch."

"Fuck you, Doc," Kenny said.

"Okay, you guys," I said, smiling. "You're relieved. See you back here at four."

They said their good-byes and left in my car, still jabbering at each other as they left.

"Well, Ms. Blair," I said, taking one of the two swivel chairs and leaning back, watching the video monitor, "are you ready to settle in for an exciting four hours?"

"Sure," she said. She pointed to the refrigerator. "Flip you to see who makes lunch."

~~~~

Part of our agreement with SPD was that together, we'd only be able to watch the house for sixteen hours per day. Today, there would be no surveillance of the house from midnight to 0800. This left a hole, but even SPD didn't have the manpower to spare for a round-the-clock stakeout in connection with a simple assault beef. Logan PI sure as hell didn't. Toni and I took the 1200 to 1600 shift, Joaquin and Kenny came back for the 1600 to 2000, and then Toni and I finished up with the 2000 to 0000 shift. The logs showed that the last car to visit the house left at 2113. Nothing particularly noteworthy all day. Did I mention that surveillance work can be monotonous?

Joaquin picked us up a few minutes before midnight. Normally, we wouldn't use the same stakeout vehicle two days in a row so as to avoid suspicion. The same plumber's van in the same position day after day will most likely attract attention. One of the beauties of the Winnebago, however, is that it's not necessarily suspicious to see a motor home parked for a few days in the same spot. In fact, that's what they do. They're *supposed* to be parked for a few days. The bigger issue for the motor home was crew transfer, but we dealt with that by parking down the block a bit and always parking so we can exit on the side opposite of our subject. Our risk of being noticed was relatively low.

Unfortunately, though, the traffic at the home had been nonrevealing on the first day of the stakeout. Certainly, there'd been no silver Mercedes.

Our plan was to leave the Winnebago in place for three days. SPD was to provide coverage on Tuesday, August 23—day two of the stakeout. Kenny met them at eight the next morning and gave them a briefing on how to use the different R/V systems. Sixteen hours later, they'd had the exact same result as us. Numerous comings and goings throughout the day. Some, even, were the same vehicles from the day before. But none were suspicious, and none involved Eddie Salazar's silver Mercedes.

Two days. Two strikes.

~~~~

In my unit in the army, only the officers were initially issued sidearms. Grunts like me were issued M4 rifles. The M4—sort of a mini-version of the Vietnam-era M16—is a reasonably good weapon: light, handy, and mobile. The brass expected them to be enough. As the war progressed, however, we learned the hard way that with the amount of close-quarter work that we did in and around buildings, lives could be saved by allowing the infantry to carry sidearms. Unfortunately, even after they figured this out, the brass didn't help us much when they issued us Beretta M9s. The gun was okay I suppose, except for the unfortunate fact that it fires a 9 mm bullet. We soon came to realize that your average hyped-up insurgent required three or four such 9 mm bullets to become incapacitated. And while you were busy trying to fill him up with the minimum number of 9 mm slugs, he was busy trying to take you out you using a gun firing a much more lethal round—usually an AK. The joke in our unit was that it was faster and safer to take out an insurgent by throwing the M9 at him and hitting him in the head as opposed to pumping him full of the requisite number of 9 mm pinpricks. After several such thrilling encounters, we didn't even bother with the Berettas; we made do with our M4s.

We were not allowed to solve this problem by carrying private weapons, under threat of severe penalty. But we eventually found something of a loophole when we discovered we were allowed to carry any officially issued weapon—not just the Beretta. Turns out the SOCOM guys were still being issued the good old Colt Model 1911A .45-caliber semi-automatic handguns. The most accurate handgun ever made with the most lethal round, the M1911A fires large-caliber bullets nearly a half inch in diameter. One hit from a "flying-pumpkin," and the bad guy was no longer a threat. We got hold of the 1911s. We loved them. We learned how to take care of them. We became inseparable.

~~~~

At seven o'clock the next morning, I was in the kitchen getting ready to go to work. This means something a little different to someone in my business because I still carry a Model 1911 nearly every day. The good news is that civilian life is not as dangerous as my time overseas was. The bad news is that in my job I still occasionally bump into bad guys that are every bit as dangerous as an Arab insurgent. Thus, the need to "gun up." In fact, I often carry a little backup strapped to my ankle. I treat guns with respect, and part of that means I follow a careful routine in caring for them.

This morning, like every other morning, I visually inspected my Les Baer Thunder Ranch Model 1911, .45 caliber. I released the magazine, thumbed off the safety, ejected the round in the chamber and locked the slide open. I confirmed that the gun was unloaded. Next, I exercised the magazine spring by thumbing out all eight cartridges, then reloading them. I did this to my two backup magazines as well. Satisfied that all appeared as it should, I replaced the magazine, released the slide, and thumbed the safety on. The gun was ready for action in "condition one"—cocked and locked. I put the gun into the Bianchi holster on my hip. Now I was ready.

At precisely that moment, the phone rang. I looked at the caller ID. Dwayne. Good timing.

"Good morning," he said, cheerfully. "You up and at 'em yet? Ready to take on the new day?"

"Of course," I said. "It's our turn to man the Winnebago. I have to drive Joaquin and Kenny out there. I was just getting ready to walk out the door."

"I think I've got someplace you might rather be," he said.

"I wouldn't doubt it," I said. "There are lots of places I'd rather be. What did you have in mind?"

"Camelot Arms Apartments," he said. "Beacon Avenue near the Jefferson Community Center."

That stopped me. "Actually wasn't thinking of that," I admitted. "Why do I want to be at the Camelot Arms Apartments?" I was suddenly curious.

"Because our good friend Javier got a phone call from a friend of his who knew we were looking. Someone saw Eddie Salazar park his silver Mercedes outside one of the apartments there and go on in. There was a pretty, dark-haired woman with him."

My adrenalin level started to climb. "No shit," I said. "When?"

"Last night, about eight o'clock. The car's still there—we've got the car and the apartment under surveillance. I'm assembling an assault team right now. We're going in at 8:15 or so to arrest Eddie Salazar. Figured you might want to be there—you know, watch the real police in action."

"You figured right," I said. "That'd be a treat. I appreciate that. Got a time and place for the rally point?"

"We're going to assemble in the Jefferson Park parking lot on the south side of the community center right on Beacon Avenue at 0745."

"I know where it is," I said. "I'll be there—wouldn't miss it for the world. I'll swing past the office and grab Toni. Then we'll head on over."

~~~~

Fifteen minutes later, Toni met me in the Logan PI parking lot and we took off. The Wednesday morning traffic wasn't as bad as it would become in another hour, but it was already starting to build.

"Maybe this is it," Toni said.

"Maybe," I answered. "I sure hope so. Hopefully, it's Gina with him and not someone else. I sure hope she's okay."

"They got no ID on the woman?" Toni asked.

"No, none that I heard. Just a 'dark-haired woman.'"

Toni thought for a second. "Well," she said, "even if it's not her, at least we'll still have him."

"True. I can't wait to get this guy in an interrogation room."

"My guess is he won't have anything to say," Toni said.

"Could be. But at least he won't be hunting for Gina anymore."

"True enough."

Except for the stereo, which was playing "Demons and Lakes" by Ravenna Woods, we drove the rest of the way in silence. We pulled into the north parking lot at the Jefferson Community Center on Beacon Avenue at 7:40 a.m.

# Chapter 14

THE JEFFERSON PARK Community Center, our rally point, is about three blocks south of the Camelot Arms Apartments, right at the on top of Beacon Hill in Seattle, just east of I-5. Technically, Beacon Hill isn't a hill at all—it's a ridge. But when Boston native Harwood Young decided to name the area in 1889, he named it after his hometown landmark Beacon Hill. The name stuck.

Today, people—mostly joggers and dog walkers—were already active in the park, even at this early hour. They slowed or even stopped to watch the assembly of heavily armed police officers that had gathered for the bust. Two uniformed officers kept them well away from the assembly area.

Toni and I were waved through—apparently Dwayne had briefed the officers regarding my Jeep. I parked, and we hopped out. We donned our vests and joined the small crowd of police officers. At 7:45 Dwayne called everyone to order.

"Okay, everyone listen up!" he called out. The police officers stopped talking and turned to pay attention. Dwayne stood before an artist-easel-type tripod to which was attached a flip-over pad. A portable blackboard was situated alongside.

"We've been informed that last night at eight o'clock, this man," Dwayne said as he pinned a copy of Eddie's picture to the blackboard, "name of Eduardo 'Eddie' Salazar, parked his silver Mercedes at the Camelot Arms Apartments complex and entered unit 109. An unidentified dark-haired woman—no other information on her—accompanied him. It's possible she might be none other than Gina Fiore. The tip came to us this morning at 6:34 a.m. We placed the apartment unit, and the car under surveillance at 7:20. The car is still there, and there's been no activity at the apartment since we've been watching."

"We have an arrest warrant for Eduardo Salazar and a search warrant with a no-knock authorization for the apartment. Salazar is wanted for the assault of a different adult female. Salazar is five feet, ten inches tall, 165 pounds, black hair and dark eyes. In addition, in the event that the woman he's traveling with is not Gina Fiore, Salazar is a man of prime interest to us regarding her disappearance. Incidentally—and pay attention to this—we also have reason to believe that Salazar is a member of the Tijuana-Mendez Mexican drug cartel. He is to be considered armed and extremely dangerous. Questions so far?" There were none.

"Good," he continued. "I want to introduce Captain Gary Radovich of SPD SWAT. In light of this character's background, Seattle SWAT is going to conduct the entry for us this morning. When the site is formally cleared, they will then turn the site over to us for processing. Captain?"

"Thanks, Lieutenant Brown," Radovich said. "First off, we've talked to the apartment manager. He says he doesn't believe that there are any children in the subject unit. He's never seen anyone there other than adults. Because of that, and because this man is considered dangerous, we'll be going in hard—thus, the no-knock. Next, we'll be using channel four for this op. Go ahead and set your radios now."

A minute later, he continued. He turned to the map and flipped to a site plan of the apartment and the surrounding street. He proceeded to lay out a complete plan for the raid of the apartment. Radovich provided both preliminary staging positions near the apartment building as well as final assault positions for each member of the entire ten-man team, along with the responsibilities of each man. It reminded me of some of the briefings we had in Iraq before moving into an insurgent building—same prep, same tension. When he was done, he asked for questions. When he'd answered them all, he broke the group and sent us to our vehicles with instructions to move to our preliminary staging points.

"Let's do it," Gus said.

~~~~

The assembly broke up and the team headed for their vehicles. "You guys ride with us," Dwayne said. Gus walked to the driver's side.

"Good," I said.

"And I want you wearing these vests," he said. He opened his trunk and handed us each a dark blue vest with *Seattle Police Dept.* stenciled in yellow on the back. "No sense anyone seeing us escorting civilians around an arrest scene," he said.

"Also, might keep us from getting shot by SPD," I said. We stripped off our own vests and donned the SPD vests.

"True," he agreed. "And here—Gus, give him your radio, just in case we get separated for some reason. We'll share." He looked at the radio and handed it to me. "It's already set to channel four," he said. "Make sure to keep the volume way down. Obviously, you guys listen only—no talking."

Gus pulled out of the parking lot and turned north. We drove in silence past a large public golf course, the home course of local-boy-made-good Fred Couples. A couple of minutes later, he turned right on Hanford and then immediately north again into an alley behind the apartment building. Two hundred yards up the alley, he stopped behind three other patrol cars already parked there.

"Game time, boys and girls," Gus said.

"Let's move," Dwayne said. "We stage right up there alongside the building."

~~~~

It's safe to say that the Camelot Arms Apartments complex was no garden spot. Though not what you'd call a ghetto, the Beacon Hill area of central Seattle was in the middle of a regentrification trend that started in the eighties and was further bolstered in 2001 when Amazon.com located its headquarters nearby. Unfortunately, the modernization hadn't yet reached the Camelot Arms. In fact, the plain, rectangular two-story building existed today pretty much as it had since it was built right after World War II. There was gray-green moss on the peeling white siding that looked as if it had never been repainted. Even the faded lavender trim paint looked original.

We joined the others at our preliminary staging position behind the east end of the building. The radio was in my pocket, its microphone clipped to my collar. It was turned down very low, but I could hear each unit check in one by one at 8:20. Soon, all units were in place, ready to move in an orderly manner to their final assault position. Radovich had carefully choreographed these movements so as to provide the maximum opportunity for complete surprise.

I was impressed with the SWAT operation. I hadn't breached a door for more than three years and technically, I wasn't going to do so today since we were only invited in after the apartment was cleared by SWAT. Nonetheless, the adrenalin rush of bashing through the door of a known bad guy was something I remembered vividly. You never really knew what you were going to find. In Iraq, our procedure was usually pretty simple. If we needed to clear a building in which we thought there was a chance of nonhostiles present, we'd use what we called the "crash and dash" technique—one guy kicks the door down, and his buddies rush in with M4s ready to hose down any bad guys. If we were completely certain that no nonhostiles were present, we'd occasionally use the "crash and blast" variation—kick the door down, and toss in a grenade. Of course, with CID I learned to refine these techniques for use in a more normal world. Still, we seldom had nine guys to breach a door.

Bottom line: Seattle SWAT was light years better than we were. I suppose they had to be, with so many civilians around. Still, with their dark Kevlar helmets and their high-tech tactical gear, they looked as though they were ready for World War III. Unless Eddie was sitting on the other side of the door with a weapon drawn, odds were good that he'd be under arrest in the next few minutes, which was all I wanted. On the other hand, if he actually was sitting on the other side of the door with a weapon drawn waiting for us, odds were also good that he'd be dead in another couple of minutes, although in that case, he might take someone with him. Hopefully, he was sleeping soundly and completely unprepared for what was about to hit him.

~~~~

Two minutes later, the radio crackled to life. "We're all here—everyone's in position," Radovich announced. "I'm moving to the CP now." He turned to the four of us and said, "Follow me. Walk slowly and quietly. We're going up behind that car over there."

We crouched down and followed him. We were all wearing soft-soled shoes and walking on asphalt, so we were able to move silently. There was no one about in the alley or the parking lot. Two minutes later we were crouched down behind a car in the parking lot, one hundred feet from the front door of the apartment.

"CP is up," Radovich said over the radio. Except for the actual breach team, he then moved the rest of his people into their final assault positions. When he was satisfied, he conducted his final status checks. "Alley One?" Alley One was one of the two two-man units stationed in the alley, directly behind the apartment. They were responsible for capturing anyone who tried to escape through one of the apartment's back windows.

"We're ready. No lights, curtains drawn, no apparent movement. But we can hear someone singing inside. Mexican, male."

"Got it," Radovich replied. Each of the remaining units checked in, ready to go.

"Okay, boys. We're ready. Entry Team, move to your assault position," Radovich ordered.

Immediately, the Entry Team emerged from their staging point on the side of the building in single file, one man directly behind the next. They moved quietly into their preassigned assault positions—two men holding shotguns aimed directly at the door locks, one holding a heavy steel battering ram. Two flankers in the rear of the line faced west and one faced east. The four men that would enter first were huddled in single file behind the battering ram.

Radovich looked at his watch. "It's 8:23. Entry Team Commander, you now have control."

The man in front of the breach line immediately started a silent finger count—one, two, three, and then pointed at the door.

Immediately, each shotgun fired a breaching slug at the door locks in what appeared to be a single deafening blast. Before the ringing stopped, the battering ram slammed into the door and blew it wide open. The next man in line tossed a flashbang grenade into the apartment. It exploded with a bright flash and a loud but muffled "clap" sound. The four initial entry members yelled "Police!" and burst into the apartment, followed by the two members carrying the shotguns.

~~~~

After the team entered, they started screaming, "Seattle Police!" and "Raise Your Hands!" over and over for several seconds. Then, there was complete silence. During this time, I considered a few possible outcomes. Although I hadn't heard anything since they blew the door locks, there was still a good possibility of gunshots. I remember registering this thought. Just as likely—maybe more so—was the possibility that they'd catch Eddie sound asleep and be on him before he was fully awake. I remember thinking of this, too. The reality, I believe, was that only fifteen seconds or so passed after the team entered before we heard the radio come to life. "Clear!" followed by "Kitchen clear!" A moment later we heard "Bedroom clear!" then "Bath clear!" Then silence. Another minute passed. What was happening?

"You hear any shots?" Dwayne asked.

"Nothing," Radovich answered.

"I didn't hear anything either," Toni said.

"There were no shots," Radovich said. "They're finishing up securing the apartment now." "Hopefully, they're putting Eddie in cuffs," Gus said.

Finally, two long minutes later, the Entry Team Commander appeared in the doorway and yelled to Radovich, "We're Code 4, Captain!" He beckoned us over. It was eight twenty-seven. A total of four minutes had elapsed since Radovich had given the word to go.

~~~~

"Come on," Radovich said to us. We popped up and jogged to the front door. When we got there, the Entry Team Commander said, "It's all secure, boss. Have a look for yourselves. Careful what you touch."

We entered the apartment through the living room. The air smelled heavily of cordite and was still smoky from the flashbang. Except for SWAT members and us, no one was there. In fact, the room was completely empty apart from a worn sofa, a Sony flat-screen TV sitting on a box, and a table that held an ashtray and a couple of empty beer bottles.

I glanced at the kitchen, where a radio on the table was blaring a

Spanish song—apparently the source of the singing Alley One had heard. A chair was missing from the dining room set. "Let's go ahead and turn that thing down so we can hear ourselves think," Dwayne said, thinking the same thing I was. One of the SWAT team members in the kitchen unplugged the radio, and the room fell silent.

Another SWAT member was standing in the doorway to the apartment's sole bedroom. "In here," he said, gesturing with his head. I walked over and looked in. Eddie Salazar sat in the missing kitchen chair facing the bedroom doorway. He was quite dead. A single bullet hole was centered in his forehead, right between his eyes. His arms were duct-taped tightly to the arms of the chair. He'd been executed. His eyes were wide open, as if shocked to see what was coming. His mouth was open and his head was thrown backward. The back of his head was basically gone. Blood, bone, and brain matter were spattered all over the wall behind him. I've seen more dead bodies than anyone should have to ever see. Still, it had been awhile. I felt a cold sweat come on. I suppressed a gag. I was stunned.

"Guess he pissed somebody off," the SWAT officer said.

I nodded—best I could do for the moment. Toni pushed me aside and looked for herself.

"Jesus Christ," she said, equally shocked.

"There's another one in the bathroom, too," the SWAT officer said. "The girl—dark hair."

I spun around and looked quickly at him as the blood drained from my face. Oh, no, I said to myself. I felt my feet move to the bathroom door. I looked inside and saw the body of a woman next to the tub, face down and turned away from the door.

"Is it Gina?" Toni asked from behind me, trying to hide the terror in her voice.

"I can't tell," I said. I moved closer and tried to get a look at the face of the young woman who'd also obviously been shot in the head, probably with a large-caliber handgun, judging from the severe damage. Was it Gina? Was it the person I'd known for more than ten years? I honestly couldn't tell. The blood and the gore and the damage from the gunshot wound made identification tough. Then I noticed the tattoo on her wrist. A butterfly.

"Oh my God," I said quietly.

"What?" Toni asked impatiently, pushing past me so she could see. "What is it?"

"It's Miss Mariposa," I answered. "Rita. Rita, from Ramon's Cantina. She's dead, and so is Eddie Salazar. It's not Gina."

PART 2

# Chapter 15

BY TEN THIRTY, the King County coroners had removed the bodies. The CSI team was inside documenting the scene while SPD homicide detectives finished interviewing the neighbors. None of the neighbors had heard anything last night except the same loud music we'd heard when we entered. Gunshots would have been a lot louder than that, and probably would have been noticed, meaning that most likely, the killer or killers had used handguns with suppressors. When combined with the loud music left playing on the radio, the sound of the gunshots would have been effectively masked.

The ME also told Dwayne that preliminarily, based on the condition of the bodies, the most probable time of death was somewhere between nine and midnight the previous day for both victims. Neither showed any signs of struggle, nor did there appear to be signs of struggle in the apartment itself. From the looks of it, the two of them allowed someone to enter and that person, or more likely, persons, subdued both of them, presumably at gunpoint. Eddie was taped to the chair, and then both were shot.

There were no other clues. No shell casings, no prints, nothing at all left behind—a real mystery.

"This is a pretty interesting turn of events—not at all what I expected," Dwayne said. "What do you say we take the rest of the day and reflect on what's happened? Gus and I are going to be busy here and then in the office for a while. This will give us a chance to contemplate what the hell happened here and why."

"Okay," I said. My mind was spinning, and I needed time to think. I offered to walk back, but he insisted on having a uniformed officer drive us to the Community Center to pick up my Jeep.

"Why don't you plan on coming by the office tomorrow morning?" he asked.

"We can't meet in the morning," Gus said. "We've got court."

"Oh shit, that's right," Dwayne said. He thought for a second, then said, "Do you know where Marinepolis is?"

"The sushi joint?" I asked.

"Yeah," he said. "Gus is on a sushi kick. He's even got me liking this crab-and-avocado thing."

"Isn't it on Fifth Ave and Valley?"

"That's the place," he said. "How about tomorrow for lunch at twelve thirty?"

"We'll be there," I said. I shook my head. "Based on all this, I have to say I've got way more questions than answers. I think I'm going to go home where it's quiet and try to figure out what the hell is going on here."

"Good idea. Call me if you come up with something brilliant," he said.

~~~~

Driving back to the office, my mind raced, unable to find a direction, unable to land on a rational explanation of today's discovery. I guess Toni was doing the same, because she didn't have anything to say either. Except for the traffic noise, it was silent in the Jeep the whole way back. We got to the office at twelve thirty, and I said good-bye in the parking lot. I didn't even want to go in.

I swung down Northlake, turned and went up the hill to my apartment. I changed into gym shorts and a T-shirt, poured a Mac & Jack's African Amber, turned on Diana Krall and went outside on the balcony, where I plopped into a lounge chair. Took less than two minutes from the time I hit the front door.

I had my last physical about a year ago. When I asked my doc about feeling fatigued more than I thought I should, she said I was fine, physiologically speaking, but that I was likely reacting to an excess amount of stress. I can't really exercise anymore than I already do since I like to run five to ten miles every morning as it is. But she told me to get to bed earlier, eat healthier, and take a nap in the afternoon. I decided to charge this afternoon off to complying with her instructions. Disregard the brew.

Son of a bitch! My main theory—my main plan—was blown! Don't get me wrong, I was delighted to see a douche bag like Eddie Salazar get his comeuppance, but I'd sure have liked the opportunity to talk to him and figure out where in the name of God Gina was. Where did this little turn of events leave her? Had he known anything about her present whereabouts? If he had, we sure weren't going to find out now.

Martinez said she was doing the angel dance, which I guess means she's dead. But I didn't know that. I didn't trust that fat asshole any further than I could toss him. All of his type lie, cheat, steal, and say anything they think will help them manipulate people to their own ends. I wasn't worried about Martinez trying to make good on his threat. But none of that helped me now when I needed to figure out what had happened to Gina. Where was she? How was I going to find her? Now that I didn't have Eddie Salazar to squeeze, I was back to square one.

I mulled these thoughts over and over as I basked in the warm sun and subconsciously watched the boats out on Lake Union. Two beers later, and I was done. The doc was right. Stress leads to fatigue, and fatigue leads to sleep. A snooze in the afternoon was something I never did. Not until today, anyway.

~~~~

In my dream, I was running. I was competing in a high school track meet I suppose, but it wasn't totally clear. Gina was in the stands cheering for me. Rita ran by my side, glaring at me. She wore a yellow T-shirt with a butterfly print. A lone runner wearing red shorts was in front of us, on the distant blue horizon, impossibly far away. Still, we were on him in an instant. We blew past, but as we did, bullets whizzed by us, and I felt my army Kevlar helmet bouncing on my head, my tac vest buckles jingling, my boots heavy on my feet. I was back in Iraq. Artillery shells boomed all around me. Boom! Boom! Boom! The noise was deafening. Gina was there again, standing on a wall in front of me, urging me on. I was confused. She shouldn't be there. I stirred and began to drift back into reality. The shelling didn't stop. Boom! Boom! Boom! Gradually, the dream-haze lifted enough for me to realize that the boom-boom-boom was not artillery shells after all. Someone was pounding on my front door. Regaining consciousness, I got up and rubbed my eyes as I went to see who it was.

Toni. She was not happy.

"Jesus, Logan," she said, walking in past me as I held the door with one hand and rubbed my eyes with the other. "I was worried shitless about you. I called here—no answer. I called your cell—no answer. I thought Martinez had sent his buddies over here to take you out."

"Come in," I said to the doorway she'd just walked through. I rubbed my eyes and yawned. "I'm alive. I fell asleep on the patio."

She looked at me, and I saw by the flames shooting from her eyes that she was really pissed. I was in trouble.

"You. Are. Alive?" she asked, saying each word slowly and deliberately. "That's what you have to say? You are alive? Oh, great. I'm so glad to hear it." She noticed my empty beer mug on the table. "You'll be just tickled to death, then, to know that while you were over here sleeping and drowning your sorrows away, I was in the office explaining what happened to the other people who work for you—people who are working their asses off on this case. I was the one telling them not to worry, not to give up. Telling them to have faith—telling them we are still going to find Gina."

She looked at me and said sarcastically, "But I'm glad you're alive."

"Give me a break, Blair," I said, walking back out to the patio. "I took one goddamned afternoon off."

"Not just any afternoon, Danny boy," she said as she followed me. Danny boy? She was really pissed. "You took off on an afternoon when you were needed. You should have come inside, reassured everyone, and then, if you felt the need, you could have taken off and gotten as piss-drunk as you liked."

"I didn't get drunk. I had two beers, for Christ's sake."

She glared at me. I avoided this by turning and staring outside and not speaking for a minute. Then I said, "You're right. I should have stopped in. I apologize. I'll apologize to the guys tomorrow."

"You'd better," she said, still worked up. "I was worried about you, you dickhead."

I looked at her for a moment. "You can't call your boss a dickhead,"

I said.

"Fuck you, then," she answered.

"Oh good, that's better." I smiled at her. She tried to remain stone-faced, but a few seconds later she cracked and smiled.

"I'm sorry," I said.

"Good. You should be. Don't wienie out like that again. We need you."

I nodded.

"We haven't had a real setback in a case like this before. I didn't stop to consider the impact it might have on the other guys. I screwed up."

She stared at me for a few seconds, studying, analyzing. Then she said, "It's okay. But we needed you today." She paused, then said, "I needed you."

"I'm sorry," I said again. Talk about feeling like a shit-heel.

"Enough," she said, "we're moving on."

Although she'd worked for me for three years, Toni had never been to my apartment before. She looked out over Lake Union and watched a Kenmore plane take off. "Nice view," she said. "Do you mind if I grab one of those beers?"

"Help yourself. The kitchen's right over there."

"You want another one?"

"Pass," I said. "I hit my limit earlier. Bring me a bottled water, will you?"

A minute later, she joined me on the patio and sat in the other lounge chair. "Any revelations come to you while you were dreaming away the afternoon?" she asked.

I told her about my dream. "I don't know what to make of it," I said. "My dreams are usually so strange that it's impossible to make sense of them."

"The ancient Chinese said that dreams are expressions of your inner desires," she said. "You must have some inner desires concerning Gina."

"She was in it, for sure, but I don't think it was about her. I haven't seen her in years," I said. "Hard to imagine that old baggage still floating around. Anyway, the dream was one of those where you find yourself running—kind of in a fog. You know, images floating past."

She took a shot from her beer, and studied me for a few seconds.

"Just because it might not seem like she was the star character in your dream doesn't mean you weren't dreaming about her. Consider that."

I thought about that for a second. "I suppose," I said. "Getting a little deep for me there, Ms. Blair."

She smiled at me. It was silent for a minute, the only sound coming from the continuous comings and goings of the Kenmore seaplanes.

"Anyway, I think she'll be home today or tomorrow," Toni said. "As soon as the press cycle runs through announcing Eddie's death. And as soon as she can confirm it."

"You think she was hiding from him?" I asked.

"Yep. Eddie's dead, death threat cancelled—time to come home."

"Unless he got to her first and killed her. In which case, she won't be coming home," I added.

"Odds are on her side," Toni said. "If she feels the threat to her is gone, she comes in, all by herself."

That would be alright with me. I'm sure it would work for her family, as well.

Toni suddenly hopped up from her chair.

"What?" I asked.

"All this heavy detective work is making me hungry. You got anything to eat here? I'll fix it."

~~~~

Toni found two steaks in the freezer. She thawed them in the microwave—something I've not mastered—and grilled them for me on the balcony as we watched the late afternoon sailboat races on the lake. We listened to music—mostly Soundgarden, watched the boats, and talked about things other than Gina Fiore or Eddie Salazar. It was nice. She discovered my emergency bottle of Opus, and we polished it off as well. Altogether, a very fine and relaxing evening. For a while, I was able to forget the fact that our case was blown. All too soon, though, it began to get dark, and Toni left. I felt somewhat more optimistic after her pep talk and her version of how things stood. The logic was sound. It made sense. Yet I still tossed and turned all night long.

~~~~

I like fish, but I'm not a big fan of sushi. I tried a piece of sashimi once when my unit was laid over in Hawaii. It looked a little suspect, and I wasn't sure I was going to like it, but I wanted to try and see what everyone was raving about. I'd no sooner put it in my mouth than I almost ralphed on the table in front of the whole friggin' group. Something about the texture, the gooey red flesh. It was all I could do to keep that bad boy from coming back up! My buddies laughed their asses off, but I was forever and permanently cured of eating raw fish. If I'm ever stranded on a desert island with plenty of fish, but no fire to cook them with, I'll starve.

That said, I can stomach some of the cooked stuff. I have to carefully inspect each piece to make sure it's not raw, and the overall process slows me down enough to where I feel full quickly. I don't eat much at a sushi joint. I'll take a hot dog or a pizza any day. But Gus wanted sushi, and here we were.

We actually got to the restaurant a few minutes early. Toni chose this particular day to wear "The Outfit"—black leather pants, black boots, and black leather vest with a little light blue V-neck sleeveless T-shirt underneath. Her dark hair was brushed down straight. She wore blue eye makeup and dark red lipstick. I'd seen The Outfit before; I'd had a chance to study its effect and slowly acclimate. This is a damn good thing because Toni could flat stop traffic with this getup. No shit, I've seen it happen. Unfortunately, poor Gus was caught completely by surprise—he never had a chance. He entered the restaurant, came around the corner, and saw Toni. She was returning from the restroom, walking slowly toward him, smiling. I'm sure that to Gus, it was like Bo Derek running toward Dudley Moore in "10." I thought we were going to lose the poor bastard right there on the floor of the sushi house. He literally stopped and almost stumbled backward. Dwayne caught him from behind and was cracking up by the time we met in front of our table.

"Ms. Blair," Dwayne said, laughing, "you do make quite an impression." He looked at Gus, who still had not quite recovered. "My partner here is speechless. This doesn't happen often."

"Thank you, kind sir," Toni answered with a southern lilt. She sat down, and we all followed.

"Sorry," Gus said, recovering. "Not used to that. Caught me by surprise there, darling."

"You flatter me, sir," Toni said to him. I'm not certain, but I think she batted her long dark eyelashes at him. I'd bet my Jeep that if she'd asked Gus to sign over his bank account and the deed to his house, he'd have stolen a pen at gunpoint if necessary to do so. I don't know if Toni did this because she thought it was fun or because she wanted to keep good relations between us and the SPD. Probably both, I suppose.

The sushi rolled past us in little dishes on a conveyer belt type of deal. We were free to take what we wanted. When we were done, the staff would tally up the damages. The three of them dug right in, but I was more selective, looking for items that were clearly cooked (preferably with grill marks).

"You all have a chance to consider what this little twist means for our case?" Dwayne asked, as he popped something long and stringy with tentacles into his mouth.

I shuddered, and then said, "Yeah, it means we're back to square friggin' one," I said.

"You okay?" he asked, looking at me. "You look like you swallowed a turd."

"I'm fine," I said, shaking my head. "I don't know how you can eat that shit."

He laughed. "Have you ever considered that if Gina Fiore was hiding from Salazar, and now she finds out he's dead, she'll probably come home on her own?" Dwayne said. "Our work here might be done."

"Yes, we've considered it, and we hope that's exactly what happens," I said. "Based on what we know, it's probably the most likely scenario. Trouble is, like Richard told me a couple of days ago, we don't know what we don't know. There could still be completely different forces at work here. As a matter of fact, the whole goddamned Eddie Salazar episode might have had nothing to do with Gina, for all we know. Might have been just a coincidence."

"One that ended badly for Mr. Salazar," Gus added.

"True. Here's to scumbags getting their proper comeuppance," Dwayne said, raising his water glass in a toast.

"Yeah. But how many times have you seen coincidences that end up being nothing more than a distraction?" I asked.

He nodded. "Plenty," he admitted. "What's your thinking? You got a new plan yet?"

"I've been working on it this morning," I said. "We assume she doesn't come back in on her own. We start back at the beginning with our ABCs, looking for tracks, cell phone records, bank accounts, credit cards—standard stuff."

"Her cell phone was in her condo," Gus said. "It won't help you."

"I know. If she left and is hiding, it's a little hard to imagine that she wouldn't contact anybody that she knows. We're going to look at the incoming side. We're going to examine the phone records of some people close to her and see if any calls started coming in, starting last Friday or so, that look out of the ordinary. If she's making calls to them, then we'll see a pattern, even though we might not be able to ID the phone number."

Dwayne had been raising another piece of that octopus-looking crap to his mouth. He froze halfway. He looked at me and raised his eyebrows. "How the hell you going to do that? How are you getting into people's phone records?" he asked.

"Better you don't know," I said. "Suffice it to say that we won't be using the information we gather as courtroom evidence. We're just looking for tracks."

"That's a long shot," he said. "That would mean someone's not being truthful with us."

"That's right," I said. "But it will also eliminate people from suspicion as well."

Dwayne thought for a second, then said, "Well, let's hope she comes home of her own accord." He returned to his lunch.

"Agreed."

After we finished lunch, Dwayne said, "Call us, and let me know what's going on. We're relying on you for the lead."

"Will do," I said.

"Oh," he said suddenly, "I just thought of something else. You may as well call Kara Giordano and tell her she can come home."

"We did that this morning," I said. "She was relieved."

"I'll bet."

~~~~

After the meeting, I went back to the office and apologized to the troops for flaking out the previous afternoon. Toni was right, team leader was one of my job responsibilities and though I didn't realize it at the time, I'd dropped the ball yesterday. I'd been deeply disappointed over the un-expected demise of Eddie Salazar, but that was no excuse. Everyone was disappointed. I screwed up.

But not today. I located Kenny and Doc and made amends.

"No problem, boss," Kenny said. "It was a big disappointment—Ed-die Salazar turning up dead. We understand you'd need some alone time. Besides, you work your ass off seven days a week. You're entitled to a little down time every now and again."

"Thanks for that," I said. "Still, I appreciate what you guys do, and I don't want to take advantage of your good nature."

They both seemed to appreciate my mea culpa, which is good be-cause I damn sure appreciate the work they do. I wouldn't want to have to try to replace either of them, especially because of a bone-headed screwup on my part.

I had Kenny start checking phone records of Gina's parents, of Rob-bie Fiore, of Reggie Campbell, and of Kara Giordano. I wanted him to look for any numbers that started popping up after last Friday that didn't show up before. If the numbers belonged to a prepaid cell phone, we wouldn't be able to track it. But at least we'd know something was up.

I checked with Joaquin to find out how he was coming with his reg-istered sex offenders.

"If I had a damn army of investigators, I could have checked out each of these sleazeballs in a couple of days. As it is, even if our whole team jumped on it, it would take a couple of months. I'm starting to think we should drop this, boss, and focus on areas where we're more likely to find her alive."

"I agree. I finally figured out the same thing this morning. Hope you're not pissed at me for having you spin your wheels on it," I said.

"No, hell no," he said. "We break out with all guns blazing. Later on, we dial it in and close the deal. That's where we are now. I'm cool."

"Good. I appreciate it."

I spent the rest of the afternoon going through notes, reviewing reports, looking for clues. Before I went home, I found Toni in her office.

"I want to thank you," I said.

"For what?"

"Thanks for kicking my butt last night and reminding me of my role. I shouldn't have needed that, but obviously I did. You were right."

"What are friends for?" she asked, smiling.

"I appreciate it. I needed it."

I looked at her and smiled. I turned to leave, but suddenly I remembered something. I looked back at her and said, "Oh, thanks for something else, too," I said.

"What?"

"Thanks for wearing that black leather outfit. It fuckin' rocks. Gus almost had a heart attack when he saw you, right there in the middle of the restaurant."

"You're welcome." She smiled slowly, then caught herself. "But you can't say that."

I was puzzled. "Why not?"

She stood up and walked around her desk toward me. "Geez," she said, "do I have to teach you everything about being a boss?" She stood in front of me and smiled. "You can't say that, you dope," she paused and poked me in the chest, "because I, as a humble employee, might be inclined to think that your comments were a form of sexual harassment. Then I'd have to sue." She winked at me and said, "You'd better get out of here before I file a complaint."

~~~~

That night I went to bed early. Despite our setback, I felt good, somewhat rejuvenated. I was ready to reengage. If Gina didn't come home on her own, I was ready to get down to some real detective work and find her.

I fell asleep easily, but then I started tossing and turning. I dreamed again. In my dream there were angels—dancing angels.

# Chapter 16

MY APARTMENT DOESN'T have air conditioning. Usually, that's alright, because most years, there are only a few days when you actually might need it. Unfortunately, yesterday was one of them, and last night I paid the price. I sweated, tossed and turned, and dreamed about everything—including Gina—all night long until, fed up with it, I finally just got up at 0400 and jumped on the Internet. I hadn't really had a chance to catch up on things for a couple of weeks, and I was eager to see what was happening in the world.

Turns out that missing two weeks of the news cycle doesn't really seem to matter very much these days. Same issues: economy sucks, home prices are down, foreclosures are up, it's nobody's fault, it's everybody's fault, Mariner's are in the cellar. Like the old saying goes: same shit, different day.

I did see one interesting story, though. The Local Section of the *Seattle Times* carried a front-page story of how a prominent suspect in the Gina Fiore disappearance case had been found murdered. They'd managed to sneak in a photographer and grab a photo of two guys from the county coroner's office wheeling one of the covered-up bodies out the front door of the apartment, complete with yellow crime-scene tape providing a backdrop. If Gina had run off because she was hiding from Eddie Salazar, then she would probably know by now that the coast was clear. She could come home now.

Yet, so far, at 7:00 a.m. on Friday, August 26, she hadn't.

~~~~

Despite my lack of sleep, I felt pretty good, and I was eager to get to work. I didn't anticipate seeing anyone official today so, given the weather, I chose my standard summer "casual day" uniform: wrinkled shorts, Hawaiian shirt, and tennis shoes. If I wasn't working, I'd wear sandals, but you can't run in the damn things. Even though I didn't expect to do any running on this particular day, I wore running shoes anytime I was on the job. You never know. It's the same reason I nearly always carry a gun in my waistband underneath said Hawaiian shirt. It was safely tucked into its Bianchi holster, even though I didn't anticipate having to shoot anyone today, either.

Thus prepared, I arrived at the office at ten minutes before eight. Richard was back in town, and we had a 9:00 a.m. staff meeting scheduled. I needed to go over my notes and look at the jobs I'd assigned everyone to. Toni arrived five minutes after I did and stuck her head in my office to say good morning. She wore blue jeans and a white sleeveless blouse with a wide collar that nicely showed off her tats. "Morning, boss," she said, smiling brightly.

"Good morning."

"Any brilliant ideas come to you last night after you left?"

"Nothing I'd call brilliant," I said. "We need to huddle up and make sure that we're all on the same page with regard to transitioning to a single premise—that Gina's hiding from something or someone we have yet to identify."

She nodded. "Good," she said enthusiastically. "Let's do it. I have some ideas I'll bring up in the meeting."

"Good."

At that moment, my cell phone rang. Caller ID: Dwayne. I held up my hand for her to wait around.

I pressed the button and answered the phone. "Good morning."

"Good morning to you," he replied. "Got some new information. Wonder if you and Toni might not mind dropping by."

"When?"

"Nine o'clock sharp. I've got some people coming by to talk to us about some recent developments."

"Okay." Damn. Scratch one staff meeting. "Any hints?"

"Can't," he said. "Just come on in."

"Great," I answered. "We'll be there." I hung up.

"We're going to see Dwayne?" Toni asked.

"Yep," I answered. "Do me a favor. Tell the other guys and see if we can push our meeting until after lunch."

~~~~

Forty minutes later, we pulled into the parking lot located beneath the Justice Building, compliments of the pass Gus had given us. We pulled right into an unassigned space next to a row of police cruisers. No hunting for spaces. No driving around. *Sweet.*

We took the elevator to the eighth floor where Dwayne and Gus greeted us in the lobby.

"We're going back down to six," Dwayne said. "Homicide."

This caused my heart to skip a beat, and Dwayne must have seen the sudden look of concern in my eyes.

He laughed and said, "Relax. It's not Gina. Just a clue. Let's go."

On the sixth floor, Detective Ron Bergstrom of the SPD homicide unit met us. He led us back to a conference room and closed the door. Dwayne made the introductions, and we took our seats.

Bergstrom was a stocky guy, probably five feet, ten inches or so, maybe 210 pounds. His hair was brown, going to gray and was clipped in a short, military-style crew cut. He wore a brown suit over a blue dress shirt. He shook my hand with his beefy paw using a grip that could have extracted oil from a hazelnut. I was tempted to check my hand for damage, but I caught myself—it probably would have been poor form.

"Lieutenant Brown's told me that SPD is working with you guys on the Fiore case," he said, as he moved to take a seat.

"Correct," I said.

"Okay then." He turned to Dwayne. "Dwayne, I assume that means you're clearing them for sensitive information?"

"Yes," Dwayne said, "already done. All of the members of Danny's team are licensed PIs. All of them have signed our confidentiality agreement. These guys are good—they're helping us a lot."

"Good," Bergstrom said. "Last week we provided information to Dwayne about the potential of a serial killer operating in the area. Our cold-case team almost accidentally discovered a pattern in the murders of four young women over the past five years. The most obvious component of the pattern is that each of the four young women had been mutilated in the same fashion: they'd each had a finger clipped off after they were murdered. The killer is apparently collecting them for some sick reason. You'd think that we'd have noticed this as a pattern before now, but we get twenty to thirty new murders per year in addition to the three hundred or so that are in the cold-case files. That, coupled with the apparent fact that this guy only kills one woman per year, makes it pure luck that we noticed the pattern at all. We've not released this information to the press because we need to be able to sort the real information from the bogus crap. And we don't want homicide victims to start popping up all over the city with their fingers cut off. That's why privacy and confidentially are so important here. Understood?"

Both Toni and I nodded.

"Good," he continued. "Now, to get down to it, last week I told Lieutenant Brown that there were four victims found in the last five years— one each August except this year."

He paused and looked at us. "There's been a change in that information," he said. "Yesterday morning, a fifth victim was found. The body of a young woman was discovered in a grove of trees just off the 520 across Lake Washington. The woman's left thumb had been clipped off after she was murdered." He paused, and then continued, "We were able to positively identify the victim yesterday afternoon. We have not released her name yet, pending notification of next of kin, but I can tell you here with 100 percent certainty that the body is not that of Gina Fiore."

Although Dwayne had said the victim wasn't Gina, I still found that I'd been holding my breath for most of that monologue anyway. I slowly released it now.

"Thank you for that information," I said. "I'm sorry to hear of the death of this woman, but I have to say I'm relieved that it's not Gina Fiore."

"That's understandable," Bergstrom said.

"Would you think that means we can eliminate this psycho from our list?" Toni asked.

"This is one of the strangest serial killer cases I've ever heard of,"

Bergstrom said. "Usually when these guys flip out and start murdering people, they seem to have such a lust for it that they can't stop. Look at Ridgway—he killed something like forty people in two years. Look at that sick bastard Richard Ramírez down in California—he killed twenty-five or so in just three months. He'd kill three or four in the same goddamned day, for Christ's sake. And then you've got our guy who seems satisfied so far to kill just one poor girl a year. Just like clockwork, but, fortunately, just one per year. That sort of control is very unusual for these nut jobs."

"I guess, at least, that's something to be thankful about," Dwayne said.

"Yeah, I suppose," Bergstrom said. "The pattern for these serial killers is that their killing spree usually gets more and more intense."

"But Ridgway managed to keep it going eighteen years," Toni said. "The story is that he went dark between '84 and '98. That, in itself, is pretty inexplicable compared to the norm—that a serial killer could start, then stop, then start again. I guess it just means that it's hard, maybe impossible, to generalize the behavior of psychotic individuals. The standard deviation of the behavior pattern of the group is so high as to almost render the predictions of the actions of a single individual moot."

"Standard deviation?" I asked. "You remember that from college?"

"Yeah," Gus said. "And what's a moot?" We laughed.

Bergstrom chuckled, and then he answered Toni. "Ignore these statistical ignoramuses," he said, indicating Gus and me. "I think you're probably right. As part of my job, I've tried to understand what makes these guys tick. I think that you can generalize a couple of things—they have no remorse—they're going to do what makes them happy at the moment—and they look at everyone and everything around them as being disposable and there for their own use. But when you try to overlay that model across their actual day-to-day reality, things become fuzzy. The outcome can look almost random, because while we may agree on a behavior model, we don't know how an individual psychotic person interprets and applies this behavior model to his immediate surroundings."

"So," I said, "I appreciate the theory. But do you think we can eliminate him?"

"Probably," Bergstrom answered. "There's a reasonable probability—better than fifty-fifty I'd say, that based on his previous history, he's sated himself this year and won't feel the urge to kill number six until next year."

"Unless he changes agendas," Toni said.

"Right. In the real world, as we've pointed out, it's hard to predict the actions of a psycho."

We thanked Bergstrom and left his office, thinking we were done.

As we waited for the elevator, Dwayne checked his watch. "Perfect. We've got one more stop," he said. "Follow me."

~~~~

We went back up the elevator to the eighth floor. Instead of turning left off the elevator and proceeding toward Dwayne's office, we turned right. Halfway down the corridor, we entered a room with no title on the door. Inside, the large room was empty except for rows of file cabinets on the outside and empty bull pen–type cubicles in the center.

"Come on back," Dwayne said. We followed him. There was a doorway at the back of the bull pen area. Dwayne knocked and said, "Cal? We're here."

A voice from inside the office called, "Come in."

We entered and found ourselves in a large office on the east side of the building. Bright sunlight streamed through the windows in front of us. Four desks, separated by partitions, were located across from the window wall. Two men and a woman were seated at a large conference table that was located near the windows. Both men were sharply dressed in dark gray business suits. The woman was dressed in a dark blue pantsuit. With my shorts and faded Hawaiian shirt, I felt like a nudist at a fashion show.

They stood as we entered.

"Good morning," Dwayne said.

"Hi, Dwayne," one of the men said as he approached us.

"Danny Logan and Toni Blair of the Logan agency, meet Calvin Tompkins of Seattle PD's Special Investigations section."

Calvin Tompkins was at least six five and probably weighed two-fifty. He was well known in Washington for his play as middle linebacker for the Huskies.

"I watched you play at U-Dub," I said. "I think you graduated when I was still a sophomore."

"Class of '05," he said with a smile. His hand swallowed mine when we shook, but he didn't have the bone-crunching grip that Bergstrom applied earlier.

"Zero eight for me and for my partner here as well, Antoinette Blair," I said.

"Pleased to meet you," Tompkins said, smiling at Toni. "I love your tattoos."

"Thanks," Toni said, fairly beaming. I think she may have batted her eyes, but I'm not sure.

"Allow me to introduce these folks," he said, turning to the others. "This is Marcus Richards and Jennifer Thomas, special agents for the FBI."

Richards was trim, average height, and had short dark hair plastered tightly to his head. Not particularly noticeable or memorable. Jennifer Thomas, on the other hand, made an impression. Blonde hair, a little past shoulder length. Blue eyes. Nobody I saw at Quantico when I was there looked like her. She looked like a cable news anchor. Hard to believe she was a federal agent.

"Mr. Logan," she said, shaking my hand. "Pleased to meet you. When we were told we were going to meet civilian detectives at the police department, I was initially skeptical, so I did a little background checking. I see you spent some time at the FBI Academy?"

"I did," I said. "I went through advanced training in Quantico the first part of 2006 while I was with Army CID."

"And then later you got your degree while you were still in the army. When you got out, you opened Logan Private Investigations. Sounds like you had it all planned out."

I nodded. "Pretty much," I said.

"How's it working out for you?"

I smiled. "Living the dream," I said, holding up my Hawaiian shirt.

She had a beautiful smile when she laughed.

I never know what to make of women when they do this. Was she just making polite small talk? Probably. Was she flirting with me and providing me the keys to some sort of secret opening that I was supposed to recognize and take advantage of? Possible, I suppose, but probably not. If there was some sort of opening for me, it was too subtle for me to recognize. Was she trying to make her partner annoyed for some reason, maybe make him jealous? Could be. He looked annoyed, but maybe he was just a tightass and was always annoyed. Was she trying to make Toni annoyed or jealous—some sort of female competition thing? Maybe, although Toni wore a quizzical look that made her appear more amused than annoyed.

My point is, I have this suspicion that women have agendas when they're making small talk like this, but it's beyond my ability to figure it out. So I just take it as it comes and try not to overthink it. This may explain why I'm twenty-nine and single. But I digress. We took our seats at the conference table.

"Would you dim the lights?" Agent Thomas said to Cal. He did. She clicked a mouse on the conference table and a projection screen dropped down from the ceiling. Another click and a picture of a middle-aged man appeared on the screen.

"The reason for our meeting here this morning is because apparently Lieutenant Brown approached Detective Tompkins about the concern that the Calabria crime family out of Chicago may have some interest or involvement in the disappearance case of Ms. Gina Fiore, who is related to, albeit a cousin removed from, the Calabrias."

She flipped open a steno pad with notes and referred to it. "Here's what we have," she said. "Detective Tompkins contacted our Seattle Field Office August 17. We contacted our Chicago Field Office the same day and asked them to keep an eye on any unusual comings and goings of the known senior members or the Calabria family. They had nothing to report until yesterday, when they alerted us that this man, Mr. Francesco Rossi, aka Frank Rossi, aka Frankie the Boot, left Chicago on Northwest Airlines Flight 784 bound for Seattle. Mr. Rossi is a first cousin of the Calabrias."

I studied the photo. It showed a big guy, probably in his sixties. He was tall, perhaps six two or so judging by the way he filled the doorway in the photo. He had a full head of silver hair. The most noticeable features were the intense dark eyes and bushy eyebrows. The eyes looked like they could bore through granite like a laser.

Agent Thomas continued. "As soon as Chicago was able to identify his destination, they called us. We were able to get an agent to the airport here, and he took the picture you see in front of you as Mr. Rossi arrived at Sea-Tac at 4:15 yesterday afternoon."

"This is pretty interesting," I said. "Do you have any idea why this guy would suddenly decide to show up in Seattle?"

"Sorry," she said. "Not a clue."

"Do you know where he went after he landed here? Where he is now?"

"We didn't have authorization to commit the necessary assets to conduct a proper surveillance operation, which would have included a tail," she said. "Our agent at the airport did manage to follow Mr. Rossi long enough to confirm that he rented a car from the Hertz counter. Presumably, he picked it up at the airport lot."

Interesting. One of Gina's Chicago mob relatives suddenly just shows up in Seattle?

"What's his background?" I asked. "Frankie the Boot?"

"Mr. Rossi was—perhaps still is—an enforcer for the Calabria family. We're not certain. Plainly speaking, he's a hit man. He earned his nickname as a young man in the organization when one of his early victims suddenly came back to life after being shot by Mr. Rossi. A group of Calabria made men were standing around the victim, apparently about to celebrate his demise, when the victim decided that he no longer wanted to be the center of attention. Gunshot wound and all, he tried to get up. Mr. Rossi apparently became first embarrased, then enraged so he proceeded to kick the victim back down. Then he stomped the poor man in the head with his boots until he literally crushed the guy's skull. In the twisted world of the Chicago mob, this apparently made Mr. Rossi quite popular. He was labeled 'Frankie the Boot' and his ruthless actions here and later in his career paved the way for his eventual rise to a very high, very trusted position in the organization. We haven't had him on our radar for a while, but who knows? Maybe Frankie the Boot's back in business."

"This just keeps getting curiouser and curiouser," Gus said.

"Got that right," I agreed.

# Chapter 17

AT A QUARTER to one, I was in the copy room of our office printing agendas for the staff meeting. I'd already prepared an agenda for what was to have been the meeting this morning. Now, four hours later, much of the information used to create that agenda was obsolete. So I restarted from scratch. I'd just finished typing a new one, and I absentmindedly fed the sheets through the copy machine.

Kenny and Doc were in Kenny's office next door to the copy room talking about girls—Kenny's favorite subject. Kenny's proud of the fact that he is a bona fide geek. He's twenty-five years old, and he looks like he's going on seventeen. He probably never got laid once in high school, and he's working hard to make up for it now. The guy has amazing luck with some surprisingly good-looking women, although most of them are quite young. He's bold, fearless, and obviously armed with an amazing intellect. He's also armed with a pretty good-sized wallet, more a result of his side jobs for the IT giants than for the relatively small amount I'm able to pay him. I'm sure this doesn't hurt the dating situation.

Doc's the complete opposite. He is the epitome of the strong silent type. And he's completely monogamous. In fact, I've only seen him with one woman, ever. While we were both at Fort Lewis, he introduced me to a dark-haired PFC he called Dot. He was completely ape-shit over her. Dot—her real name was Dahteste Belacho, was a very pretty young army private who was born on the Mescalero Reservation in New Mexico—the same reservation where Doc was born. I suppose it was natural for the two of them to hook up. I knew Doc reasonably well then. I saw them often, in fact, I never saw the two of them apart for the next few months. Dot and Doc—he was as happy and content as any man I'd ever seen, as happy as a man could wish to be. Until one morning he called my apartment early, nearly incoherent.

"What's wrong?" I asked, alarmed.

"She's gone," he said, weeping.

"What do you mean?"

"She's gone. The MPs just came by. She went out running this morning like she always does, and she got hit by a car. She's gone, Danny."

I rushed over and took Doc to the hospital. The doctor met us and told us Dot had died almost instantly at the scene of the accident.

Doc transformed almost instantly right before my eyes—I never saw anything like it. He changed from nearly inconsolably grief-stricken one instant to completely blank—emotionless—the next. One moment, he was crying, barely able to walk. The next, there were no tears, was no waver in his voice, and he had ramrod-straight posture. It was like his mind flipped a switch, and he completely sucked in his external grief. I knew him by then, and I knew the grief wasn't gone, it was just hidden away from the public. But it was still there.

I was able to arrange it, so I went with Doc back to New Mexico. We buried his woman on the sacred ground of his people. I think a part of Doc died with her, and I've never seen him with another woman since.

Four years later, I think Doc's kind of recovered. He still doesn't date, but I think he's happy. He seems to enjoy talking to Mr. Swordsman—Kenny. It seems to amuse him and, I imagine, it's somehow good for him.

"Did you see that black leather shit she wore yesterday?" I overheard Kenny ask.

"Yeah."

"I couldn't get up from my desk, if you know what I mean."

Doc chuckled.

"All I got to say is that it's too fucking bad she plays for the other team."

"What do you mean?" Doc asked.

"You know, she swings from the other side of the plate. She likes the ladies."

"Bullshit," Doc answered.

"It's true," Kenny said, "I swear it."

"You're full of shit. How do you know?"

"You ever see her with a guy?"

"That's bullshit," Doc said. "You ever see me with a girl?"

"No," Kenny answered. "I've never seen you with anybody."

"You go around telling people I swing from the other side?"

"Course not."

"Good thing. I'll cut your *huevos* off and feed them to the buzzards if you do."

"You don't dress up in black leather."

"What the hell does that mean? She looks good in black leather, you idiot. She's making an impression."

"I know. That's what I'm saying, you know."

"You don't know shit, numbnuts. You should be so lucky to end up with a woman like that. All those fucking teenaged *chiquitas* you hang with."

"Look, I know I'll never be so lucky as to end up with someone like her."

"Damn right. You stop talkin' shit."

"I wasn't talking shit," Kenny objected. "I was just talking to you. My friend. Private conversation."

"Just remember, *pipucho*," Doc said. "I like her more than I like you."

Just then, I heard Toni walk past Kenny's door. "My office is right next door," she said. "I can hear every word you're saying, you little fucker. I heard you talking shit about me. Get your ass in the conference room. It's time for the meeting."

"I wasn't," Kenny said quickly. "I was saying how nice you looked in black leather."

"Bullshit, I heard you. You're busted. You better hope you bleed out fast when Doc cuts your nuts off because when he's done, then it's my turn."

She walked toward the conference room and without slowing down, turned and looked at me, smiled, and winked as she passed by.

~~~~

"So am I to understand that we're now officially focusing solely on a voluntary disappearance scenario?" Richard asked. We were in the conference room, and I'd just brought everyone up to speed on the events of the last week or so.

"That's right," I answered. "By now, Gina's either dead or she's choosing not to come out of hiding for some reason. Otherwise, she probably would have showed up already. If she's dead, we can't help her. If she's hiding, our job now is to figure out where and why she's hiding. We need to figure out her motive."

"Indeed," Richard said. "Why would a twenty-seven-year-old woman, daughter of a successful businessman, holder of a very nice job, suddenly up and disappear?"

"Good question," I said. "Let's throw some ideas out and brainstorm a little. So that we don't fixate, I think it's important that we consider scenarios related to Eddie Salazar, and also scenarios unrelated to him. Let's recap the facts first."

I got up and moved to the whiteboard.

"Fact one," I said, "she's been missing for two weeks—since the twelfth."

"Fact two," I continued, "She comes from a good family and had a good job."

"Objection," Toni said. "We *think* she came from a good family, we don't know the inner dynamics. And even though her job looks good from where we sit, we don't really have any idea how she felt about it."

"Good point," I admitted. "I'll use green for facts, and I'll write the questionable stuff in red. We'll call this category 'observations' instead of facts. Observations, by nature, are subject to interpretation and, as such, we can get them wrong. Agreed?"

"Agreed," Toni answered, nodding.

"Fact," Doc said. "She hung out with Eddie Salazar." I wrote it in green.

"Fact," Kenny said. "She hung out at Ramon's Cantina, a nasty little place." I wrote this down as well.

"Fact," Doc said. "Eddie Salazar's toast." Couldn't argue with this—

wrote it in green.

"Fact," Kenny said. "Her family is connected to the Chicago mob. And another fact, a senior member of the mob is in Seattle." I wrote these down in green.

"I got one," Toni said. "Fact. Her personality is domineering, controlling, and manipulative. She's extremely intelligent and a very clear thinker." She looked at me as I considered what she'd said. "Use whatever color you like," she added.

"Several people have said those things about her," I acknowledged. "My own experience seems to back that up, at least somewhat. I'll use green." Toni smiled.

"I've got a couple, too, then," I said. "Fact. She's very attractive, she's got a magnetic personality, she's very easy to talk to, and she has a great body. Green, right?"

"Sounds like you're writing a personal ad for Craigslist," Toni said. "Chicks wanted."

"Write it in green," Richard agreed. "It's factual and helps round out the picture." I smiled. Toni stuck her tongue out at me.

"Okay," I said, after I wrote it all out on the whiteboard.

"Before we try to figure out scenarios that help us with Gina's motives, who killed Eddie Salazar and why?"

"One. Drug rip-off," Doc suggested. "Happens all the time."

"Two. Beef with his employer," Kenny said. "No severance packages in his line of work."

"Three," Richard said. "The girl, Rita, was married and her husband discovered them. He killed them both."

"Four. Gina killed him," Toni said.

I turned and looked at her. "No offense, but that's bullshit," I answered. "She's no killer."

"Write it down," she insisted. "It's a possibility."

"I've known her for more than ten years. I don't believe she has that in her. Besides, she went missing more than a week before he was killed. Why would she come out and whack the guy?"

"Because he was pressing her?" Toni said.

"You should write it down," Richard said. "You haven't seen Gina in five years. You don't know her all that well or what she may have become, or especially why she might be doing what she's doing. She could have hired anyone to kill him in order to get him off her back. Ironic that it could be he thought he was the bad guy and she was the weak one, when in reality it was reversed." Reluctantly, I wrote it down.

"Short of a completely random murder, which would be at odds with the crime scene, any other obvious scenarios that lead to Eddie getting killed?"

There were none. "Okay," I said. "We've recapped the facts, and we've worked through three possibilities where Eddie could have gotten himself killed—and nothing to do with Gina at all."

"And one in which she was very much involved," Toni added.

"True," I admitted. "Next topic. Why is Frankie the Boot here?"

"Vacation," Kenny said. "But I don't really believe that," he added quickly.

"Family called him in," Toni said.

"They said they'd let us know if they were going to do that in order to keep us in the loop. They haven't. If they did call him, they're holding out on us," I said. "It's definitely possible. Could also be that they plan on telling us later."

"Or they just hoped we wouldn't find out," Toni said. "How about Gina called him in for help with Eddie?"

I wrote down an abbreviated version of both of these then said, "Okay, now let's talk about Gina leaving. Let's dream up some scenarios that fit all these facts and can help us develop a motive."

"Scenario number one," Toni said. "She's stressed out from her job, her life, etc. She's throwing in the towel and she just wants to disappear. She'll come back when she pleases. Eddie Salazar had nothing to do with her disappearance, and the fact that he's dead is just a coincidence and doesn't motivate her to come home. The family's hired Frankie the Boot to come and help locate her."

"Good," I said. "But why was Eddie Salazar pissed then? Why did he want to find her and kill her?"

"Who knows," Toni said. "Maybe she embarrassed him in public. I get the impression with a little peacock like Eddie Salazar, there wouldn't have been a much bigger sin in his eyes than being publicly humiliated by an attractive woman."

"Okay," I said. "She disappeared because she's fed up with the world and she wants out. I'll go with that. It fits all the facts."

"Okay, then. Here's scenario number two," Toni continued. "The obvious one. She starts teasing Eddie Salazar and then something goes wrong. She holds out, and he gets pissed. Or they get into a lover's spat, and he gets pissed. Maybe he's no good in the sack, and she tells him to his face and, you guessed it, he gets pissed. It doesn't seem like it would've been too hard to piss off Eddie Salazar. She knows he wants her dead, so she hides out. Eddie gets popped, unrelated. Family brings Frankie the Boot out to bring her in. Now that he's dead, she'll come back soon."

"That fits them all," I said.

"Scenario number three," Kenny said. "Like Toni said, Gina strikes up a relationship with Eddie Salazar, who considers himself a world-class ladies' man—God's gift. At some point, she puts him in his place and tells him to fuck off. He takes offense. He threatens to kill her. Before he can make good, though, Gina calls in her cousins, and they whack Eddie first. Frankie the Boot, retired mob executive that he is, is simply coming in to oversee the mop-up. When the coast is clear, legally speaking, he'll give the word, and Gina comes home."

I wrote it down. "There's one common denominator in all three of these scenarios that we might be able to use," I asked. "Anyone notice it?"

"Of course," Richard said. "Frankie the Boot. In every case, we have either the family or Gina asking him to come out."

"Kenny, do you think this might create some sort of phone record trail?"

"Probably," he said.

"Then I think you should try to grab the information on Frankie's home phone and cell. See if calls took place between him and the Fiores since the twelfth. Also, look to see if any unusual calls to unidentified numbers started popping up for him after the twelfth."

"If Gina knows about things like prepaid cell phones," Kenny said, "I won't be able to trace her calls back to her even if she were the caller."

"But at least you'd see the number," I said. "Maybe you could spot a pattern."

"True," he said. "I'll get right on it."

"Other theories?" I asked.

"I have an observation," Richard said. "If our theory is correct that either the family or Gina herself called in Frankie the Boot and didn't tell us, then it's obvious that either the family or Gina or both knows more than we do and, most importantly, more than they're telling us."

"That's true," I agreed.

"They're lying to us?" Kenny asked.

"Starting to look like a possibility," I said.

"I don't know about you guys, but I'm not comfortable being the only one who doesn't know what's going on," Richard said. "Paul Newman said, 'If you're playing poker and you can't tell who the sucker is, it's you.'"

"Do you think we might be the suckers here?" Kenny asked.

Richard looked at us all, and then settled on me. He nodded.

"I think you owe another visit to the family—Robbie, in particular. It's entirely possible that they know more than they're letting on."

# Chapter 18

THE NEXT MORNING was beautiful. The temperature had cooled back down to normal, and I was comfortable in dark green khaki pants with a dark blue short-sleeved shirt. Toni wore pressed jeans and a vest over a long-sleeved light blue shirt. The sky was a deep, clear blue with only a few clouds. As agreed, we met with the Fiores at their home at ten o'clock. I rang the bell on the front door of the grand home, and we waited. Inside, we could hear music playing—sounded like traditional jazz. Outside, a lawn mower was running, either in the backyard of the Fiore home or next door. The air smelled sweetly of freshly cut grass. A minute later, the door opened, and Angelo Fiore greeted us.

"Please," he said. "Come in, come in." He led us through the entry and back to the family room where we'd met before. The glass doors to the back patio were open, and he led us outside onto the patio. Carina Fiore was seated at a wrought-iron table reading a newspaper. She stood when she saw us and greeted us warmly.

"Please, have a seat," Angelo said.

We sat. I looked around. "Is Robbie joining us?" I asked.

"I apologize," Angelo said. "Robbie had to run up to Bellingham this morning. He said the auditors are inventorying our warehouse up there, and he didn't trust anybody else with them."

"Oh, okay," I said. "I hope that works out well."

"He said it was routine. He said he'll call you tomorrow, and you guys can arrange a time to get together," Angelo said.

"Good," I said.

"Something to drink?" Carina asked, nodding toward a tray of soft drinks on the patio table.

"Thanks," I said, taking a bottled water.

"So," she said. "Bring us up to date. Robbie keeps us pretty much filled in, but we appreciate the opportunity to hear from you directly. Where are we?"

"First off, thanks for meeting us this morning," I said. "We won't take much of your time. We have been making progress. Robbie's probably told you, we've been able to uncover some of Gina's activities on the day she went missing and the next day or so afterward. We've identified some of her friends along with a man that she used to see."

"Salazar," Angelo said.

"That's right," I answered.

"Good that the bastard's dead," he said.

I thought for a second, and then said, "I agree. He was a bad man. As you know, it's been two weeks now since Gina disappeared. You'll remember that when we first met, I told you there were three basic scenarios we felt were in play. We've now eliminated two of them from our focus."

I paused before continuing. "First, since we never heard any kind of ransom request, no note, no message of any kind, we've eliminated the kidnap-for-ransom scenario.."

Angelo nodded.

"Next," I continued. "We've found absolutely no evidence to suggest that Gina was abducted by a stranger. Her condo was absolutely clean. Seattle Police sent in a Crime Scene Investigation unit into the condo, and they found nothing. If she was abducted, it almost had to have been from her condo, otherwise why would her purse and keys be there? And if she was abducted from the condo, it was either done with no struggle, or whoever abducted her cleaned up perfectly afterward. This might have happened, but probably not. None of her neighbors heard or saw anything that night. It doesn't seem Gina would have voluntarily left with someone without her purse and her keys. Nor does it seem Gina could have been easily abducted forcibly without anyone noticing—particularly because the abductor would have had to take the time to clean up and lock the door with a new key that he'd somehow managed to discover. This whole scenario seems a big stretch, so we're basically dropping it as well and moving on." I didn't mention that after two weeks, there'd be little hope of recovering Gina alive anyway.

The Fiores digested this, and I continued. "Because of all this, we feel that Gina is most likely alive and well. We feel that she's gone underground—perhaps somewhere other than Seattle. We don't know why. One of our theories had been that Gina was hiding from Eddie Salazar for some reason. We were very concerned that Mr. Salazar was looking for Gina with intent to hurt her."

"Why would he want to do that?" Angelo asked.

"That's a question we're still trying to answer," I said. "Salazar was looking for Gina. Salazar beat up one of Gina's friends, Kara Giordano, when she couldn't tell him where Gina was. He told her he wanted to kill Gina. But Gina was already gone."

"Good," Carina said.

"That's right," I said. "It also sounds just like Gina to me—at least one step ahead of this guy."

Angelo and Carina both nodded their agreement.

"But with Eddie Salazar dead, why doesn't she come home?" Carina said.

"That's the question we're trying to answer," I said. "We don't know her reasons yet, but they might be related to Eddie Salazar—it's certainly a heck of a coincidence if they're not. But we don't have a full understanding yet. And the fact that Salazar's been dead for a few days now and Gina hasn't returned is troubling. Clearly, there's much we still don't know."

I paused while the Fiores considered this news for a few moments. The only sounds were the birds singing in the trees and the muffled hum of the lawn mower outside.

"Well, even though she's not home yet, I suppose this is good news," Angelo said finally.

"Compared to either of the other two scenarios, I think so. I think she's out there—alive and well. I don't know why she hasn't come home yet, but we're determined to find out. Sometimes, our work is a process of elimination."

Angelo nodded.

"Any questions about where we're at? What we've been doing?" I asked.

Angelo looked at Carina, then back at me.

"No. You've made terrific progress. We're very grateful."

"Well," I said, "we're not done yet. We're still committed to finding Gina and making sure she's safe."

They both nodded.

"Next issue. Mr. Fiore," Toni said, "when we met here last time we asked you to notify us if you decided to ask for help from your cousins in Chicago. I need to ask you, have you asked them for any assistance with finding Gina?"

"Absolutely not," Angelo said, a little indignantly. "If I did, I would have let you know, just like I said."

"Good," I added. "We believe you. We just needed to ask."

"Why? Is something going on I don't know about?" Angelo asked.

"Do you recognize this man?" Toni asked, putting an eight-by-ten glossy of Frankie the Boot's airport surveillance photo on the table in front of him.

"That's Frankie," Angelo said. "Francesco. Francesco Rossi. He's a second cousin. He works for Johnnie and Peter."

"By Johnnie and Peter, do you mean John and Peter Calabria?" Toni answered.

"Yeah," Angelo said, nodding as he looked at the photo.

"This photo was taken two days ago at Sea-Tac," I said. "Did you know he was here?"

"Frankie's here in Seattle?" Angelo said. His surprise seemed genuine. Then it seemed to turn to anger. "Hell no, I didn't know he was here," he said loudly, plainly agitated. "What the hell is he doing here?" He stood up and began pacing back and forth.

"That's what we want to know," I said.

"Sit down, Angelo," Carina said. Angelo looked at her, and then sat back down. She turned to me. "Usually, whenever someone comes from Chicago to Seattle, they at least stop by and say hello," she said. "I don't know why Francesco wouldn't stop in."

"Well, it's got us confused as well," I said. "We're going to work on it and we'll keep you informed."

Angelo said, "Why don't I just call Johnnie and ask him?"

"We—that is, the police and the two of us—think that it might be better not to let your cousins know that we're aware of Frankie being in

Seattle," I said. "It might make it that much harder to figure out why he's here if they know we've seen him. It was only a matter of luck that we were able to spot him in the first place."

"You sure?" Angelo asked.

"Yes. It could be important in our finding and helping Gina. Please don't contact them."

"Okay. Whatever you say," Angelo said. "We'll do whatever it takes to get Gina back."

"Besides," I said. "It's very probable that Frankie's visit to Seattle has nothing at all to do with Gina. Better not to get your cousins all worked up over an airport photograph if Frankie is here for some other reason."

"That makes sense," Angelo admitted.

"There is something you can do for us, though," I added.

"What is it?"

"Earlier you mentioned a warehouse in Bellingham. I think it could be helpful if you'd list every piece of real estate the Fiore family owns—even leases. Start here," I said, "then list every piece of property you either own or lease, home or business. For example, do you have a vacation home?"

"No."

"No cabins, no condos, nothing like that?"

"None."

"No other personal real estate other than the house here?"

"None."

"How about business property?"

"Yes, we have three warehouses and probably half a dozen other businesses. We own three bakeries and two pizza restaurants. Plus, we own an excavating company in Mount Vernon."

"Could you write down the addresses and phone numbers of all of these places—anything that your businesses own or rent—and then e-mail them to us?" I asked.

"Certainly," Angelo said. "Give me an hour."

"Did Gina ever work at any of these places?" I asked.

"She's worked at our offices here the whole time she's been with the company, except for a four-month period in '09 when we bought the bakeries. Then we sent her to Port Townsend to get to know the operation there, so she'd have a better understanding of the numbers. She moved into a little apartment up there."

"Did she keep the apartment?" I asked.

"I don't think so," Angelo said.

"Do you have the address?"

"I'll get it for you and send it with my e-mail."

"Great," I said, jotting that down. "I think that does it for us. Do you have any questions for us before we go?"

"Just one," Carina said. She looked me straight in the eye. "Do you still think you can find her?"

"Yes, ma'am, I think so," I said. "We've done a pretty good job of putting events together and figuring out where she isn't. Now, it's time for us to start zeroing in on where she is."

~~~~

"He seemed sincere to me," Toni said as we drove back to the office. "I think he was surprised to see Frank Rossi here in Seattle."

"I think so."

"Do you think he can control himself and keep from calling his cousins? It really would be better if they didn't know we had surveillance on Frankie."

"That's a fact," I said. "I'll bet the Feds would be a little smoked at us if they knew we'd said anything. I sure hope he stays quiet."

We drove in silence for a second. Something was gnawing at me, something that Angelo'd said. Then, there it was. It hit me.

"Son of a bitch!" I said. I turned and looked at Toni. "He lied!"

"Angelo lied?" she asked.

"No, not Angelo. At least, I don't think it was Angelo. Robbie lied to us."

"Lied about what?"

"Last week, when we were interviewing Reggie and Cindy Dunlap in Gina's office, I asked Robbie if Gina ever worked anywhere else. He was emphatic when he said no. He said the only place she'd ever worked was at the main plant in SoDo."

"I remember that," Toni said slowly, now seeing the inconsistency.

"But Angelo just said she spent four months in Port Townsend learning about a new business they bought there two years ago—that she actually moved up there for a little while."

"That's right. Robbie remembered just fine that I had spent four hours with the family five years ago at Thanksgiving dinner, but he forgets that Gina was reassigned for four months just two years ago? Sounds a little strange to me."

"Can't wait to talk to him again," Toni said.

I agreed.

~~~~

We got back to the office, and I went straight to Kenny's office.

"What are you working on?" I asked him.

"I got Frank Rossi's numbers. I just finished downloading his cell phone records. I was just about to download his home phone records," he said.

"Good. Go ahead. Also, I want you to get the phone records for Robbie Fiore. Home and cell."

"Got 'em. I already pulled them earlier this morning," Kenny said.

"I'm downloading three months of data for each phone. I'm going to export to Excel. Then, I'll split the data into two categories: calls before August 11 and calls since August 11. I'll do a simple macro to identify all the calls since August 11 that are from a new number—any number that doesn't also show up before August 11."

"I get it," I said. "Then, if we see a pattern developing in those new numbers, it's possible it just might be Gina."

"Right, that's the premise," Kenny answered. "I'm making the assumption that this disappearance gig is a big enough deal for her that she'd not want to make calls using a phone number that she's used in the past. She'd take the precaution of assuming someone might be monitoring that number."

I thought for a second, and then asked, "What's the area code for Port Townsend?"

"That would be 360," Kenny answered. "Why?"

"Because Gina lived in Port Townsend for four months," I said. "If she was going to hide anywhere, she might feel comfortable going back there. Pay special attention to new numbers from the 360 area code."

"Give me a few minutes to write the macro," he said.

~~~~

Twenty minutes later, Toni and Kenny came into my office. They handed me a copy of a printout for each of the four phone numbers—Robbie's home, Robbie's cell, Frank Rossi's home, and Frank Rossi's cell.

"This is fascinating," Kenny said. "On average, each of these phones had one hundred calls per month incoming and about the same number outgoing. If you look here," he pointed to a heading on my report, "you'll see the new phone numbers that appear on the incoming call list only after August 11. You can see that Robbie's home had zero. His cell had two—one was a 360 area code. Frank Rossi's home had zero, and his cell had one, also a 360 area code. Look at the number."

I did. "It's the same number for both of them!"

"Bingo. What kind of coincidence is that? Suddenly, after August 11, both Frank Rossi and Robbie received phone calls from a brand-new, 360 caller—someone who hadn't called either of them in the previous two months."

"Holy crap!" I said. "Any pattern to the calls?"

"Turn the page," he said. I did. "You can see that the caller with the new number is making a call to Robbie's cell phone every other night at ten, just like clockwork."

"Holy shit! Little sister is calling in!"

"Sure looks like it," Kenny said. "And turn the page on Frank Rossi's report."

I did. There were two calls, one dated August 13, one dated August 24. "If that's Gina, she called Frank Rossi a couple of days after she disappeared and the very day Eddie Salazar was found dead."

"Unless Robbie suddenly found a friend who started calling him every couple of nights right after Gina disappeared—a friend who also happens to know cousin Frankie and decided to start calling him at the same time—then he's lying to us," Toni said.

Kenny ran the same phone analysis on Angelo and Carina Fiore's home number. No matches—no calls from the new number. I wasn't surprised. I've seen some good actors in my time, but if they could pull off a concerned parent act as well as they were, when they knew there was no reason to be concerned, then I needed to find another line of work. Fortunately, I was safe. For a while, anyway.

~~~~

With Robbie out of town, there wasn't much left for us to do. I sent everyone home at two thirty. I was in the lobby talking to Kenny and Doc when Toni walked out, ready to leave. She looked at Kenny and said, "What are you doing tonight?"

"When Danny said we had the night off," he said, "I simply referred to the black book, Saturday section, and dialed up a lucky, beautiful young redhead. I'm not certain, but I imagine that at some point, we'll end up at what I like to call Ground Zero—the king-sized bed at Casa Hale."

"You are so full of shit," Toni said, laughing. "Do me a favor. First, check her ID. Make sure she's older than sixteen. Second, make sure she's literate."

"Why?" Kenny said, feigning confusion.

Toni laughed. "And you'd damn sure better wear a raincoat."

"It's not supposed to rain tonight," Kenny said.

"Raincoat, dumbass," Doc said. "You know, the rubber variety. R-U-B-B-E-R."

"Oh, I get it," Kenny said. "Not to worry. Ground Zero is well stocked with a variety of—raincoats."

"Oh, Jesus," Toni said.

"And you," I asked, looking at Toni. "What are you doing with your free evening?"

"Well," she said, "it may interest mister ground zero here that I have a date." She looked at Kenny. "With a man."

"Really?" Kenny said. "Do you mind if I ask—"

"Stop. You're two seconds away from swimming in Lake Union," Toni said. "It's none of your goddamned business. But," she added, "I don't know why, but I'm going to tell you anyway." She paused for effect.

"He, and I repeat, he, plays for the Seahawks. He's six four and 230 pounds of solid muscle. Six percent body fat." She looked at Kenny.

"He could break you in half and not even realize he did it."

"Wow," I said. "He sounds like a stud."

"He is," she said.

"Well," I said, "have fun. You should ask Kenny if he can spare you some of his raincoats."

"There's an idea," she said. "You never know." She left.

~~~~

I got home and went for a longish sort of run—twelve miles or so. I like to do this when I need to clear my head. We were getting close. It looked like Gina was safe. Why she continued to hide, I didn't know, but I intended to find out, starting tomorrow. I was seriously motivated to find Robbie. He was lying, and I wanted to find out why. Angelo said he'd call me. If that didn't happen by ten or so the next morning, I was going looking. If he led me to Gina, and if Gina was safe, then we were about done. In which case, I'd probably owe Angelo some of his $120,000 back. Oh well—easy come, easy go.

After I got home, I showered and drove to the grocery store. I picked out a nice salmon fillet—just enough for one. Later, just as it got dark, I fired up the grill and sat out on my balcony with a cold Mac & Jack's. The seaplanes were done for the day. A few boaters were out on the quiet water, green-and-red position lights reflecting off the lake surface, dancing to the gentle ripples of boat wakes. The outside tables at Chandlers across the lake were full.

After dinner, I sat in a lounge chair and enjoyed the evening. I put a Chris Webster CD on and listened to her sing about "Something in the Water." Just after nine, my phone rang. Caller ID: Toni.

"Hey," I said.

"Hey yourself."

"Why are you home? What happened to Mr. Seahawk?" I asked.

"He left."

"Why?"

"Promise not to laugh?" she asked.

"Okay."

"He's gay."

I laughed, but quietly. "No shit."

"He's a nice guy. I've known him since college."

"Okay."

"Another thing," she said.

"What."

"I'm not gay."

I chuckled quietly. "I know that."

"I just wanted you to know. I know you heard those guys talking."

"That's just Kenny being Kenny. There was never a question in my mind. Ever."

"Good."

It was silent for a few seconds.

"Do you want to come over?" I asked.

It was silent for a few seconds more.

"I'd like to, but I don't think that would be such a good idea," she answered. "You know what I mean?"

I smiled. "You're right," I said. "Moment of weakness. Excuse me for asking."

"Okay. But I didn't mind you asking," she said. "Talk to you tomorrow." She hung up before I could answer.

# Chapter 19

DESPITE OUR DIFFERENT backgrounds, Robbie and I got along well when we were in high school. Our social groups could hardly have been more opposite. He hung with the money crowd—we called them the "Pretty People." They drove expensive cars, wore expensive clothes, and spent all their time trying to impress each other. They probably should have gone to private school instead of Ballard High.

My family had the same money as most of those families, maybe more. But I was brought up differently. When it came to money for things like cars, toys, and the like, I was pretty much on my own. My mom and dad expected me to learn the value of money by having to go out and earn it. So I did. And it worked. I worked part-time at a variety of jobs all through high school—car wash, grocery store, golf course—even a short stint at a movie theater. I drove an old Ford pickup that I bought with my own earnings when I was seventeen. I hung out with the nerdy crowd—kids like me who were more interested in college and music than impressing anybody with our cars and clothes.

Despite our differences, though, Robbie was nice to me—not condescending or judgmental like many in his group tended to be. Because we went to the same church, he knew about my family and me. He knew my dad was a lawyer, like the previous four generations of Logans before him. He knew that our family'd been in Seattle since the late 1800s. He also understood the differences in philosophy between the way he was raised and the way I was, and he was cool with it. He'd have made a good politician. He appreciated his good fortune as an anomaly, and he didn't think any less of me because I earned my own way and drove a truck instead of a Lexus. Unlike most in his group, he always seemed to consider me an equal.

Now, eleven years later, he'd screwed up. The fact that he thought he could run some sort of game on me and think that he'd not be discovered was the worst kind of condescension. It pissed me off. And, as opposed to when I was in high school, I sometimes deal with being pissed off now by getting physical. At times it's the perfect answer. That said, I'd also read Sun Tzu. I knew the advantage of hiding inside knowledge from my opponent. So, this time, I hid the fact that I was pissed off, and I played dumb when he called at nine thirty the next morning, and we agreed to meet in half an hour at his office.

~~~~

The outer door to Pacific Wine and Spirits was locked when I arrived, so I knocked and waited. Robbie had apparently been waiting inside around the corner. He walked around and unlocked it for me.

"Hey, Danny," he greeted me cheerfully as I entered.

"Good morning." I stepped inside, and he locked the door behind me.

I turned to face him and said, "You look like you're in a pretty good mood this morning."

He shrugged his shoulders and looked perhaps a little puzzled.

"Let me ask you," I said, "when you talked to Gina last night, was everything okay?" Alright, so much for Sun Tzu.

He stared at me, surprised. He started to talk, but I cut him off.

"You know, last night," I said, "your regular ten o'clock check-in call. That's right, Robbie. I know that all the time you've been talking to us, wringing your fucking hands and being worried about Gina, she's been calling in every other night on your goddamned cell phone. What do you two do, compare notes? Did you know that she's even called in the National Guard in the form of your uncles from Chicago?" He looked surprised.

I'd raised my voice and was almost shouting now. "Why are you dicking us around on this, Robbie? What's the fucking game?" I paused for a second, but he still couldn't get any words out. "Why shouldn't I call the police right now and have you explain to them why you've been making false reports? This bullshit stops now! What the fuck is going on?"

I'd taken a couple of steps toward him, and he'd backed up accordingly. He had the panicked look of someone who was suddenly way out of his comfort zone. Smiling and razzle-dazzle wouldn't help now, and he was smart enough to realize this.

He held up his hand as if to say *stop*. "Can I explain?" he finally said.

"I've got all day," I answered. "I'm here for some goddamn explanations."

He nodded and beckoned me to follow him. We walked down a hallway and entered his office. He closed the door behind us and pointed to a small sofa while he sat down in a chair across from it.

"I didn't lie," he said.

I looked at him and started to respond, but he continued. "At least, not at first. Gina was missing, and we called the police, just like I told you. They interviewed us and took their reports. We waited all that first weekend for word and there was none. When the police told us to contact you, we did. We still hadn't heard from Gina when I met in your office the first time and the next day at my parents' house. She only called that night after you'd met with my parents and already agreed to take the case."

"You're telling me you didn't know anything about the disappearance?" I asked. "You weren't involved at all? You were just some sort of innocent bystander for the first few days? That's a little hard to swallow, now that the truth is out about the phone calls."

"That may be so," Robbie said. "But it's the truth. I didn't know what she was doing. Hell, I still don't know what she's doing." He paused and looked away. "I just do what I'm told," he said, quietly, embarrassed.

"Told? By who?" I asked.

"By Gina!" he answered, frustrated. "Whatever's going on, Gina's running it. I'm probably the one who's going to get in trouble with the police for hiding stuff." He paused, and then said again, "Gina's running it. Just like she runs everything else. It's always Gina."

Wow.

"What do you mean, 'just like she runs everything'?" I asked.

"At work. She's the chief financial officer. I'm the chief operating officer. My dad's the chief executive officer. Which one of us do you think is the boss? Gina's the boss. If my father ever questions anything she does—which he doesn't anymore—she sweet-talks him into doing it her way. He goes along with her every time. I tried standing up to her once, and she had dad suspend me! For two goddamned weeks! From my own friggin' company! It was a threat. She fired a shot across my bow. She basically said 'Don't fuck with me! Don't even think about trying to take me on!' Guess what? It worked. I take it seriously. It's the Gina show now."

"How's that working out?" I said.

"Oh, business is great!" he answered hotly. "We make money hand over fucking fist. But we also roll over people. It's our way or the highway, now. No slack, no leeway, relationships be damned. Dad built this business on relationships. His word was gold. If our customers needed help, he'd help them. He'd extend them credit, increase their lines, whatever it took. For thirty-five years this worked. The business grew and prospered."

"And now your dad's saddled with a tax-evasion charge that could put him away for twenty years," I added. "There's that little detail."

"True," he said, nodding. "There was a team of people who stole from him and underreported the income to cover it up. Those fuckers at the IRS are convinced that dad was part of it so that he could skim money off the top. He wasn't. That's what the fight is all about."

"And how does Gina fit in to that?"

"Gina's the one who figured out what was happening. When she came to work with us in 2006, she discovered it almost immediately. She fired the people involved and went after them, criminally and civilly, but by then the IRS already had the scent."

"But as far as Gina's involvement," I said, "she did good by the company, right?"

"Yeah. I never said she did stuff for her own personal gain," Robbie said. "For whatever reason, she doesn't seem all that interested in personal gain. I guess she's working for the big picture, long term. She works stupid long hours for the company and the family. But she's just fucking ruthless. What she says goes. Period. Or else you can leave. Even me."

"So she called on Tuesday the sixteenth?" I said.

"Is that the same day we talked at my parents' house about hiring you? Yeah, that's it."

"Tell me about it."

"It's ten o'clock at night," he said. "I'm home watching the news

about her disappearance. The cell phone rings—it's a number I don't recognize with a blocked caller ID. I wasn't going to answer, but then, with
Gina missing and all, I actually thought it might be some sort of ransom
call or something. It wasn't. Turns out it was Gina herself."

"How did the conversation go?"

"I was surprised as hell. Probably shouldn't have been. She said she
was fine. She said she had a boyfriend she wanted to avoid, so she was
taking a few days off. I told her we'd been looking for her and that we'd
hired your company to help find her. She seemed surprised. She asked me
all about you and what I knew about what you were doing. She told me to
keep track of what you did and let her know."

"So it's safe to say that you've reported to her everything that I've
reported to you?" I asked.

"Yes. That's the first thing she asks for when she calls."

"Did she say where she was?"

He nodded. "She's up in Port Townsend."

"Port Townsend? At your bakery?"

"Yeah, I think. I know she spends some time there," he admitted.

"Does she have a place up in Port Townsend?"

"I don't know. She used to, when she worked up there. She rented an
apartment."

"That brings up another point," I said. "You lied to me when you
said she hadn't worked anywhere else other than the SoDo plant. You
knew she worked up there for four months just two years ago. Did she
tell you to lie?"

"Sorry," he said. "I thought I was helping. Hell no, she didn't tell me
to lie. When I told her I said that—about her only having one office—she
got really pissed. She said I'd left a loose end and that you'd figure that it
was a lie in about a week. I guess she was right."

"It sounds like your parents aren't in on the lie," I said.

"They're not."

"How could you keep your parents in the dark over something like
this when you know they're breaking up inside over missing her?"

"She told me not to tell them. She said it was for their own good and
that it would all be over by the end of the month."

"End of the month?" I asked. "What's supposed to happen at the end of the month?"

"I don't know. I have no idea. I told you that she doesn't include me in her plans. She just tells me what she wants me to know and gives me orders."

"Which you blindly follow."

"I don't have a choice," he said, protesting. "She's messing with something big enough where she has to hide, and she's afraid that it might spill over onto my parents. What am I supposed to do?"

I just stared at him without answering.

"Besides, much as I hate to say it, she has good instincts. Everything she does tends to work out well for us, even if it pisses me off while it's happening."

I thought about that for a moment, then said, "At first, I thought you sounded like you were intimidated by her."

"I am. She's a lot closer to my parents than I am. She runs the business. She's hard to outsmart."

"Okay. But the more I talk to you, the more I get the sense that, despite being a little intimidated by her, you actually respect her and want to protect her."

He nodded. "Respect? In an odd sort of way. She gets results. I don't necessarily like her methods. Protect her? Of course. She's still my sister."

"If that's the case," I said, "why are you coming clean now? Why not just stonewall me?"

"You have to ask?" he said. "She told me to."

I must have looked surprised.

"Last night she told me to tell you she'd meet you at the PT Croissant, that's our Port Townsend bakery, at three this afternoon."

He watched me for a few seconds. Apparently, I looked as befuddled as I felt. Slowly, a smile appeared on his face. "So," he said, smirking, "now Gina's given you an order. Are you gonna go?"

I stared at him, not knowing what to say.

# Chapter 20

AT ONE THIRTY that afternoon, I drove on to the ferry *Spokane* at the Edmonds dock for the thirty-minute ride to Kingston on the way to Port Townsend. As soon as I parked, I grabbed a jacket and made my way forward between the rows of cars to the stairway leading to the passenger deck. I went upstairs, two steps at a time. The passenger deck is an inside deck with seating, restrooms, and a snack bar. I bought a Diet Coke and went through the double doors to the open seats on the outside deck at the front of the boat. The sun was out and warmed the deck nicely. The breeze was gentle. Two seagulls were perched, one on either side of a twelve-foot-long handrail. For a few seconds, they screamed at each other, each trying to claim exclusive use of the rail. Neither would budge, so in the end they quieted down, apparently resigned to sharing.

I thought about the case. So I'd been summoned. Of course I was going to go. There were way too many unanswered questions not to. I knew Gina was most likely safe and that she was less than an hour away in Port Townsend. I will admit, realizing that she knew that I knew her whereabouts was a little odd. Maybe I'd been chasing her bread crumbs that she'd left for me all along. As if I was supposed to find these things. Gina had it all figured out, even down to the timing. Was she that good?

In the end, though, I'm not certain it mattered whether I found her, or whether she allowed herself to be discovered. Either way, I could make a visual determination that she was okay. If she wanted me to, I could escort her safely home. If she didn't want that, at least I could report back to her parents that I'd found her and that she was safe. However it turned out, the job would be done, and we'd earn our pay. I was satisfied. Move on.

Still, despite feeling that I was fast approaching a resolution that should lead to at least a semi-positive result, I couldn't escape the nagging feeling that comes when you realize that you don't know everything, you're not in control of the unfolding events, and things can still go horribly wrong. Of course, you're never in total control, but at least you'd like to feel that you had an edge. That's pretty much what Sun Tzu was all about, how to capture that edge by having the control. Fight the battles according to *your* strengths, not your opponent's. Attack your opponent where he was weak, not where he was strong.

In my case, though, I had the uneasy feeling that I had only the knowledge that Gina wanted me to have. I wasn't certain where this left me. I didn't know her game. I didn't know her motive. I didn't know what was driving her. I didn't know what I didn't know. The way she was messing with me, I wasn't even sure if we were on the same side anymore.

~~~~

The ferry docked at Kingston, on the west side of Puget Sound, at a quarter after two. Ten minutes later, I drove off the boat and was on my way. The first thing I did was grab my cell phone and call Toni at her home.

"I just tried your place," she said. "I was just about to try your cell."

"And here I am, just like magic," I said. "Must be psychic."

"Must be," she agreed. "Where are you?"

"I just got off the ferry in Kingston."

I must have surprised her because the line was silent for a few seconds. "The hell are you doing in Kingston?" she asked. Before I could answer, she said, "Wait a minute—you're going to Port Townsend, aren't you?"

"What makes you say that?"

"Don't be coy with me," she said. "You talked to Robbie, and he told you something, didn't he?"

Did I mention the fact that Toni's quick?

"I talked to him this morning," I admitted. "And yes, he confirmed that Gina does, in fact, call him every other night. He told me she was in Port Townsend."

"So after you interviewed him without me, you decided to drive on up to Port Townsend, again without me. Why?" she asked. "Oh, wait. I know. You're thinking you're going to see your mystery woman up there, aren't you. I'd be in the way, and nature might not be able to take its proper course, so best that I remain behind. Don't want to fuck with nature taking its proper course and all."

This was starting to spin out of control. "It's not like that," I said. "Let's be professional—" The word had no sooner escaped my lips than I immediately wished I could grab it and put it back before she heard it. No such luck.

"Professional?" she asked, slowly, quietly. "Professional, like you running off this morning to do an interview with a prime suspect without calling your partner? That kind of professional?" Louder now. "Professional, like you driving off to Port Townsend to potentially find our primary target—who conveniently just happens to be an old lover of yours—again without calling your partner? That kind of professional?" She raised her voice again. "You act like this case is all over, but you're ignoring the fact that a Chicago hit man has been imported here, presumably for the purpose of protecting the very person you're trying to find—a person, I might add, who, at least up to now, has not wanted to be found. That kind of professional?" Crescendo nearly complete. "Who'll be watching your back? Who's being professional? Excuse me, Mr. Professional, but you're a jackass." Very loud, this last part.

*Ouch.* Had that one coming, I suppose. My drill instructors in basic could dress you down by yelling and screaming and cussing in such a manner that could blister paint. But in your mind you always knew that it was a put-on for the benefit of the group. You rolled with it. But this was the real deal. Toni'd just made the DIs look like Cub Scouts, and she'd made me feel like a complete shit-heel—again—all in less than fifteen seconds. "I'm sorry," I said. "Poor choice of words."

"Poor choice of words. Sure," Toni said.

The line was silent for a full thirty seconds. "I didn't call you to get into an argument with you," I said, hoping to defuse the disagreement.

"No, I don't imagine you did."

It was quiet on the line, and then something changed. "I'm sorry, Danny," she said, softly, demurely. "I was out of line. You own this company. You're the boss. You can run it any way you like. I'll do whatever I can to help you."

Whoa! What had she just done? What did this mean? The Toni I know doesn't roll over and give up. This was bad. I think she'd somehow just ratcheted up the level of our disagreement by claiming to agree with me, if that was possible. She'd somehow raised the stakes by reminding me that we were not attached. She'd identified a whole new level of risk and grabbed it. This was an unfair, world-class tactic for which I had no handy response.

"Who are you, and what did you do with Toni?" I said. Cheesy, but it's all I could come up with.

She stuck with the theme. "Look," she said, very calmly, "I'm just an employee. I have no right to come down on you like I just did."

"Where's this coming from?" I said. "You know you're not just an employee. My name's on the door, but we're basically partners."

"We are not partners," she said emphatically. "I'm just an employee here. You can run the cases however you like. And if you don't like the way I do things, you can get rid of me. If I don't like the way things are run around here, I can leave. That's the way it is. No strings. No partners. No attachments."

She had me. I was screwed. The line was quiet for a second.

"Well Toni, for the record, that's not the way I feel," I said. "I'm sorry. I didn't mean to hurt your feelings."

"You didn't," she said. "Call me if you need anything, Danny. Bye." She hung up.

Oh, shit. Nice move, Logan. Way to go, dumbass. You've just jeopardized the most valuable relationship you have with the one person in the world, other than your parents, who would fall on her sword for you. Why?

What's worse, she was absolutely right. I was sneaking off to Port Townsend alone, by myself, because I wanted to see Gina. Risk be damned, Chicago hit man be damned. I didn't seem to care about any of that. I had a serious case of tunnel vision. I remembered the thrill of hooking up with Gina five years ago. I remembered the beautiful face, the killer body, the magnetic personality. I was drawn to that vision as if caught in a riptide. The fact that swimming in riptides is dangerous and doesn't always end well didn't even seem to register.

~~~~

I have a bad habit that I'll confess to. Sometimes when I'm driving, my mind will be busy rolling over a problem, and the actual act of driving gets kicked into an autopilot mode apparently controlled by something hidden within my subconscious. Some time later, I'll arrive at my destination not remembering anything about the ride. So far, this hasn't gotten me in trouble, but a couple of times, I've thought *Holy shit!* when I arrived. The idea of what I'd just done scared the hell out of me. Good thing I didn't hit anybody. I resolved to try to correct this by concentrating solely on the driving, but I wasn't always successful.

Such was the case now. I drove toward Port Townsend in a sort of numb silence. As I rolled over recent events, three things were obvious. First, I had some visceral need to see Gina. I wanted to see her face-to-face, to talk to her, to find out what she was up to. More than that, it was possible I wanted to see if now, five years gone, there was anything left of the sparks that had burst into a brief flame while I was still in the army. I had no preconceived notions, no expectation of any particular outcome. But I couldn't leave the question unanswered.

The second thing that was obvious was that at best, Toni had just fired a screaming cannon shell six inches over my bow. At best. At worst, she'd be gone when I got back. By pointing out the fact that our relationship had no strings, no attachments, she implied that she could—and she might—leave at anytime. The thought of Toni leaving filled me full of a cold dread, centered right in the middle of my chest. Something was going on there—not necessarily with her, but with me. I needed to sort things out and get my shit together on this, pretty damn quick before somebody got hurt. Like her. Or me.

Of course, the last thing that was obvious was that I was no match for Toni in an argument. No way, no how. It was clear that she could kick my ass without even looking up. A heavyweight against a flyweight. I'd best not forget the beating that she'd just given me.

My mind considered all this as the scenery passed by. I hardly noticed the forest. I hardly noticed the ocean. I didn't notice crossing the bridge at the Hood Canal—and it's a mile and a half long. Worse, I almost didn't notice the silver Ford hanging on my tail about four hundred yards back. Only when I crossed the bridge did I realize that I'd also noticed the same silver Ford on the ferry—and that it'd been right behind me ever since. In and of itself, silver Fords were no cause for concern. But I'm not a big believer in coincidence. Why was this guy stuck four hundred yards behind me all the way from Kingston halfway to Port Townsend?

Who was this guy, and what did he want—those were the two questions that immediately sprang to mind. I was armed, of course. But if he really was tailing me, then he was probably packing as well. And most likely, there was more than one of him. No sense picking a fight when you're outnumbered going in. It would have been nice to have Toni here. She was a dead shot, and she'd have evened out the odds. Oh well.

I was doing fifty-five, so I decided to pick up the pace and see how they reacted. I accelerated to sixty-five and watched. At first, I appeared to pull away from them. Their reflection shrank in the rearview mirror. Then they quickly recovered and moved back into position, four hundred yards back. I tried it again, accelerating to almost eighty. Same result. I swerved sharply to pass a slower-moving car. They followed suit. I was driving northwest on Highway 104, about five miles past the Hood Canal Bridge. If you keep going straight on 104, you'll bump into Highway 101 in about eight miles. Highway 101 is the main highway around the north end of the Olympic Peninsula that takes you all the way out to Port Angeles and beyond. Instead of taking 101, though, I turned north on Highway 19—it's a much straighter shot into Port Townsend. As soon as I made the turn, I downshifted and floored it to try and make distance on the silver Ford in the event that they, too, turned onto 19. Ten seconds later, they did. I could see that they also picked up the pace.

I hadn't driven on Highway 19 in several years, and I'd never driven while being pursued. It didn't take too long to realize that all the advantages on Highway 19 went to the powerful sedan behind me. The road was long, straight, and flat. Soon, I was fairly hurtling along at eighty-five, near the Jeep's top speed. I swerved to pass a car and when I swerved back, the Jeep's tires squealed in protest. The top-heavy Jeep leaned to the left so much that I thought I was going to roll. My pulse was as redlined as the Jeep's tach. The Jeep had great ground clearance and fabulous low-end torque. Two things the Jeepster did not have were impressive straight-line top-end speed and the ability to maneuver around high-speed turns and swerves, the kind you'd need to pass cars. In other words, there's no way the Jeepster outruns a sedan on a road like this. The silver Ford was rapidly closing the distance. If I wanted to lose them, then I needed to get off the main road.

It pissed me off that they were following me. If they were Gina's guys, she probably already knew that I was almost to Port Townsend. I knew Gina was expecting me, but I'd hoped to arrive undetected so I could scout out the area before our meeting. If they weren't Gina's guys, then who the hell were they? Eddie Salazar was dead. Did these guys have something to do with him?

I continued driving north. To the west was a valley in which were located a number of small, picturesque farms. The valley floor where they were situated was flat, but it was ten feet or so below the level of Highway 19, which meant that I couldn't just hang a quick left anywhere and go tearing across an open field. I'd have to wait for a crossroad, but if I did that, I'd not gain anything over the sedan.

To my right was a steep, heavily forested embankment. The embankment ran up to a ridgeline that paralleled the highway and was nearly as long. The valley where I was driving was on the west side of the ridge. The east side led back downhill all the way to Oak Bay Road, which ran along the shoreline of the Puget Sound.

Right after I'd bought my truck in high school, I used to drive this area with my friends looking for places to camp. I knew that the heavily forested ridgeline was laced with logging roads, some of which actually went up the hill and crossed all the way over to Oak Bay Road on the other side. I started noticing small, unpaved roads bump into the highway periodically. This was my ticket. If I could get onto one of these, there'd be no way the sedan could follow the jeep over rough terrain like that. As long as I got lucky and picked the right dirt road, I'd be able to follow it all the way over and down the other side. The Ford would lose me, and I'd regain the element of surprise.

Then again, I could accidentally pick someone's driveway instead and find that it dead-ended fifty yards into the forest. The trees were so thick you couldn't see fifteen feet straight through them. Then, instead of losing my pursuers, I'd have allowed them to pin me into a dead end with no way out.

The sedan continued to accelerate and close the gap between us. When it reached a point about one hundred yards behind me, I noticed a small, unpaved road ahead. For better or worse, that would have to do. I slammed on the brakes of the Jeep, and the tires locked up on me. No ABS on this baby. I started my turn and downshifted while the Jeep was still sliding. She leaned precariously before drifting to a stop, perfectly aligned with the side road. Every once in a while, I do get lucky. I immediately punched it. The Jeep jumped forward onto the dirt road, tires spinning wildly as it blew out a shower of rocks and dirt before we got any traction. Then, it catapulted itself up the small, rocky road. Now we were talking!

I wasn't sure if the sedan followed or not, because I never saw them after I made the turn. The road I was on turned out not to be a driveway, thank God. On the other hand, it didn't cross the ridgeline, either. Instead, after heading uphill for a mile, the road swung north and paralleled the highway for about five miles before turning west and eventually, dumping me right back onto Highway 19 again!

Fortunately, there was no sign of the silver Ford. I hoped that they were convinced I'd cross the ridgeline and were now speeding north to intercept me.

# Chapter 21

I SLOWED TO twenty-five as I entered Port Townsend. There was no sign of the silver Ford, but it didn't matter anyway now. I was looking for a parking place no matter what. If they were tailing me, they could just come on up and introduce themselves, for all I cared.

The town's commercial district is located along the waterfront on Water Street. It was built at the beginning of the twentieth century. Today, many of the historic brick buildings have been restored to like-new condition. They house an eclectic mix of trendy shops, boutiques, and specialty restaurants that attract tourists by the horde, especially in the summer. The Washington State Ferry system has a port directly on Water Street. The ferry completes a round trip to Keystone on Whidbey Island every ninety minutes or so. Each time the ferry lands, dozens of cars are dumped onto Water Street, some belonging to locals, but most to tourists. They mill about and clog things up for fifteen minutes or so, and then they either park or move on their way. Traffic on Water Street surges like the tide with ferry traffic all day long.

The heart of Water Street is just under a mile long and extends from the southwest, where I approached, to its northeastern end, where you had to turn left or else drive off into the Puget Sound. The PT Croissant bakery was located about three-fourths of the way up Water Street near the corner of Water and Taylor. The bakery was on the landward side of the street. The speed limit on pedestrian-heavy Water Street is twenty-five miles per hour, so I hoped I might have been able to scope the place out as I drove past. Unfortunately, there were too many people on the sidewalk to see inside. So I kept driving, looking for a parking spot. I drove another three blocks northeast, made a quick illegal U-turn in the middle of the street, and pulled into a parking space in front of the Jefferson County Historical Museum. I was fifteen minutes early.

Before I got out, I looked around carefully, making sure there was no tail. I wanted to see if anyone was paying an unusual amount of attention to me. No one seemed to notice or care. *Good.*

I parked on the same side of the street as PT Croissant. I wanted to approach from across the street on the seaward side so I could have a better chance to scope out the bakery from across the street before someone inside noticed me. My strategy was to blend into the crowd, so I figured I needed to look the part. I put on a Mariners' cap I keep in the glove box. I wanted to carry a backpack, but my light nylon day pack was completely empty. It would look pretty stupid carrying a completely empty backpack. Fortunately, I remembered that I always keep a RON (Remain Over Night) kit under the seat of the Jeep—a habit from my military days. The bag contains a clean set of underwear and socks, a T-shirt, a pair of jeans, a polo shirt, a razor, and some basic toiletries. Rolled up tightly, it fits into a small bag not much bigger than a shaving kit. I grabbed the RON kit and tossed it into the pack, which filled up nicely. I slipped the pack on. Now I looked like any other tourist here. I waited for a break in the traffic, jaywalked across the street, and started walking back toward the bakery.

~~~~

I read somewhere that tens of thousands of people visit Port Townsend annually, either as a destination in and of itself or as a side trip on the way to the Olympic National Park. I believe this because most of them seemed to be on the sidewalks this fine Sunday afternoon. Young, old, English-speaking and foreign-language speaking, the place was full of people shoulder to shoulder.

I had four blocks to cover, preferably in about five minutes if I wanted another five minutes or so to surveil the bakery. I needed to hurry, but there was only so much hurrying I could do without running people over. That, of course, would not be a good way to stay incognito. So I did my best to walk fast, all the while trying to make it look like I was out for a casual stroll. Just another tourist window-shopping his way down the streets of Port Townsend on a nice summer day. Pay me no mind.

As it turned out, I soon realized that I would make it with a couple minutes to spare. I stopped into a souvenir store and quickly bought a Port Townsend T-shirt with a picture of a killer whale screened on it. The shirt didn't do too much for me, but the shopping bag helped to round out my disguise. Returning to the sidewalk, I could see the PT Croissant across the street, thirty yards ahead.

Water Street and Taylor Street crossed in a perfect X with Water parallel to the water and Taylor perpendicular to it. I entered a place called the Fitzgerald Gallery kitty corner from PT Croissant, hoping that by ducking off the main street, I'd be able to watch the bakery and perhaps catch a glimpse of Gina in the few minutes I had before I had to cross over for my meeting.

When I entered, I was immediately greeted by a slender young man in his late twenties wearing slacks and a white long-sleeved shirt, rolled up at the sleeves. The collar was unbuttoned and he wore no T-shirt. He wore brown sandals with no socks. His dirty-blond hair was pulled back into a ponytail.

"Good afternoon," he said. "Welcome to the Fitzgerald Gallery. I'm David."

"Hi, David," I answered. I looked around. *Great*. I'd managed to find the only business in Port Townsend with no people inside.

"Is there something in particular you wanted to see," he asked, "or do you just want to spend some time browsing?"

"I'm just looking," I said.

"Feel free," he said. "Take all the time you want. I'll be right over here if you have any questions."

I pretended I was looking around as I made my way to the store's front window. I glanced at my watch—it was 2:55. From my vantage point, I could see the PT Croissant on the opposite corner. There were four tables outside on Water Street. An elderly couple occupied the first. The second held a happy group of four, laughing, talking, and enjoying the afternoon. A single man sat at the third table, and a single woman at the fourth—the end table. The woman had her head down reading a book, looking away from me. Still, I could see that she had short blonde hair. None of these people looked like Gina.

Because of the traffic, the reflections, and the shadows, I was just barely able to see through the front window inside the bakery. There were a number of people inside, but I was unable to make out any faces from my vantage point.

"I see you're interested in our Henry Felder lithographs," David said. I'd been focusing across the street and hadn't heard him approach.

"They're nice," I lied. "But they're a little out of my price range."

"I understand," David said. "I'd be happy to check for you—we may have the same image in a less-expensive print."

"No, thanks," I replied. "I like the real thing or nothing at all. Looks like I'll just have to save up."

I decided to cross Taylor so that I'd be directly across the street from the outdoor tables. Maybe I'd have a better view inside the bakery.

~~~~

I waited for the light to change, then crossed the street with the crowd. I took up a position in front of a bicycle shop directly across from the bakery. Music, what sounded like Jack Johnson, drifted out from a tavern window above the bike shop. I pretended to be looking at the newspaper stands on the sidewalk. In reality, though, I was scoping out the inside of the bakery. The front door was located in an inset doorway directly on Water Street. There was a secondary entrance on Taylor. A long display counter full of baked goods took up half the space inside. Small tables—maybe fifteen or so—filled up the balance. Three-fourths of the tables were occupied.

I reached down and grabbed a free *Homes for Sale* magazine, opened it up, and pretended to read it. Instead, I peered over the top of the magazine and began to examine each table inside, looking for Gina. She's short with long, dark hair and dark eyes. I thought she wouldn't be hard to miss. That's certainly the Gina I remembered. Looking across the street into the bakery, my eye was immediately drawn to a single woman sitting with her back to me who appeared to fit the description. Dark hair. Short. My hopes began to rise. Then she turned to get something from her purse, and I got a clear look at her face. It was clearly not Gina.

I looked down, turned a page in my magazine, and then resumed my scanning. Three or four tables with two elderly women each. Three or four tables with four people each. Three or four tables with couples. One single guy. Despite my hopes, nobody looked anything like Gina.

Then, I had a long-shot thought. If she owns the store—or her family does, anyway—maybe she'd be behind the counter. There were three people working behind the counter, all busy serving customers. The first was a man. The second was a middle-aged woman. The third was a young woman with dark hair. She was maybe eighteen years old. It wasn't Gina. Damn. So much for that bright idea.

I set the magazine down on top of the stand and took another look. There'd been no change in the people seated outside. Elderly couple, group of four, single man, and the single blonde with the book. As I was intent on studying them without being too obvious, I gradually realized that the blonde girl was studying me. Suddenly, she smiled and waved.

No one was behind me, so I knew she was waving at me. I looked hard for a second and suddenly it hit me: I'd been fooled by the short blonde hair. Now that she had set her book down and was looking up, I could see her face, and it was one I could never forget. Hello, Gina. It's been a long time.

# PART 3

# Chapter 22

I'D NO SOONER recognized Gina than I felt the unmistakable sharp jab of a handgun in the small of my back. I didn't lift my hands. I didn't move. I froze.

A man behind me leaned forward and with a quiet but deep, husky voice said, "I'm thinking that the lady over there'd like to talk to you. What do you think?"

I didn't move. "The one waving?" I asked, trying to buy time.

"Yeah, the blonde. That'd be the one."

I said nothing for a moment as I ran through the possibilities. My Krav Maga instructors taught me four or five ways to disarm an assailant who approaches from behind, depending on whether he's on one side or another, or straight behind. The trouble is that the probability of success with any of these techniques runs from 10 percent on the low end to as high as 70 percent on the high side, depending almost completely on the skill of the guy standing behind me. Looked at the other way, it means the odds of getting shot in the back during an attempt to disarm the bad guy run from 30 percent at best to 90 percent at worst. Which, I suppose, is another way of saying that if the bad guy with a gun gets the jump on you from behind, you're already mostly screwed, especially if he knows what he's doing. I needed more information.

"Would you be Uncle Frankie?" I asked, without turning around.

"In the flesh," he said. Odd, but now, I felt a little comfort knowing that the guy with a gun to my back was a Chicago hit man. At least he was Gina's relative, if that counted for anything.

"Is that a gun in my back?"

"No, it's my finger, dickhead," he answered. He chuckled at his own

joke, and then said, "Actually, it's a Ruger .44 Magnum. Big fucking hole.
Old-school."

"That'll work," I agreed, nodding my head slowly. *Great.* Caught flat-
footed by a mob enforcer. I figured my odds of getting shot during an
attempt to disarm him were pretty much redlined at the wrong end of
the meter—the dead end. "You know, I was just about to go over there
anyway on my own. Matter of fact, she asked me here. I really don't think
you need a gun."

"Oh," he said. "In that case, I'm thinking I'll just toss it into this trash
can here." I felt him remove the gun, but I still didn't turn around. He
chuckled again—a real joker, this guy.

"That's a nice gun," I said. "No sense tossing it. You could just give
it to me."

He laughed again. "A fucking comedian," he said. "I like that." Takes
one to know one.

"Well, that's something. Should I walk now?" I asked.

"Yeah," he said. "Wait for the green, so's you don't get splattered. I
ain't a hundred percent certain, but I'm guessing that would annoy her. I
don't want to piss her off."

So we waited for the light to turn green. Then we walked.

~~~~

Before just now, the last time I'd seen Gina was at Sea-Tac in December
2006. At the conclusion of our three-week romance, she dropped me off
at the airport on my way to Quantico. At the time, she was twenty-two,
just six months out of college. She'd cried as we said our good-byes. As
I've thought about it over the past years, I think it's very possible that I
was probably already out of her plans, and we were feeling bad for different reasons. She probably dismissed me not long after I told her I couldn't
alter my training schedule to go on holiday with her. I messed up her Hawaiian vacation plans and, in so doing, proved that she wasn't in control.
I think this was something Gina probably could not—or would not—tolerate. So, most likely, I'd already been written out of the play by the time
she dropped me off. I was standing at the airport in the rain, looking at a
beautiful young woman, saying good-bye and meaning "Good-bye. I'll see

you in ninety days." She was saying good-bye and meaning, "Good-bye, it's been swell." But oh, she'd looked good. Damn good.

The woman I saw standing at the table, waiting for me to finish crossing the street looked the same in some ways, different in others. The hair was different, obviously. She used to have long, wavy, dark hair. Now, it was shoulder length and a honey blonde shade. Better for being incognito, I guess. Both styles looked attractive, although I was more used to the dark-haired Gina, so I probably still preferred her that way. But her eyes were the same—happy, sparkling, dark blue eyes. Her prominent jaw line, her lips wide and full—all the same. Her figure, if anything, was better now than it had been at age twenty-two. She wore tan shorts and a white sleeveless blouse. Her skin was tanned as if she'd just returned from a vacation in the Caribbean. Quite simply, she was stunning. I forgot all about Frankie and his .44.

"Hi, Danny," she said happily, smiling broadly when I crossed the street. She stood up and held her arms wide. I stepped forward and hugged her. She didn't just give me one of those little courtesy hugs—the type where both parties lean in and essentially reach around each other and pat each other on the back without actually touching anywhere else. Instead, she gave me a full-body press, just short of jumping up and wrapping her legs around me. Tight hug. Her large breasts pressed against my chest. Her perfume was mesmerizing, the smell of her hair intoxicating. I started to feel dizzy—like I was being sucked into a whirlpool. Another second, and I'd be a goner.

"Gina," I said, finishing our embrace and pushing back just in time. I smiled. "It's been a long time—almost five years. You look even more beautiful than I remembered."

She leaned forward and kissed me on the cheek. Hold on, dude. Don't topple.

"You always knew how to flatter me," she said, smiling.

"It was all true," I said. "Every word."

She laughed. She seemed sincerely happy to see me.

She turned to my left and said, "I see you've met Uncle Frankie."

Jolted back to reality, I turned and, for the first time, saw Frankie the Boot. He was a little taller than me, maybe six two. He probably weighed two-forty—he was a big guy. His hair was silver, and his face was lined with wrinkles. I guessed he was probably in his mid-sixties, but he might have been a little older. He wore a short-sleeved print shirt, untucked, over wool slacks. There was no sign of the .44, but it would have been easy enough to conceal under the shirt.

"I have," I said. "We met across the street."

"Uncle Frankie," she asked, looking at him, "were you nice to Mr. Logan?"

He looked at her, then at me, then back at her.

Before he could answer, I said, "He was a perfect gentleman."

He smiled—not at me—but at her. "See?" he said.

"I'll just bet," she said. "Oh well," she said to me, "at least he didn't shoot you."

"There is that," I agreed.

She smiled and said, "It's really good to see you again. Let's sit down and catch up." She waved for a waitress. "Are you still drinking Diet Cokes?"

I said yes, so she ordered one for me, another glass of tea for herself. Frankie took a seat at the next table—where the lone man was seated. Naturally, I thought. A bodyguard team for Gina.

We sat down. I spoke first. "It's really good to see you."

"You too," she said. "It's been a long time."

"Been very long," I agreed. "I've thought about you often."

"Me, too," she said. Then she added, "Especially in the last couple of weeks, huh?"

I chuckled. "True. Do you want to tell me what's going on? Why'd you suddenly up and disappear?"

"I'll tell you everything," she said. "In due time." She saw that I wasn't happy with this answer, and she said, "Okay, in just a few minutes, actually. But I'd like to just talk to you like old friends for a bit, if that would be alright. I'd like to catch up." She paused, and then added, "We were close once, if you still remember."

I nodded, and then I smiled. "I do remember."

"Good. What's it been, Danny, five years or so?"

"Five years this December," I said.

"A lot's changed in five years," she said.

"That's true," I agreed. "You'd just graduated and started working for your dad."

"Where I still am today."

"Chief financial officer and senior vice president," I said.

"That's right," she said. "But it wasn't nepotism, you know—I earned the title."

"So I've heard."

"And you," she said, "you're out of the army now. You have your own detective agency. You always said that's what you wanted to do, and now that's what you're doing."

"Just living the dream," I said.

"Is it what you expected?" she asked.

"It's bigger," I said. "Bigger as in broader, more comprehensive. Better in some areas than I'd expected, worse in others. Probably just more real world."

"And you have employees. I hear you have a good-looking girl working for you."

"Sounds like Toni impressed Robbie," I said.

"Apparently," Gina agreed.

"She's a looker," I said. "She's been known to impress the guys."

"Are you with her? Are you with anyone?"

"I'm not," I said. "I'm single. You?"

"Single, independent, unattached," she answered.

"Independent," I laughed. "From what I remember, I think you'd probably be independent, whether or not you were attached."

She laughed. "Maybe," she admitted. Then she smiled and said, "Maybe I was just never attached to the right person."

"Take a hell of a guy to make you want to give that up," I said.

"True," she agreed. "I don't mind being in charge."

I laughed. "Spoken like a master of understatement."

She laughed again. "You were always witty," she said.

"It's not being witty. It's being truthful. No offense, but you were always a bit of a control freak."

She shrugged, neither agreeing with nor denying the statement. I think we both knew it was spot-on.

"Anyway," she said, apparently changing subjects, "I've wondered how things worked out for you after our time together."

"Me, too," I said.

She smiled. "I thought about how you were probably the most hardworking, dedicated guy I'd ever seen. You were a genuine war hero, for starters. You had a plan, a goal, and you were going after it. I never doubted you'd have your own agency, just like you planned." She laughed. "I really never thought my own parents would hire you to track me down. But I guess I shouldn't have been surprised when you zeroed in on me so fast."

"I like to think we're pretty good at what we do."

"It would appear as though you are," she said.

She studied my face intently. "The years have been kind to you, Danny. You look more handsome than ever. I always knew you were a sleeper."

"Thanks, I think. What's a sleeper?"

"Yeah, a sleeper," she said. "You cruise around in high school, not involved, not into anyone that I could tell. Totally good looking but totally shy. You were a sleeper. A late bloomer. You didn't even know how good you were or how good you were going to become. But I knew."

"Stop, I'm blushing," I joked.

"See—that little comeback is something you'd have never said in high school. I guess it took the army to give you the confidence to really see your own strength. I think the army brought out the man in you." She smiled. "And, from where I sit, it looks like they did a damn good job."

"Thank you, ma'am," I said. "Flattery will get you everywhere."

"I certainly hope so," she said coyly. "We'll see."

I felt like I was playing tennis. She'd fire a witty line to me. I'd return a witty line to her. Fun—at least for a while.

"I was always confident," I said. "You were the only one that gave me butterflies."

She smiled. "But you're over that now."

I looked into her eyes. "Not a hundred percent."

There was silence for a second, like the tennis ball had been hit into a high lob and everyone was watching, waiting for it to come down. She broke the silence. "I missed you, Danny."

She may have been manipulating me, I'll never know. But I do know that right then, right there, I was hers.

"Me, too."

"Let's go on back," she said, setting her drink on the table and pushing out her chair. "We've got a little office in the back where we can talk privately. I have a lot of things I want to share with you."

I nodded. "Okay."

We stood, and Frankie started to get up as well. "Frankie," she said, "I'm alright. Stay out here."

Frankie the Boot looked at her, and then he looked at me, and then he looked back and nodded one time.

~~~~

The inside of the bakery was busy, even at three thirty on a Sunday afternoon. I followed Gina as we passed through the seating area and then through a door marked Employees Only. If the workers noticed us, they pretended not to.

She opened a door marked *Office*, turned on the light, and went inside. I followed. Once I was in, I took off my baseball cap and slid my backpack off while Gina closed the door behind us. I put my pack on a chair and turned back around.

Gina threw her arms around my neck and kissed me. This time, it wasn't on the cheek. It was a full-throttle lip-lock that went on and on and on. My head was spinning. I saw stars. I was just about to reach down and sweep all the shit off the top of the desk so I could throw her down and make a woman out of her when she broke it off—just in time.

She stepped back and said, nearly breathless, "Goddamn. I've wanted to do that since Robbie told me you were involved in the case. That surely brings back memories of our time together, doesn't it?"

I nodded. I don't think I was able to speak just yet.

"You're a terrific kisser," she said.

"You too," I answered, nodding. "Want to do it again?"

So we did. A little less passion this time, a little more tenderness. A little less loss of control.

We broke it off, but I continued to hold her, my face tilted down to her, our lips inches apart.

"That was awesome," she said.

I nodded. Then I kissed her on the forehead. I held her for a full two minutes, memories flooding back, lost in the moment. Gradually, I started to remember that I wasn't here on vacation—I was actually working. I leaned back and looked into her eyes. "Why am I here, Gina? Why've I been summoned? You could have had this from me anytime in the last five years. Just for the asking. I'm helpless around you. Why now?"

She stared deep into my eyes. "I guess I should fill you in, shouldn't I?"

I nodded.

"Okay." she said. "Let's sit down. This will probably take a while."

We broke our embrace, and she walked to the chair at the desk in the tiny office. I sat on the other side.

"From the beginning," I said.

"You sound like a detective."

I smiled but didn't say anything.

"Oooh, okay," she said, mock seriously, "from the beginning."

She gathered her thoughts, and then said, "First, let me say that I'm going to tell you some stuff you might not like to hear. You and I—we have a little history, but we don't know each other all that well. Despite that, I need to bring you into my confidence."

"Okay," I said. "Your secret's safe with me."

"We'll see," she said. "What's your feeling about marijuana?"

"Marijuana?" I asked. "I don't inhale." What a joker I am.

"No kidding," she said, seriously.

"No kidding? I guess I don't have any feelings about marijuana," I said. "I don't think about it. I don't smoke pot. I don't care if anyone else does. I'm not a cop."

"Did you know that law enforcement spends over sixteen billion per year to stamp out the marijuana business in America, and in the process arrests eight hundred thousand Americans every year for simple marijuana possession?"

I thought about it for a second, and then said, "Big numbers. I suppose that bothers me on a couple of levels. I don't see huge differences between pot use and alcohol use. Both get you stoned. As a cop in the army, we busted people for both. I saw a lot more functional problems with booze, though. Alcohol problems seem to have a much higher tendency to spill out onto the street. The idea that nearly a million people a year are put into jail for simple possession of pot is insane."

"Good, I think so, too. It bothers me," Gina said. "Next, did you know that in our state, marijuana growth is the number two cash crop, just behind apples?"

"I heard that somewhere."

"And did you know that the vast majority of that crop is controlled by the Mexican drug cartels?"

"I heard that, too."

"Does that bother you?"

"Which, that it's number two behind apples, or that the Mexicans are making all the money from it? I'm starting to see a pattern to your questions. I think it might bother me for a different reason than it bothers you."

"Explain," she said.

"It bothers me because it's against the law—it's an illegal crop."

"Legally, that's true. Morally, what's the difference between that and a vineyard? Both grow drugs that get you high. You already said that the concept of marijuana use didn't bother you. If the use doesn't bother you, why do you object to the cultivation?"

"I don't know. I suppose I just haven't thought it through and worked it out in my mind."

"Well, I have. And I've come to the conclusion that pretty soon, the federal government is going to wake up and say, 'Hey, we can kill not two, not three, but five birds with one stone. If we make pot legal and tax it, we can stop spending sixteen billion a year to prevent it, we can stop arresting a million people a year trying to prevent it, we can start earning a truckload of tax revenue, we can shut down the Mexican cartels on our side of the fence, and we can start a whole new legal agricultural business right here in America.'"

I thought about it for a moment. "Interesting theory. But people have been trying to legalize pot for forty years or more. No luck so far."

"The country's never been broke like we are now," Gina said. "Look around. Every statistic I gave you is true. I know the clowns in Washington, D.C., are brain-dead, but I don't think that they're that brain-dead. Eventually, they'll choose to take this issue on as opposed to cutting money and services from their constituents. They'll do this because the path is a lot easier and besides—they don't have a choice. They need the money. What this means to me is that the window of opportunity to make some real money on a venture that's technically illegal, yet morally correct, is open. But only for so long."

"You sound convinced," I said. "Knowing you, you must have some sort of plan."

She smiled. "Of course. My plan is to create a team using my family ties in Chicago and a Mexican drug cartel. They grow. We distribute nationwide. We split profits. This works until the Feds pull the plug and change the laws. There's a bucket-load of money to be made in the meantime."

I paused to digest what I'd just heard. "I have to say that you even considering this is pretty mind-boggling. And telling me about it is like way over the top."

"I figured you'd need some convincing," she said.

"Fire away," I said. "Frankly, I'm having a little trouble with this—even conceptually."

"Okay. Sometime—end of April, start of May—I started seeing in my mind how this could work. I did my research and put together a business plan. I went to Chicago and met with my uncles. I laid out all my numbers. They were impressed. They should be. I think we can split more than three hundred million dollars a year with a single cartel. When I drove home the fact that the Mexicans were making all this money right now, coming to our country, illegally, and using our land to grow marijuana to turn around and sell to Americans, I got their patriotic juices sizzling. They may be crime bosses, but they're Americans, and they don't like the idea of someone sneaking over and stealing what they consider to be their profit. If anyone's going to sell drugs to Americans, it's going to be them. Based on this, I signed them on to my plan."

"My problem, though," she continued, "is that I didn't know anyone with contacts with a Mexican drug cartel that was already in the marijuana business here. I didn't know how to contact them, or why they'd even listen to me."

"Speaking of which," I said, "what's in it for them? If they're making all that money now, why would they agree to split it?"

"Two reasons," she said. "First, my uncles can put together a wide distribution network, particularly through the East Coast, where retail prices are double West Coast prices. This will increase gross profits significantly. The second reason was left unspoken. It's basically if they don't agree to cooperate, they should no longer expect the U.S. organized crime families to sit on their hands while they take hundreds of millions of our customers' dollars out of the country. With the cocaine and the heroin business, they provide the product—we distribute it. We're comfortable with that arrangement. Ultimately, this business will be no different."

"In other words, you use the carrot if you can, the stick if you can't," I said.

"Exactly."

"So how'd you go about finding a contact in a Mexican drug cartel? Let me guess—that would be the lately deceased Mr. Eduardo Salazar."

"Poor Eddie. That's right. I met Eddie in June. I figured that if I wanted to meet someone connected with the Mexican drug cartel, then I should start hanging out at places where they hang out. I started going to Mexican lounges and bars. Sometimes I went by myself, but usually I went with a friend. I know a girl named Kara Giordano from work. She runs the finance department for a customer of ours."

"I've met Kara," I said. "Eddie beat her up trying to find you."

"Robbie told me. I'm very sorry she got hurt." I assumed she was being truthful, but she barely slowed down before continuing. "Anyway, one night Kara and I go to this crappy dive of a bar called Ramon's Cantina."

"We spent a very lovely evening there ourselves," I said.

"I'll bet. We hadn't been there an hour when I get hit on by this skinny little Mexican guy who thinks he's god's gift to women. He was so completely full of shit that it was laughable—corny lines and little innuendos—he'd have been blown off instantly in any respectable place. It was pathetic. But the thing was, I noticed that everyone in the place acted like they were afraid of him. They treated him with respect, were almost subservient. Naturally, I was intrigued. I worked him a little. He wanted in my pants so bad that I soon had him bragging that he was a lieutenant in the Tijuana-Mendez drug cartel. Bingo! Actually, I'd have never believed him, but judging from the way other people treated him, I thought maybe he was telling the truth."

"When you say you worked him, what do you mean?" I asked.

"Worked him? You know, I flirted with him. I chatted him up. I made him think I was impressed by his bullshit while I tried to figure out if he was connected."

"Okay," I said, "you dangled the bait."She smiled. "Exactly."

"Then what happened?"

"We went back to the bar several times in June, maybe once a week or so. Eddie apparently practically lived there, so each time he'd come at me with his crazy stupid pickup routine. Each time I let him think I was a little more interested and that he was a little closer to payday. Then, one night in late June, I'd ground up a Quaalude and poured it into a pen container, just like the spies. When he went to the bathroom, I dumped it into his drink and stirred it up. He drank it when he got back. As soon as he was done, I told him to take me to his place."

"I barely got him inside before he basically passed out. I'd seen him with a little notebook he'd use when he'd get phone calls. He kept it in his shirt pocket, and it seemed pretty sensitive to him. While he was sleeping, I found it and saw that it contained hand-drawn maps of each of his grow sites—there were about twenty of them that he was in charge of—along with phone numbers of the guys who worked for him. I used my cell phone to take pictures of each page. Then I put the notebook back in his pocket. I wrote him a sexy note that told him I had a great time and that he was a wonderful lover. Then I left and took a cab home."

"You're bad," I said.

"I know," she smiled.

"The very next time I went to Ramon's, I got Eddie by himself. I told him that I was connected to the Calabria family and that we wanted to meet to talk about a business proposition. I gave him a card with my name and an e-mail address. He laughed and said forget it. So I turned over one of his grows to the DEA. I left an anonymous message from a pay phone and three days later, the Feds busted it."

"You didn't tell Eddie, did you?"

"Hell no, he'd have killed me. Instead, I just bugged him again the next week. Left another card. This happened three more times. Same result—another field turned in. I turned in a total of four of his fields."

"I saw the busts in the paper. You made the DEA very happy. You were playing with fire. Weren't you worried that he'd eventually catch on?"

"Oh, yeah. But poor Eddie wasn't the sharpest pencil in the box. Even so, after the fourth time, I finally got an e-mail, but it wasn't from the cartel—it was from Eddie. He said that he needed to see me about something urgent. I figured my luck must have run out, and he'd finally put two and two together. So I decided to disappear and keep working on him."

"And that's when we got called in."

"Right. That was a bit of a surprise. I never thought the police would actually suggest that my parents hire a private investigator. I just expected them to do nothing because I'd read that they won't look very hard for a missing adult. I figured my deal would be concluded by the time anybody actually did anything to try and find me."

"Oops."

"Damn right, oops. You guys got started and almost immediately picked up my trail."

"That's what we do," I said.

"I can see that now," she said.

"So what happened to Eddie?" I asked. "Who shot him?"

"We didn't do that," she said quickly. "I think Eddie finally told his bosses what was happening because two things happened right about that time."

"Go ahead."

"First, I got an e-mail. Eddie finally gave my card to someone who mattered. The e-mail said that they wanted to talk to me."

"What was the second thing?"

"The second thing was that Eddie got killed. I didn't see that coming, either."

"Bad news for Eddie."

"True, but I'm sure you know that Eddie was a sadistic little prick. I didn't expect him to be killed, but there's no doubt in my mind that he would have killed me once he figured out what I was doing if he'd found me."

"I agree. However he got there, we're probably all better off without Mr. Salazar. So did you meet with the cartel?"

"Yes. They sent a man named Francisco Miranda. He's a high-level guy in the cartel. We met this past Thursday. I ran him through the whole proposition, and he relayed it to his bosses."

"And? What next?"

"And there's going to be a meeting tomorrow morning between the bosses of the cartel and my uncles to close the deal."

"They're meeting here?"

"At the Jefferson County airport, in a hangar. They both fly their planes in, taxi to the hangar, park, meet, agree, shake hands, and then leave. The airport is uncontrolled. No tower, no FAA. I think the cartel is flying in from Vancouver."

"Holy shit," I said. "So you've pulled it off."

"I think so," she said, smiling broadly. "All that has to happen is the principals need to meet each other and shake hands. Then, the lieutenants will work out the details, and we'll have a deal."

"Damn," I said. I thought for a minute and suddenly wondered what my role in all of this was. "Back to my original question," I said. "Why am I here? Why did you summon me to Port Townsend, sandwiched in between high-level meetings with the Tijuana-Mendez cartel and the Calabria family?"

"Simple. You were getting too close to be left alone," Gina said. "My genius brother told a lie after I specifically gave him instructions not to, and you caught him on it. You were closing in. My deal happens tomorrow morning. I've been working on it for four months. I couldn't risk you doing something to blow it up at the last minute. So I brought you in."

"Where you can control me," I said.

She smiled but didn't disagree.

"How did you plan on controlling the rest of my team?" I asked.

"I'm counting on you to do that," she answered.

"And you're convinced that I won't blow it up, even now?"

She smiled as she got up and walked around to my side of the desk. "Yes," she said, putting her arms around my neck. "I am convinced that you won't blow this up. You have no reason to. Like you said, you're not a cop." She kissed me lightly on the lips. "I'm also convinced that you'll go home with me now and stay with me tonight. Tomorrow, I'll go back to Seattle with you. You can tell the world you found me. That's what my parents hired you to do. That's what you did." She kissed me again.

"Should be great for your firm's reputation."

She must have sensed by the look on my face that I wasn't sold.

"Besides," she said.

"What?" I asked.

"We still have a lot of catching up to do tonight. I can't wait."

I started to get a little light-headed again, intoxicated by her perfume, the smell of her hair, even her breath. No harm in doing a little catching up, I supposed.

# Chapter 23

THE QUIMPER PENINSULA juts out to the northeast from the top of the Olympic Peninsula like a hitchhiker's thumb thrust from a fist. The peninsula is bounded by Discovery Bay to the west, the Strait of Juan de Fuca to the northwest and north, Admiralty Inlet to the northeast, and Townsend Bay to the southeast. Port Townsend is located at the far northeast corner of the peninsula. Gina said the house where she'd been staying was six miles directly west, on the Discovery Bay side of the peninsula. I agreed to follow her.

She dropped me off at my Jeep, where I tossed my pack in the back and fell in behind her silver Lexus SUV. From Water Street in downtown Port Townsend, we took Tyler Street west until it turned into Discovery Bay Road. She turned right on Hastings Avenue. The small town quickly dropped away, showing that we were on a long, straight road with very little traffic. The posted speed limit was fifty, but Gina drove at sixty-five for several minutes. The surrounding area was half forest, half rural-type residential.

The terrain rose slightly, peaking near the centerline of the peninsula, before falling back toward the sea on the western half. A couple of minutes after we'd crested the ridge, Gina turned right on a small, unnamed dirt road. The forest was thick on both sides of the road. She proceeded about half a mile until she came to a gated entry, complete with two attendants who, despite not wearing uniforms or showing visible weapons, were clearly guards. If I had to guess as to whether or not they had weapons nearby, my money was landing on yes. In any case, they smiled at Gina when she approached. She stopped and talked to them. I saw her pointing back to me. Both guards nodded. After she drove through, I approached.

"Good afternoon, Mr. Logan," the first guard said without smiling. "Please follow the Lexus up ahead. Stay right with her."

"Okay," I answered simply. These guys acted like government guys— they were serious. Sometimes you crack jokes. Other times, not. This seemed like one of the other times. I followed Gina.

She wound through the trees, and after another two hundred yards or so, she disappeared around a corner. Rounding the corner myself a few seconds later, I saw a magnificent lodge framed by huge cedar trees. Beyond the trees, the sky and the brilliant blue waters of the Strait of Juan de Fuca served as a backdrop. The lodge was constructed with rocks and timbers and featured a large, twenty-foot-tall porte cochere. A circular drive wound around a well-manicured lawn the size of a long par-three or maybe even a short par-four golf hole. Flowers of all colors surrounded the lawn and the home. I thought I'd been transported to Yosemite and was looking at the Ahwahnee Hotel. It was jaw-dropping.

I pulled up beside her and stopped. Hopping out, I said to her, "Where do you stay when you're not slumming?"

She laughed and said, "Pretty nice, isn't it? It belongs to my Uncle Peter. He doesn't use it very often. He welcomes family as guests, so whenever I'm up here, I like to stay."

"I can see why," I said, grabbing my backpack. "This is where you've been hiding out?"

"Yeah. Just leave your keys in the car. Someone will park it for you in the lot over there." She pointed past me. I looked and saw several cars including three silver Fords of the same type that had followed me. Looks like my hosts were making sure I arrived safely.

"Would you like me to show you your room?" she asked.

"That'd be great," I said, wondering exactly what she had in mind.

"I'd be happy to," she said. She laced her hand through my arm and led me inside, through two of the largest doors I'd ever seen. Each must have been six feet wide and fifteen feet tall. The doors were carefully counterbalanced so that they swung open and closed at the lightest touch. Which was good, since they probably weighed four hundred pounds each.

"Is your uncle a really big guy?" I asked, peering at the giant doors as we passed through.

She laughed. "Actually, he is. Not this big, but big. You'll meet him tomorrow." *Really?*

"He had this built?"

"No, he bought it already built about three years ago from a techie billionaire who was having money problems. He fixed it up the way you see it now. Like I said, Uncle Peter doesn't come here often, but he definitely likes it up here. He said he always wanted a place in the Pacific Northwest."

"Nothing like starting at the top and working your way up," I said, as I took in the grand scale of the home.

We entered what would normally be called a foyer in most homes, but in this case that term was wholly inadequate. Here, the entry had to be called a lobby. Directly in front of us was a large living room and behind it, an enormous plate-glass wall spanning the entire length of the room. Through the windows was the Strait of Juan de Fuca, framed by large cedars. On the far distant horizon, the Canadian city of Victoria was visible on the edge of Vancouver Island.

"Wow. I may have made a serious mistake with my career choice," I said, blown away by the view.

Gina laughed. "There's more, trust me. Come on, I'll show you your room."

I followed her down a hallway with doors lining both sides, like you'd find in a hotel.

"I don't see any room numbers," I joked.

"You're down here at the end," she said. She opened the door to what looked like a hotel room inside—clearly a guest room.

"Very nice," I said, entering and looking around. "Even has its own bathroom." I pretended to be confused. "Where's the minibar?"

Gina laughed. "You're a regular comedian, aren't you, Danny Logan? I don't remember that about you."

I looked out the window and watched a large freighter inbound for Admiralty Inlet. "I'm actually just blown away by your Uncle's little vacation home here. I think I've landed in Never Never Land."

"It's real," she said.

I turned to her. She walked up to me and put her arms around my neck.

"It's real," she said again. She reached up and kissed me lightly. "Why don't you get yourself cleaned up? We'll have dinner around six. Come down to the family room anytime. It's right back up the hallway on the other side of the entry. You can't miss it."

"I don't know," I said. "I forgot to bring my GPS."

She laughed. "See you in a bit."

~~~~

I took the opportunity to take a quick shower and change into the clean clothes in my RON bag. I also figured that in a place like this, I could probably find a laundry room somewhere to wash the clothes I wore today so that they'd be clean tomorrow. I'd learned in the military to take advantage of things like showers and laundry facilities when they were available. Later, I might find that I needed one, and I might not be so lucky. Even clean, and maybe even pressed, my wardrobe was almost certain to fall short of the other meeting attendees. Unfortunately, there was nothing I could do about that now.

I walked outside onto the private balcony. I could see other rooms—probably other guest rooms. It appeared that each guest bedroom had a similar patio-table-and-two-chairs arrangement. I sat down in one of the chairs and leaned back, the better to enjoy the sunshine and the view. Under different circumstances, this would have been a hell of a vacation spot.

Almost immediately after I sat down, I heard Gina's voice coming from the next bedroom. Her balcony door was also open. She was inside, speaking on the telephone, unaware that anyone might be outside listening.

Out of courtesy, I started to go back inside so I wouldn't be tempted to eavesdrop. I'd only taken a step, though, when I heard her say. "Yeah, he's here. I brought him here just a little while ago." She must have been talking about me. I stopped. Who was she talking to?

"Trust me, it's better to have him here where we can keep an eye on him as opposed to letting him wander around on his own. They've done a better job than I expected so far. Faster, too. He'd likely come strolling right into the middle of our meeting tomorrow." This was consistent with what she'd told me.

"Yeah, we're set up for ten. You'll fly in, taxi to the hangar, unload, and walk right in. Any problems, you turn right around and walk right back out. After the meeting, you hop on your plane and you're out of here." She must be talking to her uncle.

"Yeah, my agreement was we each get four guys outside and two guys inside, plus me and Francisco Miranda. Not counting the two of you and the two Mendez brothers, of course." Was she referring to security arrangements?

Gina continued. "Yeah, Francisco Miranda's the guy I already met with here. He's a pretty high-level person on their side, about the same level I am on our side.

"I'm just going to count him as one of our security guys." (Probably referring to me.) "We'll be okay. Frankie will be our other guy.

"It's all set up. They're ready. He said everything's a go." The Mexican side is ready?

"I think we can count on it. He'll talk. That's the point." No idea. Who'll talk? What's the point?

"Good. I'll see you tomorrow. I really appreciate what you're doing. Love you, bye."

I stepped inside and quietly closed the doors in case she decided to go outside on the balcony. No sense in letting her know that I'd overheard half her conversation.

But what had I heard? Her story to her uncle was consistent with what she'd told me in the bakery. Though now it sounded like she was factoring me into the security equation. She should be careful here. I might be okay for helping her fill out her meeting quota, but she'd best not count on me for backup if the Mexican cartel and the Chicago mob got into a beef and decided to solve it with gunplay. I'd most likely be heading for the exit. I didn't have a horse in this race, and I wasn't about to start shooting someone if things went sideways. Unless, of course, someone started shooting at me. The whole damn thing was illegal anyway. The last thing I wanted to do was to remove the ability to claim innocence by doing something stupid like joining a side. As things stood now, I could always claim I was coerced if everything went to hell and we all ended up getting busted.

From what I could hear, it sounded like the Mexican side agreed to the terms and was ready to conclude a deal. The only thing I couldn't even fathom a guess about was who was supposed to talk. Gina'd said, "He'll talk." Who will talk? What will he say? Someone must have had information that Gina wanted, and she wanted him to talk to about it. That let me out. I didn't know anything. Certainly, I had no secrets from her anyway. Except maybe that I overheard her telephone conversation.

~~~~

I left my room at five thirty and walked down the long corridor past the entry and into the family room. A large flat-screen television was built into the opposite wall. The kitchen was to the right, separated from the family room by an eating bar that must have had ten barstools in front of it. A large stone fireplace was on the wall opposite the television. It was not lit. A wet bar was located opposite the kitchen, next to a dining table.

"Good afternoon, Mr. Logan," said an English-accented voice from behind me. I turned and saw a middle-aged man on the other side of the bar as he polished stemware with a white linen cloth.

"Hi, there," I said. "Very beautiful home you've got here."

"It is, isn't it?" the man said. "My name's Randall. In addition to being a relief bartender, I'm the home's manager."

I was intrigued. "Glad to meet you, Randall," I said. "I'm Danny. I'm curious, what does a home manager do, anyway?"

"Certainly, sir," he said. "Homes of a certain size require diverse staff of different capabilities. For example, at this home we employ two gardeners full-time, two maids, a chef, a chauffeur, and myself. Seven of us, altogether. I am responsible for the overall condition and state of the home, including the management of all the staff."

"Fabulous," I said. "And this happens whether or not Mr. Calabria is here?"

"That is correct," he said. "Our duties change, of course, when the family is in residence. But we're always prepared." He finished polishing his wine glass and set it down. "May I offer you something from the bar?" he asked.

"Do you have Mac & Jack's?" I asked.

"African Amber on tap?" he asked.

I smiled. "Oh, we're going to get along famously, Randall," I said.

He smiled, and then pulled me a glorious ice-cold pint and passed it across the bar. "Please feel free to enjoy the grounds, Mr. Logan," he said. "Ms. Fiore has let us all know who you are. We're pleased to have you as a guest for the evening." He turned to leave.

"Thank you," I said. "Say, Randall, before you hurry off, would you be the one to talk to about getting some laundry done?"

"I'll pass the word," he said. "It will be taken care of immediately."

"Thanks," I said. "I appreciate it." I turned and walked down the steps into the family room. The glass walls that separated the room from the outdoors were pushed back on tracks so that the entire outdoors became an extension of the room. Warm sea breezes floated up the cliff and into the home—mesmerizing. Looking to my left, I noticed a table in the corner of the patio, nearly invisible from inside the home. Frankie Rossi sat at the table, alone, drinking a beer, apparently enjoying the view. He noticed me and waved me over.

"Mr. Comedian," he called, smiling. "Come have a seat."

"Thanks," I said. I walked over and pulled out a chair. "Pretty nice digs, here, huh?"

"Yeah," he said. "Terrific. I'm thinking the view here's almost as good as from my place."

"In Chicago?" I asked.

"Of course. I got a condo on Sheridan, just north of Lincoln Park. Looks out over the lake. 'Course, we get our sun in the morning, and here it's in the afternoon." He pondered this for a moment, then said, "Both are nice, I guess."

I nodded. "This is pretty fabulous. I don't think I've ever seen anything quite like this."

"Yeah, the family's been around a long time. They know how to live." He paused for a moment. "Oh, shit. By the way. Meant to tell you, sorry about the gun in the back this afternoon. I didn't know who you were. Got my ass chewed big time for that. Promised I'd apologize. She asks— and she sure fucking will—you tell her I said I was sorry. Got that?"

"Got it," I said, amused. You don't often meet hit men, and especially not the type that look like they're afraid they're about to be castrated. "No problem about the gun. Glad you didn't shoot me." I paused for a second, then added, "Do it again, though, and you and me are going to have issues."

I smiled when I said it, but he wasn't sure what I meant. He gave me a cold, hard stare for a moment. I returned fire. Then, he chuckled. "You're a funny little prick," he said. Then realizing that he might just have insulted me, he quickly added, "No offense."

I laughed, "None taken. Here's to your self-restraint." We clinked glasses.

"Big day tomorrow, huh?" I asked.

"Yeah, it looks like. Got the family flying in."

"Do you know why I'm here?" I asked.

"Just that she told me she wanted to keep an eye on you," Frankie said. "I'm thinking that you make her nervous. Besides which, I'm thinking she likes you."

"She likes me? Why are you thinking that?"

"Way she talks. She talks like she's impressed by you." He shook his head like he didn't understand.

"Well, no accounting for taste, right?"

He shrugged. "You don't seem all that bad," he said. "That a four- or five-inch 1911 you got on your hip there?"

I smiled. "Good eye, Frankie. It's a four-inch."

Thought so. "I carry a five sometime," he said. "I shoot a tighter group with a five."

"Me, too, but from three feet, what difference does it make?"

"Fuckin' a," he said, smiling and raising his glass again.

"There you are." Gina walked into view from the family room. "I've been looking. I checked your room, and you were gone."

Frankie and I both stood when she approached. "Sorry about that. I didn't know where you were," I lied, "which room is yours. So after I took a quick shower, I decided to walk down here and see the home. Only just got started, and I bumped into Uncle Frank."

"Are you being nice?" she asked him.

"I am," he said quickly. He looked at me.

"He is," I confirmed. "He even apologized for pulling his gun on me this afternoon. He needn't have apologized. He's a very loyal man, and I'm certain you're in good hands with him watching out for you. No offense whatsoever. We're good."

Gina looked surprised. "How about that," she said. Then she added, "Uncle Frankie, if you'll excuse us, I've arranged for a private dinner with Mr. Logan."

"Good meeting you, Uncle Frank," I said reaching forward to shake his giant hand. "You take care of yourself."

"You, too."

~~~~

When the sun begins to go down in the Northwest, even in August, it gets cool—especially if you're on the water. Or in this case, above the water, since the house sat on a cliff fifty feet or so above the ocean. The sun was just above the horizon shortly after eight thirty, and all the warmth from it was gone. Gina and I sat huddled in a blanket outside at the fire pit and watched the end of the day. A large supply of split pine was stacked nearby, and we were working our way through it. The pine logs burned brightly and quickly and smelled wonderful.

Gina had arranged to have dinner served on the patio. We polished it off along with a bottle of Silver Oak cabernet. Later, she chose coffee while I worked on a bottle of Fiji water. I had my arm around her as we stared off across the water. The lights of Victoria were visible in the twilight on the northwest horizon.

A breeze filtered up the hill off the water. She shuddered and snuggled closer to me.

"You cold?" I asked.

"A little."

"Big day tomorrow."

"I know," she answered.

"You nervous?" I asked.

"A little."

"But you're all set up?"

"Yes."

It was quiet a moment, and then I said, "Tell me again why I'm here."

"I told you. If you're here, you're not there."

"Very funny."

"If you're already here, you can't come barging in and blow my deal."

"But you must know that I'd have never discovered this place by tomorrow morning."

"I most certainly did not know that. You've surprised me throughout this ordeal. I couldn't take that chance."

"That's it?" I asked. "That's the only reason?"

Instead of answering, she reversed the conversation. "Let me ask you something," she said. "You tell me. Why are you here? Why didn't you tell me to go to hell and just leave? Why didn't you turn me in?"

"Would you have let me leave?" I asked.

"Would it have mattered? Did you need my permission?"

"No, I suppose not."

"You could have overcome poor Uncle Frankie."

"Probably," I said. "And the rest of your army here? Maybe. But okay. My first answer? I'll be honest. I was intrigued."

"About?"

"About you. We had something once. I remember it to this day. It was short, but it was intense and it was memorable. I was intrigued to find out if there was a chance to reopen that. To go there again. There. I suppose that's why I came. I suppose that's why I'm still here. And I'm damn sure not going to turn you in. You're probably committing some kind of 'conspiracy to misbehave' offense that I can't name at the moment. But I'm not thinking about that. That's someone else's job now.

"Second answer," I continued. "I was curious about what the hell you were doing. Now I know."

"You satisfied now?"

"As to the second answer? Yeah, I suppose so."

"As to your first answer?"

"No. No resolution on that one yet."

She looked at me, and then we kissed gently. "I'm afraid we might not be able to resolve that question tonight," she said.

"I understand," I said. "Tomorrow's a big day."

We watched silently as the sun began to set. Out on the water, a large freighter moved steadily eastward, Seattle-bound.

"Let me ask you something," I said. "What are your feelings about the time we had together?"

"Same as you," she answered. "I have very nice memories of those three weeks. Who knows where things might have gone?"

I kissed her again and hugged her tighter.

"What are you doing tomorrow night?" she asked, smiling. "Got plans?"

"I don't know yet," I said.

"Look," she said, wriggling free and suddenly pointing to the western horizon. "Look at that." The sun was dipping below the horizon.

"Beautiful," I said.

"Do you remember what I wanted to do five years ago before you had to go off for training?"

"I do," I said. "You wanted to go to Hawaii."

"And?"

"And watch a sunset together."

"And?" she asked again.

"As I recall, there was something about getting naked and making love so passionate that the building would fall down around us."

She laughed. "I don't remember it quite that way, but it sounds fun."

It was quiet as we both relived the memory and contemplated the possibilities.

"Hawaii's nice this time of year," she said.

"So I hear."

"Maybe we should think of finishing that date."

"Really?"

"Tell you what," she said. "My deal closes tomorrow. Let's not wait. Tomorrow night, let's go to the airport together. I'll buy the tickets."

I smiled.

"Was that a yes?"

Before I could answer one way or another, she said, "I'll take that for a yes." She stood up. "And," she said, "on that happy note, I'm going to my room to finish getting ready for tomorrow. I'll see you bright and early."

~~~~

I lay in bed with the balcony door open and listened to the sound of the ocean crashing into the cliff below the house. My mind was a blur. I was well and truly under the intoxicating spell of Gina Fiore. I was tempted to run next door and seal the deal.

But I was having trouble visualizing a relationship between a private investigator who'd basically been a cop most of his adult life, and a woman who brokered deals between Mexican drug cartels and the Chicago mob. Something was fundamentally wrong with that picture. The part of me that recognized this wanted to get dressed and sneak out.

In the end, I did neither. I didn't go next door—and she didn't come over. Nor did I sneak out and go home in the middle of the night.

I listened to the sound of the ocean for about fifteen minutes. Then I fell into a deep, deep sleep. I dreamed again. More dancing angels.

# Chapter 24

NEXT MORNING I woke up feeling uneasy. I'd tossed and turned to bad dreams all night long. I got out of bed at six thirty and went outside on the balcony. I took my phone, checked my e-mails, and looked at the news websites. I was showered and dressed by seven thirty. When I'd returned to my room after dinner the night before, the clothes I'd been wearing when I arrived had already been laundered, pressed, and placed at the end of my bed. I don't know if the olive khakis and Hawaiian print shirt had ever been pressed—certainly not since I'd bought them. I looked at the reflection in the mirror and was impressed by what I saw. One used, somewhat conflicted, but still-in-good-condition private investigator, vintage 1982. Six one. One seventy-five, maybe 180 pounds. Sandy hair. Sharply turned out in well-pressed duds. As good as it gets. For me, anyway. Still, I had an uneasy feeling in my stomach.

I left my room and walked to the family room, where I smelled breakfast already in progress. I turned the corner and, to my surprise, found eight armed men seated at the twelve-person dining table, talking quietly among themselves and working on hearty breakfasts being served buffet-style from trays on the serving bar. It reminded me of pre-mission meals in Iraq, except the food looked better here.

Uncle Frankie was seated in the middle of the group. When he saw me, he said, "Hey fellas, listen up!" When he had everyone's attention, he said, "This guy here—" he pointed at me, "this guy—" he paused and looked me up and down, "this guy who I'm thinking must think he's in Hawaii or something, his name is Danny Logan. He's a high school friend of Ms. Fiore's, and he's coming with us today. That means you can't shoot him. Got that?"

The men nodded or grunted, and then returned to their breakfasts.

I looked for Gina, but she was not there yet, so I grabbed a plate and helped myself.

"Come sit over here," Frankie said, pointing to an empty chair opposite him.

I sat down. "Thanks for the introduction."

"Don't think of it," he said. "These are my boys. Say, you get a good night's sleep? I always find it helps to get a good night's sleep. I sleep like a baby."

"I tossed and turned all night long," I said. "Bad dreams."

"That's too bad. You okay? You ready to go?" he asked. "You don't look too good."

I laughed. "This is as good as it gets, man. Besides—what am I going to do? Sit on the sidelines and stay out of the way. I still don't even know why she wants me there."

"I'm sure she has her reasons," Frankie said. "She's keeping tabs on you."

"So you've said."

"Don't sweat it, kid," he said. "By lunchtime today, you'll be on your way home."

"Good," I said. I meant it.

~~~~

After breakfast, I had thirty minutes to kill before our 8:45 departure time, so I walked outside and found a path that meandered down to the railing at the cliff's edge. A hidden bench had seemingly been hewn from the stone. I sat down and looked out over the water. Last chance. I desperately needed to sort things out in my mind.

What was I doing here? Why was I going to an organizational kickoff meeting between a Mexican drug cartel and the Chicago mob? Was I being coerced or was I a willing participant? They didn't take my gun, so I must be willing. But I'm a decent, moral, law-abiding citizen. I had no business being within ten miles of this shit, except to move in afterward and throw people in jail. But I wasn't in the army anymore. I wasn't a special agent anymore. I didn't throw people in jail anymore. I was right when

I told Gina it wasn't my job.

But that didn't mean I was cleared to sit happily back and watch a major illegal drug deal get structured right in front of me—as if I wasn't even there? This couldn't be right, even if it wasn't my job, even if I didn't particularly care whether people smoked pot or not. Even if I thought that the law enforcement efforts amounted to a waste of money on the one hand and the persecution of thousands of otherwise innocent Americans was ridiculous on the other—right was right. Wrong was wrong. The law was the law.

Or was it? Suddenly, it became clearer to me as two things sprang into focus, one right after the other. On the one hand, law enforcement officers have it easy. For them, the law really is the law. They're compelled to enforce it to the letter. Black and white, no gray area, no room for interpretation. A law enforcement officer follows the law and doesn't question its effects, its reasons, or its underlying morality. Those questions are left to the public and the politicians. Law enforcement pins on the badge; they do their job. Period. Because of my CID background, I'd been looking at things in this manner for a long time. Yet, since I was no longer a cop, perhaps it was time to change, or at least reexamine, my perspective.

On the other hand, for the public—people who aren't cops, which now included me by the way—there's an ocean of gray between black and white, or at least there can be, maybe even should be sometimes. Even the boundaries are fuzzier. Of course, the essentials are the same: right is still right, and wrong is still wrong; laws are still laws. But the picture expands to include a big hunk of gray that doesn't exist for lawmen. Things like the effects of a given law—intentional and unintentional—and the underlying morality of the law are now open to examination. If the law is bad, is obsolete, has unintended negative consequences, then it needs to change, and it's up to the general public—not the cops—to see that it gets done. Rational, thinking people understand this.

Finally, the fog began to lift. At least in regard to the nature of the problem, if not the solution. I was bumping into an internal conflict between the black-and-white perspective of the cop side of me and the gray-area perspective of the non-cop side that believed the federal pot laws were archaic, damaging, and would inevitably be changed. I'm not saying I had the answer to this conundrum, because I didn't. My cop instincts were, and still are, strong. But at least I better understood the nature of my dilemma. And I was more comfortable with the reasons why I felt uneasy.

Of course, the second thing I figured out while sitting on the bench overlooking the ocean was that when I'm near Gina, it's as if I'm intoxicated. I say and do stupid shit. When I'm able to back away from her and get to a point where I can think clearly, like now, then I realize that I'm actually saying and doing the stupid shit that I didn't recognize I was saying and doing when she was around. It's embarrassing. It's like Gina comes around, and snap—brain short-circuits. Worse, I think it's always been that way. It's entirely possible that Gina has never even seen the real me. She's only seem some sort of mind-numb roboton with stars in his eyes who does and says what he thinks will most impress her. I needed to suck it up and sort that shit out.

Conflict or no conflict, I needed to let somebody know where I was. That was just good procedure. Toni was already pissed at me, but I had to let her know what was up; otherwise, she'd have reason to be even more pissed. I dialed her number.

"Good morning," she said when she answered the phone. She sounded okay maybe?

"Hi."

"Did you find her?"

"Yes, I did. She's alright. She's up here in Port Townsend."

"I imagine there must be a good story behind all this?"

"Oh yeah, I'll tell you when I get back."

"Okay. Are you still in Port Townsend then?"

"Yes. There's a meeting I'm going to attend this morning at ten at the Jefferson County Airport. I'll be coming home afterward, probably early afternoon."

"What kind of meeting?"

"I can't tell you over the phone," I said. "I'll explain it all this afternoon."

It was quiet for a second. "Are you okay?"

"I'm fine."

"Do you need backup?"

"No, I'm good."

"I'm worried about you," she said.

"I'm okay, really."

Again, the line was silent for a second. Then she said, "Where'd you stay last night?"

"Let's talk about that this afternoon, too."

"Okay," she said quietly. Then she added, "Your Aunt Thelma called." I don't actually have an Aunt Thelma, but no one knows this. It's a secret code. The movie *Thelma and Louise* came out in 1991 when Toni was something like six years old. Still, it's one of her favorites. She especially likes the character played by Susan Sarandon, Thelma Sawyer. Toni admires Thelma's tough, no-nonsense qualities. Inspired by the character, Toni developed a coded emergency message she calls Aunt Thelma. The way it works is that if either of us mentions that Aunt Thelma called, it's really our secret way of asking if the other person is under duress, such as might be the case if they were being held prisoner and not able to speak freely. If the answer is, "Tell her I'll call her back," it means yes, I'm in trouble—call out the cavalry. We'd never had reason to use it before now.

Fortunately, I was able to say, "I'm good. No problems. Still armed and dangerous."

"Good," she said. "Dwayne called. He wants you to call him."

"I will. I'll see you this afternoon."

"Danny," she said, "Be careful."

I didn't know what to tell Dwayne and I didn't want to lie to him, so I decided to call him back after the airport meeting was over. That should be two hours or so. Is that a form of a lie? I hope not. I rationalized it by thinking that by then, I'd have a lot more information, and I'd be in a lot better position to know what to tell him.

~~~~

At 8:40, I returned to my room and grabbed my pack. My intention was to throw it in my Jeep so that all my stuff would be in one place. I walked over to the garage at 8:45 just in time to hear Frankie assemble his "boys."

"Here's the deal," he said. "Philly and Mike, you two are going to stay here at the house. House guard. Stay at the gate, both of you. Got it?" The two men nodded.

"Berto, you're inside the house. Don't leave."

"Francesco, you're the roamer. You're the boss in charge of the house." Francesco nodded.

"Steve, Johnnie, Carmen, Salvador—you're all going with us to the hangar. You'll all be outside, playing footsies with the spics, got it?"

"Yeah," they said.

"You're armed with AKs, and they're armed with AKs; but they're all hidden in the car. I'm thinking anything goes down inside, or outside for that matter, you fuckers open up with your handguns and hose those motherfuckers. Then work your way to the car for the heavy iron. Beat 'em to the draw. Got it?"

They nodded.

"You're Americans," Frankie added. "You gotta' be better than they are."

"You gonna be inside, boss?" one of the four asked.

"You bet. John and Peter will do the meeting. Gina's gonna be the MC. I'm gonna be inside with numbnuts, here." He pointed. I was numbnuts.

"They got the same numbers, boss?"

"Yeah. Exact same numbers. Four outside guards—that's you guys, plus two inside. That's me and him," he said, again pointing to me. "Two principals and one assistant each. Gina's our assistant, even though she's the one really puttin' this thing together. They got that kid who Gina met with last week as their assistant. Bottom line—there'll be five people inside and four outside from each party."

"I'm thinking there shouldn't be any trouble," Frankie said. "Gina and the Mexican already worked out all the details. This here's supposed to be just a meet and greet, shaky-shaky, and seal the deal. There ain't no money here, and there ain't no drugs, so there's no reason for anybody to get all twitchy. Except that this is a high-level meeting between the highest-level bosses you're ever gonna see. So stay the fuck awake! I don't want no chitchat outside."

"No problem, boss," someone said. "We don't speak Spanish." Everyone laughed.

"Laugh it up now," Frankie said. "When we get there, we're all fucking business. Remember, you're representing the USA. You damn well better make us proud, or I'll personally put a cap in your fucking ears. Got it?"

"Yeah," they said in unison. One joker started chanting, "U-S-A!, U-S-A!, U-S-A!" and the rest started laughing.

Gina walked around the corner into the garage at that moment. She looked spectacular. She wore dark blue jeans, creased. She had on a simple white long-sleeved blouse over which she wore a lightweight navy blue jacket. She wore a single strand of pearls around her neck along with pearl earrings. Her lipstick was a deep red.

"Did I miss something?" she asked.

"We're ready to go," Frankie said.

"Good. Let's not be late," she said.

~~~~

I rode with Gina in the Lexus SUV to the airport, while Frankie and the boys followed us in a gray van. Once we turned onto the paved road past the edge of the property, Gina picked up speed and headed east on Hastings Avenue.

"You look really pretty this morning," I said.

"Thank you," she answered. "You look pretty dapper yourself, in an island-casual sort of way. Let me guess—you're getting a jump-start on our vacation."

I laughed. "I'm not completely certain that was a compliment, but I'll take it that way. Actually, when I left home yesterday, I didn't know I'd need my dress-ups."

She laughed. "You look fine," she said. Then she added, "Did you sleep well?"

"Tossed and turned all night long," I said.

"Me, too," she said. "Must be nerves."

"Probably."

"You know, I half expected you to come to my room last night," she said.

"Really?" I said. "I didn't think the time was right, for a lot of reasons."

"Such as?"

"You said you needed to get ready for this morning. I figured you'd be nervous and preoccupied. Hell, I was nervous and preoccupied."

"It will be good to get past this, won't it?" she asked.

"True," I said.

We drove in silence for a moment, past houses and small farms. She said, "You're not at all comfortable with this, are you?"

"Honestly," I said, "I'm torn right down the middle between 'Holy shit—this is illegal and I have to do something' on one hand, and 'doesn't matter to me—rather see you with the dough than the cartels' on the other hand."

"Which hand prevails?"

"For this meeting, the latter," I said. "I guess I'm really not a cop anymore. I'm not doing anything. I'm just along for the ride. If anyone asks, I'll tell them I thought we were going to look at an airplane."

She laughed. "No one will ask."

Gina reached Discovery Road and turned south toward the airport.

"But you are right about one thing," I said. "I'm definitely not comfortable with this. I suppose I should be jumping up and down for you saying congratulations on all the money you're going to make, but I'm not. Like I said, I'm torn."

"Well," she said, "maybe things will be clearer to you after the meeting."

"Maybe." I said, though I didn't know why that would be the case.

A few moments later, she said, "Danny, whatever happens today and beyond, I don't want you to change, you know?"

"I don't think I could change now if I wanted to," I said. "Maybe evolve a little, but no wholesale changes coming. Too old. Too set in my ways."

"Yeah, you are getting to be an old fart," she teased. Then, seriously, "I envy your ability to see things in black and white. No hesitation, no questions, no self-doubts. That's the opposite of me. I always liked that about you. I'm jealous."

I laughed. "That's funny," I said. "I was just thinking this morning of the need for me to expand my thought process so that I can understand the vast gray area in the middle. I have trouble with that."

"Well, don't overthink it," she said.

"No, but it's important to understand the whole picture," I said.

"You trying to rationalize what I'm doing?" Gina asked. "Trying to find a way to get on board with me?"

"Yeah, I suppose," I admitted. "Trying to figure out why I'm willing to go to this meeting with you instead of calling it in. I have to say, I was pretty goddamned baffled by the guy who looked back at me in the mirror this morning."

"I figured that might be a problem. That's one of the reasons I wanted you to stay with me last night."

I smiled. "You mean so you can work your charms on me?"

She smiled back. "Something like that."

"Well," I said, "I'm here. I didn't try to bust out last night. I'm here because I want to be." I paused, and then added, "Because of you."

She smiled again. "I'm glad," she said. "Really glad."

"I'm not making any promises in the future—about what my conscience will allow and what it won't," I said.

She laughed. "Relax, Danny. I'm not asking for any commitments here. If nothing else, I can use the extra protection. I'm just glad you're here with me this morning."

"Glad for business reasons?" I asked. I played back in my mind what I'd just said. Oh, Jesus! Listen to me fishing for compliments like a complete jackass. There it happened again—snap! Brain just shut off.

She smiled. I was hooked, and she knew it. "Partly business," she said, "partly personal."

# Chapter 25

IT'S FAIR TO say that the Jefferson County International Airport looks quite a bit different in reality than it sounds to the ear. It's so small that it has no terminal, no boarding gates, no security—not even a control tower. Amazingly, in this day of TSA body scanners, X-ray machines, and genital-groping pat-downs, the Jefferson County International Airport doesn't even have a fence. You can drive right onto the tarmac. Technically, Jefferson County International is an international airport only because pilots can call ahead if they're flying in from British Columbia. U.S. Customs has an office on the field—normally vacant. A customs officer will drive down from the harbor at Port Townsend and meet the flight. The fact is that Jefferson County International is a VFR–only general aviation airport—the kind where private pilots drop in for the proverbial hundred-dollar hamburger-and-pancake fly-ins. In other words, it's sleepy quiet.

Which made it perfect for the meeting Gina had planned. An airplane lands and taxis to a remote hangar at a tiny, out-of-the-way airport without filing a flight plan and without telling anyone where they are or where they came from. Another airplane does the same thing. A high-level meeting is held, then the principals hop back on board their respective airplanes. Fifteen minutes later, they're gone with nobody the wiser except maybe for a couple of airport bums—guys who spend all their free time hanging at the airports swapping lies. But these guys wouldn't be paying attention to the men or the meeting. If they were interested in anything at all, it would be the airplanes themselves. Most likely, though, they wouldn't even notice the planes unless someone flew in and landed in a 1938 Beechcraft Staggerwing biplane. Short of that, they've pretty much seen it all already.

The runway is quite short, so whoever was flying in wouldn't be doing so in a jet. Most likely, the meeting participants would fly into a nearby jet-capable field, maybe Sea-Tac or Boeing in Seattle, perhaps even Vancouver. Then, they'd change planes to a short-field aircraft capable of landing and taking off from small airports. This airplane switch-ola would have the side benefit of making them nearly impossible to follow without advance notice.

We approached the airport on Highway 19 from the north. We reached the sign announcing the airport's entry at five minutes after nine. Gina turned west onto Airport Road and then, after driving through the main airport entrance, she turned right and continued driving west. She drove around a row of hangars to another building that was hidden from view from the airport entrance. Three large hangars had been built near the approach end of runway nine at the far western edge of the airport. The front of the middle hangar actually faced west, directly away from the entry to the airport. We were completely screened from anyone who might have wanted to look. Didn't matter—we didn't see a soul once we entered the airport.

"We're here," Gina said.

*Great*, I thought. *Let the games begin.*

~~~~

Two dark blue SUVs were already parked nearby when we rolled up. Gina pulled around and parked next to them. Just as we were the advance guard for the Calabria family, apparently these fellows were the advance guard for the Tijuana-Mendez cartel. As Gina opened her door, a door opened in the closest SUV and a very well-dressed Mexican man, probably in his mid-thirties, stepped out. He wore a charcoal pinstriped suit with a white shirt and a dark lavender tie. His dark hair was slicked back, his face tanned. He approached Gina.

"Gina," he said with a dazzling smile. "At last! The big day is here."

Gina walked up to him and hugged him politely. It was not the full-bodied bear hug that she'd given me, and that made me feel pretty smug.

"Francisco," she said, "so good to see you. You're right. This is a big day for both of our families." She looked around, and then said, "Is everything on track on your side?"

"Everything indeed. They called about fifteen minutes ago and said they're about forty-five minutes out. No problems."

"Wonderful. We are ready on our side. My uncle called me and said that they would also be in about twenty minutes before ten."

"Perhaps the two aircraft will taxi in together, eh?" he said, laughing.

"Perhaps," Gina answered. She turned to me and said, "Francisco Miranda, allow me to introduce Danny Logan. Danny is the private investigator I told you about that my family hired to look for me while I've been in hiding."

"Good to meet you, Mr. Logan," Miranda said, reaching to shake hands. "I've heard a lot about you from Ms. Fiore, and I've taken the liberty of doing some background research myself. You have an impressive résumé."

"Thanks," I said.

I watched as six other well-dressed Mexican men emerged from the two SUVs. These guys looked sharp. But despite their stylish business-suit turnouts, all six men looked big and hard, like former military. No weapons were visible, but I imagined all carried sidearms beneath their neatly tailored suit jackets. They took up positions, three in front of each of the two vehicles.

On cue, Uncle Frank and his boys emerged from their van. Miranda seemed to recognize Frankie. Gina beckoned him over.

"Mr. Francesco Rossi," Miranda said, beaming and holding out his hand, "please, allow me to introduce myself."

"Uncle Frank," Gina said, cutting in, "this is Francisco Miranda. Francisco, my uncle Francesco Rossi."

"Delightful!" Miranda said, smiling broadly. "Dos Frankies!"

I thought I saw Uncle Frankie cringe, but he hid it well.

"Pleased to meet you," he said, shaking the much smaller man's hand.

"The pleasure is all mine," Miranda said. "We've heard much about you, Frankie the Boot, if I may call you that. Your reputation is very distinguished."

"Thanks, but I'm thinking there are three things about that," Frankie said.

"What would they be?"

"First, everything you heard happened a very long time ago."

Miranda laughed. "Of course. Time is the enemy of us all. And the two other things?"

Frankie stared hard at him for a moment. Then he suddenly smiled and said, "Everything you heard was a lie."

Miranda laughed again. "I understand. We have a great many such misconceptions about our family as well. I find myself spending far too much time defending my family against such false allegations. What is the last thing you wished to mention?"

"Simple," Frankie said. "No one calls me Frankie the Boot."

Miranda's face dropped—he looked mortified. "I apologize, señor. My information was bad. I'll see that it is corrected at once."

"Relax, Francisco," Gina said. "Uncle Frankie, you are to stop terrorizing this young man at once. Got it?"

Frankie smiled. "Got it." He turned to Miranda. "No offense."

Before Miranda could answer, Gina said, "So Francisco, your side is clear on the rules?"

"Of course," he said, trying to quickly regain his composure. "Four men to remain outside from each party, no weapons showing. Three people inside from each side, plus of course the two principals from each side. You are the chief negotiator for your side as I am for mine. Mr. Logan and Mr. Rossi will be your side's internal security. In addition to me and our two principals, we'll have two security men inside as well."

"That is the agreed arrangement," Gina said. "As soon as the principals arrive, we can begin."

~~~~

We didn't have long to wait. Fifteen minutes later, a large single-engine aircraft flew over the center of the field from north to south. It circled to the east and swung gently around onto the final approach for runway two-seven. The airplane, an executive version of a Cessna Caravan turboprop, landed and taxied all the way down the runway before exiting at a taxiway abeam our hangar. A little zigzag and the pilot pulled up onto the tarmac in front of the hangar. The pilot gunned the engine while holding his left brake, and the airplane did a sweet little pirouette and turned to face the opposite direction—the better, I suppose, to make a hasty exit if the necessity arose.

While this was happening, the second airplane, a larger Pilatus PC-12 single-engine turboprop, repeated the routine. It overflew the airport from south to north, turned to join the traffic pattern and landed heading west on runway two-seven. It also taxied the full length of the runway and pulled off abeam the hangar.

Meanwhile, the right side door on the Caravan opened and a set of stairs unfolded. Two men disembarked. The first man was of medium height and weight in a navy suit with a yellow tie. With his silver hair trimmed short, he looked like he could be the CEO of a Fortune 500 corporation. Instead, I recognized him to be John Calabria, former head of the Calabria organized-crime family. The other man was very tall, perhaps six four or so, and probably weighed two-fifty. He was dressed in a dark charcoal suit and he, too, had short, trimmed silver hair—Peter Calabria.

Frankie and Gina walked over to greet them, while I watched and waited with Francisco Miranda. Frankie shook hands with them while Gina received warm hugs from each. They talked among themselves for a couple of minutes, Gina pointing to me and to the hangar. Satisfied, the group walked over to where I stood.

Gina did the introductions. "Uncle John, Uncle Pete, this is my good friend Danny Logan. Danny, these are my uncles, John and Peter Calabria." We shook hands.

After we'd said our hellos, John Calabria looked at my Hawaiian shirt and khakis and quipped, "Nice suit."

"Apologize about that," I said. "I just popped up yesterday on a whim—didn't know what I'd find and didn't know I'd be staying. Sure didn't know I'd be invited to your meeting."

"See," Gina said. "I told you. He was going to find me either today or tomorrow anyway."

"Good thinking," Peter Calabria said. "Better that he's here." He turned to look me over. "You sure this guy can be trusted?"

"I'm sure of it," she answered immediately. "I've known Danny for years. He's an honorable man—a war hero, even. He told me that he was okay with this. If he says we can trust him, we can trust him."

"Besides," Frankie said, "I talked to the kid. I'm thinking we understand each other, him and me. He's alright."

"There you have it, then," John Calabria said, smiling. "You come highly recommended by my two most trusted advisors. You must be golden."

"Thanks," I said. "I made a commitment to Gina. I'll stick by it."

"Good," he said.

"Uncle John, Uncle Pete," Gina said as she turned to Miranda, "Please allow me to introduce Mr. Francisco Miranda. Mr. Miranda is my counterpart with the Tijuana-Mendez family."

"Mr. Calabria," Miranda said, practically bowing as he reached to shake hands with John Calabria. "*Mucho gusto*, señor," he said. "I am very honored to meet you." He shook hands with Peter Calabria and said, "For the longest time, my family has dreamt of joining forces with an organization such as yours. We feel that the advantages to both our families could be tremendous. We were very excited to hear from Gina with her ideas."

"Good," John said. "We're excited, too." He turned to watch the Pilatus taxi up to the hangar. "Looks like your bosses are pulling up now."

Like the first aircraft, the second spun around to face the outbound direction before the pilot cut his motor. Shortly afterward, the door on the left side of the fuselage opened and the stairs were extended. The first man off was middle-aged, with dark hair brushed back and tinged with silver. He wore a beautifully tailored pinstriped suit in a color I think is called taupe. His tie was dark blue. He stood perhaps five ten and was solid, but not heavy—perhaps one seventy-five or one-eighty. He looked like a CEO as well. No doubt about it, we were plain swimming in crime lords dressed up as CEOs this morning. An older fellow with thinning hair followed him. He, too, wore a suit, but his was a little more rumpled.

I had to stop for a moment and remember that I was definitely not looking at CEOs. Instead, I was looking at two of the FBI's most wanted criminals. Hector and Luis Mendez were both on the Ten Most Wanted list for little things like racketeering, murder, drug trafficking, kidnapping, and extortion. And I had both at arm's length, right in front of me. Well, actually, me and fifteen bad guys armed to the teeth. I'd made a commitment to Gina not to call this meeting in to law enforcement, and I was duty-bound to honor that commitment. But still, watching these two guys get off the plane was damn hard to take.

As I thought about it, I had no underlying issue with the Calabrias—they'd made their mistakes in the past, and they'd both done their time to pay for it. Gina, of course, had no criminal history—yet. She was still in the clear. As to what they were proposing today—I now understood the reasons for my confusion. Although what they wanted to do was technically illegal, it was at least arguable as to whether or not it was morally bad. There's that gray-area thing.

The Mendez brothers, though—they were a whole different story. I was 100 percent black and white with these guys—no confusion at all. They were cold-blooded killers, unrepentant bad guys. They thought nothing of blowing up a sheriff's station and everyone inside it, or running a truck bomb into a shopping mall. These were the kind of guys that settled business disputes by cutting off your head—and the heads of your immediate family, just for good measure. Gina had an odd sense of acceptable business partners. I guess they were a necessary evil, but that didn't excuse things.

For my part, seeing these two guys snapped me back to reality and brought things into sharp focus. Seeing the Mendez brothers walking toward me—smiling, seemingly with no cares in the world—there was no conflict in me; I was suddenly galvanized. No part of me could tolerate the Mendez brothers—they were pure evil. And while I had no choice but to play along with this little powwow today, I resolved right then and there that the Mendez brothers were going down, and I was going to be the one to take them down. Not today, but soon. Sorry, Gina.

~~~~

Francisco Miranda practically ran over to greet the Mendez brothers warmly as they descended the stairs. As the turboprop whirred to a stop, Miranda shook their hands and talked to them. He pointed at our group and at the hangar. He pointed at the airport and the runway. Finally, he accompanied the brothers over to our group.

"Mr. John Calabria and Mr. Peter Calabria," he said with a flourish, "please allow me to introduce Mr. Hector Luis Mendez and his brother, Mr. Luis Ramon Mendez."

"Pleased to meet you, gentlemen," John Calabria said as he stepped up and shook hands with each of the Mendez brothers in turn.

"We, as well," Hector Mendez said in heavily accented English. He turned to Gina. "You must be Gina Fiore," he said.

"I am," Gina said, reaching over to shake his hand.

"You are a very impressive young woman," Mendez said. "Very brave and very resourceful, too. Not many would have thought to approach us in the manner you chose."

"Sorry if my methods were a little severe," Gina said. "I was pretty sure I had a good idea that would appeal to the leaders of both families."

"And sometimes, stupid people stand in the way," Mendez said, apparently referring to the late Mr. Salazar. "I'm glad you figured out a way around that particular obstacle."

"Thank you," Gina said.

"It did cost us four grows," Mendez said. "Perhaps we can speak about this?"

"We can, and we will," Gina said. "And trust me when I say that I believe when we're finished talking, you will not be concerned about the loss of these four fields. Instead, I believe you will consider this loss to be a bargain price for admission to a whole new level of distribution channels in the United States. The potential profits from these new channels will make you quickly forget about the four lost fields."

"I like the way you think," Hector Mendez said.

Gina smiled. "Thank you, sir. But please," she said, "let's move this discussion inside. We're all set up for you gentlemen in the hangar here."

Gina pointed the way to the hangar and, except for the four outside guards from each side, the rest of us went inside.

~~~~

The gigantic airplane door was closed, of course, so we entered through a normal-sized door built right into the edge of the airplane door. The hangar was large, perhaps sixty feet square. Inside, four hanging mercury-vapor lights lit the interior of the empty hangar like an operating room. The shiny, white, epoxy-painted floors reflected the light back against the white insulation on the walls. I felt like I should have brought sunglasses—it was as bright inside as it was outside. Fortunately, even though it was already warming up outside, inside the hangar was cool and quiet.

A two-story office had been built into the corner of the hangar opposite the entry door, but the lights inside were off, the door was closed, and the office did not appear to be occupied. Instead, centered in the middle of the hangar floor were two eight-foot fold-up tables pushed together and covered by a royal blue linen tablecloth. The tables were surrounded by six chairs—two on each side plus one at either end. A smaller table, also covered by a blue tablecloth, held water carafes and a coffee pot.

When I was in the army, I attended dozens of meetings of all types—staff meetings, planning meetings, briefing meetings, you name it. Many of these meetings were held in impromptu settings, and more than once in airplane hangars. The layout here was one that I'd seen many times before—it felt like old times. I was ready to jump up and salute when the general walked through the door. Except now it wasn't generals—it was drug lords and mob bosses. My, how times change.

"Gentlemen, please have a seat, and we'll get started," Gina said. The Calabria brothers took the chairs facing the door while the Mendez brothers sat across from them. Francisco Miranda took the seat at one end of the table and, once everyone was seated, Gina sat at the other end next to an easel, which held a flip chart. Frankie and I sat behind the Calabrias, while the two Mendez guards sat behind their principals.

"Thank you all for coming today," Gina said. "This is a very important day for both the Tijuana-Mendez organization and the Calabria family. I believe that we truly have an opportunity here where the combined effort of our two organizations is much greater than the sum of the individual parts." Gina paused to let her words sink in. Miranda nodded his agreement.

"Briefly stated," she said, as she looked at the Mendez brothers, "your team is a world-class master in the art and science of creating a very profitable, renewable product that is in high demand—that is, high-grade marijuana. Our family," now she looked at the Calabrias, "has local contacts and a distribution network second to none. You create the high-quality product, we can move it for you at prices and in quantities that you'd otherwise not be able to achieve. This is the essence of our proposal. If you'll allow me, I'd like to show you the details." She turned to the flip chart behind her and flipped the cover over to reveal a chart labeled Business Plan.

Gina spent the next thirty minutes leading the group through a detailed financial business plan showing numbers of fields, percent loss to law enforcement, delivery costs, profit comparison for different distribution strategies. She concluded by detailing bottom-line profits.

"So subtracting the thirty-million-dollar production costs from the equation leaves a total net profit of approximately $337,000,000 a year. I've proposed a fifty-fifty split. Half for the Tijuana-Mendez organization, half for the Calabrias—about $169,000,000 a year for each of us."

The hangar fell silent as everyone studied Gina's chart and absorbed the information. She'd gone through the numbers like a corporate VP pitching a new project to her CEO. Except that I don't think corporations usually make three hundred million per year on thirty-million-dollar annual investments.

After a couple of minutes, Hector Mendez spoke. "I know I speak for my brother when I say that we have always wanted to work with the great families of America," he said. "For many years, we have dreamt of the humble Mendez family being thought of with the same respect and honor as is granted to the great American families such as the Calabrias."

John Calabria acknowledged the compliment with a nod.

Mendez continued. "For too long, the Mexican cartels and the Colombians before us have acted in an uncivilized fashion. This has caused us to be looked upon as amateurs and thugs. Our compatriots around the world view us with scorn and disdain. In the words of your comedian, 'We don't get no respect.' Truthfully, sadly, we've done little to earn the respect we desire. My countrymen have turned my beautiful country into a killing zone. Their greed is limitless. There is plenty of money to go around, but, alas, they have not even learned life's simplest lessons—including how to share. Luis and I mean to see this change. We wish to take our place among the world's most respected criminal organizations and, in so doing, begin to show the way to my countrymen. We wish to bring them to the table of respectability, even if we have to drag them there.

"We wish to thank you, John and Peter Calabria, for honoring us with this meeting this morning. We want to assure you that we hold your organization in the highest respect, and we would like nothing more than to work together on this venture. But we have some questions that need to be answered first."

"Please, Mr. Mendez," Gina said. "Feel free to ask any questions you'd like."

"Thank you," Mendez said. "By my own calculations, at a wholesale value of one thousand dollars per plant, acting alone, my organization would net about $250,000,000 per year. By joining forces, our share falls to $165,000,000 per year. Fifty million per year difference seems a lot to give up for something that's already our product."

John Calabria said, "Fifty million is a lot of money, for sure. But I think you might want to look at it another way—that is, you'd be completely out of the distribution business. You deliver the crop, period. We take it from there. We can pay the equivalent of fifteen hundred per plant and you're out of it. You don't have to deal with lower-level people at all. Right now, you're operating wholesale and retail. My guys will do what they're best at, which is running the product through distribution and putting it in the retail places that pay the most."

He paused for a second, then continued. "And another thing, believe me when I tell you, we appreciate the opportunity to work with you guys as well. We don't know squat about growing marijuana. Never done it. Never want to. You guys are good at it. But like Gina said, we've had distribution channels in place since Al Capone and prohibition—more than eighty years. We can easily move the product anywhere in the country. That does two things for you. First, it allows you to take advantage of better pricing on the East Coast than you're getting now. Second, it allows you to focus on ramping up production. And that's where the real money will be."

I noticed Gina smiling as her uncle spoke. She'd obviously briefed him well in preparation for the meeting.

Mendez nodded. "In truth," he said, "I'd probably be willing to part with fifty million per year simply in order to establish a partnership with the Calabria family. I think the enhanced respectability brought on by the relationship with your organization will be worth at least that much in our other businesses."

Calabria nodded. "Thank you for the compliment," he said.

Mendez nodded. He turned to his brother. "Luis, I like these gentlemen. I think we should do this deal. What do you think?"

"It's good," Luis said, nodding. "I'm with you."

"We think it's a good deal as well, right, Pete?" John Calabria said.

"Damn right," Peter Calabria answered, smiling for the first time. "I always wanted to be in the pot business."

Gina smiled. "Excellent. Gentlemen, I think we have the basics of an agreement in hand. I think Francisco and I can meet and polish off the details later—the mechanics of the deal."

"That sounds good," John Calabria said, standing up. "Probably best for all of us if we don't linger around here anymore than is necessary."

"Agreed, amigo," Hector Mendez said. "Next time, we can meet in my country. I can take you fishing for yellowfin tuna on our boat."

"It's a date!" John said, reaching across to shake hands with Mendez.

At that instant, a huge explosion ripped through the hangar. The blinding white flash and the thundering noise echoed off the hangar walls. My ears went instantly numb, and I was completely blinded.

# Chapter 26

MOMENTS LATER, THE deafness was replaced by a loud ringing in my ears, the kind you get after you've been to a loud, all-day rock concert and sat a little too close to the PA. Smaller but equally bright orange-yellow stars floating back and forth across my vision replaced the bright flash that had at first caused everything to turn black. The acrid smell of cordite was strong, and the smoke burned my eyes. After a few seconds, the ringing in my ears diminished, and the stars in my eyes began to shrink in size and intensity. My vision started to clear, and I became aware of my surroundings again. I emerged into a complete state of pandemonium in the hangar. All around me, I heard the footsteps of people running in heavy boots. "Get down!" they shouted. "Down on the floor!"

Before I was fully functional and able to come up with a coherent action on my own, I was roughly grabbed from behind and literally thrown to the ground. I barely caught myself before face-planting on the cold, concrete hangar floor. As it was, I bashed my knee on the floor as I went down. It hurt like hell, but the sharp pain had the side effect of snapping me back to reality. As my vision returned to normal, my vantage point gave me a great view of boots—black tactical boots—running back and forth. Lots of them. I turned and looked in the other direction, and I was able to make out the fact that the boots were connected to the legs of black-helmeted men clothed in black tactical uniforms with the letters *DEA* stenciled on their backs in bright yellow. *Great.* I was right in the middle of a bust. This was definitely not good.

"Nobody move," a loud voice commanded us.

I didn't move. But I was able to ascertain that Frankie was sprawled out on the ground to my right. I could see the Calabrias in front of me, but I couldn't see Gina from where I was lying. It seemed like dozens of black-uniformed men were visible. Where'd they all come from?

For a few moments, the room was silent. Suddenly, I felt the presence of a man standing behind me. I couldn't see him, but I heard him walk up. "Well now, that was fun, huh guys?" the man said. His voice was deep and confident. "Loads of fun. Big bang—nobody hurt. Allow me to introduce myself. My name is Special Agent Regis Jackson of the Seattle Office of the United States Drug Enforcement Agency. I'd like to thank you all for coming to this little party this morning. Such a—a difficult location, and you all made a special trip. I am impressed." Wonderful. I was going to be busted by Officer Joe Sarcasm.

"I do want to apologize that our refreshments are a little lacking at our party this morning," he continued. "But not to worry. I'm certain you'll all be impressed with our overnight accommodations. I'm told that the food served there is, shall we say, unforgettable." Several of the men laughed.

"Yes, yes indeed," he said, now laughing himself. "But this is not fair. I've introduced myself to you, yet we don't know who you are. Let's get a proper introduction going. Jimmy," he called out, "push that green button there, open up that main hangar door, and let's clear the smoke out of here. Make sure you tell the guys outside to stand clear before you do." He paused, and then said, "Mikey, starting with this shithead right here—" Wham! He kicked me hard, right in the butt, before he continued, "Let's stand them up one at a time, pat them down, and cuff them. Get a little introduction. May as well be polite, right?"

Two hands grabbed each of my arms and roughly lifted me to standing. They quickly and professionally patted me down and took my wallet and my 1911 before zip-tying my hands together. I looked around for the first time. Smoke still hung thick in the air, but I had no trouble seeing at least two dozen heavily armed, black-clad DEA agents in the room. The door to the office in the back of the hangar was wide open. Had they all been hiding in there?

The Calabrias were in front of me, still on the ground. Miranda was on the ground to my left. I couldn't see the Mendez brothers, but I could see the Mexican guards behind them, sprawled out on the floor with four DEA agents right behind them, rifles pointed and ready for action. Looking to my right, from my vantage point, the only part of Gina I could see were her legs. The table hid the rest of her body. Uncle Frankie was still lying on the ground on my right side.

The large hangar door began to lift upward like a giant garage door as the agents moved clockwise around the table, meaning the next ones to get stood up would be the Calabrias. Agent Jackson walked past me, and I could see that he was a tall, well-built black man, probably in his late thirties or early forties. He was also wearing tactical clothing.

"Daniel Charles Logan," he said, reading my driver's license as another agent handcuffed me. "Thirteen thirty-six Dexter Avenue, Seattle, Washington. Local boy, huh?" He flipped through my wallet. "And what's this? A CCW permit and a PI license?" He looked at me. "Mr. Logan, or should I say Detective Logan, I have no idea what you're doing here, but my friend, you are definitely guilty of being in the wrong place at the wrong goddamned time. We'll see what else you're up to." His men laughed again.

He walked past me and pointed to the Calabrias. "These guys next," he said. He watched as the Calabrias were simultaneously jerked to their feet, facing away from him. Both were frisked and cuffed. He had his men turn them around to face him. He acted in mock surprise. "John Calabria!" he said. "I recognize you." Then he turned and said, "And Peter Calabria! What a treat! Gentlemen," he said, turning and addressing his fellow agents, "the Chicago mob is in the house!" A couple of the other agents gave mock cheers. When the cheers died down, Jackson said, "Guys, honestly. I'd have thought by now that you fellas would be out of this shit. You should be sitting on a beach in the Caribbean by now. Soaking up rays, playing hide-the-salami with some sweet young things, and enjoying your golden years. What the hell are you doing working with scum suckers like these cartel idiots here?" he said, pointing to where the Mendez brothers still lay on the ground. The Calabrias said nothing, they simply stared back. "Cat got your tongues, eh? Well, you'll have plenty of time to figure out where things went wrong, won't you? Cuff 'em."

After Francisco Miranda was cuffed, the Mendez brothers were next. They were stood up and searched, then handcuffed. Did I say they looked like CEOs? I take that back. Not anymore. Now they looked like angry, psychotic killers, the kind that would not have been happy unless everyone responsible for this raid was tortured and executed, along with their families, their acquaintances, their whole towns. They were pissed, but they said nothing. Instead, they glared. They had really nasty glares, like angry rattlesnakes poised to strike. Luis Mendez decided to try out the glare on one of the agents. "A little stink eye? Very cute, fuckface," the agent said just before he slammed his elbow into Mendez's gut.

"Mikey," Jackson called out to the offending agent, "Play nice. Don't forget these men are our guests."

Unable to manipulate the DEA agents, the Mendez brothers next glared at Francisco Miranda. This worked better, as it had the effect of making Miranda immediately piss himself. The man's face was sheet–white, and he looked like he expected to be executed sometime within the next seven seconds, which, in Mexico, would probably have been the case.

"Well, bless my soul if it isn't Hector and Luis Mendez," Jackson said, walking around the table to the Mendez brothers after they were cuffed. "You are the Mendez brothers, aren't you?" he asked. He held up Most Wanted pictures of each against their faces. He made a show of looking at the poster, then at the men, then back at the poster. "Yeah, that's you alright. Looks just like your photos, guys. Gentlemen, welcome to America! We've wanted to make your acquaintance for so very long. And now, here you are, our guests."

Luis Mendez muttered something incoherent, still trying to catch his breath after being doubled over by an elbow to the gut.

"I'm sorry," Jackson said. "I didn't get that. What'd you say?"

"He says, I respectfully request to speak to my lawyer," Hector Mendez said.

"Oh, well, since you put it that way," Jackson said. "Fuck you. You'll get your chance."

~~~~

Finally, they stood Gina up. For the first time, I was able to see her, and I was surprised. On many occasions, I've seen people who are unaccustomed to trouble with law enforcement get busted their first time. Most of these people are in a complete state of shock—eyes wide open, legs trembling to the point of having trouble standing; sometimes they've even vomited. The mind short-circuits when faced with an ultra-stressful situation. People lose control and don't act rationally, or certainly not in a way they normally would.

This definitely did not describe Gina. Don't get me wrong—she didn't look happy about the situation, but she certainly didn't look like she was in shock or terror, either. Hers was a look of grim determination, like she had a job to do and, by god, she was going to do it. She didn't look pissed off like the Mendez brothers did, but she didn't look the slightest bit afraid either, even after she was searched and cuffed, even after Luis Mendez tried the glare on her. She simply stared right back and shot him a "go fuck yourself" look, which was pretty gutsy considering whom she was staring down.

Last to go was Uncle Frankie, but before the agents reached him, the hangar door suddenly groaned and made a loud bang! People jumped and ducked, and then turned to look at the door. It was stuck about three-fourths of the way open. Beneath the door, I had a great view of the four Mexican and four Chicago outside-guards all lying on the ground, hand-cuffed and completely immobilized. Another dozen DEA agents guarded them and the airplanes' pilots.

"Great," Jackson said, "Door's broke. Let's see if we can work that cable loose," he ordered. Several agents jumped to comply, including those on my side of the table who had been guarding Uncle Frankie.

Frankie noticed right away that everyone was looking at the door and not at him. Knowing he wouldn't be left untended for more than a moment, he quickly jumped to his feet. Instead of trying to escape, however, he put his hands behind his back as if he were already cuffed. Then he simply stood there. I was the only one who'd noticed.

I looked at him and tilted my head and tried to arch an eyebrow, as if to ask, *What the hell are you doing?* He responded by nodding back at me and giving me a glare, indicating that I was to mind my own goddamned business, thank you very much.

This was going to be interesting. In fact, this was turning into a regular laugh a minute.

~~~~

The moment ended quickly as the agents muscled the door cable back into position. The door then completed its upward swing. Jackson turned back and looked at us. "Now," he said, "where were we?" He paused for a second, looked us all over, then said, "Oh yeah, we were completing our introductions. We'd just reached Ms. Gina Fiore, the architect of this happy little joint venture."

Gina glared at him.

"And without whose cooperation, this meeting could have never taken place," cracked one of the agents next to Jackson.

Whirling quickly, Jackson said, "Shut the hell up, Matthews. What's wrong with you?"

Matthews froze and the color drained from his face as he realized what he'd said.

I was shocked. I looked first at Jackson, and then at Gina. What the hell? What cooperation?

Gina looked stunned at what the agent had said. Her mouth had dropped open, and her eyes seemed to plead the question, "Why?"

"Cooperation?" John Calabria said, looking first at Gina, then at Jackson. "What fucking cooperation?" He turned to look at Gina. "Gina, what the fuck is he talking about?"

She looked at him but didn't say anything.

"What cooperation?" he repeated.

"Shut up," Jackson ordered.

"Fuck you," Calabria said, not taking his eyes of Gina, eyes that were flashing with rage and hatred. "Did you set us up, Gina?"

Gina shook her head no, but remained speechless.

"Did you do this?" he screamed.

"Enough of this," Jackson said. "Boys, let's get these assholes out of here. They can settle their internal squabbles on their own time. They're going to have plenty of it."

His men started to grab each prisoner by the shoulder.

Suddenly, Frankie yelled out, "Gina, you bitch! You rat out your own flesh and blood!" In a flash he pulled his Smith & Wesson .44. Before anyone could react, he fired a single shot that ripped into Gina's chest.

Gina's eyes flew wide open in complete shock for an instant as the force of the bullet's impact shoved her over backwards. Blood and gore flew from her back and spattered on the floor behind her. She fell onto her back and lay on the white concrete gasping for breath, her hands clutched tightly into fists at her side, her eyes full of terror.

Almost immediately after the shot, two agents tackled Frankie and threw him to the floor. They cuffed him and left him there. "Son of a bitch!" Jackson yelled.

Two agents jumped in to try to help Gina, but she was beyond help. She looked at me and weakly gasped, "Danny, tell my parents—" She wasn't able to complete the words before the muscles in her face and arms went slack, and she died, right there in front of me on the floor of the hangar. Her blood was bright red against the white concrete.

~~~~

My mind went numb. I stared at Gina's body and felt the blood rushing out of my head. My face tingled and the ringing returned to my ears. I felt the whole world close in. Yesterday, two weeks after she'd gone missing, five years after I'd lost her, I'd found her at last. We'd reunited. We'd talked. We'd even kissed. Today, I'd lost her all over again. She was dead. Gone.

I looked around. Everyone in the room was in a state of shock. The DEA agents had their guns leveled. Francisco Miranda was frozen, mouth wide open. He'd turned sheet-white and looked as though he were ready to faint. The Calabrias stood wide-eyed, staring at Gina, then at Frankie, then back to Gina. The Mendez brothers had a look of alarm on their faces. I imagine they were thinking, We know that's how we'd handle things, but we didn't know the Americans handled things the same way.

I took all this in for a few moments, and then I guess I just snapped. The agents had just finished lifting Frankie to his feet when I turned and looked at him. He stared back. "Motherfucker!" I screamed. I kicked him in the balls with everything I had. He gasped, and when he staggered forward, I kneed him right in the nose. He went down like he was the one who'd been shot. Blood flew everywhere from his shattered nose. I was lucky I didn't have my gun—Frankie was lucky I didn't have my gun.

The DEA agents grabbed me and yanked me away. "Cut it out!" they ordered. "That's enough of that," one of the agents said. "This asshole will get taken care of in prison."

"Frankie, you fucking asshole!" Jackson yelled. "This idiot over here didn't mean she knowingly cooperated with us. She didn't. We were already tracking Eddie Salazar when we stumbled onto Gina and her plans. She had nothing to do with us. Jesus Christ!" He stood frozen in place, transfixed for several moments. He recovered quickly and yelled, "Get these people out of here, now!" He paused for a moment and stared at Gina. "Cover her up," he said.

~~~~

The agents hustled us out of the hangar and made us stand in a line, facing away from the door. They kept Frankie off to himself, with four men guarding him. My mind was still numb as I tried desperately to come to grips with the events of the morning. I wasn't worried about my legal predicament. I was essentially an innocent bystander. At least, that's how I saw it. There was no law against being in the same room as a mobster or a member of the Mexican cartels. Although those guys had discussed a criminal venture, I sure as hell hadn't. I sat in the back and didn't say a word. I thought I was on pretty solid legal ground.

Emotionally, though, I was a wreck. I never liked to see anyone get killed—even bad guys in Iraq and Afghanistan. I accepted it. I recognized the necessity. I was grateful that it was them, and not one of my buddies or me. But I didn't keep score or keep a PBC—personal body count—like some guys I knew. I didn't hold anything against these guys—they were normal, everyday American boys trying their best to deal with bizarre life-and-death situations that were so far beyond their normal upbringing and experiences that they defied reconciliation. These boys were doing what they needed to survive, just like all of us over there. But I wouldn't say I liked it.

But here—seeing someone that I actually cared for get killed—this was everything bad about Iraq magnified a thousand times. This was way different. I mean, at one point, I thought I loved Gina Fiore, thought I had since the first time I saw her in high school. I certainly was captivated by her—her bewitching smile, her beauty, her engaging personality. Now, she was gone. Watching her get blown away was something I'll never forget. Maybe never get over, I don't know.

The agents searched each of us again, much more carefully this time. They read us our Miranda rights individually. Then we were formally arrested. In my case, they told me I was being arrested for Conspiring to Violate Federal Laws regarding the Trafficking of Marijuana.

I had no time to think about it, though, because three minutes later, our group was split up and loaded into DEA vehicles. They loaded the guards from the Mexican and Chicago mobs into separate vans with three or four prisoners per van accompanied by the same number of armed agents. The Mendez brothers were split up and each taken alone in a car, along with three agents apiece. The Calabrias and Frankie were handled similarly—one to each vehicle. I was loaded into a car by myself with two agents. We pulled out of the airport for the long drive south through Tacoma, and then back north to Seattle.

On the way out of the airport, as we passed the entry, I noticed a vehicle entering marked with the words *Jefferson County Coroner's Office*. I shuddered. I was worried about being arrested but, much more painful than that, I was devastated about Gina.

# Chapter 27

THE TWO-AND-A-HALF HOUR automobile ride from Port Townsend to the Seattle headquarters of the DEA went past in a hazy blur. The agents elected not to take the ferry, instead traveling south in a caravan of vehicles on Highway 3, through Tacoma, then north on I-5 to Seattle. Fortunately, the agents had taken my handcuffs off and recuffed me with my hands in front at the start of the ride. Still, the immobility had my joints screaming before we were halfway there.

But that wasn't what hurt the most. My mind was numb the entire way. Gina was dead, shot to death right in front of me. Just like that. I could not escape the stark vision of her lying on the shiny white hangar floor, gasping for breath, staring vacantly at the ceiling as the dark red blood slowly spread from beneath her. "Tell my parents . . ." The vision haunted me. I felt a profound sense of loss and dread—I wanted to scream. I felt like I was the one with the hole in my chest. Then I got mad.

Goddamn that stupid fucking DEA agent. Why had the idiot said what he said? How could that bastard have been so goddamned incompetently stupid?

And goddamn Frank Rossi! Why? Why kill her? She was family! Was his loyalty to the Calabrias so great that he felt compelled to simply blow Gina away without any proof at all? He hadn't even known if there was a legit case against the Calabrias. And he sure as hell hadn't waited to find out. He just pulled that massive .44 Magnum cannon of his and blew her away.

And goddamn my own stupid self. I could have stopped Frankie by saying something when I saw that he was not cuffed, but the last thing I expected him to do was to shoot Gina. Jesus Christ! I was still so angry at him that it was probably a good thing that we were both incarcerated. That way at least, I couldn't get to him and get myself into real trouble. As it was, I'd have to satisfy myself with shattering his nose when I'd kneed him. Better than nothing, but nowhere near good enough. I shook my head to try and clear my mind—too many fucking questions. This was going to take awhile.

We arrived at the federal building on Second Avenue in Seattle just before three in the afternoon. The agents cuffed me behind my back again and led me upstairs through their offices and into an interrogation room. There, they removed the handcuffs and left me to sit by myself for a little over an hour. I suppose they wanted me to sweat it out and get nervous. It's what I would have done.

The room was empty except for a metal table and six metal chairs. There were two television cameras mounted in domes in the ceiling, one at either end of the room. The wall opposite the door was completely mirrored. No doubt the other side of the mirror was another room, probably occupied by a half-dozen federal agents who were observing and recording everything that happened on my side.

Eventually, two new agents—Stephen Boyd and Ken Sawyer—entered and proceeded to spend the next hour trying to persuade me to talk to them without a lawyer present. I tried to be polite. Really. I was almost as pissed at the DEA as I was with Frankie, so it wasn't easy. After all, if they hadn't shown up, Gina would still be alive. Still, polite or not, I had no intention of talking to them without my lawyer. No way; no how. So I told them the same thing over and over, "I'll be happy to tell you everything I know as soon as my lawyer is here. So the sooner you let me call him and get him down here, the sooner I'll talk. Until then, leave me alone."

They tried to bullshit me by saying that if I needed to lawyer up, then I must be guilty of something—that sort of crap. Their argument: only guilty people needed lawyers. What was I trying to hide?

Unfortunately for them, I knew their lines as well as they did because I'd used them myself many times in the past. It's complete nonsense, of course, but the police use the tactic all the time and sure enough, people routinely give up their rights to have an attorney present during their questioning. They're either deluded and think they're going to outsmart the cops (good luck), or they believe what the cops are telling them and think they'll look guilty if they ask for an attorney. So they start talking. And then they hang themselves. My experience is that it's about twenty times more likely that someone acting on their own talks themselves into trouble than if they'd had an attorney present. Hell, even people who are completely innocent usually make their lives much more difficult by not waiting for their lawyers. They'd almost always be better off if they waited. But they don't. People like to talk. And the cops are good listeners. Real good. But I wasn't talking. Period. Not yet, anyway. I held firm and eventually, they had to relent.

Almost exactly an hour later, at six, my lawyer, J. David O'Farrell, was led into the interrogation room, red-faced and out of breath. David is an old friend of the family's. He's my father's age but, unlike dad, David continues an active law practice. He's tall, lean, and has a full head of silver hair. Like his father and his grandfather before him, David is one of the best criminal lawyers in Seattle. I pay him a small monthly retainer, which buys me the privilege of keeping him on permanent standby, just in case I—or someone on my staff—runs into legal trouble. Kind of like now. I'd never had to use his services before, but I felt damn lucky to have him on my side now.

"Hello, Danny," he said, as he entered. "I'm so sorry to hear about Gina Fiore. Are you alright?"

I nodded. "Thanks."

"Good," he said. "I apologize that it took so long for me to get here." We shook hands. He turned to the agents and said, "Gentlemen, I'm David O'Farrell with the firm O'Farrell, Darnell, and Associates."

The agents introduced themselves.

"Agents Boyd and Sawyer, my client will be ready to speak to you in exactly thirty minutes. During this time, he'll need to speak to me—and only me. Do you have a place he and I can speak privately?"

They moved us to another room where I filled David in. Thirty minutes later, we reconvened with the agents and David had me repeat the story I'd told him from start to finish—all about being called in by the family to help Gina. The agents had several questions.

"Why were you there at the meeting?" Boyd asked.

"Because I was asked to be there by Gina Fiore. I was looking for her on behalf of her family. I'd just located her, and I wanted to make sure she was okay. Besides, once I got there, I'm not completely certain they'd have let me go anyway."

"You mean Gina Fiore wouldn't have let you go?"

"Frankie Rossi. And the other eight or ten guys there." I paused. "And Gina Fiore. She seems to have been the one in control."

"Why? At any point did they tell you that you couldn't leave?"

"Not in so many words. But I got the impression."

"Were you held hostage? Did they take your gun away?"

"I don't know for sure if I was a hostage. That's what I just said. And no, they didn't take my gun away. If they'd have done that, then I suppose there wouldn't be any questions about whether or not I was being held, would there? But then again, they didn't need to take my gun."

"Why?"

"Because they had at least ten people there, probably all armed. I was way outmatched. Are you asking could I have shot my way out of there? I think if I'd have tried any macho bullshit with my gun, I'd almost certainly be dead now. So, bottom line, I suppose you're right—I could have tried to leave. I did have my gun. But the question is whether I'd have been allowed. I had the distinct impression that I would not have been—that I was a concern to them and that they felt the best way to deal with that concern was to bring me in close where they could keep an eye on me."

"You've heard the old saying to keep your friends close and your enemies closer, haven't you?" David asked.

"Sure," Boyd said. "Did you attempt to call law enforcement when you found out about the meeting?"

"No."

"Why not?"

"Because I felt that doing so could have very well endangered lives."

"Why would you say that? Don't you think that law enforcement could have handled the situation?"

"Handled the situation?" I asked, incredulously, jumping up from the table and leaning forward. "Did you happen to notice what happened to-day, you fucking idiot? Handle the situation like that? In case you haven't figured it out, bad things happen when people get together in enclosed spaces with guns. Certain people, like that stupid fucking DEA agent, say

the wrong thing at the wrong goddamned time and someone who's supposed to be working on your side suddenly gets themselves killed! What
did she do to deserve that? Are you completely fucking stupid, or what?
Handle the situation, my ass."

David also jumped up and grabbed me from behind. Boyd remained
seated and simply stared at me.

"Sit down, Danny," David said, pulling me back to my chair.

I stared at Boyd for a moment, then sat back down.

"I meant no disrespect," Boyd said. "I apologize for my choice of
words, and I'm sorry for what happened today. A mistake was made, and
I apologize."

I stared at him for a moment more, and then I nodded. I calmed
myself, and then I continued. "Today was relatively controlled and still
somebody got killed. Yesterday—last night—it was a completely uncontrolled, unscripted situation. A bust could not have been arranged at night
in the short time available within what I felt to be acceptable risk. I spent
several years in the army CID making the same sort of judgments, so I
know a little bit about assessing risk. Last night would have been too risky.
There were a dozen heavily armed men at relatively high alert on duty last
night. Mistakes would have been made and lives—maybe mine—might
have been jeopardized. And for what benefit? To maybe stop a potential
meeting to discuss a potential marijuana trade? That's not good enough
for me to risk my neck. I made the judgment call that I wasn't going to
endanger any lives—including my own—by trying to be a hero. It made
no sense and besides, it's not my job anymore."

"Did you intend to report it afterwards?"

"No need to answer that, Danny," David interrupted. "That question—what my client may or may not have intended to do in a completely
hypothetical situation calls for speculation on his part and is neither relevant nor is it appropriate. As a matter of fact, gentlemen, unless you
have anything else of substance to add, I think that's enough questions
for today. We've been answering questions for nearly an hour. Mr. Logan
has been in this office now since 4:00 p.m."

"Three," I said, correcting him.

"Three," David said. "As you can see, my client has had a long, stressful day. One of his dear friends has been murdered, right in front of

his eyes. He told you he'd tell you everything he knows. He's done that. Throughout it all, I haven't heard a single crime he's committed. At the very worst, he's guilty of being in the same room at the same time as some bad characters. But that, in and of itself, is no crime. He didn't set up the meeting. He didn't contact the bad guys. He didn't speak at the meeting. He didn't even go to Port Townsend with the knowledge that a meeting was going to be held. He showed up in Port Townsend, where he was basically kidnapped and dragged to the meeting. Next thing he knows, the person that brought him is dead, and he's under arrest. He's done nothing wrong. Now, if you don't have anything to charge him with, it's time to let him go. By the way, he's not going anywhere. He lives here, as you know. His family has been here for more than a hundred years. If you need to talk to us again, we'll be happy to comply."

The agents excused themselves for about five minutes before returning. "We talked to our superiors. We'd like to be able to contact you in the future about what happened."

"Already agreed," David said.

"Then you're free to go," Boyd said.

"I want my gun back," I said.

"Swing by tomorrow. It'll be released then," Boyd said, suddenly nice again. "Again, we're sorry about Gina Fiore."

I nodded, and then followed David out of the building.

We no sooner stepped out of the front door when I heard voices say, "There he is!"

Immediately, we were blasted by powerful lights from half a dozen local television cameras, all pointed in my direction. Microphones were thrust into my face, and I was hit by a barrage of questions: "Mr. Logan, what happened?" "Mr. Logan, were you with Gina Fiore?" "Mr. Logan, is it true that the Chicago mob arranged Gina Fiore's murder?"

"Ladies and gentlemen!" David yelled out, "Please!" It grew quiet.

"There is an ongoing federal investigation, and we have been instructed not to speak to the press until the DEA issues a statement, which we are told will take place tomorrow morning," he said, recounting what Boyd had told us. "I am authorized to say that Mr. Logan spoke to federal agents this afternoon. He cooperated fully with them and is not a suspect in anything that's happened today. Any other questions must be directed to the United States Drug Enforcement Administration. That's all we are allowed to say."

Immediately, the reporters continued with their onslaught of questions, but David used a heavy grip on my upper arm to propel me through the throng and to his car, where we made our escape.

~~~~

My Jeep was still in Port Townsend, so David dropped me off at my apartment a little after eight. He made me tell him I was okay before he drove off. I went inside, turned the light on, and grabbed a beer from the refrigerator. If ever there was a good night to get drunk, tonight was it. My plan was to make a short beeline to the patio. I'd barely finished the thought when the phone rang. Caller ID: Toni.

"You're home," she said, relieved, when I picked up.

"I am."

"I've been calling and calling."

"My cell phone's off," I said.

"I know. I heard what happened on the news. Jesus, Danny," she said.

"Yeah."

"Are you alright?"

"Yeah, I suppose. I'm okay."

"Where've you been?"

"The Feds had me. I've been in interrogation since three. David O'Farrell finally got me just a little while ago."

"Holy shit," she said. "Did you get hurt today?"

"No."

"And you're okay now?"

"Yeah. I just got home. I've decided that I'm going to get drunk."

"Okay. Good. I'll be right over."

I didn't really feel like seeing anyone, but I didn't feel like arguing about it, either. I had the feeling that if I said no, I'd start a fight, and I was in no mood to fight. Easier just to give in. Besides, it would take her fifteen minutes to get to my apartment and with a little effort, I could suck down a whole six-pack by then.

"See you in a few," I said.

~~~~

It turns out that I wasn't in a full-race, green-flag drinking mode after all. More of a somber, yellow-caution-flag mode. Slower, more thoughtful. I was only halfway done with my second beer when Toni got there. Thoughtfully, she'd brought another growler of Mac & Jack's, just in case. She hugged me for a good long while when she walked in. It felt good—not in a sensual way, but in a comforting way. God knows I was ready for some comforting. Toni knew me better than anyone in the world. She could tell where I was hurting and why—maybe even better than I could. If anyone could help me sort things out, she'd be able to. Maybe not tonight, but over time. She grabbed a beer and walked over to my CD player where she picked out one of our favorites, "Bleach" by Nirvana. We walked out to the patio together.

In the past few weeks, the days had begun to shrink. Three weeks ago, it would have been bright and sunny at eight thirty. Now, it was definitely twilight. Still warm with a nice, gentle breeze, but the sky was darkening and the lights across Lake Union were clearly visible. I lay back in one lounge chair, and Toni took the other.

Neither of us spoke, until she finally said, "Talk to me."

I was quiet for a minute, drinking my beer slowly, staring at the water. Finally, I gathered my thoughts and said, "Heavy shit today."

I saw her nod out of the corner of my eye. "Were you right there?"

I nodded. "Yeah. I was six feet away. I watched her die." The vision of Gina on the concrete floor was back in my brain. "She was trying to ask me to tell her parents something when she died." I was quiet for a moment. "I guess she probably wanted me to tell them that she loved them."

"That makes sense," she said. "What happened, Danny?" she asked. "What went wrong?"

I started at the beginning and walked her slowly through the whole chain of events, up to the point where I was arrested along with the others.

"Jesus Christ," she said, quietly. "What a clusterfuck! That idiot DEA agent opens his big mouth, and the mobster just blows her away? That's unbelievable."

"It's like it happened in slow motion," I said, "like in a dream when you're trying to run in water. You could see the whole thing unfolding, and there wasn't a goddamned thing you could do about it. As soon as that asshole said what he did, I knew Frankie was going to shoot her, and there wasn't fuck-all I could do to stop him. It was bing-bang-boom! Gina's dead."

"Then, of course, I fucking lost it and kicked him in the nuts so hard he'll probably be singing soprano for the rest of his life. When the bastard doubled over, I kneed him so hard in the face that I'm sure I flattened his nose permanently."

"Well done," Toni said, lifting her beer in a toast.

"Doesn't bring her back, though," I said. "If I'd have been a few seconds quicker—if my brain would have acted a little faster, then maybe I could have stopped him before he fired. It felt like I was in quicksand. Just couldn't engage fast enough."

"It sounds like the whole thing was just a couple of seconds."

"Something like that. The DEA guy talked, and then I think John Calabria said something, and then Frankie yelled at her and shot her, almost at the same time. It was quick."

"Nothing you could have done," Toni said.

I thought about it for a second. "Probably not. I knew Frankie wasn't cuffed, but I wasn't going to point that out. He was on his own with that. I was curious as to what he was going to do. I had no idea that ten seconds later the whole fucking thing would blow up in our faces like it did. I think he must have just snapped."

Neither of us spoke for a moment, and then Toni said, "Do you think there's a possibility that Gina actually set this whole thing up with the Feds like the guy said? Is that why the agent fucked up and said what he said?"

"They said not, but who knows?" I said. "Why would she? Why turn her own relatives over now? That makes no sense."

"I suppose not," Toni said. "I was just looking for something to give to her parents. Some sort of explanation. You're going to have to talk to them, you know."

"Thanks for reminding me. I'm not looking forward to it."

"You did all that you could," Toni said. "All anyone could, under the circumstances."

"Thanks for that," I said, raising my bottle.

"You're welcome," she said, clinking the neck of hers against mine.

We sat without talking for a few minutes, listening to the music. Eventually, I said, "This is going to take a while to get over."

"I don't expect you can get over this," Toni said. "It's not something you get over. I think it's something you get accustomed to. You learn how to live with it. Gradually, time patches it over a little."

"I imagine," I said. "I hope so, anyway."

We drank our beers and listened to the music and watched the day turn to night.

Kurt Cobain sang about needing a friend. I understood. The lyrics and the melody soaked into my brain. Somehow, I felt better, comforted. "Toni," I said, "thanks for being here."

She smiled. "Where else would I be?"

She left around ten thirty, and I went to bed shortly afterward. I tossed and turned again. Two hours later, I woke up in a cold sweat. I'd been dreaming—nightmares, really. I'd dreamed of demons—of explosions, of sheer terror, of seeing friends killed in Afghanistan and Iraq. I dreamed of a faceless woman, bleeding out on a cold, stark-white floor. It was so real that I could hear her gasping for breath. And at last I dreamed of angels—white angels dancing across a deep blue sky.

~~~~

Next morning first thing, I called Robbie. I told him how sorry I was. He didn't sound good. Why would he? We made an appointment for Toni and me to stop by at eleven. Robbie said there was a houseful of people already, but that his parents had said they wanted to talk to me.

Toni and I arrived a few minutes early. Toni had to park fifty yards up the street because of the traffic. We found a space and walked back to the Fiore house. I was dressed in a dark suit, while Toni wore a long-sleeved, very proper black dress. We walked up the path from the gate to the porch. Several people sat out on the porch, talking quietly. A few of them clearly recognized me. Gina's death was big news and, apparently, the people here had seen my television "interview" last night or maybe the front-page follow-up picture in the *Seattle Times* this morning. No one said anything, though. The door was open, so we went in without knocking.

Almost immediately, Robbie saw me. His eyes were red and swollen, but he wasn't crying at the moment. He came over, and we shook hands first; then he wrapped his arms around me and hugged me. I patted him on the back, doing the best I could to comfort him.

He stepped back and said, "I can't believe she's gone."

I didn't know if he expected an answer, but I didn't have one. I just nodded.

"Robbie," Toni said, "we're so sorry about what's happened. We're devastated. It's such a waste."

Robbie nodded. "Thank you," he said. "If I'd had any idea that something like this could have happened, I'd have never gone along with her. She seemed like she had everything under control."

"No one could have known what was going to happen," I said. "I couldn't even do anything about it, and I was standing right there—six feet away. It happened too fast."

He nodded.

"You have quite a houseful," Toni said, looking around at several dozen people crowded into the home.

"Lots of friends and relatives," Robbie said. "Everyone's been on edge since Gina disappeared three weeks ago, and now this." He looked around and surveyed the crowd. Then he turned back to me and said, "My mom and dad asked about you already this morning. I know they want to see you."

"We want to talk to them, as well. Is there a place we can talk privately?" I asked.

"Yeah. I kept the door to dad's study closed so that no one would go in. Come on."

He led us through the entry and down a hallway to the study. The heavy double doors were tall—probably ten feet. He pushed one open, and we entered. No one was inside.

"Robbie," I said, "this would be a real good time for you to tell me what your parents know. For example, do they know you'd been talking to Gina for the last couple of weeks?"

He looked at me. "Yes," he said.

"I thought you told me they were in the dark on that."

"They were. After our meeting Sunday at the office, I figured I'd better tell them before they heard it from you instead."

I nodded. "Good thinking. So there's nothing else—no other secrets I should know about?"

"Nothing," he said.

"Good," I said.

"Wait here," he said. "I'll go and get Mom and Dad." He closed the door behind him.

"He's not doing as bad as I would've thought," Toni said.

"Hard to say," I said. "I've seen people handle grief a lot of different ways. Some people, it spills right out. Others keep it bottled inside. To each his own, I guess."

I looked around the room while we waited. The furnishings were masculine—heavy carved wood with leather inlay on the desk and leather upholstered sofa and chairs. One wall had floor-to-ceiling shelves full of books and keepsakes. Another wall was made of windows and opened on to an outside garden with French doors. The wall across from this had a huge painting, modern style, of shapes and colors that looked like a schoolchild had drawn.

"Holy shit," Toni said softly. "Look at this. This painting is by Jasper Johns. I've never even seen it before. If it's real, it's probably worth millions."

I looked at it. To me, it looked like a drop cloth in a kindergarten class on finger-paint day. I guess I couldn't appreciate fine art. At least not then.

I'd just started to answer Toni when the door swung open and Angelo Fiore entered, followed by Carina and Robbie.

I walked over to Angelo and shook his hand. He, too, had red, swollen eyes. Carina dabbed at her eyes with a handkerchief. She reached up and hugged me, and then Toni.

"Thank you both for coming by this morning," Carina said.

"We wanted to be here," Toni said. "We had to talk to you."

Carina nodded.

"Let's sit over here then and talk for a few minutes," Angelo said. "It's getting loud out there and now, of all times, I could use a little peace and quiet." He motioned us to the sofa and chairs.

"I'm so very sorry about what happened," I said.

Both nodded.

"I don't know what you know or what you've been told."

"I'd like to hear everything from you," Angelo said.

"Okay," I said. I walked them through each step in the chain of events that led me to Port Townsend, including my meeting with Robbie where he confirmed Gina's location.

"It's unfortunate that Robbie was put in that position by Gina," Angelo said. "I understand his loyalty to his sister. I wish it hadn't been at our expense—and I mean that literally—but I understand. I've forgiven him for misleading us, but I commend him here in front of you for trying to protect his sister."

I looked at Robbie and nodded. "I understand," I said.

I continued and explained how I'd located Gina and been taken to the house outside Port Townsend. I told them the exact plan for getting into the marijuana business that Gina had spelled out for me. I went on to explain what happened. I left out the grim details, but I did say, "I was with her when she died. Her last words were 'Tell my mom and dad that I love them.'"

We all cried now, even me. Toni handed me a tissue.

"Sir, there was nothing I could have done," I said. "It all happened so fast, it was over in just a few seconds."

They both nodded. Angelo said, "Well, at least you put Frank Rossi in the hospital."

I looked at him. "I did?"

"Yes," he said. "That's what the man from the government told us yesterday afternoon. He said that you'd broken his nose so badly that he needed surgery."

"I lost my mind," I confessed.

"Good," he said. "Too bad you didn't kill him."

"Angelo," Carina said.

"I mean it," Angelo said. "The bastard killed my daughter."

It was quiet for a second, then Toni said, "Well, I'm certain he'll be going to prison—probably for the rest of his life—when he gets out of the hospital."

Angelo nodded. "That's something, anyway."

"Mr. and Mrs. Fiore," I said, trying hard to hold back my tears, "I feel like I failed you. You hired me to find Gina, and I take that to mean find her and protect her. Even from herself. The fact is, I failed. I'm so sorry."

Angelo looked at me.

"Young man," he said. "You didn't fail. And I don't like or appreciate your self-pity. Self-pity tends to fit like a poor suit. That is to say, badly. My wife and son and I will come to grips with Gina's death, as will you. I realize that you had feelings for Gina in the past and that those feelings might still have been present even yesterday. But none of us can afford to wallow in self-pity. This was not our fault. This was not your fault. This was partly Gina's fault for putting herself into that position. My cousins may have been partly at fault for the same reason. But the real culprit—the one who's really at fault here—is Frank Rossi. He killed my daughter. Not you, not us, no one else. He pulled the trigger. Him. I'd prefer that you not try to deflect the blame for this heinous action onto anyone other than him. Certainly not onto yourself. You and your people did a fantastic job."

I looked at him for a moment, then said, "Thank you. That helps a lot."

Toni smiled at him and said, "We're supposed to be trying to make you feel better, not the other way around."

"None of us feels too good today," he said. "But it will get better. Trust me."

# Chapter 28

GINA'S FUNERAL SERVICE was held at ten o'clock on Friday morning, September 2, at the Calvary Catholic Cemetery. It was a breezy day, partly cloudy. Although it was technically still summer, the temperature was noticeably cooler than it had been a month ago. The sun didn't have the same warmth that it had before, and I was comfortable in my dark suit.

I was surprised that the Fiores had opted for a simple graveside ceremony instead of the full-blown Catholic funeral mass. I knew that they were active members of St. Joseph Parish on Capitol Hill, because my family were also members. As active parishioners, the Fiores were certainly entitled to the full-dress ceremony. If I'd have had to predict, I would have thought that they'd have gone big.

Instead, they downplayed the funeral. They told everyone that there would be a small, private ceremony for immediate family members only, although they invited Toni and me. The only thing I could think of was that they were embarrassed by the nature of Gina's death—so much so that they didn't want to make a big deal of her funeral.

Not that I objected. I'm Catholic, but I'm not exactly what you'd call devout. I don't go to church often, and I particularly try to avoid funerals. I've had more than my share of close friends die, and I've found that for me anyway, I prefer that my last thoughts of my best friends be the happy memories I have of them—not the sad ones like watching their parents crying at their funerals. So, given my druthers, I'd normally prefer to chicken out and not go.

That said, most of the time I end up feeling compelled to attend out of a sense of duty to my deceased friends. I figure that they'd want me to be there to help comfort their parents, just as I'd hope they'd do for me if it were me in the box instead of them. So I sucked it up and went for them.

The coffin was bronze-colored and sat on a rack made of stainless steel. A dark green carpet, made to resemble grass, covered the hole beneath the coffin. Covered chairs were lined up behind the coffin. Altogether, there were a total of maybe twenty people at the service, including the Fiores themselves, a few other people who looked like family members, the priest, and Toni and me. That was it. Angelo Fiore stared somberly at the coffin while Carina dabbed at her eyes with her handkerchief. Robbie simply stared at his feet.

Promptly at ten o'clock, the priest began the service. He offered up a benediction prayer and then introduced Robbie.

"Thank you for coming," Robbie started. "I'll be very brief." He spoke extemporaneously. He paused, gathered his thoughts, and then started. "You all knew Gina; there's not much for me to add to that. You all knew that not only was she beautiful on the outside, but she was beautiful inside as well. Full of life, caring, take-charge, in control. I can say that this past Monday, I lost not only my sister but also my best friend. My mentor. She was always there for me. I'm—I mean I was two years older, but it always seemed like she was the big sister. She took charge of everything she touched. She always had everything under control. But she couldn't control what happened this past Monday.

"As you know, Gina went missing three weeks ago. We believe that she left on purpose for reasons that are still not entirely clear to us. And though we know what happened this past Monday, we'll probably never know exactly why things happened the way they did. We do know she died trying to assure my mom and dad that she loved them—in fact, those were her last words.

"We don't know why she'd gotten involved in the things she had, but we ask you to please remember Gina as we do—a loving daughter, a caring sister, a true friend. My family believes firmly that when people like Gina die, they ascend to the right hand of God. There's no doubt in my mind that that's where Gina is right now, seated at God's right side. And, knowing Gina, she's most likely explaining to God exactly what He could be doing to improve things up there."

~~~~

After the service ended, we walked over to the Fiores and gave our condolences.

"Nice words, Robbie," I said.

"Thanks," he said. "I guess words and memories are all that's left."

I nodded. "I suppose. Still, I'm sure Gina would have liked what you said about her."

"I hope," he said.

"Mrs. Fiore, we're very sorry about the ways things turned out," Toni said to Carina. Toni had tears in her eyes, and I think this made Carina start to cry again.

She smiled and choked back a sob. "It's not easy burying your little girl," she said.

Toni stepped over and hugged Carina. "I can't even imagine. And I know there's nothing we can say to make this better," she said. "Only God and time can do that. I'll pray that God is kind to you all and that the time to heal is quick."

Carina smiled. "That's very kind of you, dear. Thank you very much." She thought for a second, and then said, "You never even knew Gina, did you?"

Toni shook her head. "I didn't," she said. "I've heard enough, though. And the biggest thing for me is my partner here," she poked me. "He always held her in the highest regard. I trust his judgment. If he thought Gina was tops, then she was tops."

"Thank you," Carina said. She turned to me. "Danny, I know you were close with Gina once. And I know that because of your commitments to the service, your relationship ended abruptly in what might not have been the best of circumstances. For all of her good qualities, Gina was not always very patient or understanding. But, what I'm saying, what I'm hoping is that after you found Gina last Sunday, the day before she died—the night before she died, did you get the chance to find some closure? Were the two of you able to talk?"

"We talked," I said. "But not too much about the two of us. It was mostly about what she was doing and why she was doing it. And why I was there and what was I going to do about what she was doing—that sort of thing." I didn't want to bring up Gina's and my conversation about going to Hawaii. I didn't know how I felt about it. I'd never agreed to it, and it would be too hard to explain. Instead, I said, "I guess that on a personal level, I'd have to say no, we didn't have time for any closure."

Carina looked at me. "I'm sorry to hear that," she said. "I'm sure Gina thought very highly of you as well."

Angelo said, "We all do. I understand now what she saw in you. You're an honorable young man. Thank you so much, both of you. You did a better job than anyone could have expected, given the circumstances. We'll always be grateful."

I thanked him for the nice words and then we said our good-byes. I asked Robbie to call me next week. I wanted to discuss how to return the overpayment of the fees that Angelo had paid us when we started.

~~~~

"So," Toni said as we drove west on forty-fifth back to the office, "you going to be okay?"

"I am," I said, confidently, changing lanes to pass a Subaru so covered in bumper stickers that I was amazed the driver could even see out. "I'm strong, and I've got good friends, like you." I smiled at her.

She smiled back. "Really?" she asked, challenging me.

"What?"

She hesitated, and then said, "I think of all the people I know, I'm closer to you than I am to anyone—even closer than I am with my sister and my mom—or at least, a different kind of close. And I think you feel the same way, right?"

"You know how I feel about you," I said. "No one knows me the way you do, that's true. And I think I understand you pretty well, although you're probably way more complicated than I am."

"You're a man. That goes without saying," she said, smiling. "Anyway, I think you might call us best friends, agreed?"

"Of course," I said.

"And best friends are honest with each other, right?"

"Agreed."

"Then listen to me. Danny, I know you. I know what this has meant to you. I know what you're going through. You may think you're okay, but you're not. I think you've got some healing to do."

I shrugged.

"Maybe you should take a few days off. I can run things in the office for a while. We've got these three little surveillance cases, and they're all easy. The boys and I'll finish them up over the course of the next week. You should take the Jeepster and head out to the forest. You seem to like it out there. You do well out there."

I thought about it. I hadn't had a day off in over a month. A week between jobs might be nice. I could load up some camping gear and drive up to the Olympic National Park. Take my guitar and find a quiet spot where the only sound was my music, the wind in the trees, and the running water. And mosquitoes the size of blue jays, but that was just a recreational hazard that you had to get used to. I agreed, the trip sounded like a good idea. Only one thing might make it better.

"Come with me," I said. "You haven't had a day off in God knows how long either. I could use the company."

She looked at me and smiled. "You're not thinking straight, Danny," she said.

"Why?"

"For starters, you're forgetting a few things," she said.

She waited for me, so I said, "What?"

"We're friends, remember? We work together. I think neither of us wants to take a chance at screwing that up."

I nodded. If I were thinking straight, I'd have probably agreed.

"Besides," she said, "even if I didn't work for you, I'm no rebound baby. If you want me, you'd have to do it properly. Not 'someone dumps you, and you turn to Toni' or 'someone dies, and you turn to Toni'—no disrespect to Gina. You need time to get your head straight all by yourself, not twisted around by me or anyone else. You need to do this on your own."

I was quiet for a few seconds as I thought about it. She was probably right, at least about her last point. "Can't blame me for bringing it up," I said.

She smiled at me. "I don't," she said. "In fact, I'm flattered."

# Chapter 29

I LEFT THE next morning at eight. Courtesy of the army, I'm able to pack quickly and efficiently. It took about ten minutes to load up the Jeep with tent, sleeping bag, my Martin D-28 guitar, and my backpack. One more sack of supplies, and I was on my way. I'd called Toni the night before and thanked her for what she'd said and for being my friend in general. She deserved that and more from me. Much more.

I told her I'd take the Edmonds–Kingston ferry to Highway 104, and then take that to the 101. Highway 101 circled the top of the Olympic Peninsula and would take me to the park's main entrance at Hurricane Ridge near Port Angeles. My intent was to drive all the way back to Lake Mills and then find a nearby camping spot on the shores of the lake. It was remote enough that even on Labor Day weekend, I should be able to find a nice quiet spot all to myself. I'd be home on Tuesday, maybe Wednesday. On the way, I'd be damn certain to skirt Port Townsend. I don't know if I'll ever be able to visit there again.

I didn't tell Toni that I was going to stop first at Gas Works Park on the way. In fact, I didn't even think of stopping until I pulled out of my condo, but the damned Jeep seemed to have a mind of its own. It turned north on Westlake, crossed the Fremont Bridge, and then hung a quick right on Northlake. Three minutes later, I pulled into the nearly empty parking lot at Gas Works. I locked up and walked to the park entrance.

Because of the hour, the park was very quiet, only a few people out. A young couple held hands and sat on the grassy slope, staring at the water without speaking. An elderly lady threw crumbs to a flock of Canada geese, the birds honking excitedly around her. I walked past and made my way south down the hill to the water's edge. I found the exact bench where Gina and I sat on Thanksgiving Day, almost six years ago. I had a seat. I looked south over the water and took in the vista. I thought about everything that had happened over the past few weeks, particularly last Sunday and Monday. My emotions were completely jumbled. As I remembered Gina, tears formed in my eyes.

"We used to sit on that bench together."

I looked quickly to the side. The old woman who'd been feeding the geese was talking to me. She was plainly dressed in neatly pressed khaki slacks and a dark green jacket.

"I was saying," she repeated, when I didn't respond, "that we used to sit on that bench, together, my Harold and I."

"Really?" I asked, wiping my eyes. "I'm sorry. Would you like to have a seat here now?" I started to get up.

"Sit down," she ordered, waving me down. She sat on the edge of the bench and looked at the water. Then she turned to me. "You know, Harold and I sat right on this very bench fifty-five years ago," she said. "He proposed to me, sitting right where you're sitting now. Told me he didn't have a penny to his name, but that he was dedicating himself to making me happy for the rest of my life. And he did, too. Leastwise, for the rest of his life, anyway. Harold's been gone since 1998 now, but I still come here, and I remember. For me, this will always be a happy place. I come here often."

I smiled. "That's a nice story. What's your name?"

"I'm Helen. Helen MacReedy," she answered.

"Hi, Helen," I said, holding out my hand. "I'm Danny Logan."

"Hello, Danny Logan. I'm glad to meet you," she said, shaking my hand.

"Believe it or not," I said, "this bench has special meaning for me, too. Six years ago, I spent three weeks with a girl who I'd known in passing in high school five years before that. I had to go away for a bit, and she and I spent some time on our last day together on this very bench. Be six years this Thanksgiving Day."

"Really? Was it a happy time?"

"It was very happy. We didn't know what was going to happen between us. Turned out we ended up not getting back together afterwards. I was in the army then, and I had to go one way, and she went another.

Our three weeks together was all we had. Then, by chance, we managed to reconnect for one day last week. Last Sunday. And the next day, she died. We buried her yesterday morning."

"Oh, my," she said. She considered this for a minute, and then said, "That's a very sad story, Danny. I'm very sorry for you."

I nodded. "Thank you."

"Are you alright?"

"I'll be okay," I said, nodding again. "Thanks for asking. I've got good friends—people who care about me. I'll be fine."

"Well, you look like a very strong, handsome young man," she said. "I can give you a couple of pieces of advice from an old woman who's been through the crap, as they say," she said, "but only if you're interested in hearing them. I don't want to barge in where I'm not wanted."

I smiled. "Feel free, Helen," I said. "I could use some good advice."

"First off," she said, "you've heard it before, but time really does help to soothe the pain of passing. When Harold died, it hurt, believe you me. But I had two things working against me that you don't have to deal with. First, Harold and I were together more than forty years—most of my adult life. He's all I ever knew. When Harold died, I felt like half of me had just been ripped out. I'd really never even been on my own. It took a long time to get over that. In your case, although you might not feel it now, your recovery will be much easier simply because you weren't together very long."

I nodded.

"And second," she said, "when Harold died, I was sixty-three years old. I suppose I could have remarried, but I'd already had a full life with Harold. I had a history that I was comfortable with, and I didn't want to add another chapter with someone new. Too damned hard to train one man—I sure didn't want to have to go through it all over again. Besides, I never was much of a looker—starting over might have been a problem for me. You, on the other hand, you look like a movie star."

I laughed. "Helen, you're beautiful now. Fifteen years ago, you must have been a knockout. If we were even close to the same age, I'd be asking you for a date right this second."

She laughed. "Smart aleck. I was never that smooth with the words, either," she said. "So you're what, thirty years old?"

"Twenty-nine," I said.

"Twenty-nine," she waved her hand at me dismissively. "You're still a baby. You're not even broken in yet. You're just about the right age to find yourself a nice young woman and settle down—find someone to train you. Your whole life is still in front of you. Trust me, Danny Logan, you're going to be fine."

She got up. "I've got to go. I have a date every Saturday morning, and I can see he just got here."

"I thought you said you weren't interested in a new man?" I asked.

"I said I wasn't interested in getting remarried. See that old man over there?"

I looked and saw a tall, silver-haired man walking toward us. "Yes," I said.

"That's Adam. He meets me here on Saturday mornings, and we feed the geese. We're not getting married," she said, "we just fool around. Big difference."

I laughed.

"Good luck to you, young man. Remember, God built you to face forward, not backward. Your future is in front of you, not behind."

I smiled. "Thanks for the advice, Helen. It was good advice. You have a nice morning."

"You too, Danny," she said, turning to walk off. Suddenly, she stopped and turned back. "Hey, Danny Logan," she said, "I saw you on the TV news a couple of nights ago. You looked good then, but you're even more handsome in person." She waved, then turned around and left.

~~~~

I chuckled to myself. First Toni last night, and now Helen this morning. How could I feel bad?

After she walked away to join Adam, I turned to look south, out over Lake Union. Funny how on the one hand, the view had barely changed at all in six years; yet on the other hand, it was profoundly different. The water looked the same as it did six years ago. The city to the south was the same. I-5 still framed the view on the east, and the houseboats where *Sleepless in Seattle* was filmed still framed the view on the west.

Yet today, everything was different. Six years ago, I was holding Gina, wondering how I could be so lucky, still unaware that we were not destined for each other. At that moment, six years ago, everything seemed perfect.

Today, not so perfect. More real, more pure, more ups and downs, more joys and hurts, but not perfect. I guess that's what you get when life happens. You get bashed. You get knocked down. And, if you're made of the right stuff, you get back up, wiser for the experience. It's not perfect, but it's real.

Gina was gone, and I was sad. But, there wasn't a damn thing I could do about it. It hurt, but at least according to Helen, one day it wouldn't. For me, I guess it was time to think about getting back up.

# PART 4

# Chapter 30

FOUR MONTHS PASSED—four months in which I grew accustomed to the fact that Gina was gone. Toni and Helen had been right—time was beginning to patch over the hurt. I hadn't had a bad dream in over a month. Christmas 2011 came and went, and now we were four days into the new year. Life fell back into something of a normal rhythm. We'd been able to pick up a half-dozen new cases: mostly simple surveillances plus one skiptrace. They paid a little, but if Angelo Fiore hadn't called me and told me to keep the balance of his retainer—that I didn't owe him any kind of refund—we'd have been hurting. I objected when he said this, but he insisted. Oh well, it came at a good time. As it was, I was starting to get a little nervous. I had personal cash reserves, but I wanted to keep them in reserve. One thing I never had to worry about in the army was meeting a payroll. It's not my favorite part of owning the agency.

In fact, it would be nice to get lucky and stumble onto a "gold mine" case—one that paid so well that I wouldn't ever have to sweat paying the rent again. I have a few friends who are PIs. One of them did some work for a software company some time ago. He was paid in the form of a stock option because they were tight on cash. Then his client went public. Overnight, he was wealthy. Today, he works only because he likes it. He sure as hell doesn't need to work. I should be so lucky.

On the good news front, Toni and I were fine again—back to our old selves. We talked and laughed and joked and occasionally hung out a little together. I still didn't really feel like going out with anybody romantically, so mostly, I just stayed home. Sometimes, Toni would come over, and we'd drink a few beers and listen to music. It was mostly too cold and usually too wet to sit out on the balcony now, so instead we'd just sit around inside and hang out—maybe watch a movie. She continued to go out on dates with the gay football player when he had time, and I continued to tease her about it. She took it well.

Overall, I was content. On Wednesday morning, January the fourth at ten, I sat at my desk, reading the *Seattle Times*. Outside, it was pouring. Not the usual Seattle drizzle—this was real honest-to-God rain like they get in the Carolinas. Big, heavy, wet drops the size of small water balloons. A couple of direct hits, and you were soaked. It was cool—probably mid-thirties, and it was blustery. All in all, a good day to be indoors. I sipped my coffee and looked outside and watched the rain.

Toni knocked on my door and walked in. She sat in one of the chairs, looked at me, and said nothing at first.

"What?" I said. "What do you want?"

"How are you doing?" she asked.

I looked at her, confused. "I'm doing fine. Why? What do you mean, how am I doing?"

"I mean how you are doing getting over Gina Fiore."

"I'm over it," I said. "It's history."

"You're not seeing anyone," she said. It was a statement, not a question.

"You know I'm not seeing anyone," I said. "Why? Do you want to go out on a date? What's this all about?"

She ignored me. "Are you still having the dreams?"

I looked at her, and then smiled and said, "Toni, you know the only person I dream about nowadays is you. There's usually a fireplace." I stared off into the distance, like I was recalling the dream. "You're wearing this short, see-through little sexy thing—" I paused and stared at the wall, as if I had a picture in my mind's eye. "My God!"

"Freeze the picture, you jerk," she said, laughing. "That's as close as you're going to get." She got up and started to walk out.

"Wait a minute," I called out to her. "Don't you want to hear about the rug? There's this bearskin rug in front of the fireplace!"

She laughed as she left my office. Does this make me sexist? I don't know.

From down the hall, I heard her call out, "Read the newspaper, moron."

Read the paper? What did she mean by that? That's what I'd been doing. I looked at the *Seattle Times* on my desk and picked it up. The paper was dominated by coverage of the New Hampshire primary. The Iowa caucus had been held the day before, and the results were spread all over the front page—something that interested me not at all. I churned through the front section, then tossed it aside when I was finished. Nothing interesting there.

I started reading the second section—local news—and almost immediately stopped. "Wow!" I said out loud. The front-page article of the second section was headlined "IRS DROPS CHARGES AGAINST FIORE." The article went on to explain how, after a four-year investigation, the IRS agreed to a small monetary adjustment in the prior years, but that all criminal charges had been dropped. Apparently, the IRS now felt that there was not sufficient evidence that Mr. Fiore had committed a crime. All that the IRS felt he was guilty of now was misclassifying revenue numbers. They wanted this fixed, but that was it. This was good news. This would have made Gina very happy.

I hopped out of my chair and walked next door to Toni's office.

"This is good news," I said happily.

"Good news?" she said, questioning. "What article did you read?"

"About the IRS dropping their tax evasion charges against Angelo."

She looked at me, and then said, "Give me that." She reached for the paper. She turned to the next page and handed it back. "Read that," she said, pointing.

The article:

## CHARGES DROPPED AGAINST CHICAGO MOBSTER IN FIORE CASE

Robert Miller, U.S. Attorney in Seattle, announced today that all charges against known Chicago mobster Francisco "Frankie the Boot" Rossi in connection with the murder of Gina Fiore have been dropped. Citing insufficient evidence to continue the case, Miller said that Rossi was to be released immediately. . .

I stopped reading.

"Holy shit!" I read some more, and then said, "Holy shit!" again. My vocabulary seemed to have shrunk. "Insufficient evidence?" I said, incredulously. "Insufficient evidence? Jesus Christ! There were thirty people standing right there! Twenty of 'em were Feds, for shit's sake! What the fuck? This bastard's just going to walk?"

I couldn't believe what I was seeing. I stared at the paper for several long moments without saying anything. Slowly, I turned and walked back to my office. I walked inside, closed the door, and sat at my desk. I spun the chair around so that I could look outside at the rain.

No justice at all, it seemed. Frank Rossi released because of "lack of evidence." I was stunned. I sat there and stared outside for ten solid minutes, reliving the events of that morning, looking for answers and finding none.

~~~~

My phone rang, breaking my contemplation. I picked it up, and Toni said, brusquely, "Come out here, Danny."

The tone of her voice told me she was serious, so I snapped out of my funk and hustled outside to the lobby. Toni was there, along with two men in long, gray raincoats.

"Mr. Logan," one of them said, "you may remember me. I'm Special Agent Regis Jackson, U.S. DEA Seattle. This is Special Agent Mike Hamilton."

I looked at him. "Sorry," I said, "hard to recognize you guys when you're not fucking up an operation and getting someone killed. Funny you should show up today."

He stared straight at me for a few seconds. "Let me guess," he said, "you've been reading the newspaper."

"That's right," I said, shaking my head in disbelief. "How could the U.S. Attorney drop charges against Frank Rossi? Insufficient evidence? Holy Christ! The son of a bitch was surrounded by Feds when he shot Gina! You yourself were standing right there, not eight feet away. What would he have had to do to actually get indicted, drag her to the U.S. Attorney's office and shoot her in the goddamned lobby?"

"I understand your frustration," Jackson said, "but we're here this morning to explain things. Is there a place where we can talk privately?"

"Our conference room," I said. "But excuse me if I don't trust you guys completely. I want my partner here to be with us."

He nodded. "We met Miss Blair on the way in," Jackson said. "Suit yourself."

I led everyone back to the conference room.

Toni said, "May I offer you gentlemen a cup of coffee? Bottled water?"

We all asked for coffee. "Do you need help?" I asked.

She shook her head. "Got it."

When she came back, Jackson started.

"I need to explain something to you that's confidential—we'd have to deny it if it ever leaked out. Still, you need to know."

"Go ahead," I said. "I'm all ears."

"Sometime near the end of last July, we were approached by Gina Fiore with an idea," he said. "She wanted to make a trade. Gina's idea was essentially to use her position within the Calabria family as an inducement to get the Mendez brothers to travel from Tijuana to the United States for a meeting where they could be arrested on American soil. Gina figured that the opportunity for the United States to arrest one or both leaders of the Tijuana-Mendez cartel would be highly coveted by the Department of Justice. Both of these men were on the FBI's Ten Most Wanted list. Gina designed an entire operation around this concept and presented it to us."

I was stunned. Jackson continued.

"I ran her idea past my superiors, and they were indeed impressed. Surprisingly, they agreed within a week. The Mendez brothers were such a notorious, high-value target that their potential capture—especially in a presidential election year—really seemed to get their attention.

"Although we didn't know it, Gina had actually started working this plan more than three months prior to the time she ever contacted us, probably in April of last year. I guess she wanted to move the operation beyond the hypothetical stage before she presented it to us.

"Initially, she needed a contact within the cartel. Where do you go to establish such a contact if you're a young woman, an accountant at that, with no contacts with a Mexican drug cartel? She'd already studied up on the cartel operations in the United States—marijuana-growing operations, in particular. She knew that Washington State is a hotbed for this type of activity. So she came up with the idea that, since she was young and good-looking, she could hang out in a popular Mexican bar and hopefully locate someone involved in the cartel drug trade. Essentially, she went fishing and used herself as the bait. It was a long shot, but by using what amounts to good acting and brilliant undercover detective work, combined with a fair measure of luck, she ferreted out none other than Eduardo Salazar at Ramon's Cantina. She flirted with him, dangled herself in front of him, and cozied up to him. Finally, one night, she promised him a home run but instead she slipped him a couple of Quaaludes when he wasn't look-ing. He fell fast asleep."

"And while he slept," I said, "she copied his notebook with her cell phone."

"She told you, then," Jackson said. "I suspected she had."

I nodded.

"Well, that's right. She copied his notebook. That notebook con-tained GPS coordinates—actually latitude and longitude—of forty sepa-rate marijuana grows here in the state of Washington—complete with sketches. Salazar didn't know it yet, but with this information, Gina had him nailed to the cross. In early July, she explained to Mr. Salazar who she was and the nature of her Chicago relatives. She told him that her fam-ily wanted to create a joint venture with the Tijuana-Mendez cartel that would allow them to move the marijuana being grown here more profit-ably. Initially, Mr. Salazar's ego wouldn't accept her in this new position. He couldn't wrap his head around it, so he just blew her off. I guess he wasn't a very big thinker. Anyway, Gina responded by anonymously turn-ing in one of Salazar's plantations to our office as a way to turn up the pressure on him. It also had the effect of establishing future legitimacy with us, although we had no idea what was going on at the time. She had someone other than herself make the call to us on an untraceable cell phone, so we didn't even know whom the tipster was; but we checked it out and got a large bust as a result. We were happy.

"This same scenario repeated itself three more times over the next month and a half before the light finally went on in Salazar's pea brain, and he made the connection—he realized that Gina was the one turning in the fields using his own data against him because he had refused to work with her and make the connection with the cartel that she wanted. Things started happening fast. Salazar exploded and began searching for Gina. Gina was a step ahead of him, though. She'd gone into hiding a week after the last bust, just in case. And, at about that time, she talked to us and proved that she was the one providing the tips. Our top brass was already inclined to give this a shot, but now that they were really convinced of her legitimacy, they gave the green light on the operation to set up and arrest the Mendez brothers."

"And that's about the time we were called in by the family to help find her. Apparently, they were unaware of all this," I said.

"Correct," he said, "they knew nothing." He paused and sipped his coffee.

"Unfortunately for Eddie Salazar, by this time, it was already too late for him. Eventually, it must have occurred to him that his bosses might add two and two and figure out that the only fields being busted were his. They would not be pleased. They'd think he was either dishonest or incompetent. Neither would be conducive to long life in a Mexican drug cartel. He undoubtedly started fearing for his own skin, with good reason. We figure he decided he'd better call his bosses and do a mea culpa. They probably said thank you very much for the update. Then, because they are who they are, we figure they had him executed. Stupidity is not tolerated in those organizations.

At the same time, they sent an e-mail to Gina. As it turns out, Gina'd been right all along. The Mendez brothers were very interested in venturing with the Calabria family. Weren't too happy about losing four marijuana grows, but they were very excited to partner up with a famous American crime family like the Calabrias. Ironically, if Salazar would have simply turned over the contact originally instead of getting all puffed up, he'd still be alive today."

"Trust me, we're better off without him," I said.

"No argument there," he said. "There was a flurry of e-mails between Gina and the cartel representative, Francisco Miranda, which eventually led to a planned meeting of the principals in Port Townsend last August."

"At that point, Gina had all her pieces put together. All that remained was to actually set up and conduct the meeting between the principals. We were working with her by this time, so we knew everything that she was doing."

"What did she want in exchange for setting this up?" I asked.

"In exchange for setting up the meeting with the Tijuana-Mendez brothers, essentially luring them to America on the pretense that they would be arranging a business transaction with the Calabrias, she wanted all IRS charges against her father dropped."

Again, I was stunned. "Really? That's it? There was never any intent on her part to go into the marijuana business?"

Jackson smiled. "Certainly not. That was the ruse. All she asked was that her father be cleared of his tax problem. She felt that there was a strong possibility that he might die in prison, so she came up with this whole entire plan to keep him out."

"That means the Calabrias were never going to team up with the Mendez brothers?"

"Of course not," he said.

"And their arrest?"

"Like yours, just for show."

"Goddamn," I said, shaking my head slowly.

"My sentiments exactly. It was a very noble action on her part," Jackson said. He continued. "The days after Salazar was killed were the days when Gina was conducting her e-mail conversations with Francisco Miranda. At the same time, your team was closing in. When it became apparent that you'd caught Roberto in a lie, Gina assumed that you'd soon break him and force him to spill secrets. So she instructed Robbie to go ahead and invite you to Port Townsend. She figured that in light of your past relationship, it would be an offer that you couldn't refuse. She felt that with only one day to go until the meeting, it would be better to have you close where she could keep an eye on you, rather than have you potentially show up randomly."

"Well, it looks like I played my part perfectly," I said.

"Don't beat yourself up," Jackson said, smiling. "I never met a more resourceful young woman. She had the entire thing planned."

I thought about it. "Except for getting shot," I said.

He simply looked at me. "Which brings us to the topic at hand, which is, what you've seen today in the newspaper. Bottom line—Gina did her part. She told us that she would lure the Mendez family to America, and she did. They're busted, and they'll never get out. As a matter of fact, the entire Tijuana-Mendez organization seems to be crumbling. The factions within the organization are fighting among themselves rather than coalescing around new leadership. Anyway, yesterday, as you can see in today's newspaper, the IRS formally dropped all charges pending against Angelo Fiore. He's completely exonerated. Which means that we've now done our part as well."

I nodded. "That's something," I said. "I'm sure Gina would have appreciated it, though I'm equally positive that Angelo Fiore would say it's not been a good trade."

"I understand," Jackson said.

I was quiet for a moment, thinking. Then I said, "Of course, all this—this ruse—makes Gina's death all the more tragic. It seems like the only one other than myself who wasn't in on it was Frankie. And now the charges against him have been dropped. How did that happen?"

"I truly don't know," Jackson said. "Not my department. I haven't been involved with that end for several months. I'm sorry."

The room was quiet. Jackson looked at Toni, and then at me. "We wanted to stop by and explain, knowing the newspaper articles were coming out today. Do the two of you have any other questions I can answer?"

Neither of us said anything, so he and the other agent stood to leave. "We appreciate your time this morning. Hopefully, I've been able to shed some light on things, maybe provide some explanations. I'll leave you my card. Feel free to contact me anytime." He handed me his business card, and the two men left.

~~~~

Neither Toni nor I spoke for a minute. We stared outside at the rain.

"That's incredible," I said. "Here I thought that she was doing it for the money, and she was really faking it all along, her only intent being to keep her father out of prison. You gotta admit, that's pretty damn noble."

Toni was staring outside, lost in thought.

"Toni? Did you hear? I said it was pretty damn noble."

Suddenly, she was laughing to herself. "Wow," she said softly, "was I stupid, or what?"

"What?" I asked. "What's so damn funny?"

"I guess it's okay, because you were even stupider," she said, laughing.

"What?" I asked again, more agitated.

"Don't you see? This guy just said twice as much by what he didn't say than by what he did!"

"What are you talking about?"

"Think about it, Danny. He's the agent in charge, and he doesn't know why Frank Rossi wasn't charged with murder? Like you said—it happened right in front of him. They're going to make decisions about whether or not to release or charge Frank, and Jackson's not going to know about it? Come on!"

I looked at her. "What's your point?"

"My point is, I just figured out why Frankie wasn't charged with murder. Do you want to know why?"

"Yeah. Why?"

"Because there was no murder! You've been squibbed," she said.

I looked at her. "Squibbed? What do you mean, squibbed?"

"Squibbed. As in Hollywood. Fake-ola. As in a fake gunshot and a fake gunshot wound. Gina Fiore isn't dead, Danny. She's alive and well, and I'll be goddamned if she's not still controlling this whole fucking thing, four months after she's supposed to have been in the grave."

I was speechless for a second, and then I managed to say, "That's crazy talk."

"Really? Think about it. The DEA is smart enough to sneak up and catch eight people without making a sound outside the hangar, and then somehow infiltrate a couple dozen guys into the hangar right under your nose, and then nab the whole meeting without firing a shot, but then they go and screw up and leave someone uncuffed and unsearched inside the hangar while all of them conveniently turn their backs and fiddle around with a goddamned stuck door? They forget who they'd cuffed and who they hadn't? And the person who is left uncuffed just happens to be Frank Rossi—Gina's confidante. Hell, Danny, Frank didn't *kill* her. *He was her fucking co-star!* He shot her with a blank, made a flash and a big bang. She triggered a couple of squibs designed to look like gunshot wounds— one in her chest, one in her back. Blood and gore spatters front and back. She grabs her chest, and then she falls over and mumbles a couple of words; then holds her breath for a second, while they hustle everyone out in cuffs. Worked just like that, didn't it?"

I said nothing. It was just like that.

"Blanks and squibs would have looked and sounded just like what you saw and heard. That, combined with a very small amount of acting experience, could convince anyone that she'd been shot. Did you take her pulse?"

"I couldn't. I was cuffed."

"Did you see anyone take her pulse? Did anyone check her at all?"

"No, they didn't need to. She was obviously fucking dead! They just covered her up with a sheet."

"Of course, they did. Let me guess: there just happened to be one lying around, right? In a goddamned airplane hangar? She could only hold her breath for so long. Did you see an actual exit wound?"

"No. She was lying on her back."

"Of course. Think about it, Danny. It's perfect. She doesn't know what the cartel's going to do after she sets up the bust. Eventually, they'd suspect her and come looking. This way, she doesn't have to worry about retaliation for herself or her family because—"

"Because they think she's already dead," I said, slowly catching on.

"And you told me you overheard her talking to her uncle on the phone and saying 'he'll talk' and you didn't know who she was talking about? She was talking about you! You were there, not because she wanted to keep you close, like she told you, and like this clown just said, but because she needed someone independent to talk to the public to help bolster the story that she'd been killed. She knows the cartel watches the news. How many television interviews did you do that week—four? Five? You were perfect. Believable as all hell because you were telling the truth—as you knew it. Gina couldn't have scripted it any better.

"And one other thing," she continued. "I always wondered why the funeral was so small and private. Angelo Fiore knows half the people in the state of Washington. They'd normally have all been there by the hundreds to pay their respects. Except the Fiores must have known Gina wasn't dead. That's why they kept the crowd down."

"Goddamn," I said slowly. Could it actually be that way? The more I thought about it, we'd either been duped or there were about eight massive coincidences happening at the same time. "We were played," I said. "I was played. Gina got to have her cake and eat it, too. She freed her dad, and she walks away."

"Sort of walks away. She may have to hide for a while, maybe not depending on whether or not the cartel implodes. I don't hold it against her that she freed her dad, or that she walked away. I'm not too happy that she didn't seem to care about getting people hurt and using people to make it happen."

Toni was silent for a few seconds, and then she said, "You know what? You're going to hear from her—probably today since all this shit seems to just be breaking loose," Toni said.

"Why do you think that?"

"Because she still has the hots for you, of course. If you'll let her, she's not done playing with you, yet. As a matter of fact, knowing her, I'll bet she left instructions with the two clowns who just left to call her the moment they stepped out of our office."

The words were no sooner out of her mouth than my computer chimed, indicating a new e-mail. We looked at each other for a second, and time seemed to freeze. Then we both bolted for my computer.

"No, you don't," I said, shouldering her out of the way.

I moved the mouse, and the screensaver disappeared. There, on the monitor, was an e-mail with a postcard from the Grand Hyatt Kauai hotel. The picture showed a beautiful white beach set against an unbelievably blue sea. Palm trees swayed seductively overhead. On the beach was a single brilliant-red towel, but no people. The message said, "You still owe me a sunset. No interruptions this time. G."

~~~~

We stared at the screen, both with our own thoughts. Finally, Toni said, "I'll get you reservations this afternoon." Her voice was different. Before, she had been alive—animated—in her element. Now, it was a different Toni. She was much more subdued.

"Why?" I answered. "I'm not going."

"Yes, you are."

"Fuck you. I'm not going."

"I'll kill you myself if you don't go, damn it," she said. "There are too many open issues. You need to go get them resolved."

"I don't have feelings for her," I said.

"Bullshit, Logan. I know you. I don't care what you say; I know what you feel. You sure as hell do have some sort of feelings for her. You have to go over there and see what that's all about. Who knows? She might be the one and only person in the whole wide world for you."

I looked into Toni's eyes. "I doubt it," I said.

She was quiet for a second, then she looked away. "Well, we'll never know unless you go, will we?" She looked back at me. "Please. Just go."

~~~~

So I went. I went to Hawaii looking for something—what, I wasn't exactly sure. I was either going to start something or to end something, I didn't know which. Someone was waiting for me, but I wasn't really sure who. Was she the one? I guess that in order to find out, I had to go. So I went.

# Epilogue

*January 5, 2012*
*1:30 p.m.*

TONI BLAIR SAT at her desk at Logan Private Investigations, working hard on completing a case report for surveillance on an unfaithful husband. Caught him red-handed with still photos through the bedroom window. Note to philanderers: pull the goddamned blinds!

Toni was not in a good mood. The case report wasn't due until Wednesday, but today Toni had a special reason to kick the productivity motor into high gear. The harder she worked, the less she thought about Danny, or more particularly, Danny in Hawaii with "the bitch." She halfway kicked herself for insisting that he go yesterday. She'd even arranged his airline flight last night. But in the end, her head had overruled her heart. Danny needed to sort things out and in order to do that, he had to be face-to-face with Gina.

Personally, Toni felt like strangling the manipulative little bitch. The fact that Gina had done what she'd done for a pretty noble cause—helping her aging father—didn't even the score for how she'd used Danny. She almost got him killed! Hopefully, Danny was levelheaded enough to recognize this.

Toni had never known someone like Danny before—completely brilliant in certain aspects, barely better than adolescent in others. Clear insight in certain areas, barely able to see to the end of his nose in others. Then again, she thought maybe that was a pretty good description for men in general. No doubt, though, Danny had more good points than bad.

Toni knew that Danny had an internal, unwritten rule about office romance. She believed that Danny's self-discipline was the only thing that kept him away from her. It was damn sure the only reason she stayed away from him. And who knew, it was probably a good thing. She didn't need the complications. Just look at how she felt now—and they weren't even together.

She finished her report and set the file aside just as her e-mail notification chimed.

She looked and caught her breath when she saw who the sender was: *dlogan@loganpi.com.*

She steadied herself, and then opened the e-mail:

*Dear Toni:*

*Got in yesterday afternoon local time. The hotel is beautiful. Thanks for your help in arranging everything.*

*I found my room, and I found Gina. We had a good, long talk. I had plenty of time on the long flight over to help sort things out in my mind. That, plus the night spent lying on the beach by myself, looking at the stars, is helping me to think clearly. After talking to Gina, here's what I think:*

- *I had a crush on a girl named Gina in high school;*
- *This crush took a long time to run its course—longer than it should have;*
- *That crush was based on a vision as seen through the eyes of a young kid;*
- *Through those eyes, Gina was damn near perfect;*
- *I'm not a young kid anymore. I see more clearly now;*
- *As an adult, I barely know Gina;*
- *Now I can see that she's just like everyone else—she has her good points and her bad;*
- *I could never be with Gina. She's far too controlling for me—look at how she used me for her own ends last year without even a second thought;*
- *Talking to her last night, I learned that she's already on to her*

*next scheme;*
- *I'm not interested;*
- *She doesn't like to sit around, drink a beer, and listen to music. She doesn't even like Nirvana.*

*Bottom line, you were wrong when you said Thomas Wolfe was wrong. I think he was right—you really can't go back again. That's because our perspective of "back" changes as we change. It isn't the same as it once was. In this case, my past wasn't bad—it was fun at the time. But my present looks a whole lot more appealing to the man I've become.*

*I'm coming home. I get in at ten fifteen tonight. Do you mind picking me up? I'm eager to see you.*

*—Danny*

Toni reread the e-mail, and then she printed it and read it again. She smiled to herself.

"Kenny!" she yelled out.

"What!" He was in his office across the hall.

"I'm taking the afternoon off," she announced.

"Good. Why?"

"That's just none of your damned business. But, if you must know, I've got a date tonight." She smiled at the thought. "I'm going home early to get ready."

~~~~

# Acknowledgments

*Angel Dance* required a great deal of research and specialized information, which I was fortunate to obtain through the efforts of the following people.

To my friend Phil Johnson, for setting me straight on high school athletics in Washington State. I am now clear on the differences between "cross-country" and "track."

To Officer Tony Falso of the Mukilteo Police Department, for his detailed critique of the police procedures used throughout the story. Any remaining procedural errors are mine alone.

To Gabe Robinson, for helping to identify and bring out the real story hidden in the jumble of words that was my original effort.

To Brynn Warriner and Carrie Wicks, for helping me take what I (mistakenly) hoped was a finished manuscript to a manuscript that now really is finished—a humbling but necessary experience. Brynn and Carrie both work in Seattle; they also provided sound advice and assistance on specifics of the novel's Seattle setting.

To Ellen Johnson, Jennifer Norton, Liz Spiller, and Rebecca Eli, for reading early versions of *Angel Dance* and providing valuable feedback.

Finally, to my wife Michelle, for her constant support in this and all my other endeavors.

# About the Author

M.D. Grayson is the author of Angel Dance – the first of the Danny Logan mystery series. He lives on an island near Seattle with his wife Michelle and their three German shepherds.

Before becoming a full-time writer, Mr. Grayson worked in the construction industry, as an accountant for six l-o-n-g weeks (square peg-round hole), and as a piano player on the Las Vegas strip. When he's not writing, he loves zooming about on two wheels-bicycles and motorcycles alike. In addition, he's a pilot, a boater, and an accomplished musician who's always ready for a jam session!

## Connect online:

Blog: http://www.mdgrayson.com.
Twitter: http://twitter.com/md_grayson
Facebook: http://facebook.com/mdgraysonauthorpage

17161853R00200

Made in the USA
Lexington, KY
28 August 2012